The
WORK
of
WOLVES

Also by Kent Meyers

The Witness of Combines

The River Warren

Light in the Crossing: Stories

Kent Meyers

The
WORK
of
WOLVES

HARCOURT, INC.

Orlando   Austin   New York   San Diego   Toronto   London

www.HarcourtBooks.com

Library of Congress Cataloging-in-Publication Data
Meyers, Kent.
The work of wolves / Kent Meyers.—1st ed.
p.   cm.
ISBN: 0-15-101057-9
1. Triangles (Interpersonal relations)—Fiction.
2. Ranchers' spouses—Fiction.
3. Horse trainers—Fiction.   4. South Dakota—Fiction.
5. Ranch life—Fiction.
I. Title.
PS3563.E93W67   2004
813'.54—dc22   2003026365

Text set in Dante
Designed by Linda Lockowitz

Printed in the United States of America
First edition

A   C   E   G   I   K   J   H   F   D   B

In memory of
Tom Herbeck and Stewart Bellman

The
WORK
of
WOLVES

Prologue

WHEN HE WAS FOURTEEN YEARS OLD, Carson Fielding, having just received his driver's license, walked outside on a fall morning, threw his schoolbooks into his father's pickup, climbed in, started the engine, drove around the Quonset hut, backed up to the horse trailer, got out, wrestled the horse trailer hitch over the pickup's ball hitch, snapped the coupling, climbed back into the pickup, eased the rig over the ruts the tractors had dug into the gumbo during the spring rains, and clanged away up the driveway. His parents were finishing coffee. They heard the empty trailer boom. They scraped their chairs back and watched through the kitchen window as their son turned north on the county road, going away from the school in Twisted Tree.

"What's that kid doing now?" Charles Fielding exclaimed. He banged his cup down, sloshing coffee on his forearm, and reached for his hat. But Marie Fielding stilled him with a hand to his shoulder. She took the dried and stiffened dishrag hanging on the kitchen faucet and dabbed his forearm, then moved the rag in a slow circle on the counter.

"He'll come back," she said, leaning down to watch the pickup and trailer disappear over the top of the first hill to the north, leaving a scrim of brown dust against the morning sky. A strand of hair fell over her eyes. She brushed it back, held it as she watched the dust thin and disappear.

"But where the dickens is he going?"

Marie Fielding began to gather the breakfast dishes from the table. She picked up the plates, balanced the silverware and cups on top of them, brought them to the counter. Outside, Carson's grandfather appeared in the frame of the window, coming from the old house. He walked to the middle of the driveway and stood gazing northward, his blue jeans crumpled around his boot tops, barely hanging from the belt above his narrow hips.

"I don't know," Marie said. She nodded at the old man standing in the driveway. "But I'll bet Ves does."

Charles Fielding stared at his father.

"No doubt about that," he said grimly.

He turned away from the window, rammed his hat onto his head.

"Charles."

But her husband strode across the floor. She listened to the back door open, then thud. She stood looking down at the pile of dishes. The stack of cups trembled. She reached out, touched the top one, then removed it from the stack, set it by itself on the counter. Rotated it, watched the handle point one way, then another.

Through the walls she heard the old Case tractor turn over, then stop, then turn over again. She stopped breathing, waiting. Her thumb and forefinger stilled the cup, as if she were going to lift it, sip the emptiness there. Then the tractor coughed and roared, and she breathed again. She opened the hot water tap and held the dishrag under the faucet. The rag's stiffness dissolved in her hand. She dropped it, reached out, dipped the cup into the suds. On the driveway her father-in-law turned his head in the direction of the running tractor, then looked back again at the hill over which the horse trailer had disappeared.

CARSON RETURNED IN THE EARLY AFTERNOON with his first horse. He'd driven fifteen miles to Magnus Yarborough's ranch to buy it. When the wiry, sandy-haired adolescent with the thin nose stepped from his stonepitted pickup and announced: "I'm Carson Fielding. I called about the horses," Magnus Yarborough checked his watch. The deep and confident voice on the phone the other day had said its speaker would be out at ten, and this kid had the same voice and claimed the same name. Still, Magnus had expected an adult and couldn't believe this was the same person. But his watch read 10:05, and he kept it set five minutes fast so he wouldn't be late for things, and the kid was sure enough standing in his driveway.

"Well well," Magnus said.

He didn't put out his hand. He'd anticipated a hard bargain when he'd heard the voice on the phone, and now his anticipation had turned into a joke, but it was a joke only he'd get. He was going to fleece this kid. It was in the nature of things, the way runoff follows a draw. Magnus walked around to the passenger side of Carson's pickup, got in, slammed the door, and waited for Carson to understand that he was meant to get behind the wheel and drive and follow directions.

The horses were pastured five miles away. Magnus and Carson didn't say a word to each other during those five miles. A prairie falcon left a power pole and flew low over the orange-brown expanse of a milo field, and a hen pheasant came out of the road ditch grass and returned. A jet labored across the sky and disappeared, and its contrail disappeared. But other than those things and the racket of the empty trailer and Carson's hands moving on the steering wheel and the rustle of Magnus's jeans shifting on the cracked upholstery in a quiet abrasion of denim on vinyl, nothing happened. By the time they got to the pasture, Magnus had convinced himself he was about to do Carson a favor, teach him a lesson that might keep him from being ripped off in a big way when he was older. The kid ought to be in school, so why not school him?

"Here," Magnus said, and nodded at a field approach. Carson turned off the gravel road and stopped the pickup with its bumper nearly touching a gate made of four strands of barbwire.

"Go ahead. Open it," Magnus commanded.

Carson stepped from the pickup, leaned hard against the post that stretched the four strands of wire, flicked up the loop of smooth wire that held it to the anchor post, leaned the loose post down, pulled it out of the bottom loop, and carried it into the pasture, the barb wire catching and scraping in the grass. He returned to the pickup and, still silent, drove into the pasture.

"You weren't thinking you should shut that gate?" Magnus asked.

"Ain't no need."

It was true. The horses, below the hill, weren't about to sneak past the pickup and escape. But it irked Magnus that the kid had decided that for himself. Before he could reply, though, the pickup crested a rise and stopped. A herd of twenty horses appeared below, standing in yellowgreen grass, all of them looking up. Then the kid spoke what ought to have been Magnus's words.

"There they are."

"They sure as hell are," Magnus growled. The kid acted like he was pointing them out as a species that Magnus had never seen.

But Carson had opened his door and was stepping out. Magnus's words flitted right past him. By the time Magnus realized the damnfool kid was going to walk down the hill to look at a bunch of half-wild horses, the kid was twenty yards away.

"Kid! You can't just."

But Carson continued down the hill.

"Christ!"

Magnus stepped to the ground and started after the kid but found himself strutting through the grass with his butt pointing this way and that—reminded himself of those racewalkers he'd see in the Olympics, looked like they had a sandbur between their cheeks they were trying to shake. And Magnus would be damned if he was going to run. He stopped, figured he'd at least take some pleasure in watching the horses spook. Maybe the kid was dumb enough to take off running after them, a goddamn track star in cowboy boots.

But the horses didn't run. The kid got closer than Magnus had ever been to the bunch, and the horses did not spook. But then, there it was. A shiver ran through the herd, as if a cloud of passing wasps had touched each animal briefly in its passing. The horses were going to break. A roiling would now go through them, as of disturbed water, some great thing moving beneath the surface. There would be a moment of confusion, animals cutting through each other's paths, all positions changed, and then the herd would be gone, their tails strung behind, lifting the earth from itself with their hooves. The kid would be left standing in the dust.

But right then he lapsed into stillness—not the sudden, rigid stillness of a frightened animal but the stillness of a boat cutting power, a stillness that seems an extension of movement, another kind of floating. It suspended the whole herd. Magnus's mouth dropped open. The kid stood on the hillside and looked at the horses, close enough to throw out a long rope and snare one, close enough to breathe their breath and the evaporation of their pores. The horses churned and eddied. But didn't run.

Then the kid was walking up the hill again, right up to Magnus, and stopping and turning and looking down at the horses for a while. He pointed with his chin.

"I guess maybe that roan there."

"What roan where?"

"One out there at the edge a the herd. Watchin us."

Christ on a crutch—the kid walks down the hill like he's going to look at horses and puts on a damn good act of looking and then walks back up and says he'll take the sorriest-ass piece of horse meat down there, a rawboned, knobheaded, razorspined, wildeyed, stiffkneed, stupidass yearling that probably couldn't be broke, and if it could it'd put you on dialysis in a year, shaking your kidneys up with that gait, and bite you if you turned your back, just for something to do.

Let school begin.

"Cost you some money, that horse will," Magnus said. "I don't mean any insult, but you're young, that's not too hard to see, and I wonder if maybe that horse is a bit more than you can afford."

Fools inspired him. If the kid's dumb enough to show a preference for a horse, go along with it. Pretend it's better than even he thinks. If one of those Greek muses wasn't named Idiot, it sure ought to have been. Thinking these things, Magnus missed for a moment what Carson had said.

"If I can't afford that one, I can't afford any of 'em. Hafta shoot one a them other horses to make it cheaper'n that roan. Several times. Just to be sure."

Before Magnus digested the meaning of this, Carson was saying something else:

"I don't mean a be tellin you your business, sir." He was look-ing at Magnus now, and he'd turned into the ugliest damn kid Magnus figured he'd ever seen, gangly as hell, with sandy-colored eyebrows that didn't quite do the job of pulling his eyes in and keep-ing them from staring. He was polite as all hell, but Magnus couldn't hardly think with those pale eyes gazing at him and that polite voice going on.

"I mean, they're your horses'n all. An if you want a sell me one a them other ones, alive, for less'n I want a pay for that roan, that's your business. But the truth is, I don't know if I ever seen a more worthless animal since I been born. Which, I admit, maybe ain't that long."

For the first time since he'd started buying and selling things, Magnus Yarborough had no words. Always have words was his rule. Always have something to say. It didn't matter what, as long as he opened his mouth and let something come out, for distraction's sake if nothing else. But, staring at Carson, Magnus felt that if he opened his mouth he'd talk in word soup, like he'd once heard from a homeless schizophrenic man in Denver, a meaningless babble that drove Magnus crazy as he walked along behind the man, trying to make sense of it.

He couldn't tell if the kid was serious or trying to be cute. And if it was cute, was it cute cute or insulting cute? Magnus couldn't let it be either. The kid's pale eyes just looked at Magnus, and his voice sounded like it was making an observation, something you couldn't help but agree with.

"I got 450 bucks," Carson went on. "An I'm about outta gas. An half hungry. Bit a gas an a sandwich at Kyle's Corner, that's maybe 25 bucks. An that roan's the only horse in that herd's worth only 425 bucks."

"Four-hundred-and-twenty-five bucks," Magnus said, pronounc-ing each syllable, the mention of a specific price giving him his voice. "You pulled an empty trailer out here, and you're going to pull an empty trailer back. Waste of gas. Four-hundred-and-twenty-five bucks."

"All right," Carson said. "You think you can get more from someone else, I guess you got the right to try."

He walked away, got in his pickup. Sat there. Magnus stared at him. What was this? No counteroffer? Nothing? The kid drives out here with a certain amount of money and finds a horse to match it, instead of finding a horse he likes and then seeing if he can get a price? What kind of ass-backwards thinking was that? Then he makes his single offer and quits when it doesn't go? Goes back to school? Got to get there for recess?

"You'll be wantin a ride back to your place?" Carson called through the window. "Or was you thinkin you had some work to do out here?"

Magnus ambled over to the pickup and put his elbows in the open passenger-side window. "Look, kid," he said. "You haven't ever done this before. So I'm telling you. A guy makes an offer and it's refused, he makes a counteroffer. Four-hundred-and-twenty-five bucks. I mean, hell. But if you offered me, say . . ."

He didn't finish. Didn't want to set the price himself and so lose the chance to push it up.

Carson looked at him, then through the dusty windshield at the horses, then back at Magnus.

"True," he said. "I ain't never bought one before. But I know how it's supposed to work. Trouble is, all I got's 450 bucks. An I do need gas."

He stared through the windshield at the horses grazing below them. Magnus let him look. Let the kid's desires work. Let him want.

"I do need gas," Carson repeated.

Magnus said nothing. He had him.

"An the truth is," Carson finally said, never taking his eyes from the horses, "that roan ain't worth an empty stomach. Which is all I got to bargain with."

Magnus couldn't believe it. He looked down at the ground, then turned his head sideways to gaze at the herd, letting the brim of his hat hide his face from the kid. The roan was the only horse down there still watching them, suspicious and rawboned. Magnus wouldn't miss a meal himself for the rangy bastard. The kid and the animal deserved each other.

"Four-hundred-and-twenty-five bucks," he said, still guarding his face from the kid's eyes. "Shit. Take the ornery sonofabitch."

He heard a rustle, looked up, found a greasy wad of bills right under his nose.

Part One

BEHIND
LOSTMAN'S
LAKE

The Careful Indian

~~~~~

EARL WALKS ALONE LOOKED UP from the cone of light where his calculus book lay. Through the kitchen doorway, he could see his grandmother at the far end of the living room, watching television and beading. Earl liked to wait until dark to work on calculus, liked the small reading lamp on the kitchen table, the way dark seemed to crowd in upon him and the way the light reflected off the pages, the equations clean and precise there. But he felt restless tonight. The equations jumbled in his brain. Black and meaningless marks. He looked from his island of light through the intervening dark to his grandmother sitting in her own island of light, the soft incandescence of the floor lamp bathing her face.

Her hand dipped, a bird's head, the silver needle a beak, bobbing into the tray of beads, stringing eight of them like droplets of colored ice that slid down the invisible thread. From Earl's view the beads seemed to float in the air, following each other, until his grandmother's hand pulled them taut against the moccasin in her lap, then circled toward the tray again. Earl didn't dance in powwows, but it seemed to him the real dance in those moccasins was what his grandmother did. How could someone not dance well, wearing all that movement she poured into them?

Earl's mother was in her bedroom, preparing to sleep. His grandmother had the television turned so low it was barely a murmur. In the silence Earl heard the wind outside shaking the trees his father had planted around the house. Earl's mother claimed the sighing of those trees was his father's voice. But it sounded to Earl like wind and leaves. What good was a voice you didn't understand? If Earl heard anything at all in that sound, it was just an old, old argument between things that stayed and things that moved. Stone and wind. *Inyan* and *Taku Skanskan*. His uncle Norm would claim, of course, that there was no argument. Just different ways of being, the rock that gets kicked into life. But, Earl thought, even if every fall the trees let a part of themselves fly with the wind, rove the world, that part was brown, dead, lifeless. Not a model for leaving a place, Earl thought. Better to leave on your own volition—not pushed, and not dead.

He turned back to his equations. The green line on the graphing calculator his mother had bought him curved upward through its matrix. A green and curving road, approaching something, never reaching it. And the never-reaching was the solution. Everything just an infinite approach. Earl touched the OFF button with the eraser of his pencil. The line dimmed, disappeared. Its reddish afterimage floated for a moment in the air. With the eraser Earl pushed the calculator around, back and forth, then in circles, then in opposite circles. The wind blew, the leaves chattered. It all made Earl restless. He glanced sideways at his grandmother again, far away in her little light.

"I'm going to go out," he said.

His voice carried across the room. His grandmother turned her face to him. The lenses of her black-rimmed glasses were glazed blue by the television's light, then cleared in an instant as the angle of reflection changed, and her dark eyes shone through. She nodded. Her hands swooped again into the tray of beads. Eyes of their own.

Earl's mother appeared in the living room, holding a hairbrush, a shadow in the darkness. She heard whatever she wanted to hear, no matter where she was in the house. Her long black hair was spread about her shoulders. Earl could barely see her face. She lifted the brush over her head, swept it down and then outward. Earl heard the faint, static sizzle and in the dark saw the myriad sparks within her hair. Then it fell from the end of the brush.

"Be careful, Earl," she said.

Earl closed the calculus book. Careful: that should be his name. Careful Walks Alone. Who else in the senior class, Indian or white, was doing homework on a Friday night? And not even homework he had to do, but extra work because he felt like it. He picked up the book, stuffed the calculator into its case, stood, walked into the living room and past his mother without looking at her. He kept his face impassive. In his bedroom he found a nylon windbreaker, shrugged into it, slipped on Nikes. The wind gusted harder. His mother brushed her long, dark hair every night, but sometimes Earl wanted to ask her why. What was the point? Who was she brushing it for? He knew: his father. Cyrus Walks Alone. Earl knew roads could have sudden endings. He knew if light grew bright enough it could be the hardest thing in the world. But he wanted to tell his mother, sometimes, not to be so careful. And not to expect it so much from him. As far as Earl knew, his father had been careful. What good had it done him?

Earl stopped his thoughts. He meant no disrespect by them. He just got tired of his father's residence in his mother's eyes, his father's story in everything his mother said. Why couldn't Cyrus just be his father—absent father, dead father, even unremembered father if he had to be—instead of always a lesson?

Earl walked back out to the living room. His mother was still standing there. She watched him go to the door. Earl turned the knob, then stopped. Couldn't go out like this.

"I'll be careful, Mom," he said. "I just got to get out, you know?"

She held the brush toward him, made a little circle of concession. He went. Beyond the grove of trees around the house, the wind was snorting through the dark. Huffing. Rising and falling. But here, near the house, the air hardly moved. The trees in their bending took the wind into themselves. Earl glanced up. Even the stars were distorted by the restless atmosphere. He got into his mother's car and drove up the short gravel drive. The moment he left the circle of trees, he felt the wind strike the car, angling across the highway into Twisted Tree. Earl held the steering wheel against it, keeping the car straight. A great blob of white came rolling out of the sky and flattened against the windshield with a sucking sound. Earl jumped, then saw it was only a plastic grocery bag. It reinflated immediately and sailed away, a prairie jellyfish.

Four empty cattle trucks banged down the highway that divided Twisted Tree. North of the highway was county land, south of it

the reservation, so that the town lay half-in and half-out of the rez.
Earl turned the corner near Donaldson's Foods. His headlights
swept over Eddie Little Feather and one of his friends sleeping near
the Dumpsters. Meal-and-a-nap, Earl thought. The men were tangled together, limbs askew, breathing each other's sour breath, having shifted in their drugged sleep toward each other.

Earl circled the town aimlessly. Caught in the stunted and dying
trees in the cemetery and on the barbwire fence that encircled it
and on the stiff stalks of yucca and sage that grew on the hillsides
above it, more plastic bags flapped, ballooning away from the wind.
A few years earlier, Donaldson's Foods had switched from paper to
plastic. It had taken those years for the bags to accumulate, but now
they occupied all sharp and jutting edges in the town, leaving nothing for new bags to catch on. Through the closed windows of the
car, Earl heard the bags' chattering. Impaled and visible ghosts.
From the corner of his eye, he saw them waving in the cemetery,
but he refused to look there. He made a U-turn outside of town and
drove back in. Another empty cattle truck, clangorous on the pot-
holes. On top of a rusty pile of machinery in the empty lot where
someone had once tried to start a manufacturing business, a single
plastic bag fluttered. Earl saluted it—a new edge discovered—and
drove on by.

He turned onto a gravel side street. Might as well entertain
Bambi. A pit bull mutt appeared in his headlights, its mouth moving, its teeth flashing white. Earl drove straight toward the dog.
Bambi had once managed to stop a tourist's motor home, the driver
afraid to run him over. The story was well-known. When the motor
home stopped, Bambi advanced to a position right under the
bumper, barking madly, growling ferociously, slobbering prodi-
giously. The driver tried backing up. Bambi followed, and the driver
couldn't gain enough speed to leave the dog behind. Bambi finally
cornered the motor home when the driver missed the turn at the
end of the block and ended up in Roger Robideaux's yard. Roger,
retrieving a beer from his refrigerator, looked up and saw the motor
home's back end heaving hugely over the washout at the edge of
the gravel street and then catapulting across the dusty yard toward

his window. By the time it stopped, Roger could see nothing but white and the ILDER of WILDERNESS painted across the back. He heard Bambi's snarling, realized what was happening, and laughed so hard he forgot to open his beer. He walked out his door, around the motor home, and right up to Bambi. Planting his left foot, he kicked the dog in the ribs with his right. Bambi yelped and slunk away. Roger stepped to the side and with a broad, two-armed sweep-and-bow and a toothless grin showed the terrified driver and his wife their freedom. As the motor home passed him, Roger looked down, saw the beer in his hand, twisted the top, and, greatly satisfied, took a deep drink, already thinking how he would tell this story. With his head still tilted back, he thought of the line he would end it with: "The trouble with being a tourist is you never know which dogs you can kick." The saying had become part of Twisted Tree's folklore.

Earl pinned Bambi between his headlights and maintained his speed. He watched the dog grow in size before him, eyes shining redly, saliva a silver spray in the reflected light. Suddenly the dog snapped its mouth shut and hobbled arthritically to the right. It barely avoided the wheel and disappeared beside the car, then reappeared in Earl's rearview mirror, red in the red dust of his taillights, a wooden dog, joints locked, lumbering and pained and then dust-swallowed.

"Some day, Bambi," Earl spoke to the dust in the mirror, "you won't move fast enough."

Counting cattle trucks and plastic bags, playing chicken with deluded dogs: nightlife in Twisted Tree. Nightlife, at least, for the careful ones. Earl often entertained himself by thinking of his life like one of the documentaries his grandmother watched, as if there were a hidden camera following him and a narrator explaining things. At the stop sign by the abandoned bowling alley he looked up and down the empty stretch of road. *The Careful Indian,* he thought to himself, *stops at all stop signs before proceeding cautiously onto the highway. Trucks can come out of nowhere and run the Careful Indian over.* Earl stepped slowly on the accelerator and crept onto the highway. *The Careful Indian is also a favorite prey of policemen.*

Three blocks away the stoplight at the intersection of the highway and Main Street changed from green to yellow to red and back
to green again, regulating traffic that didn't exist, going about its
precise and useless business. As he drove slowly toward it, Earl
thought of going out to see his uncle, Norman Walks Alone. But
even Norm might not appreciate Earl's driving up to his wheelless
motor home at this time of night. Earl stopped at the light, watched
the empty intersection change colors. He didn't move when the
light went green. *The Careful Indian would rather stop than go. He believes that two green lights are twice as safe as one.* On the second green
he pulled away. As he did, the solution to the calculus problem he'd
been working on when he looked up at his grandmother earlier in
the evening flashed into his head. He could go back home and start
the next problem.

Earl made a U-turn in the middle of the highway and went back
through the stoplight on a red. *At times the Careful Indian can change
into the Mathematical Indian, and when this happens he can lose all cau-
tion. This is when his life is most in danger. Driven to do math by forces
deep inside himself, the Mathematical Indian will sometimes exceed the
speed limit.* Earl watched the speedometer rise to 66 miles an hour,
then held it there. He approached the grove of trees that marked
his place, a dark circle on the prairie. He thought of the parties
going on tonight. He was never invited, but he knew of them.
Heard the talk. There was one out at Larson's stock dam, mostly
white kids, and one on top of Tower Hill, mostly Indian. He slowed
down as he approached his driveway, thought of his mother in the
house, gone to bed, listening even in her sleep for the sound of the
car door, and his grandmother, for whom darkness and light did not
correspond to sleep in any established pattern, staring into the TV,
her face bluely lit, her hands dancing, ordering beads.

He let the car coast past the driveway. *This behavior is something
absolutely new.* Earl put his foot back on the accelerator. He looked
into the rearview mirror, saw the grove of trees diminish. "Why
shouldn't I?" he said, watching them.

A few miles later he turned off the highway onto the gravel
track that paralleled Red Medicine Creek into Antelope Park. Under

the cottonwoods far back from the highway, other cars were parked. Earl stepped out. The drumbeat of music came from the hill above him, filtered by leaves, and the red lights of the television and radio towers blinked on and off high among the stars, disconnected, the towers themselves invisible. A softer, nearer spread of firelight lay along the top of the hill, an orange glow through the trees.

Indistinct voices. The chuckling of the creek. A single frog's clarinet calling. Smoke drifting down the hill, into the smell of cattails and water. Shaking cottonwood leaves. The sharp, clean smell of cedar cutting into the deep and fishy smell of Lostman's Lake from across the highway. Earl kept his hand on the roof of the car and gazed up the hill. He thought of the empty town. He thought of his mother sleeping. Of the cemetery ringed with plastic bags. Wasted souls. The expectations of the dead.

Ssshhh. He shook his head. No thoughts like that. No disrespect. He took his hand from the car and started up the hill.

It looks like the Careful Indian is in unfamiliar territory. Notice how he seems lost?

Earl thought of peeing on a bush. Marking territory. For the camera.

HE STOOD IN THE DARK OF THE CEDARS on top of the hill. About twenty young men and women, many of them in high school, stood or sat on the flat space surrounding the towers, where the NO TRESPASSING signs and the threats of prosecution had been defaced so long ago that even the inspiration to add new layers of graffiti had been defeated. Orange-tinted and shadowed faces bobbed in the rise and fall of flame: Ted Kills Many, Meredith Remembers Him, Gerald Dupree, Angie Long Feather, the Lemieux brothers. The only pure white kid was Willi Schubert, the German foreign-exchange student, who was eager to do anything Indian. As if drinking, Earl thought, was a different experience in Lakota than it was in any other culture. The great leveler: tip a bottle often enough and everyone becomes the same.

Talk and laughter, the Budweiser cans tipped up, set down. *Well,* Earl thought, *here I am.* But so was the story that had controlled his life for as long as he could remember. Headlights in the wrong lane, filling all space. That story was here. It was anywhere Earl went. He could defy it, but he couldn't walk away from it. At least not this easily. He thought to himself that he could still turn around, go back home. No one knew he'd come. He could watch, then leave.

Earl remembered the way his mother had looked when he brought home his first driver's license, proud of having passed the test, not a single written answer wrong and only a few points taken off for driving, not looking over his shoulder to check the blind spot once. His mother had taken the license from his hands, holding it by a corner, far from her face. She hadn't smiled. She hadn't even commented on the photograph. She'd just looked at the license as if it were some mildly unpleasant object, an unexpected bill perhaps. Her dangling red-bead and feather earrings shivered as she gazed.

"Just be careful," she said. And handed the license back. Earl shoved it into his pocket, felt its clear rectangular edges there. He'd been going to tell his mother how well he'd parallel parked, how the examiner had praised his precise following of instructions. Instead he'd mumbled, "I will be, Mom."

In another year he'd be gone from here. Maybe then he'd be far enough away to be gone from that story. Because maybe the story was here and not in him. Maybe it was in the way the roads went to the tops of hills and then curved abruptly down. Maybe it was in the way people held their beer cans in one hand and steered with the other. If the story wasn't in Earl, he could ride test scores away from it as far as he wanted to ride them. One of the coasts if he wanted. Maybe that story wouldn't survive ocean air, the salt in it, the humidity. Earl had a vague vision of something surrounding him like a veil, a gauze, disintegrating under the influence of salt spray and waves and his hard concentration upon differential equations. Sitting on a beach, book in his lap, and becoming only himself. Cleansed. Pure.

He stepped into the firelight. Heads turned. Stillness came. *The Careful Indian has decided to join the others. Notice how they look at him. They're wary. They don't know what to do.*

Then Ted Kills Many, a twenty-five-year-old there, drinking with the high schoolers, raised his beer can in mock salute.

"Earl Walks Alone! You lost?"

Earl stuck his hands in his pockets, shook his head. "Just figured I'd see what was happening, you know?" he said.

"Maybe you're lookin for your homework. Thought the wind blew it up here, enit?"

"Just seeing what's happening."

"This is what's happening." Ted snapped a Budweiser out of its plastic ring and flipped it over the fire at Earl. It came tumbling out of the smoke end-over-end. Earl fumbled it, managed to catch it before it hit the ground, then stood looking at it in his hands.

"You know how to open one a those?" Ted hooked his finger, pantomimed flicking the snap top.

"Thanks, you know? But I'm not drinking."

"Not drinking?" Ted mimicked. "You come up here to work out some equations, then? Calculate how many Indians it takes to drink a case? There an equation for that?"

Earl wished he could be smart without everyone knowing about it. Being smart was almost a disease. Except that no one blamed you for having a disease. No one took it as an insult. He looked at the ground, unable to think of any response to Ted.

"Leave 'm alone, Ted."

Meredith Remembers Him spoke quietly, not so much in Earl's defense as in just not wanting to listen to this. She ran her fingernail around the top of her beer can, in the little groove inside the lip. Then she lifted the can and took a swallow.

"Leave 'm alone? Earl wants a beer. Just don't know it yet. Go on, Walks Alone. Have that beer."

"If Earl don't wanna drink, he don't hafta. Set it down, Earl."

Ted was angry Meredith had stopped the nervous laughter and sheepish grins Ted had started in the group at Earl's expense. Ted reached down to his side, ripped another Bud from the plastic ring, popped the top, and sucked the foam that erupted.

"What the hell's he doing here, then?" he growled. "This's a drinkin party, enit?"

Earl wished Meredith had stayed out of it. She wasn't really interested in him. Now, no matter what he did, he was taking sides. Following someone's orders. Drink or not, he'd be winning someone's argument. He looked at the can in his hand. A simple snap of the finger, the metal edge breaking cleanly, sinking into the foam. Nothing to it.

"Earl's goin places," Meredith said. "He don't need this shit."

"Yeah. Apples don't roll straight, but they roll. Right off the rez."

"That's old, Ted."

Meredith sounded tired, and the whole thing made Earl tired. He hadn't come up here to be discussed as if he didn't actually exist. But then, why had he come? He walked away from the fire and sat down on one of the concrete slabs anchoring the radio tower. He leaned his back against the steel frame. No one followed him. He shut his eyes and felt the cold steel against his spine. Then he opened his eyes again. *The Careful Indian,* he thought, *has retreated to observe the group.* But he found even this monologue boring now, and not very funny.

Against his back the steel skeleton of the tower vibrated in the high wind. Another almost-voice. Earl looked away from the fire at the land below him. He could see the metallic surface of Lostman's Lake across the highway, bluewhite in the moon, no more depth than polished stone. Water shimmered white over the spillway. Someone changed the rap music in the boom box to an Indian drum group singing powwow music. *You can't get into the drum group if you're drinking,* Earl thought, *but with modern technology you can bring the drum group into the drinking.*

Over the rim of a hill above the dam something white moved. Earl dismissed it, but it came again, a signaling from out there in the darkness, dimmer than fireflies or faint stars. Like something waving to him. He stared but could see nothing. He averted his gaze for better night vision, and after a bit the firelight left his eyes. Then he saw what was out there. Barely visible in a pasture above the lake, dim and indistinct shapes, three horses stood in the dark. Earl gazed at them. He didn't know it then, had no idea at all—but he had just stepped into Carson Fielding's story.

A Fall

WHEN CARSON PULLED AROUND the curve in the driveway with the roan horse in the trailer behind him, his grandfather had been waiting near the barn. The old man pushed away from the peeling paint and weathered wood and ambled to the corral gate as Carson swung the trailer around. In his rearview mirror Carson saw his grandfather undo the chain holding the gate and push it open.

The old man was peering into the trailer when Carson got out of the pickup. They stood next to each other, looking into the dim interior where the roan horse stood as far from them as possible, pressed against the other side.

"He a good one?" the old man asked.

"I think so. Is Dad around?"

"You think, huh? Well, let's see 'm."

Carson's grandfather walked to the back of the trailer and knocked up the lever holding the trailer door shut. The door swung open.

"Is he around?"

The old man shook his head. "Drillin wheat," he said.

"Oh. I was hoping maybe he'd . . ."

Carson looked around as if he might find his father walking toward them.

His grandfather missed the boy's disappointment. "Been in that field all day," he said. "C'mon outta there now."

For several seconds the roan didn't move. Then the trailer clanged, a set of huge and dissonant cymbals, and the animal burst from it, running flat out. It barely managed to turn itself at the sudden apparition of the corral fence looming. It flowed around the far perimeter of the corral, turned, and flowed back the other way, seeking an opening, avoiding the two human beings.

They watched in silence. The old man nodded, reached into his shirt pocket, removed a pack of cigarettes, shook one out, stuck it in his mouth, replaced the pack.

"Looks like a pretty good one," he said around the cigarette.

"I thought he looked OK. You think Dad'll like him?"

"He know you bought 'm?"

"I never said."

"Maybe he won't even notice. Anyways, won't like 'm any more or less 'n another horse, I guess. Your dad never was much for horses."

"Maybe he'll like this one, though."

"Nervous sumbitch."

The roan was now trotting back and forth along the far fence, watching them, head raised, nostrils flared.

"Seems like."

"Give us sump'm to do."

The old man removed the unlit cigarette from his mouth, held it out, and looked at it.

"I been needin sump'm," he said. "Your ma's after me to quit smokin. Says it'll kill me. I been tryin a make her happy. She cooks better when she's happy. Been makin sure I got no matches on me. Other day, though, I tried a light one a these off a catalytic converter. Crawled under the pickup and stuck it against the converter when the engine was runnin. Didn't work though. Hadn't a been for the tailpipe leakin, I wouldn't a got no smoke at all."

He stuck the cigarette back in his mouth and nodded in the direction of the horse. "Trainin that there animal'll keep my mind off inventin ways a killin myself."

The horse had quit roaming the perimeter of the corral and settled into a corner, not frenzied, just alert and a little hateful.

"Got a name?" the old man asked.

"The horse?"

"I assume you ain't havin babies."

"Guess I ain't thought've a name yet."

They both had their chins on the top corral rail, their wrists dangling, two heads watching the animal. Ves opened his fingers and dropped the unlit cigarette into the corral.

"There ain't hardly anything more worthless than a cigarette you can't light," he said.

"Cept one you can."

"Your ma tell you that?"

"Thought it up myself."

"Well. Sounds like sump'm she'd say."

"Whyn't you just not carry 'em with you? Don't make no sense, seems like, to have 'em if you ain't gonna light 'em."

"Never know. Hate to go cold turkey. Catalytic converter mighta worked. Or I might get struck by lightning. Got 'em on me, I can take advantage. But still be quittin. You believe that story?"

"What story?"

"'Bout the catalytic converter."

"Probly not."

"I probly don't myself. Could be true, though. Either way, probly best your ma don't hear it. She can be half-gullible. She got to believin somethin like that, no tellin what she'd do."

LATE THAT AFTERNOON Marie Fielding drove out to where Charles was drilling wheat to get him for supper so he wouldn't have to drive the Case back. She waited for him at the end of the round, the tractor rolling toward her, chased by its slow cloud of dust. It reached the fence line, and the drill heaved out of the ground on its hydraulic rams. Charles parked it, walked over to the pickup, knocking dust out of his clothes with his palms, climbed in.

"Is it going OK?" she asked.

"Nothing broke."

"That's good."

"Unusual."

Marie put her hand on the gearshift and moved it back and forth without engaging it.

"Your son bought a horse today," she said.

"I didn't figure he was pulling that horse trailer around the county for the fun of it."

She looked at her fingers wrapped around the gearshift. The way the light came through the windshield and whitened her knuckles. The diamond on her finger, its brilliance. The dry skin on the back of her hands.

"It's important to him, Charles," she said.

"He skipped school. Took the pickup and trailer without asking."

"I know."

"So you want me to tell him what a nice horse he got?"

She shrugged, tried to smile him out of his mood. He looked away from her, at the land uncoiling to the horizon, the gray shapes of the Badlands against the far sky.

"He did."

"Did what?"

"Get a nice horse."

She smiled at him again, and when he met her gaze he couldn't quite sustain his anger.

"Christ!" he said, trying to inoculate himself against her light-heartedness.

She put the pickup into gear. They bounced over the ruts of the field toward the road. A covey of quail leapt from the fence line grass, torpedoed away, disappeared into the ground. They might have burrowed right through it so sharply did they descend, so suddenly disappear.

"It's a waste of his money, Marie. He should be saving money. Thinking about college. He's not too young."

"I know. It's just . . ."

"Just what?"

She waited until she'd pulled onto the road, shifted into high.

"He's so proud of it," she said.

Charles watched a jet lay a contrail in the blue. He watched it for a long time, until it was directly above the pickup and he couldn't see it. Marie glanced over at him. She reached out her hand, touched him on the shirt sleeve, so lightly he didn't notice. Then she put her hand back on the steering wheel. When Charles looked back down, she was just driving.

"Proud of it," he said. "Well, fine."

Then, a half-mile later, he said: "I been going back and forth in that field all day. Neither one've 'em ever even thought've comin to relieve me."

AS IT TURNED OUT, cigarettes did cause Ves Fielding's death, but not in any way that his daughter-in-law had imagined or warned against, their role in that death being so momentary that, to all but Carson, who had seen it, they seemed less cause than coincidence, and Marie would come to say, with humor and affection, that Ves Fielding had died of sheer orneriness. And that, too, would be true. Ves's death became a memory that pinned Carson to a moment, to a spot of time and land, to snowfall, to blue morning light strained and crystalline, so that for years afterwards, even in the heat of summer, just before he woke he would believe he was standing in a bluegray place streaked with lines of white, and when he woke he would find himself confused by the square and stationary edges of his room.

He and his grandfather took up training horses together. Carson would come to remember standing by the corral, waiting, and his grandfather coming out of the old house morning after morning, a stub of cigarette between his yellowed fingers, his breath in the winter indistinguishable from the smoke he exhaled, his words of greeting made of cloud, and he would saddle up a horse with creaking leather and swing a leg over. But he refused to accept his age— the ornery part—refused to cede to his grandson the raw horses, so that on a snowy November morning in his eighty-fifth year and Carson's sixteenth, the old man's leg didn't swing quite high enough, and the bump of his heel against the horse's haunch caused his snowcrusted boot in the stirrup to slip, which—like some perverse Rube Goldberg machine—caused his stub of smoldering cigarette to drop from his mouth onto the horse's withers, which caused the horse to startle and jump, which caused Ves's foot to slip clear out of the stirrup, and he fell down alongside the horse's flank.

Final cause was never officially determined. The coroner could not or would not say whether death came from the broken neck when Ves hit the ground with the back of his head or from the fractured skull where the horse's hoof connected as he fell past its flank in the descending snow.

But Carson, seeing the hoof flash up, knew beyond any need for autopsy or official statement that his grandfather was dead before his skull struck the ground. He was coming out of the barn with a rope in his hand when the accident happened. He saw it all. He saw the old man's head jerk sideways as he fell, the abrupt, strange, quick movement parallel to the ground, angling across the lines of snow. Carson heard the sound. The horse, freed, bucked away from the body. Carson did not run, and he did not raise his voice. Even if things could not be made better, they could be made worse, and a horse wild in the corral was worse. He opened the corral gate slowly, walked to the animal, speaking. Took the reins. Tied them to the fence. Only then did he go to his grandfather, the horse huffing behind him.

Carson put one knee on the ground, put his elbow on the other one. Blood, like fluid too bright from an engine, leaked out of the old man's head onto the snowy, hoofmarred ground. In later years, recalling it, trying to know what he'd seen, Carson would think that the old man's head and neck looked like a tennis racquet he'd once seen shattered and abandoned on a street—that kind of twisted, wrongful look that proclaims beyond all doubt that this particular kind of broke is final. The smell of the old man—cigarette smoke and Copenhagen and age, and the pungent smell of unwashed sheets slept in so many weeks that Marie would periodically give in from asking Ves to bring them to her and sneak into the old house, holding her breath, and peel the greasy things from the bed, laying clean ones beside it, and swear to never do it again, though always the old man's indifference to the sheets' dirt and smell outlasted her will—came up, mixed with the metallic smell of blood and the cold distillation of snow in the air.

Though the old man's head was twisted like an owl's or doll's, there was a smile on his face. But Carson knew that it was a mere betrayal of muscle, that the old man saw no humor or satisfaction in his own death other than, perhaps, the satisfaction of dying within his own activity, of being bested in fair competition by an animal he had many times bested and, by so dying, of leaving the world without giving money to the sonsabitches who made their livings herding old people from room to room. Other than that, the old man had no wish to die, took no pleasure in it, saw no humor in its finality. Carson, even at sixteen, standing in the corral with the horse blowing behind him and the rope he'd carried from the barn still in his hand and snow drifting out of the sky, knew, seeing the smile on the wreck of the old man's face, that the smile was not the old man's joke but instead a joke played upon him and that his grandfather would have preferred to spend eternity—if he could—stinking and farting and riding and cursing the things he hated in the world he loved.

Carson watched snowflakes melt on the old man's face. Then turned away, not wanting to see the first flakes that would not melt. He didn't hurry to the house, and when he entered he did not call out but walked from room to room until he found his mother. She was in the spare bedroom getting Christmas ornaments out of the closet a month early. She turned when Carson entered the room, holding a cardboard box of glass bulbs and porcelain figurines.

"You're quitting already?" she asked.

He removed his work gloves, put them in his back pocket, stepped to her, lifted the box from her hands, stepped back again, set the box on the carpet, stood again. He reached up, removed the wool Scotch-plaid cap from his head, held it down near his knee, flicked it in the direction of the box.

"Didn't want you to drop that," he said. "Somethin happened. Grampa's had 'n accident. Tryin a ride that Scooter horse an fell. It's bad, Mom. He's dead."

It wasn't the first or the last time his mother would wonder who this son of hers was. She stared at him, the way he stood before her, holding his cap, watching her.

"You said dead," she said.

He nodded.

"But . . . Oh, my God!"

Only then did her hands fall, which all this time had been lifted as if she still held the box, and Carson saw that if he hadn't removed it she would indeed have dropped it.

She rushed toward the doorway, but he was in the way. She ran into him, was surprised to find him there. Her hair swung forward past her cheekbones as she rebounded, and then she was like a broken, motorized toy which, thrown off course, limps in circles. To Carson she was suddenly a stranger who had bumped into him and who stood flustered for a moment, giving him a brief second to observe her and wonder who she was. And perhaps because his grandfather lay dead only yards away in snow already covering him, near a horse that, having killed him, was already sleeping standing up in the slanting snowfall, Carson saw his mother as both beautiful and old. Perhaps she was both because she was so suddenly lost and fragile.

He dropped his cap on the floor and reached out with both hands and took her upper arms. He intended only to stop her shimmering, her circling within herself. He grasped her in the oddest way he'd ever used with her, as if he were grasping a railroad tie to set it firmly in place in a fence post hole he'd dug.

"Mom," he said. "What are you doing?"

"We've got to call an ambulance."

He'd reached out to her in gentleness, but the look on her face, the desperation there, and the hope, disturbed and angered him. With his arms fully extended, he gripped her triceps and pushed her downward. A week later he would notice black and blue and yellow marks of fingers on her upper arms as she washed her hair in the kitchen sink—a habit left over from the time when she had lived in the old house without a shower—and he would almost ask her how the hell and who the hell. His mind would race, trying to think who might have done that to her, his father beyond possibility—and then he would realize the answer and stare at his thumb and finger on the handle of his coffee cup and scrape back his chair and go outside, where the sun had not yet risen, and wind was driving snow across the pastures, and Venus was alone in the eastern dark.

He gripped her hard and drove her down against the floor. Her knees almost collapsed.

"I didn't say hurt, Mom. I said dead. He's dead. He's laying out there dead."

Surprise and pain bubbled for a moment to her face, then went. Suddenly her eyes became clear and unclouded.

"You did," she whispered. "Yes. You did say dead."

She was back. Here. He needed her here. He relaxed his grip on her shoulders, his forearms trembling. She stumbled, caught herself. Steadied. Pushed back a strand of hair.

"But how do you know?" she asked.

He grunted. Now she'd turned sly. A riddler. Looking for the right answer to death's recognition, and if he got it wrong she would insist again that the old man lived.

But her eyes remained steady and clear. Carson saw the question was only what it was: a desire to know if he'd passed a hand over lips, felt the neck for a pulse. Carson was baffled. There were no such details to provide.

"I know dead, Mom," he said. "I've seen dead."

She pursed her lips, then nodded, the barest gesture of assent.

"I suppose you have."

It calmed her, this certitude of his, that he could look at death and know it and not require confirmation. Yet it disturbed her too. Such confidence, in such a thing. What kind of son would reason so? Her son: She didn't know him—didn't know what he'd seen to recognize death like this. A stranger beyond her perimeter, taught by experiences she'd never learn of. How had he leapt so far beyond her knowledge of him?

"I need to call the hospital. They'll send an ambulance."

"Mom! Jesus!"

To have her believe and then retract: It nearly broke him, nearly turned him back into a child. For the first time that day, his eyes burned.

She reached out and touched his cheek.

"Oh, sweetie," she said. "I believe you. But do you think anyone else will?"

She ran her fingers from his jawbone to the end of his chin, twice, then let her fingers drift into air. She stepped into him and wrapped him in her arms, and they held each other. Snow rattled on the window pane. She let him go, stepped around him and through the door. He heard her footsteps descend the stairs, heard the phone lifted below, her voice speaking, pausing, replying, the receiver being returned to the cradle. He picked his cap off the floor, pressed it for a moment to his eyes: wet wool, straw, horses. He lifted his face, stared about the room like a man lost, then stepped over the box of Christmas ornaments to the snow-struck window. With his foot above the box, he thought of stepping right into it: the explosion of the hollow ornaments, the grind of glass. He lost his balance and had to fall forward to keep from doing what he had imagined. He missed the box with his upraised foot, but his trailing boot caught its top edge and tipped it over as he stumbled to the window. There was a ruckus of glass. Several ornaments rolled past him, hit the baseboard under the window, rebounded off-kilter.

"Might as well a let her dropped it," he murmured.

He stood looking out the window at the cold, parched light. The wind drove snow in slanting lines, skewing the world. He could see the horse standing where he'd tied it, asleep, its saddle filled with snow. A cold rider.

"That's right," he whispered. His breath momentarily obscured the window. "Sleep. You won't be doin any more work today."

That quick, bright hoof. It had come up in a sudden contortion of the horse's flesh. Carson had seen his grandfather swing his leg up, had heard the bump of boot on flesh, heard the intake of his grandfather's breath and seen the cigarette glow bright, then drop. He couldn't see the cigarette butt against the snowy landscape. Could see only the flame. An orange spot of heat, floating down. Wavering. And his grandfather's face at peace, not yet having registered the way things had gone wrong. After eighty years of riding, there was not a right or a wrong way to mount a horse. There was only the way.

Yet it had gone wrong. Not because the old man had made a mistake. His body had. His old body. Time and age. Those old betrayers.

And then the fall, and the horse's back taut and arched, the rear hoof snaking forward, random and chaotic. It could have gone anywhere: intentionless, purposeless. Kicking just to kick. Yet it had met his grandfather's skull.

From the window Carson tried to make out the old man's body. Either the corral fence hid him or the snow had already so covered him that he'd become another lump on the ground. Carson felt no need to change that. Snow or cloth might cover the old man, and he would surely prefer snow, and would prefer the open corral to anywhere else they might now move him.

Through a gap between the outbuildings, Carson saw his father's pickup creep over a hill in the pasture, coming in from hauling hay to the cows out there. The pickup was a blur through the thickening snow, disappearing in a squall and then reappearing further down the hill, so that it seemed to move in jerks, in sudden annihilations of space.

"Goddamn," Carson said.

His own breath obscured the pickup. Then the cloud on the window evaporated inward from the edges, and he watched the pickup until the barn hid it. He turned back to the corral, to what was no longer visible there. He thought of how his father would receive the news, as something from a foreign sphere. He'd gone out to the pasture in one world, would return to another.

"Wasn't nobody's fault," Carson murmured.

Still, he wanted to blame his father. For not being there. For being somewhere else. For anything that might have changed if he had been there.

"Nobody's fault," he said again.

In a few more minutes, his father would arrive at the door below and be told. In Twisted Tree an ambulance was setting out. In some minutes its siren would be heard, if they used it, wailing behind the hills, and if Carson stayed at this window he would see the red lights, if they used them, setting off a circle of flaming snowflakes. Then below him he would see much activity, doors opening and closing, efficient movements, a regimen enacted, his father standing up in the corral where he would have gone to direct them over. Snow brushed away.

All those things to do, mostly useless.

At the moment there was only one useful thing to do. Carson turned from the window to go back downstairs to unsaddle and care for the horse.

Trespassing

∧∧∧∧

WIND HUMMED IN EARL'S SPINE, the television tower throbbing like a musical instrument deep below sound's register. Near the fire the party went on, but no one looked Earl's way. He'd become invisible. A part of the background. A lump. A stone. Earl leaned his head against the steel framework, then turned and pressed his ear for just a moment hard against the tower, heard a hollow, wordless bellowing. Wind and iron. The lights of Twisted Tree illuminated the sky to the east, a muddy glowing. Earl thought of Bambi asleep in his plywood house, dreaming of stilled vehicles—the dog's rote and ceaseless hope.

The fire threw the shadows of the partygoers into the cedars, crooked spokes from a hub of flame: bent, wavering, twisted. Or maybe the lighted areas were the spokes and the shadows the spaces between them. Earl tried to see that wheel, but the shapes of light were meaningless, and he looked again to Lostman's Lake and the intermittent flashing of white from the hill beyond it, the barely discernible shapes of the horses. He didn't know what he was doing here.

He stood. No one looked at him. *The Invisible Indian,* he narrated silently, *can't even be seen by other Invisible Indians. We're not even sure we're filming him. Maybe all we're filming is a television tower.* Earl might have made it entirely away if he'd looked down and noticed the empty beer can. Instead, he kicked it, and it whanged along the ground, and all eyes turned to him.

"Leaving already, Walks Alone?"

Ted Kills Many was a little more drunk now, his voice more surly. Earl kept walking. He tried to believe what his mother said, that people like Ted felt threatened by him because they were weak. That's why they tried to knock him off the Red Road, Lorna said. But Earl wasn't sure he was on the Red Road. Wasn't sure he was on any road at all. And if Ted was weak, he sure had a way of seeming strong, of seeming solid and significant—like Goat Man, the shape-shifter that people sometimes saw in their headlights or mirrors, huffing down the highway in long strides, immense and muscular and smelling of earth, like air from a cave or wind from a swamp.

The fire had died down. A current of smoke streamed out and for a moment obscured Ted's face. Earl let himself imagine that Ted was disappearing. Fading. A mirage being eaten by the air. He thought of the men who had hunted Goat Man, the story they told of finding themselves on a windswept plain, deep in the reservation at the edge of the Badlands, their dogs whining and slavering and straining at their leashes, but not to go forward, even the pit bulls cowering and urinating in fear, leaving thick, yellow stains in the snow. But the men had borne forward and had finally seen a gray-brown shape, cobwebby and distorted, within a single tree a hundred yards away. Out of this shape two eyes stared and over this shape horns curved. The scent came to the men, like stagnant water at the edge of a stock pond where cattails grow and cattle have trod and shat: moss, algae, dead fish, fermented vegetation. One of the pit bulls broke its leash and tore away toward home, quaking so violently it couldn't run a straight line but snapped back and forth like a rag in the wind.

The men gripped their rifles, resolved, and dragged the remaining dogs forward. The dogs sat on their haunches, bracing against the pull, or scratched the frozen ground until their paws bled, leaving a flattened path in the snow, raked with red. Then the men stopped. The form in the tree had disintegrated. The shape was there and then it wasn't, and no one could say when it disappeared. Or how. The dogs rose on bleeding paws and panted.

But Ted Kills Many didn't disintegrate, in spite of Earl's imaginings.

"Gotta get home an study?" he said. "Check in with your mother, enit?"

Earl shut his eyes and thought of Goat Man peering out of the tree, and for a moment he saw the men and dogs through Goat Man's eyes, strange and frightening creatures with dire intent. Maybe it wasn't Ted who was like Goat Man at all. Maybe it was Earl. *This looks like a sober Indian, but it's really a creature called Goat Man.*

He opened his eyes, looked away from Ted, and through a gap in the cedars saw a flash of white from the forehead of one of the horses beyond the lake. "I'm going to look at those horses," he said, to divert attention from himself.

He jerked his chin in that direction. Everyone looked but couldn't see anything. Gerald Dupree struggled up and came over and stood next to Earl for a moment, then went back to the fire and collapsed near it.

"Greggy Longwell will arrest you, you go up there," he announced. "That's Magnus Yarborough's land."

"That won't bother Walks Alone," Ted said. "He'll just say it was our land first, and Longwell will let him go. Hah, Walks Alone? That right?"

"Ha-uh, ha-uh, ha-uh." Gerald Dupree made sounds in his chest without opening his mouth. Every high school student in Twisted Tree could imitate Greggy Longwell's two-note grunting laugh. Most of them had heard his flashlight tapping on their windows, had seen its beam in their faces, illuminating the interiors of their cars, seeking alcohol or drugs or nakedness, and then his questions, and the three two-note grunts of laughter that dismissed all answers.

Earl walked away from the fire. Shucked them all off. On Monday, in school, a few people would make fun of him for coming up here, but then they'd forget, and he'd be back to his careful and invisible life. And if he was careful, he could keep it invisible. Or if he stayed invisible, he'd have no trouble being careful. He'd made a little mistake tonight. If he was quiet enough, it would correct itself.

He was in the shadows of the trees, almost out of range of firelight—almost back to his life—when a voice called out, "I am coming with you."

WILLI SCHUBERT, WOULDN'T YOU KNOW? The German foreign-exchange student lived with the Drusemans, a white family, but he spent as much time as he could on the reservation, participating in Lakota activities. Every summer Europeans, Germans in particular, appeared in Twisted Tree to "Experience Lakota Life." It was all one phrase, and it was always, even spoken, capitalized. Willi made Earl feel like a research project. On the other hand, Willi spoke Lakota, which Earl and most of his classmates couldn't do, and Willi had studied Lakota history and stories until he knew them with a disconcerting and uncanny accuracy.

Earl kept walking, putting tree after tree behind him, until the shadows thickened and stabilized and he could no longer tell his own shadow from the shadows of the trees. The music faded, absorbed by cedar needles. Then Earl heard the sound of footsteps behind him. Then the sound of breathing.

"Who is Magnus Yarborough?"

Willi's English was nearly perfect, his *ss* just a bit heavy, his constructions sometimes, but seldom, reversed. Earl didn't answer him. He didn't turn his head to look at Willi. Instead of being rebuffed, Willi walked a little faster, dodging trees, until he was alongside and a little in front of Earl.

"These horses we are going to see," he asked, breathing hard. "Magnus Yarborough's horses. Who is he?"

Earl looked down the moonlit hill. "Just a rancher, you know?" he said. "A rich one."

"And Mr. Longwell is police? Would he arrest us? For seeing these horses? If he knew?"

"I guess Yarborough doesn't like people on his land."

"But why would he care if you are just looking at horses?"

"I don't know. Why are you following me?"

"To see the horses."

"You think I'm going to talk to them?"

"Talk to them?" Willi looked back at Earl, his eyes wide and curious.

"That's what Indians do, you know? Talk to horses."

Willi missed the quiet sarcasm in Earl's voice. "Do you know about horses, much?"

"Why were you at that party?"

The question confused Willi. For the first time he sensed Earl's mood. "Angie Long Feather invited me," he said, a little defensively.

"So you could see a bunch of Indians drinking?"

Earl knew what he was doing wasn't fair. He was angry at Ted, and he was angry at himself for letting Ted make fun of him, and now he was taking it out on Willi just because he could. For that matter, Earl was angry at his mother and probably his father, and certainly the man who'd been on the wrong side of the road that long-ago night. And he was angry at the party makers above him for their drinking, and angry at people who thought Indians did nothing but drink. And Willi, here in the darkness, was just a little weaker, a little more vulnerable, than Earl himself. An easy target. Earl couldn't look at him. He asked the question and then looked away down the hill, as if to take the question away, dilute it, pretend he hadn't asked it.

Willi stopped walking.

"If you do not want me with you," he said, "I will go."

"Why not see a bunch of cowboys drinking, you know? There's a cultural experience for you."

"I think I will go back."

Earl shrugged, staring down the hill. Willi brushed past him. Earl heard his footsteps climbing upward. Then he heard them stop.

"Why did you go to that party?" Willi's voice asked.

Earl turned around. Willi stood above him, moonlight illuminating his hair so that it frayed brightly around his head.

Earl shrugged again and answered more honestly than he had intended. "Because I wasn't invited, I guess."

"OK. The next time I get invited, I will invite you. So you can stay home."

Earl stared at Willi. He didn't know whether Willi was serious or joking, but the statement was so absurd, yet so dead-center, that it broke Earl's sullen mood, and he laughed. Willi grinned uncertainly.

The wind rushed through the cedars around them and a moment later hit the tower high above, and the bass throb of the guy wires descended to Earl's gut.

"I just wanted to get away from that party, you know?" he said. "I wasn't even gonna look at them horses."

"I should not have invited myself to come with you."

"On the other hand, I did say I'd look at them. I should do what I say."

Earl met Willi's eyes, then started down the hill again. Hearing nothing behind him, he turned back. Willi hadn't moved. Beneath the incandescence of his hair, his face was in shadow.

"You coming?" Earl asked.

THEY EMERGED FROM THE CEDARS covering Tower Hill onto the highway running south and west into the Badlands and then the Sand Hills of Nebraska. In the dark the highway looked like a fossilized river whose banks had eroded away, raising it above the land. The sky opened up, the Big Dipper vast and bright in the north. Their footsteps rang on the asphalt.

"It is so quiet here," Willi said. "In Germany even the quiet places have noise. Because all the people go to find the quiet. And here it is so dark. With stars."

Earl paused in the middle of the highway. He'd never given the darkness and quiet much thought. He looked at the sky, trying to see it new, like Willi did. The lights of Twisted Tree were hidden behind Tower Hill. Even the Little Dipper was distinct and clear.

"The second star in the handle of the Big Dipper is a double star," Willi said. "Some American Indian tribes call them the Horse and Rider."

"Huh," Earl grunted. "Horse and Rider, huh?"

Willi nodded.

"You know it's actually a double double?" Earl asked.

"Double double?"

"Two pairs. Each star revolves around its partner. Then each pair revolves around the other pair."

"I did not know. It is a big dance up there. It is a star powwow."

"Or gravity," Earl said.

He walked across the highway onto the dirt drive leading to Lostman's Lake. In another minute the lake came into view, stretched out in the moonlight, lapping against its earthen berm and against the sand the Corps of Engineers had hauled in to form a beach and boat ramp that no one ever used. Earl's uncle Norman said it was just like the Corps of Engineers to dam a stream and then try to appease the Indians by building a boat ramp even though no one had a boat and even though the Indians opposed the dam not for their own sake but the stream's. Norm periodically threatened to get a modern-day war party together to hijack one of the yachts being carted across the country on I-90. "Wouldn't that be something, Earl?" he said. "One of those big old yachts on that little lake and a bunch of Indians with war paint on, drinking out of cocktail glasses."

"This is a pretty lake," Willi said.

"I don't know. They didn't drown any villages here, I guess."

"What do you mean, drown villages?"

"You been to Lake Oahe?"

"My family took me there. It is the biggest earth dam in the world."

"Why do you think those walleyes get so big there? My uncle says it's because they're living in Indian houses. There used to be Indian towns along the Missouri. They're under water now. They just dammed the Missouri up and told people to move. But hey, the walleye fishing improved. My uncle says everyone else is feasting on Indian, so why not give the fish a chance?"

Willi's moonfaced attentiveness encouraged Earl to go on. "Once they got to building dams, they couldn't stop," he said. "First they dammed all the rivers, and when they ran out of rivers they went to little creeks. Like this one, you know? Norm—my uncle— calls it a bad case of addictive behavior. He thinks the Corps of Engineers and the Bureau of Reclamation need to attend Dam Builders Anonymous."

At a powwow Earl had once talked to a tourist from Florida who told Earl he'd come to South Dakota to go scuba diving. Earl had thought the man was joking until he described going into Oahe, sinking beneath the waters into silence. Then he saw, opening through the murk below, the rooftops of houses, gray rectangles, silt-coated, strange in the dimming light. He felt he was entering another world where time had ceased, suspending the forms of things. He descended fifty feet toward those roofs: a world cold, austere, and lifeless. He stood, finally, on a rooftop and looked into a murky street and then dropped off and floated down, and when he hit the bottom dirt clouded up in a slow, roiling storm. An open door awaited him, the gaping interior of a house. He wanted to walk through those abandoned houses, watch the bubbles of his breath rise to the ceilings, roll upward on the slightest slopes. He wanted to touch the furniture abandoned there, to sit in rocking chairs, sway them against the water's resistance. He wanted to pretend to smoke a pipe or read a paper. But he couldn't enter the house. He stood in the doorway and felt a power forbidding him. He looked down the gray, receding street, and fear entered him. As if here, even with air, he could drown.

When Earl was twelve, Norm had taken him to the top of the dam here at Lostman's Lake. Earl pointed out the NO TRESPASSING sign to his uncle, but Norm strode past it. "Two things, nephew," he said. "The first is, your mother isn't happy you're with me at all, so you're already stepping outside the lines. And the second is, that's a government sign."

Norm wiped sweat from his eyes and walked along the top of the berm until he got to the very center. He stared across the twenty acres of stilled water, hooking his thumbs in his pants pockets. Earl, standing next to him, did the same.

"They've sure got that creek shut down, hey?" Norm asked.

Earl nodded, unsure how to respond.

"But I guess we knew that without strutting up here to have a look. Just thought you ought to see it."

Norm walked away, and as he passed it he grabbed the NO TRES-PASSING sign in his large hands. His shoulders bunched beneath his T-shirt, and with a quick jerk he twisted the sign clear around so that the post looked screwed into the ground and the NO TRESPASS-

ING BEYOND THIS POINT faced inward and seemed to be speaking to people born on top of the dam, keeping them off the hills beyond. The post torsioned back and forth when Norm let go of it, and the sign made curious, catlike crying noises, sheet metal under stress—whing, whing, whing—as Norm strode away, long black braid swinging on his back.

No one had ever bothered to straighten the sign. Earl saw it shaking off moonlight, scattering it into bits and pieces, as he and Willi walked past the dam. *Like a lost code for wind,* he thought, *some equation no one understands.* He'd trespassed onto the face of the dam that day with Norm, and when Norm twisted the sign to face the other way, it was like he'd trespassed off again. Alien everywhere he went.

A BARBWIRE FENCE demarcated the end of public land and the beginning of Magnus Yarborough's spread. Hung over every fourth fence post were old tires with PRIVATE PROPERTY: KEEP OUT hand-painted on them in white. Earl used one of the tires to steady himself as he climbed over the fence. Willi followed, teetering as he swung his leg over, the steel post shaking under his weight. He jumped down and turned around.

"Where are the horses?"

This was an adventure for him, a new experience.

"Loud as you are, probably in the next county by now," Earl said.

But as they topped the rise above the lake, the horses came into view, standing in a depression invisible from the road. The animals stood inside a second barbwire enclosure fifty yards away—unmoving, and so close together they might have been a single, three-headed animal carved from rock. A small plume of steam rose behind them, and the sound of trickling water reached Earl's ears.

"Take it slow," Earl said.

They approached carefully, the animals alert and nervous. One of them left the group and moved to the far side of the small enclosure, then returned, bobbing its head. Dust rose from the grass, turned silver in the moonlight, a low, metallic, shining cloud. The animals glowed within it.

"See?" Earl pointed to a white diamond on the forehead of one of the horses. "That's what I saw from up there."

He looked back at Tower Hill. He could see the faint glow of the fire illuminating the treetops and above the trees the red lights snapping on and off high in the stars.

The horses backed away as Willi and Earl approached—not so much fearful as careful, waiting to see what they would do. Earl saw the source of steam and waternoise. A small artesian spring trickled out of the ground, collecting in a small hole hastily dug near the fence, its excess heat dissipating in clouds of vapor. Earl walked around the pen to where the water pooled. Willi followed. The horses circled the other way.

Earl held his hand over the water, felt the steam against it, then dipped his fingers quickly in. The water was hot but not unbearable. He pulled his hand out, shook the water off.

"This is kind of odd, you know?" he said.

"How is it odd?"

Earl looked around as Willi stooped and felt the water. The pen was maybe thirty yards across, perfectly square, made of wire so new the points of the barbs glittered. The only land Earl could see in any direction was the top of Tower Hill, which meant the pen was invisible from anywhere but that point, sunk behind the rolling rises around it.

"I don't know," Earl said. "Just odd, you know? A brand new fence. No rust. The fence posts are all straight yet. Why would anyone build a pen like this and stick three horses in it? With just that to drink?"

Willi pulled his hand out of the water, shook it, wiped it on his pants. The wire gleamed softly in six parallel lines, and the white tops of the steel fence posts punctuated the darkness in neat and regular array, anchored at the corners by wooden posts smelling of creosote. Earl watched Willi pick a tuft of dark hair off one of the barbs, rub it between his fingers, let it go. The wind caught it, carried it into the darkness.

His own words had made Earl vaguely uneasy. "I ought to be going home," he said.

"Why is that horse standing funny?"

The horses had settled down. The veil of dust they'd raised from the grass had dropped, and their scent came more distinctly, like old wool soaked in vinegar. Earl had turned to leave, but he turned back now and looked where Willi pointed. The horse with the white diamond on its forehead stood with its back left leg curled up, putting no weight on it.

"Likes to stand that way, I guess," Earl said.

Willi walked around the fence toward the horses. As he did they moved slowly away, the diamond-marked horse holding its rear hoof off the ground.

"Look how it walks, Earl."

"It limps a little. I got homework to do, you know?"

"Is not it odd that horse is, what did you say, limping?"

There was curiosity and excitement in Willi's voice. Earl thought of what his mother would say if she knew he'd gone to the party on Tower Hill, even if he hadn't taken a drink. And if he got caught out here. It was true, they were just looking at the horses, but the place made him feel he shouldn't be here. Made him feel that if they were caught here, bad things would happen. He tried to shake it off with a little internal narrative. *The Careful Indian doesn't like what he sees. Notice how he shies away from the fence, while his companion, the Wannabe Indian, approaches the horses.* But it didn't work. Earl couldn't rid himself of the feeling the place gave him.

"Horses limp for a lot of reasons," he said.

"I think this is very odd, Earl."

"But you probably think a lot of things are odd out here, you know? Anything can make a horse limp. Maybe this pen is to help it heal. So it won't run."

"I don't think so, Earl. I think there is something wrong here."

A stubborn tone had crept into Willi's voice. Earl realized he was in an argument. He'd once heard a Belgian man who had come to live on the reservation challenge the way a naming ceremony was performed. The man insisted he'd studied the ceremony, and it had been done incorrectly. No one could convince him that the way it was done in real life was more correct than the way it was written down. But the Belgian held captive the men he argued with. They felt the need to convince him he was wrong, and as long as they felt that need, he controlled them. Earl didn't want to give Willi that power. This fence and the horses penned within it might make perfect sense, as Earl had just said, but he wasn't going to argue the point.

"All right," he said. "If you say it's odd, it's odd. I'm going home."

He turned, leaving Willi and the horses behind. When he crested the rise, Lostman's Lake appeared below him, a brilliant, ragged oval of water filled with the moon. Against that lighted surface, the silhouette of a bat suddenly appeared below Earl, its wings folded. An instant, and it was gone. It startled Earl. Then he heard the sound of wings, a soft clacking in the air coming from all over, an unintelligible conversation murmurous and strange, and he realized the bats were all around him, that he was walking through a storm of them, invisible in the darkness. From nowhere, air rushed against his ear, and he heard the suck of wings inches away. Earl imagined the bat tumbling upward over his head, its small, tight face following the myriad reflections of its own voice. A white moth floated by, then suddenly disappeared, but Earl could not see the bat that had swallowed it.

The Rememberer

∿∿∿∿

WILLI WATCHED EARL'S HEAD, shoulders, and torso rise out of the darkness of the hill to be silhouetted against the background light of the southern stars. Then he watched Earl's shape sink down again. He looked again at the horses, and he knew that Earl was wrong. Horses might limp for many reasons, and there might be a reason to pen them up, but Willi knew that *odd* was not the right word for what he saw before him. That required a darker word that conveyed the foreboding Willi felt, the sense that his heart was made of some elastic material that had been thinned and stretched and was leaking downward through his chest. It was the same feeling he'd had when he first visited his grandmother. That, too, had first seemed merely odd.

The white diamond on the horse's forehead bobbed up and down. In the darkness that white diamond seemed almost a bird. A white bird flying up and down within a cage.

He remembered his grandmother's pale white hand, the finger she raised from the arm of her chair. "Look around you," she said. "Cages are everywhere."

"No," he told her. "You're wrong."

But here he stood, having crossed land and water both, before a cage. He could almost hear his grandmother's voice. *You expected something different?*

"ARE YOU SURE YOU WANT TO GO?" his father had asked him.

Willi nodded.

"A year is a long time."

"I know."

"What do you hope for?"

His father was speaking like the history teacher he was, as if Willi were one of his students writing a research paper and his father were quizzing him on what he expected to find. Distant. Reserved. Aloof. Examining his student's reasoning.

Willi pinched the leather on the arm of the chair where he sat, saw the leather bunch between his thumb and finger. He released it, pinched again. "I don't know," he said.

"You must have something?"

"I want to know about the Lakota people."

"What about them?"

"Their rituals. Their ceremonies. Their language."

"Why do you want to know these things?"

Willi felt resentful. Did there have to be a reason? "We've made such a mess of the world," he finally said.

He looked out the big window behind his father at the city of Koblenz. Over the lower edge of the window, he could just make out a partial curve of the Rhine, moving gray and swift. The smoke stack of a boat labored from one edge of the window to the other, working upriver. On the walking path along the far bank, a pedestrian appeared in a gap between trees, indistinct, male or female, coat open and flapping, then disappeared again.

"You think the Indians have an older knowledge," Willi's father said.

Willi pinched the chair again, watching his fingertips turn white as the blood was pressed from them. "Maybe," he said, defensively. "At least they haven't destroyed things."

"You have your books. Your *Indianer* club. Its powwows. That's not enough?"

"That's still us. Germans pretending to be Indians for a while."

"Us," Willi's father repeated. He gazed at Willi. Willi met his eyes for a few moments but couldn't hold them and looked out the window again, now just sky and trees and edge-of-river. Finally his father spoke again: "If you wish to go, I have no objection, Willi. I just want to be sure you're sure. You may find, though, that people are the same everywhere. That there is not the difference you think between us and them."

"I know what difference there is," Willi almost said. He almost told his father about his visit to his grandmother a year earlier, the secret he had kept from his parents all that time. But his father, now that he had agreed to letting Willi go to South Dakota, had opened the book in his lap again and was reading. As if everything were settled.

IT WAS ONLY AFTER HE LEARNED that his father's mother was alive, and met her, that Willi began to think that his first memory was one he couldn't possibly have. Whenever he remembered meeting his grandmother, he was always across from her, looking out of his own eyes. He remembered *her:* her withered hand on the chair arm, the smell of lavender and cleaning fluid and disinfectant in her house, the way her finger came up, pointed to the bird in its cage, the dry and humorless voice that emerged from her moving lips. But when he thought of his first memory, he saw *himself,* at different angles and distances, in different lights. But if he was seeing himself, then which was he in the memory, the one seen or the one seeing?

He began to realize that with all his other memories the memory of the memory itself was traceable. It left a clear track in his mind that he could follow back through the years and know that five years ago he had remembered such a thing, and five years before that. But his first memory had no such continuity. There was a break in his memory of remembering it. He could remember remembering it when he was twelve. Ten. Perhaps nine or eight. But there he lost the trail.

It begins with a child's screaming. It is his own screaming, but he hears it from a distance. He remembers being in the back seat of a car, but what he sees is not what he would have seen: the back of his mother's head, her short, curled hair above the headrest, and the vast reaches of the auto, the dome light far away, and his own fat hands in front of his eyes. Instead, it is all reversed, as if he is somewhere within the dome light, peering out at himself: his red, scrunched face, his taut tongue.

The tires strike the bump of the driveway. *Chunkchunk.* He may have heard this from anywhere. But he remembers his mother's worried face and himself in the backseat behind her, the nubs of his teeth. Is he standing on the car's hood, peering through the windshield?

For no reason at all, she has told him. *You just started crying for no reason at all. I couldn't get you stopped. So I turned around and took you home. You must have felt something. Children do that sometimes—know when something is wrong.*

But Willi can't remember discomfort or unease. How can he remember the sight of his own red face but not remember the feeling that caused that crying?

He also has a mental picture, which surely cannot be a memory, of his father upstairs in a darkened room, on a bed covered with plastic sheeting. On the dresser is a photograph at which his father stares. Then his father glances away, surprised, and sees himself in the mirror across the room, pressing a pistol against his forehead. He sees himself only because the headlights that surprised him shine briefly through the uncurtained windows as the tires bump up into the driveway. His wife and son were not supposed to return for hours. But now the headlights show Willi's father his reflection in the mirror, while for a moment they reflect off the glass of the framed photograph on the dresser in such a way that they block the photograph. For the briefest spasm the photograph is nothing but reflected light, and the unsmiling face of the man behind it, which has stared out of that frame for years—since Willi's father removed it from a bureau drawer and placed it there, in spite of his wife's attempts to remove it (telling her, *Leave the bastard there. I don't want to give him the satisfaction of forgetting*)—that face is for a moment obliterated.

Willi doesn't know of this argument between his mother and father over the photograph, and he doesn't remember how his father went through the house after he and his mother left in the car that night—doing the dishes, folding newspapers in the living room, putting his office in order, straightening the pages of an unfinished article manuscript, looking at what he has written before squaring it on his desk, finally climbing the stairs, shutting off lights behind him. Willi doesn't remember these things, though he has reconstructed them so clearly that what he remembers and what he knows but doesn't remember have mingled to form a coherence that perhaps he cannot trust and that, under the force of examination, turns to dust, an insubstantial architecture that nevertheless bears everything.

His father climbed the stairs, carrying a packet of painter's plastic, which he unfurled over the bed. An unbearable neatness. He went to the bureau and removed a pistol from a drawer. He checked it for cartridges, saw them snuggled inside. Neat. Waiting. Smelling of oil and brass. He closed the chamber, took the pistol to the bed, lay down.

The plastic rustled. A watery sound. He turned to the photograph on top of the bureau and placed the barrel to his head. *Your own pistol,* he said to the photograph. *This is the end of your ugly dream. Of what you tried to make me.*

He gathered his breath. He heard linden leaves outside the window. He heard traffic. American rock music from a passing car. And then, muted by the walls of the house, the *chunk* of tires on the driveway, and the room momentarily filled with light. A crying child, a point on a distant road where a car is turned around, the angle of light, the exact moment when he presses the barrel to his forehead—it all forms an equation impossible to calculate.

The black windows: Willi's mother was filled with dread. She slammed on the brakes in the middle of the driveway, and Willi was startled out of his crying. He remembers silence—as if the world were suddenly shut off—then his wail again, louder than before. His mother bolted from the car, took one step toward the house, and was paralyzed. She looked from the dark house to her crying child and could not move toward either.

Then she stumbled back to the car, jerked open the back door, fumbled with the belt holding Willi, hoisted him out.

And heard a shot.

She screamed, lost her hold on him. Willi's head slipped toward the concrete driveway. His mother fell to her knees to get her arms around him and managed to recover him inches from the ground. Willi remembers some of this, but again from the wrong perspective. He doesn't remember the shot and doesn't remember the stars shaking as he lay in his mother's arms, or the world turning upside down as he fell headfirst toward the pavement, or the abrupt jar of being caught, or the underside of his mother's jaw as she ran toward the house, or her tears falling on his face. What he remembers instead—as if he stood on the steps of the house and watched her come up the driveway carrying him—is how she fell to her knees to catch him, the open car door behind them, an insect flickering through the light of a street lamp, brilliant and fleeting, his mother's knee bleeding in two long rivers down her leg as she ran toward the house, and one of her shoes, fallen off, lying on the driveway alone. And how it lamed her. How she ran clumping toward the house, trying to kick the other shoe off, and then burst through the door, clutching her child, calling her husband's name, and started up the stairs and then suddenly stopped, sobbing, unable to go on. She swayed, nearly fell backwards, grasped the banister with one hand to keep from tumbling down. Remembering this, Willi finds that he has somehow migrated, that he sees his mother in that memory from below, her hair swinging around her head as she nearly falls, and his own head bobbing and swaying when she catches herself. His helpless and powerless neck.

Then she heard plastic rustle. She jerked her face upwards. Her husband appeared on the landing above her, holding a pistol at his side, his feet bleeding. He pushed the smell of cordite out of the bedroom with him, pushed it down the stairway. That moment of illumination canceling the past and revealing the present had been enough.

When he thinks of it, Willi doesn't know what he remembers. He remembers his parents talking, though he knows he didn't understand language. And he remembers that they spoke in eerily quiet voices, though he can't remember when he stopped crying, that such whispers could be used.

"You're bleeding," his father says.

His mother looks at her knee, sees two streams of blood running down both sides of her right shinbone, pooling for a moment in the concavities of her ankle, falling to the floor. She wipes her face with the ball of her thumb.

"You too," she says.

Willi's father—in Willi's memory—looks puzzled. He follows her gaze to his feet, widens his eyes in surprise at the lacerations there, the blood soaked into the hallway carpet. He lifts his foot. It glints as he lifts it. Then he removes a long sliver of glass and holds it up. Glass stained with blood, redly transparent. They all look at it—mother, father, and the rememberer, who stands somewhere below them now, though Willi must have been in his mother's arms.

Then Willi's father places the bloodstained glass on the ledge at the top of the stairs. Gently, not to break it. He steps toward his wife, but she retreats downward, keeping herself and her child safe. He understands a new beginning is necessary.

"You're right," he tells her. "I was going to do it. But you came back. The lights from the car." He gestures, helpless.

"I shot that photograph instead," he says. "That's why." He lifts his bleeding foot.

"He would get the last cut in," he says.

She lets him descend and touch her and their child. They are strangers, their touching formal and careful, seeking the boundaries of what they have lost, what they have gained. But they hold each other, and a little familiarity returns.

"Why did you come back?"

She looks down at the sleeping baby.

"He wouldn't stop crying," she replies.

"Thank God for that."

They have told Willi he was sleeping. Yet he remembers his father's words.

Of course, he can't remember them.

And neither can he remember—a different kind of impossibility—what he most wants to remember: whether he was crying because he knew, because he felt something terrible happening and so saved his father's life. Or whether it was just chance: teething, the straps of the car seat binding him.

"EARL?" WILLI CALLED WEAKLY into the foreign night.

Earl had gone beyond the reach of any voice. But Willi wasn't alone. Because he'd been standing still for so long, cast back into his memories, the horses had settled down, come closer, and Willi felt warm breath against his shoulder. He turned. The diamond-marked horse blew its breath out again, over Willi's face. He breathed that breath in, the condensed grassiness of it. He reached out, and the horse let him touch it. He stroked it. Then the other two crowded close, and he stroked them. The gleaming barbwire stood between them.

"Cages," his grandmother had said, "are everywhere."

And this place was more than odd. No matter what Earl said.

The air was speaking, clicking and stammering. The artesian spring bubbled and gurgled. Willi stared over the bowed heads of the horses at the steam rising off it. He shivered. He drew closer to the horses, to their large warmth. "I will help you somehow," he said. He didn't know how. Didn't even know for sure they needed help. But that hot water springing from the earth, dissipating in vapor, seemed horrible to him. To be caged with that, night and day.

The Old House

~~~~~

Few weeks after he graduated from high school, Carson
Fielding moved out of his parents' house into the old one. In
the two years since his grandfather's death, Carson had
walked past the old house every day, on his way to doing something
else, but he stopped at the broken steps one late summer evening,
bowed his head for a moment, then put his hand on the doorknob,
opened the door, and stepped into the empty rooms where only
the smells of his grandfather remained: stale cigarette smoke, dirt,
sweat.

Carson's grandfather had never resisted cleanliness but had
never considered it necessary either. After his death, Marie and
Charles had washed the floors, vacuumed the threadbare carpets,
unplugged the appliances—and then wondered what the point was
and stopped. Carson stood in a cleaner version of the house his
grandfather had stepped from the morning he died. The meager
furniture stood where Ves had arranged it. Carson had never known
a space that so much framed an absence.

The next day he began to carry his few possessions from his
room in the new house down the stairs and across the yard into the
old one. From the office where she was keeping the ranch's books,
Marie watched him go up and down the stairs. When he stopped
for a glass of water, she came out of the office and stood in the
doorway to the kitchen.

"You're moving into the old house, Carson?"

He tilted his head, drained the water, set the glass soundlessly
on the counter, nodded.

"You've talked to your father about this?"

"It's been standin empty for two years. Might as well live in it."

"Your father was going to tear it down. He just never got around to it."

"Tear it down? Grampa built that house."

"There's nothing there, Carson. And it's falling apart."

"Only because no one's keepin it up."

"Some things aren't worth keeping up."

"It ain't a thing."

"It's old, Carson. It was old when we were living in it. Before Lucy and Ves moved back."

"Old's OK with me."

He smiled at her, but Marie wasn't shaken from her serious mood. "I've lived in it," she said. "Your grandfather wasn't an architect. That house is more a windbreak than a house."

But Carson only grinned. "Well, Grampa knew how to break wind."

WHEN HE WAS FOUR YEARS OLD, Carson left a game his mother had thought he was absorbed in and wandered out the door and across the yard. By the time his mother discovered him gone, he had disappeared behind the barn. She followed her fears—first the road, then the stock pond. By the time she got to the pond, Carson had left off playing at the water's edge and rounded a bend in the draw. Had she known what to look for, she might have seen where his feet had muddied the water and the bent-grass trail going away from the water's edge.

Having seen nothing, frantic, she ran back to the house, got in the car, and bounced over the section line road to the field where Charles was working summer fallow. They hurried back, neither of them voicing their fears: the wideness of the country, the water Marie's voice had traveled over when she stood at the stock pond's shore.

Charles started the two ATVs they owned, and they searched, calling. But they were both too worried to think clearly, and they ended up circling, covering ground they had already covered. When they met back at the house, Marie was in tears, Charles tight-lipped.

Carson's grandmother had called the CENEX in Twisted Tree and lo-
cated her husband. Returning home, Ves found his son and daughter-
in-law almost paralyzed, having looked, as they thought, everywhere.
He listened to their story.

"Wonder what he was thinking?" he said.

He meant it literally. He went to the door of the old house,
squatted down to get Carson's four-year-old perspective, and gazed
at the country. A long time. He tapped a cigarette from a pack, stuck
it in his mouth, lit it, and gazed as he smoked. Finally he rose, went
to the barn, and saddled a horse, waving off his son's offer of an
ATV. He rode to the stock pond. He saw what Marie had missed.

A few minutes later Carson looked up from where he had spent
a long afternoon playing under the steep bank of the draw to find
the old man sitting the horse and watching him. Smoking. Saying
nothing. Carson went back to playing. The old man sat and watched.
Unhurried, unexcited. Carson might have been a mule deer the old
man had spotted. A pheasant or grouse. A cone flower. A badger or
blade of grass.

After a time Carson climbed out of the draw and walked to the
horse and waited for his grandfather to reach down and loft him,
his feet leaving the ground, that long float up. The old man secured
his grandson in the crook of his arm, clucked to the horse, and
turned it without urgency toward the house. Carson dozed within
the sharp and sweetish smell of his grandfather's embrace. When
the horse stopped moving, he half-woke but kept his eyes closed.
Marie came across the yard with upraised arms, her face tear-
streaked.

"Give him to me, Ves."

Carson's eyes fluttered at the sound of her voice, but glimpsing
her broken expression through the slits of his lashes, he knew he'd
done something to hurt her. He didn't know what, but he quickly
closed his eyes again.

"Boy's sleepin, Marie," his grandfather said. "I'll go on ridin with
'm. He was jus playin, but he's about wore out. I'll ride 'm around,
let 'm sleep, and when he's awake I'll bring 'm back."

Carson heard his mother's sob. He knew he should reveal himself as awake, leap down to her. But he couldn't. He let his grandfather turn the horse away. Through fluttering, narrow lids, he saw his mother floating backwards, and he could feel the horse's muscular, rocking body. It felt to him as if the horse were the one still thing in a moving world.

"He's not sleeping."

It was his father's voice. Carson had seen his father standing behind his mother, unmoving as she walked toward the horse. His father in the background, waiting, watching. How did he know the truth?

Ves let the horse continue walking.

"He's not sleeping, Dad," Charles said again.

But Ves didn't turn around, and Carson didn't open his eyes. If his father had told him to, he would have. But his father said nothing more. So, complicit, Carson let his grandfather take him away.

NOW, AS THEN, CARSON FELT A GULF between himself and his mother. Not an estrangement—just a quiet gulf that he couldn't bridge. Nothing she said about the old house seemed to him an argument not to live in it. He didn't mind wind, or even cold, that much. When he'd wandered away at four years old, he'd not intended to hurt his mother. That had just happened. But he'd never been lost. She'd just thought he was, and her grief had confused him. And here again she seemed to be insisting he was lost when he wasn't.

He'd never told anyone what he'd seen or done the day his grandfather died. He thought of telling her now. But he didn't know how to say it: how he'd seen the horse's hoof connect with his grandfather's skull and that instead of it making him bitter toward the animal, he'd left the bedroom window where he'd watched the snow falling in slantwise lines and gone out to the animal and untied it and led it into the barn and removed the saddle and bridle and laid his ear against the large, calm ribs and heard the faraway, slow thump of the heart. He'd broken a hay bale and fed the animal and watched it eat, then gone back into the snowstorm, where near the corral the ambulance squatted, and men were bending down.

He had watched them for a moment, then found a bucket, taken it to the mudroom of the house and drawn warm water, added detergent, returned to the barn through the snow. The ambulance had its back door open, and the men were carrying a stretcher. He had looked at the stretcher and what was on it but had not stopped—had gone back to the barn and with a rag ripped from a pair of his grandfather's old denims washed blood from the horse's hoof. The next day he'd ridden the Scooter horse out to the draw where his grandfather had found him when he was four and dug a hole in the frozen earth and buried the bloody rag. Wind had blown and snow had fallen, the world indifferent, going about its vast and austere business, beyond all human grieving.

Carson thought that if he could speak of these things his mother might understand why he wanted to live in the old house. But he couldn't even begin. He thought of horses. Of how they moved singly or in groups, of how their hoofbeats drummed the earth. He thought of how, when he trained them, he breathed their grainy breath and how, in arenas, their hooves cut into the earth and back out with so much power that spectators were dirtied high into the stands with flecks of mud. Of how, when horses turned around the barrels, their bodies leaned as if gravity could be suspended—and how he could train them to so suspend it.

But of this, too, he found he could not speak.

A MONTH AFTER VES DIED, Charles had wanted to tear the old house down. "What use is it now?" he'd said. "Leave it stand, it's gonna be nothin but a mouse hotel. Or a temptation for lightning."

But Marie had stopped him. "We can't be that practical about it," she said. "It's hard enough for Carson, Ves being gone. If you tear that house down, too? Wait a few months."

But things had come up, the needs of the ranch, relentless and ongoing. They took Charles's attention and energy. Distracted him. Only once had he actually found time to start the demolition. "Tomorrow," he'd told her, "I'm goin a start takin it down. Try to save some've the lumber, maybe use it for something else." She'd agreed.

Enough time had passed. But the next morning, while Charles was doing chores, the Case had died, and he spent two days fuming and fixing it, and by the time he was done other things took over.

And then they just got used to it. Almost forgot it was there. Until now. Strange, Marie thought, how empty structures can become a part of your life. How you can simply not notice them. And then you quit imagining what you'd see if they weren't there. Quit imagining the space you'd see, the sky. Or the flower bed you might plant. The tree. Instead you just let the empty structure stand. Let it occupy the space you'd thought to use. You go about your business. Yet she wondered how much the empty structure made a difference. Its standing there. Its witness to what had been—how much did that matter, even though they'd quit noticing? She wished she'd let Charles tear it down when he'd first wanted to.

She had watched Carson and his father grow apart. It wasn't animosity but more a giving in. A sense of the inevitable. Carson had grown attached to Ves, and Charles had seen how they worked the horses together, how good Carson was at it. Charles had refused to fight it. He could see that Carson loved it. But at the supper table, when Ves bragged about Carson's instincts, Marie noticed how Charles nodded. She knew that he heard another thing, unsaid: that he himself had never been that good. And she knew that his own silence, his mere nod, sprang from his deep, unspoken sense that he should be the one bragging about his son. The one showing him the world and taking pride in how he grasped it.

Marie thought now that if Carson moved into the old house, it would be another instance, like when he'd gone to buy that horse without asking, of choosing Ves over Charles. Neither Carson nor his father would think of it that way. But she knew that Charles, whether he named it or not, would feel it.

Looking at her son, so confident, so sure what he wanted to do, she wondered if she should tell him how hard Ves had made Charles work when he was young, how single-minded Ves had been. The grandfather Carson knew, the patient, slow-moving teacher of how the world worked, had been a long time in the ripening. It had taken Marie years to warm to him, and she believed that warming—her warming—had been part of what had softened Ves. If he loved Carson, Marie suspected he'd loved her first because she had so steadfastly refused to be intimidated by him, until he'd finally laughed at himself. And loved her for allowing that laughter.

He'd come banging on the door of the old house one rainy night in the first years of Marie's marriage—this before Carson was born, before Lucy, Charles's mother, had insisted that Marie and Charles move with their new baby into the new house while she and Ves returned to the old. He'd come banging on the door and before Marie could answer had barged into the kitchen, dripping water on the floor.

"Marie," he'd exclaimed. "Goddamn. We got cows broke out up north. Get your clothes on and come out and help chase 'em."

She was dressed in a bathrobe, doing nothing but reading a book. He turned to go, assuming she'd do as he commanded.

"Goddamn no," she said to his back.

A glass pane seemed to descend invisibly from the ceiling, and Ves ran into it. He stopped so fast he appeared to rebound. His hat spun water off its brim as he turned back to her.

"No?"

"You're a crazy old fart," she said. "You don't come barging into someone else's house until they answer the door or call you in, even if you did build the damn thing. You don't dribble all over their floor. And you don't go chasing cattle at night in the rain when your neighbors will help you chase them tomorrow when the sun's shining. Where do you think they're going to go? There's no highway up north they're going to get out on. So no. Goddamn no."

She turned back to the paragraph she'd looked up from. Ves stared at her through the water still dripping off his hat brim.

"I'm a crazy old fart?" he asked. "Is that what you said?"

"At least you're not a deaf one, too."

"Jesus! I ain't that goddamn *old!*"

He'd gone from the house, laughing a storm. She heard him call into the darkness: "Chuck, goddamn, come in outta the rain. Marie says it's crazy to be chasing cattle right now. She says I'm a crazy old fart!"

His laughter was louder than the rain. The next day he was still laughing. It got so he couldn't see Marie without smiling, and the more she teased and insulted him the more he laughed and returned it. Marie would come to believe that night was the first time anyone had claimed a thing that Ves considered his by right of effort and will. He'd had the new house built for Lucy but had never relinquished his claim on the old, not even when his son and daughter-in-law moved in. But that rainy night he'd been confronted with a woman calm and unmoved within walls she'd decorated, space she'd created, even if he'd first formed it. He'd felt himself an intruder. In his laughter he'd admitted the old house was hers. He'd let it go—perhaps the first thing in his life he'd ever relinquished completely and without stipulation. He'd never again entered her home without knocking. He would stand on the steps until she opened the door, even if she called him in, and not out of irony but because he knew no other way to change. There were no subtleties, no gradations, to his giving in.

And because he'd learned to relinquish his claim to a thing he considered his, he was prepared, when Carson was born, to be a grandfather, to accept what others had labored over, the fruit of others' dreams and wills—to accept those things as gifts. He held his newborn grandson, when Lucy handed him over, as gently as he'd hold a newborn calf dropped in a snowstorm, and with far more wonder.

Who would have thought—Marie didn't at the time—that anything of sad consequence could come of that? The one person who couldn't benefit from Ves's change of heart was Charles. No matter what the Bible said, Marie thought, prodigality—and there could be a prodigality of control—would have its consequences. You can't just change your life and expect everyone to be happy with it. Expect everyone to forgive. To eat the fatted calf, drink the wine. To glory in the fact that you can now relent, love, live your life, without demanding that everyone live theirs the way you want them to. Ves had demanded so much of Charles. And maybe because of that, Charles had never managed to claim the land as she had the house, to take it from his father, put his own stamp on it. He worked endlessly but like tires slipping in gumbo mud, unable to imprint himself fully upon his work.

And then, when Charles had a son, with visions of raising that son in a different image than he'd been raised himself, Ves changed. He had lived a life of hardness against others, and then a life of gentleness—and had managed to claim, maybe, more than his share of each. Charles was still Carson's father—but in some ways Ves had stolen the boy from Charles. Stolen him by patience. By laughter. By horses. By affections Charles had intended to show his son, as he'd not been shown them.

Marie knew that Charles wanted nothing so much for Carson as that he get away. Go somewhere other than this ranch. But Charles, though he would not choose the things Carson chose, could not demand Carson be anything but what he was. In this way he was, after all, the father he had always intended to be. But in letting Carson choose his own path, choose his grandfather, Charles became aloof from them both. Without realizing it, he made that sacrifice.

Maybe if Charles had gotten the old house torn down, Carson would have less reason to stay. Marie looked at her son, so confident and sure of himself, and she had an odd and disconcerting thought: She wished she could plant in him a seed of discontent. Wished she could make him more needy. She used to buy him toys when he was young, and he would play with them for a while but would soon go outside, and she'd see him throwing stones or walking toward the stock pond to fish or watch for birds. She felt now some of the same sadness she'd felt when she would eventually put away the toy she'd bought, knowing he would never play with it again—a sense that she could not reach him and a guilty desire to make him need what he did not want. To make him less secure. Less content.

Marie thought of the old house as a barren pile of lumber. Walls tacked together. But her son, she knew, would be happy there. It would be enough for him. But how much, Marie wondered, might that limit him? She knew young men who were becoming old men out here—men who stayed on their family ranches because they loved the life, but unless they were very lucky and found a woman who also loved the life, they ended up divorced, like Burt Ramsay,

Magnus Yarborough's hired hand, who used to ranch nearby, or they never married at all and either became quirky and silent and almost unable to speak, closed in on themselves with only a vision of sky and horizon in their eyes, or else they spent their nights at the Ruination Bar, excessively loud, with excessively loud men like themselves and women who didn't care for quiet voices.

Charles had found a woman willing to live here. She remembered when he'd first shown her the old house and she'd realized she'd be living in it if she married him. She had already decided to marry him, but the house had been enough to make her ask herself if she was, after all, not entirely sane. But what if Charles hadn't been lucky? He had not told her until they'd been married a full year that he had once thought of being an airplane pilot. When he did tell her, he joked about it. As if to say how naïve he once had been. But she heard the serious note beneath.

"Why didn't you?" she asked.

He was embarrassed that she wouldn't just let it go—a revelation he wanted her to have but didn't want her thinking about. He waved his hand.

"The ranch," he said.

"You decided to ranch instead?"

He didn't affirm the statement, didn't deny it.

"Dad needed help," he said.

"I bet he did."

"What do you mean by that?"

She heard defensiveness. But she wasn't accusing him of not resisting his father. She meant it both ways: that there was always work to do on the ranch and that Ves would demand help whether he actually needed it or not. Need was a word with shifting borders. She knew it wasn't easy to say no to a father who put a claim upon that word.

"Nothing, really," she said. "Just there's always work to do."

He nodded. "I used a put together these plastic model airplanes," he said. "Don't know how much time I wasted as a kid gluing those things together. Painting 'em. I'd work on 'em at night when I was supposed to be in bed. Musta had fifteen of 'em or more. And I knew the names and speeds and all of every one of 'em."

"What happened to them?"

"One night when I was about sixteen, the Russians and the Americans got 'n a dogfight. Not a single one of 'em survived."

"You mean you wrecked them?"

"Like I say, a big dogfight."

He laughed.

"I'd like to have seen them," she said.

"Just kid stuff."

She imagined a wastebasket full of painstakingly painted airplane parts, shattered. The kind of thing you don't put back together. But Charles was trying to be cheerful. Pretending it meant nothing. Pretending he'd simply outgrown a childhood hobby.

Now, with Carson before her, turning to the kitchen faucet again, filling another glass of water and draining it, preparing to finish moving into the old house, she wondered, if she told him this story about his father's desire to fly planes and how at sixteen, unable to escape Ves's demands, he'd despaired of it, would that story be enough to counteract the land's pull on Carson? Ves's pull. Enough, at least, to make Carson think? To see possibilities within himself beyond this ranch?

Marie almost thought it might. She had this thing, this story, that might just rivet Carson. Pin him to her. Make him yearn for what he didn't have, as she sometimes wished he would. And maybe, in that yearning, he would turn to her. Need her. For advice at least. For guidance. But she wasn't sure she had a right to tell the story. Carson wanted the land's pull. Wind. Animals. Emptiness. Space. He'd never wanted anything else.

An Agreement

∧∧∧∧∧

EIGHT YEARS LATER Carson sat at the kitchen table in the old house, listening to the wind outside and seeing in his mind the eyes of two hawks cutting amber swaths through air. Those swaths seemed as senseless as the flight of fireflies. As empty. He thought of a piano, never played, so coated with dust it seemed the shape of a piano only, which any touch would shatter. He saw his hand going out to it, but he had no idea what music that hand might play, and it seemed that if it ever reached the keyboard, the world would fall apart. Or already had.

When the phone rang, he started. For just a moment, until he caught his bearings, the ringing seemed to come blaring from that other world. As if the piano in his mind had played of its own accord and visited ruin here. He dropped his feet off the table and reached the phone in two strides. Then he paused, put his hand on the receiver, and caught his breath. He tried to calm his voice.

"Hello. Carson Fielding."

"Carson. This is Willi Schubert."

Carson's mind went blank. He stared at a kinked coil in the phone cord.

"Willi Schubert?" he said.

Then he remembered the German exchange student Allan Druseman had brought out for riding lessons a few months ago. Carson had taught him the basics of riding, but the last thing he wanted to do right now was give another riding lesson. He tilted his head back and shut his eyes and saw again the eyes of the hawks like flaming brands inscribing meaningless messages upon the sudden darkness.

"Oh yeah, Willi," he said. He opened his eyes and fingered the kink in the phone cord to bring himself back to where he was. "Been a while."

"Are you still giving horse riding lessons?"

"Not much. It's a busy time."

He hoped the response would be enough to keep the German kid from asking to resume the lessons.

"I suppose it is always a busy time on a ranch."

"Pretty much."

"I am not, however, calling about riding."

"No?"

"I am calling about some horses."

"Some horses."

"That is right."

"Buying horses, you mean?"

"No. I could not fit them in my luggage when I went back to Germany."

Willi said this so seriously it took Carson a second to laugh, but it broke his mood.

"I guess not," he said. "What's up, then?"

"Some horses that we found," Willi said. "Maybe they are hurt. Maybe you could look at them."

"Hurt how? Sick?"

"There is a limping one."

"That's it? You want me to go look at a limping horse?"

"It is odd. There is a little pasture. There is hot water coming out of the ground. What do you call it?"

"Artesian water?"

"Yes. Artesian. And these horses are penned up. There is not much food, I think, for three horses."

Carson reached blindly for something to steady himself. His hand hit the refrigerator, and he held onto it as the world reeled and his ear's pulse yammered against the receiver.

"Three horses?" he said thickly.

"Yes. It is three horses. And they are penned up."

Carson leaned his forehead against the cool, enameled steel of the refrigerator, felt the motor humming in his skull.

"Where'd you find these horses?"

"Behind Lostman's Lake. It is, how do you say his name? It is a rich rancher."

"Magnus Yarborough," Carson said dully.

"That is right. We found them on Magnus Yarborough's land."

"Jesus!" Carson whispered.

The refrigerator motor shut off, rocking on its loose mountings, and clunked into silence. Carson realized he had his eyes shut, and he opened them and stared at the blank, undifferentiated whiteness of the machine. He turned slowly, put his shoulders against the refrigerator, and stared at the small confines of the house, the dusty drapes covering the windows, the old wooden table he used to sit at, drinking lemonade, watching his grandfather smoke and drink coffee and talk about animals. Carson let his knees go limp. His shoulders slid down the refrigerator. He sat on the floor and stared at the worn wood between his feet.

"Carson?"

"Yeah, Willi," he whispered. "Yeah. I'm here."

HE'D NEVER WANTED TO train Magnus Yarborough's horses. It had been his father's idea. They were walking through the door of the Quonset machine shed, talking about other things, when his father suddenly said, "Magnus Yarborough called yesterday. Needs some horses trained."

The wind caught the broken rolling door of the shed and banged it against the frame. Steady as a slow drummer. Bang. Bang. Bang. The whole building echoed.

Carson walked to the ancient Case that they'd been using since he was a kid. He checked the oil. "How many's he got?"

"Said three."

Carson stuck the dipstick back into the tube, noticed the fan belt on the tractor was cracking. He hooked his finger in the belt and pulled, pretending to assure himself it would hold for another day. Then he stepped to the ladder and swung up to the tractor's cab.

"When's he wanta bring 'em over?"

He had the door to the cab open and was about to step inside, but his father didn't answer. Carson looked down at him. Charles met his eyes.

"He wants you to go over there," he said.

"You tell 'm I don't do that?"

There were trainers who traveled, but Carson wanted the horses brought to him. His grandfather had often said it was the rider needed training as much as the horse. Carson agreed, and if the rider was willing to come with the horse, he'd train the rider, too. But he wouldn't go where horse and rider both had developed bad habits and by so going fight animal and human and surroundings all. Hard enough, he thought, to work with two of the three. And he had his own ranch to work. He didn't need to beg for jobs. If people didn't want to bring him their animals, they could find someone else.

"I told him," his father said.

"Well, then. Guess that takes care've it." Carson stooped inside the tractor cab and sat down. He reached to pull the door shut.

"It's Magnus Yarborough," his father said.

"If it was the governor, I wouldn't travel to Pierre."

"It's only fifteen miles. Easy to go and come back."

"Easy for him to bring 'em, then."

Carson had started to close the door when he heard his father say, "I already told 'm you'd come."

A blackbird flew in through the open doors and, confused by the sudden loss of sky, fled to the far, dark rafters and flitted in circles there.

"You told 'm I'd come?"

"Dammit, Carson. You looked at beef prices lately?"

"I know what beef's worth."

"Then you know it's piss poor. And wheat ain't much better. We'll be lucky to break even this year."

"Next year might be better."

"And it might be worse."

The blackbird blended into the shadows of the shed's rounded peak. Carson pushed the cab door all the way open. He gazed over

his father at the stock pond downhill below the house, a small flock
of ducks there leaving intersecting wakes. The broken door banged
in the wind.

"Me training a few horses or not ain't gonna make much difference," he said.

"When I told him you don't travel, he offered twice the price.
When I still said no, he doubled that. That's four times. That's more
'n just a few horses. I figured it wouldn't hurt you to get off this
place for that kind of money."

"Why's he want me?"

"Said he wants the best. Heard you were it."

"He heard that, huh?"

"Says so."

"Well, you told 'm I'd come. Guess I'm bound."

He pulled the cab door shut. He leaned over the steering wheel,
found the glow plug button, held it in. He had no desire to go to
Magnus Yarborough's ranch. Enough work to do right here. But his
father had already made the deal. And maybe he was right. But it
wasn't his deal to make. Why was it that every time he and his father talked they seemed to disagree? Carson reached the end of the
count, let go the glow plug, turned the ignition. The engine ground,
then started.

HE STOOD ON MAGNUS YARBOROUGH'S PORCH. Twelve years ago he'd
been met on the driveway, which hadn't been paved then. He couldn't
remember if the brick walkway had been laid; nor could he remember the stained glass panels inserted above the doors and windows
of the house. Carson turned his back to the door and looked at the
outbuildings: two red-and-white steel machine sheds, chimneys
emerging from their roofs and rolling power doors high enough to
drive a combine into; a red-and-white metal barn with steel gate
corrals; the stock pond beyond it, a small boat with a trolling motor
tied to a firm plank dock; and beyond it all, the land, Yarborough's
ranch, that went at least as far as Red Medicine Creek. Carson wondered how much land was enough. How much of the world did a
person like Yarborough need to have pointing back at him? Every

time a rancher retired, Yarborough was there to make an offer on the land. He owned land in Nebraska and Wyoming as well as South Dakota, and the more he owned, the more he seemed to need. For a guy like him, satisfaction was a horizon slipping away, always visible, never reached. Carson couldn't comprehend it.

He rang the bell and waited, heard footsteps beyond the door. Then it opened, and Magnus Yarborough stood behind the screen. He had a toothpick in his mouth. The morning sunlight through the screen silvered a ring of hair above his ears. The rest of his hair was dark, cut short. He gazed through the screen at Carson for a moment, eyes impassive, gray as distant water. Then he removed the toothpick with his left hand and with his right pushed open the door and stepped onto the porch.

"I'm Carson Fielding."

"We've met."

Carson thought Magnus was referring to a chance meeting in Twisted Tree. He tried to recall the moment. He'd passed Magnus at various times on errands but couldn't remember talking to him.

"How'd that horse treat you?"

With a start Carson realized that Magnus was referring clear back to when he'd bought his first horse. That was years ago. He'd been how old? Fourteen? An age ago. Why would Yarborough remember that?

"Oh," he said. "Worked out OK."

Magnus nodded. "Worth your four-hundred-twenty-five bucks, then?"

He stuck the toothpick back in his mouth and gazed at Carson. He not only remembered selling the horse, he remembered the price.

"I'd say."

"Worth more, maybe?"

"Wouldn't say that."

Magnus removed the toothpick with his thumb and forefinger and flicked it off the porch into the grass.

"Hear you're good at training horses."

"It ain't mine to say how good I am."

"Modesty won't get you a job."

"I ain't lookin for a job."

"If you don't know how good you are, who does?"

"The horses."

Magnus's eyes sheared away, then steadied, came back.

"The horses," he said. "Well, I'll be sure to ask the horses, then."

"I ain't never yet managed to train one to talk."

Magnus's cool eyes regarded Carson. Then he shook his head, stepped off the porch.

"At least you grew some eyebrows," he said.

Carson had no idea what he was talking about.

WHILE THEY STOOD ON THE PORCH, three pickups had driven into the yard and parked by the first machine shed. Magnus's hired men—Lonny Youngman, Wagner Cecil, and Burt Ramsay—got out and stood talking, drinking coffee from big, plastic truck stop mugs. Carson knew and liked Burt Ramsay. Burt had operated his own ranch for years, and Carson had helped him with branding, but Burt ran into financial difficulties after his wife divorced him. He sold out to Magnus, then started working for him. Carson knew Lonny Youngman less well. Lonny was in his thirties and had tried various jobs—highway construction, driving a Mount Rushmore tour bus for Gray Lines out of Rapid City—before coming back to Twisted Tree. Carson didn't know Wagner Cecil at all, except by face, name, and rumor. Wagner was about five years younger than Carson and had dropped out of school his junior year, disappeared for a year or two, then showed up in Twisted Tree again, tight-lipped about where he'd been and what he'd been doing. For a while he'd been a fixture at the Kwiker Fill convenience store, playing video lottery, but had finally taken this job with Yarborough.

"The horses are in the barn," Magnus said. "I'll be there in a minute. Got to give my hands their instructions."

Carson nodded at the three men as he walked past them. He heard Magnus talking to them, their brief responses. As he neared the barn, Magnus caught up to him and passed him: a big man, with a slight paunch visible in profile, torso shaped like a sledgehammer but gone soft around the edges—a man whose activity had decreased while his consumption hadn't. He reached the barn ahead of Carson and stepped through the door, leaving it hanging open. By the time Carson stepped into the dim interior, he saw Magnus walking between rows of steel pens, toward three horses watching them from the rear of the barn.

Magnus leaned on the gate penning the horses in, and when Carson walked up he nodded at the animals. "There they are," he said.

Carson put both hands on top of the gate, leaned his chin on the back of his hands, put one foot on the bottom rail, and observed the animals. They stood as far from the two humans as they could—not frightened but wary. If they'd had more space, they'd have used it, but they knew what space they had.

"Nice animals."

"Ought to be."

"A bit shy."

"Bought them up in Harding County. Eighty-year-old rancher wouldn't quit. His kids visited, noticed things falling apart. Figured he was losing it. They sold him out."

"Sold him out?"

"Got power of attorney and had an auction. I went up and bought these animals. Worked out well for me."

"What happened to him?"

"Who?"

"The old guy."

Magnus shrugged. "Probably ended up in a nursing home."

"Nice kids."

Carson thought of the old man staring out a window, remembering the space he used to roam, until he just crumbled, a nurse coming along one afternoon and finding a pile of dust in his chair and calling the janitor over with a vacuum cleaner. And his kids getting a call in the new houses they'd built with his money, hearing their father had just evaporated. Why not let the old guy wander around his ranch if that's what he wanted to do, until he fell into a gully and died?

"I need them broke," Magnus said.

"I don't break horses."

Magnus turned to stare at Carson, but Carson watched the animals. He didn't look them in the eye or challenge them but observed how they held themselves.

"You don't break horses. I been paying you for a half-hour now to stand in my yard and lean on my fence, and now I hear you don't break horses?"

"I train horses. An I don' take pay by the hour. I take it by the horse. Time ain't a factor. My dad didn't explain that?"

"All I know is I'm paying you a hell of a lot."

"You are. Wouldn't pay myself that much. Truth is, you'd a asked me, I'd said bring the horses to me or find another trainer. But my dad agreed to this, so I'm here."

Carson said this matter-of-factly, but Magnus tensed, leaned away from the fence, hooked his thumb in his belt.

"I guess you got definite ideas."

"Long as I'm workin with 'em, these horses are mine. I ain't a hired hand, an I don't follow orders. I do things my own way, an at my own speed. You don't like what I do, it ain't like we compromise. You either like it or you pay me what we agreed on to quit. You can watch, but you ain't allowed a give suggestions."

Magnus's jaw hardened. His fingers at his belt curled. Then he opened them and smiled humorlessly.

"I heard you knew what you were about," he said.

Carson turned back to the horses. The bay with the white diamond on its forehead was the most intense. It hadn't once, in all the time Carson had watched, put an ear back to catch a sound from another direction. The other two had relaxed, the black gelding even eating from a hay feeder. But the bay remained suspicious and alert.

"There's one other thing," Magnus said.

"What's that?"

He wished Magnus would leave. He wanted to be alone with the horses now.

"My wife wants to learn to ride. I thought, since you were training the horses, it'd make sense to teach her at the same time."

"A lot a people could teach her to ride."

"There isn't much sense in having two people out here working around these horses."

Carson nodded, considering it. At the movement of his head, the bay grew more alert, its spine hardening.

"OK," Carson said. "Same rate. Make it another horse."

Equilibriums

∧∧∧∧∧

WILLI CLICKED OFF THE PHONE. He'd told Carol Druseman, his host mother here, that he was going to call his parents in Germany. Instead he'd called Carson. Why had he told that small lie? And should he now call his parents so it wouldn't be a lie? He lay on his bed and stared at the ceiling. He thought of the huddled horses, the taut lines of gleaming wire: the order, the neatness, the perpendicularity of the posts against the ground. And that steaming water, pouring out of the earth with a life of its own. Its gurgling in the night. Willi thought of drinking that water, the hot liquid sliding down his throat. He thought of never being able to move away from that sound, of that endless bubbling from deep inside the earth, occupying his waking and sleeping, trapping him even in his dreams.

An air of secrecy pervaded that pen behind Lostman's Lake. And he'd heard in Carson Fielding's voice confirmation of his own suspicions. He thought of telling the Drusemans. He imagined their kind and open faces, the way they would listen to him. But in the end they would be like Earl—thinking he didn't understand something. They would try to explain away the pen and the horses and the steaming water. He would never be able to explain to them what troubled him.

Willi traced the half-circles in the plaster ceiling with his eyes. Ceilings were different here, he thought. Light switches were different. Even beds were made up differently. But secrets were the same.

WHEN WILLI WAS EIGHT YEARS OLD, he'd grown curious about the fact that he had only one set of grandparents, and he'd asked his mother.

"Yes," she said. "It is a terrible thing. Your father's parents were in an accident on the autobahn a long time ago. They both died."

Willi wanted to ask more about his father's parents, but his mother turned her back to him and began to stuff groceries into the refrigerator. "This refrigerator is too small," she said. "We really need a new one. I've told your father that." Willi peered around her briefly at the neat, lighted space of the refrigerator with its milk and juices and glowing cans. He couldn't tell whether they needed a new refrigerator or not, so he said nothing and never asked about his grandparents again.

One evening when he was fourteen, his father answered the phone and listened without responding. He hung up and went into the living room, picked up the newspaper without a word of explanation. Later, from his bedroom, Willi heard his parents talking to each other, his mother urgently, his father with a toneless doggedness.

The next evening during supper, his father's sister Marti burst into the house without knocking. She'd never done anything like that before. Suddenly the door was open, and there she was, standing among them. Willi's father dropped his fork when she whirled into the dining room. He held up his hands as if to ward off a spell. He waved his hands back and forth, his fingers blurring like fan blades.

"How can you do this?" Marti cried, without even saying hello.

"Don't say another word!" Willi's father shouted.

He pushed his chair back so hard it tipped over. He rushed around it, his pants cuff catching for a moment on a protruding chair leg so that he stumbled, and his head went down, and he looked for a moment like a wounded bull charging Marti. He barely managed to right himself before he reached her, and then he glanced back at Willi and positioned himself between Willi and Marti, shielding Willi from her—from Marti, soft and overweight, who was always talking in a distracted way about her troubles finding a decent man, who spent the Christmas holidays with them, lounging all day in her bathrobe until it glittered with sugar flaked from pastries, and who spoke of peace as something real and not just a word in holiday lyrics.

"Your own father!" Marti cried, her voice hoarse. Over his father's shoulder Willi, still at the table, could see her swollen eyes, her short hair in punctuated disarray about her head.

"Stop, Marti," Willi's father commanded. "Not in this house."

"I'll say what I want. I won't go along with this any more. Your own father, and you won't go to his funeral."

"Not another word. You're not welcome here saying these things."

"I don't care about welcome. Good God! Are you my brother? You have to honor him at least in death."

Willi had his head down, staring at the table. His mother had placed a bouquet there. One of the flowers had a bent stem. He saw how the tiny fibers had torn, how they protruded from the break, how the stem was white instead of green where it bent. He didn't want to hear his father and Marti shouting at each other. He wanted to be invisible.

His mother, sitting next to him, reached over and covered his hand with hers. But Willi wouldn't look at her. He stared at the flower's broken stem.

"You can still leave, Marti," his father said. "You haven't caused complete damage yet." His voice had gone gray, no longer shouting, just a grim and desperate argument.

"I didn't think you'd stay stubborn this long, Hermann. You're just like him."

"Don't ever say that."

"I'm through not saying things."

They faced each other. Two bulldozers. If they collided, they would ruin each other. They would tear each other apart. End up a tangled and ruined pile where they stood. That's what Willi felt. He didn't know either of them could be so massive, so obstinate, so deeply iron, and so willing to destroy themselves over whatever lay between them.

Then his father bowed his head. As if he were giving into something he knew all along he would never defeat. He looked back at Willi. His face was gray, wet paper, sagging. Then he stepped aside. His eyes went to the floor. Willi was exposed to whatever Marti carried.

"Willi," she said.

Willi stared at the bent stem in the bouquet. He didn't want to see Marti's tear-swollen face. Didn't want to hear her earnest, pleading voice.

Then his mother spoke. "Marti."

She said only the name, but it halted Marti. Startled her. Willi glanced up and saw Marti's blue eyes wide in surprise, as if she hadn't known anyone else could be in the room.

"Whatever you think your responsibility is," Willi's mother said, "it's over. The rest is up to us. You've given us no choice. If that's what you intended, it's been done."

She never raised her voice, but her eyes never left her sister-in-law's. Marti's eyes suddenly had no focus. They darted around the room. As if she didn't know where she was. Then she saw her brother again, and her face and posture sagged. They stood looking at each other like paper statues disintegrating in rain.

"Hermann," she said. "I'm sorry. I just can't believe. You're not even going to the funeral. I just can't."

She thrust her hands into the bulky bag she carried everywhere. She rummaged in it, emerged with a tissue. She blew her nose, then waved the tissue in a tiny, helpless gesture.

"He was your father," she said in a small, little-girl voice. "No matter what."

Willi's father shook his head. A dull, mechanical movement. His neck didn't look strong enough to support the weight of its moving. He just stood there, shaking his head. As if there was a weight inside, rolling aimlessly about.

"Mom's in terrible shape," Marti said. She wiped tears from her face with the back of her hand. Her handbag slipped off her round, sloping shoulder, caught in the crook of her elbow. She grabbed at it, caught it, readjusted it on her shoulder, hitching it up. She looked around for a place to throw the soiled tissue.

"I don't care."

Willi had to look at his father to be sure it was his father speaking. It was a worn and old man's voice. Then Willi saw it was a worn, old man who spoke.

"My God, Hermann. She's our mother."

Willi's father's neck stiffened. He came out of his slump, stood erect. His head no longer wobbled, and he looked at his sister, then shook his head.

"No," he said. "Your mother. My well of life."

AFTER MARTI LEFT, Willi's father put on his coat. Willi saw him through the gauze curtains, a shape striding down the sidewalk, the Rhine far below him, and a train speeding down the tracks along the bank. Head down. A man who might walk onto the street and be struck by a car and never notice. Maybe never care.

Willi's mother cleared the table. She had her back to him, standing near the dishwasher, when she spoke.

"We'll talk later," she said.

"I had a grandfather who died? I have a grandmother who is alive?"

"Later. First I have to talk to your father. Now go and do your homework."

HIS MOTHER CAME TO HIS ROOM without turning on the light and sat on the edge of the bed. For a while she just sat there. Then she said, "We didn't want you to find out this way, Willi."

She stared over him, silent. A statue, bronzed by distant street-lights.

"Your father didn't get along with his father." It sounded as if she'd found the words in the glowing light. Words without emotion, like a fairy tale. And she was sitting on the edge of the bed, like she did when he was little and she read to him: a fairy tale about a father and son who didn't get along, maybe a cottage and a boat.

"Just tell me," Willi said. "I'm old enough."

"You know about the Nazis," she said. "Your grandfather was one of them. SS."

Willi had heard about the Nazis so much in school he'd grown tired of them. He thought he should be shocked—his own grand-father—but he wasn't. It seemed like a common, worn-out story.

"What did he do?" he asked.

"He was a member of a killing squad in Poland. An *Einsatz-gruppe*. He was a little man. He escaped punishment."

Willi sat up. He didn't like lying down while his mother sat. He leaned his head against the wall so that his eyes were level with hers. The cover on the bed crackled as he moved. In the darkness small, static sparks ignited in the fibers. His mother reached out to touch him, but he didn't respond. He sat unmoving, waiting. She let her hand drop from the air.

"Your grandparents tried to hide it from your father and your aunt Marti," she said. "But when your father was about your age, he found a photograph that made him wonder. His father in an SS uniform. He started to ask questions. And look in old documents."

She looked down at her hands on her knees. White, pale hands in the dark. "Marti never forgave him," she said.

"Her father?"

Willi's mother shook her head. "Yours," she said.

"She never forgave Papa? Why?"

"She didn't want to know. She's always been angry at having to know. Sometimes she pretends not to know. Pretends not to believe, at least."

"Why wasn't she angry at her father?"

She sighed. "Marti wants to love the people she loves," she said. "She wants to believe it is enough."

"And it isn't."

He was stating a realization, not asking a question.

"It should be, I suppose," his mother said. Then: "Or maybe it shouldn't."

They sat in silence for a while, contemplating love's sufficiency or insufficiency.

Then Willi's mother said, "Your father tried to kill himself once, Willi. You were young. You don't remember."

But once she said it, he did remember: vague outlines of light and noise, himself crying.

"You saved his life." And she told him what had happened: how he'd begun crying without reason, forcing her to return home, and all that followed. But even as she told of it, he remembered. And it seemed that he had remembered it before, though he hadn't known until now what he had been remembering. He had thought it was a dream. When his mother was done, Willi felt he'd become someone else: someone—now—whose grandfather had done vague and terrible things in the long-distant war; someone who had saved his own father's life, though perhaps without intending to; someone whose first memory was the memory of so doing.

"Was it because of what his father did?" Willi asked.

"What?"

"That Papa tried. Tried to."

"No. Not only that. At least I don't think so. He was always searching. Always looking in documents. I think he found something new."

"What?"

"I don't know. I think, for him, it's too terrible to tell."

"What did he mean when he said his mother was his well of life?"

"I don't know, Willi. I've never heard him say anything like that before."

"Did Papa love his father?"

His mother expelled her breath in surprise. "I suppose he did," she said.

"But he hated him, too."

"Maybe more for his silence than for anything else. For never admitting anything. He might have hated him less if his father had spoken."

"Why didn't you make Papa tell you what he found? The new thing?"

His mother bowed her head and thought for a while. "I'm a little like Marti, maybe," she finally said. "I was just so glad to have him here. I knew there was something, but I didn't want to ask for fear it would disturb him. I thought he would tell me when he was ready. Then a kind of equilibrium set in. Life went on. I didn't want to disturb the equilibrium. I decided to let it be his secret. Maybe he decided the same. Not to disturb my equilibrium."

They sat for a long time without speaking. The moon sent its light into the dark room, and the shadows of tree branches moved down the wall as the moon rose. Willi's mother reached out and stroked his arm, then his shoulder. He allowed it, but he didn't respond.

"I had a right to know about them," he said.

He was a little surprised when his mother didn't apologize or affirm his implied accusation.

"Maybe," she said. "Parents have to make decisions for their children. After that night when you and I came back to find him, your father visited them once. And said he never would again. I agreed. Even now, it isn't that easy to know we were wrong."

Willi lay awake for a long time after she left the room, thinking about the grandmother he now had. Thinking he had a right to know her. And to know what his father knew, even if the knowing disturbed an equilibrium his parents had worked to maintain. For that equilibrium made him a stranger to himself.

Four years later he lay in his borrowed bedroom in the middle of a foreign continent, staring at patterns on the ceiling and remembering how he'd done the same thing after his mother left his room. Here too, he thought, an equilibrium had settled, and here, too, he was a stranger. But to what he wasn't sure. His call to Carson Fielding had perhaps disturbed whatever equilibrium was here. Whatever silence. But Willi knew it had to be disturbed.

Horses and Men

~~~~~

ARE YOU WAITING FOR SOMEONE, *takoja?*"

Earl's grandmother could bead, carry on a conversation, observe the weather outside the window and in the hearts of her daughter and grandson, and watch television, all at the same time. She was watching a baseball game when she spoke, and her eyes never left the screen, so that when Earl glanced at her he had the impression she was speaking to the pitcher, calling him *takoja*, "grandchild," and wondering when he was going to throw.

"I don't know," he said.

"You don't know if you're waiting for someone."

"No."

"Then you're waiting to find out."

"I guess so."

His grandmother nodded. The needle rose in her hand, then dipped downward into the loose beads and ordered them, making tiny clucking sounds, like a small, content bird, as it found the holes and then looped another eight beads into the air, dots of light running down the thread until they tightened against the moccasin into pattern. Earl knew his grandmother wouldn't pry further, but if he wanted to tell her she would listen. She had asked the question that opened the door. Now she would wait. The pitcher raised his leg, wound up.

Willi had called the night before and told Earl that he and Carson Fielding were going back to the pasture behind Lostman's Lake. Earl had spent the weekend at home, writing scholarship applications and helping his mother cook, and on Monday at school he had controlled the jokes directed at him about his excursion to the top of Tower Hill by smiling and not responding and pretending to be focused on the teacher or his books. It wore him out, maintaining defenses. But by the afternoon, no one was saying anything about his amazing feats of drunkenness, his craziness under the towers. New gossip had already started in the halls. Earl didn't understand how stories could spring full-fledged to life between the first bell and lunch, but he was grateful for that mystery. Walking home from school, he felt relieved, like he'd shed that Friday evening, allowed attention to drift elsewhere.

Now, when Willi called, Earl could think of no response. It was like finding gum on your shoes after leaving school—an irritating little reminder of a place you'd rather forget.

"Oh," he said. "You and Carson Fielding."

He had heard of Carson Fielding, though he'd never met him.

"We will pick you up. At eight tomorrow."

"What?"

"Eight in the evening."

"I'm not going back up there."

"You found them, Earl."

Earl's mother was working late, and his grandmother, as always, had the television on. Nevertheless, Earl stepped around the corner into the kitchen and lowered his voice.

"You can't find something unless it's hidden," he said. "Seeing something and finding something are different, you know?"

"We will come at eight o'clock, Earl."

Now it was approaching eight. Earl had tried to do the advanced calculus problems Mr. Edwards had given him. He had seen classmates go off to college, with relatives wishing them luck and giving them gifts, and he had seen them return, washed out within a semester, claiming it was all worthless, all a bunch of bull, hiding their failure behind bravado, grinning about it, claiming they had better things to do. Earl didn't want to be one of those people. But he couldn't concentrate tonight. He kept listening for the sound of a vehicle. It was nearly dark when he heard tires slowing down on the highway. He was glad his mother was attending a school board meeting. If she were here, he'd have to explain what he was doing. All his grandmother said, when he went toward the door, was,

"I guess you were waiting for someone."

"I guess."

"It's good, if you were waiting for someone, that they showed up."

"Yeah. I guess. Goodbye, Grandma."

"Be safe, *takoja*."

Earl walked out the door. He'd go with Willi tonight, but he'd make it clear this was the end for him. From behind the windshield of the idling pickup, Carson and Willi watched him impassively. He opened the passenger-side door. Willi moved to the center of the pickup seat, and Earl got in. They adjusted to the closeness, the three of them packed together, trying not to touch at the knees and hips.

Willi and Earl exchanged hellos, and Earl and Carson nodded to each other. Earl raised his hand across Willi's chest, but Carson ignored the gesture, put the pickup into gear, and started up the driveway. Earl let his hand drop, rubbed his knee with his palm, trying to make his attempt to shake hands look like something natural. He didn't know whether Carson hadn't seen his hand or had deliberately ignored it.

Earl looked out the side window at the basketball hoop his uncle had erected for him when he was in elementary school. It was the only time Lorna had allowed Norm on the place, and then only because Earl was unrelenting in his begging. He'd had such visions of being a basketball player, and he needed a hoop to practice at. Now the ragged net, shredded by the wind, flapped back and forth under the splintered plywood backboard.

"Didn't know you were comin," Carson said, not glancing at Earl. "Don't really need three've us for this."

It was exactly what Earl had been thinking, but the comment made him flush. Carson was polite, but reserve and politeness could hide a lot of things. It was almost an art form, the way people used politeness. Earl had experienced it from store clerks and wait-

resses—that quiet aloofness that both formed and withheld judgment at the same time. Earl often wished that if people didn't like
Indians they'd just say so right up front and be done with it so he
didn't have to guess.

"'Well," he said, "I guess we're all three here."

He remembered Norm working on the basketball hoop that
day, talking about everything and anything. Earl had been a fourth-
grader. He'd stood looking up at his uncle on the ladder, waiting for
him to ask for a socket or wrench, eager to show him he knew what
the tools were. Earl felt his mother's eyes inside the house, so he
stood a little distant from the ladder, but he watched his uncle's
every move and listened to every word he said. Norm was talking
about his time in the Army, the training he'd gone through, the people he'd met. He told Earl about a white kid from Philadelphia
who'd never met an Indian and had a hard time believing Norm was
a real one. "Wondered if I lived in a tipi," Norm said. "And when I
said I lived in a house—this was before I was living in my motor
home—he thought I was just pretending to be Indian. Any real Indian, he thought, had to live in a tipi. When I asked him if any real
white man had to live in a castle, he didn't know what I was talking
about. But we got along good. The Army turned us both into grunts
anyway. Which is what the Army does best. Hand me a ratchet,
wouldja?"

Earl hurried to Norm's toolbox. He loved the way the tools were
arrayed, all their gleaming forms, the endless choices they implied.
He found a ratchet and handed it up and watched as Norm attached
a socket he'd pulled from his pocket and tightened the nuts that held
the backboard up, his hand spinning the ratchet in quick half-circles,
so quick the silver handle looked like a propeller blurring the air.

"'Course, things're changing," Norm said. "It's getting so people now want to be Indian. Or think they do. And I got to say some
of them get pretty good at being Indian. But there's one thing someone who's not Indian can't fake, and they can't fake it even if they
marry an Indian and get adopted by an Indian family and get an Indian name and do genuine Indian arts and stand in line for genuine
government commodities. And what is this thing, nephew? I'll tell

you. Get into a pickup with two white guys in South Dakota, and if you're still Indian then, you're a real Indian. Hanh."

At the time Earl hadn't understood what Norm meant. Now, though, he wished he'd kept his hand held up until Carson either shook it or clearly refused to. He stared out the side window of the pickup as they rode, unspeaking, tires rumbling on the highway. They pulled into Lostman's Lake and parked near the boat ramp. Carson cut the engine and lights. They got out, the gravel crunching under their feet, the waters of the trapped creek lapping the shore. Carson pushed the pickup seat forward and retrieved a large flashlight.

"They up there?"

He spoke to Willi, but Earl answered. "Yeah. Up there."

Carson turned and set off up the hill. Willi followed him, but Earl held back, watching them disappear into the darkness, blending into the hillside. He thought he'd maybe just stay here. Let the white guys do their thing. He didn't want to be here anyway.

Then he thought of what Norm would say: "That's right. Stand there and pout. I always enjoy a good pout myself."

He pushed away from the pickup. He remembered a TV documentary about pigeons called pouters. *The solitary pouter,* he thought, *decides to join the flock.*

AT THE BORDER OF MAGNUS YARBOROUGH'S LAND, they once again clambered over the fence hung with its painted tires. "Trespassing again," Willi said, swinging his leg up. "When I get back to Germany, I will tell them about this sport." He wobbled on the fence wires, then jumped down.

Earl had caught up to them halfway up the hill. He'd heard them talking quietly ahead of him, but when he joined them the talk ended. Chance, perhaps. Carson's face, when Earl glanced at him, was devoid of emotion. He seemed to emanate silence and distance. But at Willi's comment Carson laughed. Earl had no idea this somber cowboy could have a sense of humor.

"Better 'n soccer, huh?" Carson asked.

"If you mean football, no," Willi replied. "No sport is better than football. Real football. Not your American kind."

Carson laughed again. But as quickly as his laughter came, his face closed down, and he turned from the fence and started uphill. But Earl, watching him, saw a new thing emerge for a moment behind his eyes and mouth, and he realized suddenly that what he had interpreted as aloofness or even prejudice might be something else entirely. For Earl saw a catch, a hitch of pain, some fear or grief, in Carson's face in its transition out of laughter. For just a moment in the starlight, Earl saw Carson bright-eyed, his features distorted, cartoonish in some interior sorrow. It was eerie. Carson glanced at Earl and might have seen that Earl saw, for he turned away like a man angry and found out.

That was not laughter, Earl thought. He shivered in the warm night. In the daylight he wouldn't have seen that momentary distortion of Carson's features. The darkness and shadows, the diminished light, had exposed it: a possession cracking through the mask that Carson maintained, a being from a different realm.

"WHERE ARE THEY?"

"They are over this next hill."

"You mind if I go over alone?"

Earl and Willi looked at each other.

"They'll be less skittish, we don't all three come prancin up on 'em."

Earl listened for a moment to the night. He heard no bats, and no wind blew, and silence seemed a profound and lasting thing, and even the moths of a few days ago had deserted the world or been devoured completely in that storm of dark, invisible wings. What Carson was asking made sense, and he was the horseman, and he should know. But Earl felt something shaping itself on this hillside, far different from anything suggested here, from anything written in the way the three of them stood. He looked at the Great Bear, its legs loping through half the heavens, and he wondered: If he and Willi and Carson were a constellation the Bear looked down upon, what would it form? What was it forming? And the horses, too?

But he didn't know, and it was too late if he did. Stories in points of light. If you looked at the skies in a Lakota way, you saw one set of stories, and if you looked at them in a European way, you saw another. Yet the stars were the same. And if you had no way to look, you saw nothing but stars. Nothing connected. Here they stood, the three of them, in their own constellations, but some new picture was being formed, was somehow already formed—if you had the way to look at it.

Which he didn't. But he did know that stars don't move. Don't wander out of their constellations, don't choose, however random their site in the heavens might be or however ordered, to take another place.

"Go ahead," he said to Carson.

"It is OK with me, too," Willi said.

Carson turned and went over the rise. Earl stood in the dark, with Willi next to him: the silent world, with only each other's breathing in it, and over the hill the sound of large animals moving, and the murmur of a human voice. Earl thought of that sorrowful and haunting look that had flashed in Carson's face. He turned, saw the red blinking lights of Tower Hill away in the high dark. He felt helpless. He knew what he'd tried to deny was beyond denial. There was no randomness in the fact that the small pasture could be seen from nowhere but where he'd seen it from. There was randomness only in the fact that he *had* seen it. Or maybe not: maybe *he* had put the constellation together. Maybe he had ordered it.

So was he star or eye? And of which place, and in which story? He should walk away, he thought—down the hill, across the fence hung with its NO TRESPASSING tires, back to nameless and public land. He imagined taking the steps, and the steps themselves were possible. But taking them somehow wasn't. He couldn't bring his feet to move. He stood. And it wouldn't matter anyway. At what point along this chain of circumstance had certain possibilities tipped into impossibility? And others into certainty?

He heard Carson's voice calling, and a sudden surge of panic and dread struck him, and he thought, *Here it is. What I don't want to know.* Then, starlike, he quelled the feeling and walked with Willi up and over the hill. It seemed as if the horses rose out of the earth, their ears like far-off mountains in the night, and then the shapes of them, the heads and dark dragon necks, their rich and earthy smell rising before them. And Carson standing in the pasture among them like the first man who had ever tamed a beast and endeared it to him. The earth trembled under the nervous movement of hooves.

It overwhelmed Earl. He had left his house in the real world, but this seemed now a dream, a strangeness, a reverse wakening. He and Willi walked up to the fence. With Carson standing among them, the horses didn't retreat. Carson held them with his quiet voice. Earl and Willi walked up until they were standing under the horses, and the horses' heads rose above them, replacing whole sections of stars and sky.

"You're right," Carson said, bluntly and without prologue. "The son of a bitch is hurting them."

The words were broken and raw and vulnerable, uncontained, without forethought of containment, and Earl knew: It wasn't just the horses being hurt. It was Carson, too. Or maybe all of them. Earl had walked off Tower Hill into someone else's story. He wasn't meant to be here. Or maybe he was. Maybe it was his story, too. He felt he was standing in a time before tools, before races, before languages, and before even that—a time when the genes of horses and men had not yet differentiated, and there was only potential and spirit and fealty, and wind, and a raw, new earth.

Hers

∧∧∧∧∧∧

CARSON HAD GONE OVER THE RISE, and there on the other side was the new, brief fence and the three horses in the dark, all with their ears forward, waiting for him. As he walked down the hill, they came from where they'd huddled on the far side of the fence. They crossed the small space of pasture that was theirs and reached their necks over the barbs to him. He walked into the pale of those outstretched necks and raised his arms to their bony heads, as if to gather them into himself.

"Jesus, Jesus," he whispered. "They are. They're hers."

Part Two

The
PHILOSOPHY
of BROKE

∧∧∧∧∧

Angle of Spin

~~~~~~

REBECCA YARBOROUGH HAD APPROACHED so quietly on the third day of training that Carson didn't know she'd come until Orlando rolled his eyes back in his head. By then Rebecca was opening the sliding latch on the gate and pushing the gate open and stepping into the corral. Carson stood there with the rope in his hands, feeling Orlando vibrating at the end of it. He almost shouted at her to get out of the corral, but Orlando hadn't heard loud or angry words from him yet, and Carson didn't intend that he should. When the gate banged shut, the horse would have jerked the rope out of Carson's hands if he hadn't prepared for it.

"Mind if I watch?"

She folded her arms and leaned against the gate. Though he'd never seen her in town or anywhere else, Carson had heard that Magnus Yarborough's second wife was young enough to be his daughter. The stories were true. She looked to be in her late twenties, Carson's age or a year or two older. From the way she leaned against the gate, settled in, she was clearly not interested in his answer. Or she assumed she already knew it.

"Don't mind if you watch at all," he said. "Long 's you do it on the other side a the fence."

She smiled but didn't move.

"I'm Rebecca Yarborough."

"Even introductions are best done across the fence."

She smiled even more. "If you won't introduce yourself," she said, "I'll just have to make assumptions. You're Carson Fielding, the horse trainer. Quite a guess, huh?"

"Ma'am, you need a open that gate and go stand outside the fence. Once I introduce you to Orlando, you can be in the corral all you want. But right now Orlando don't want you here."

The smile disappeared. She lifted her chin, keeping her arms crossed, and met Carson's eyes with a hard stare. She had a heart-shaped face, cheeks a little full, deep green eyes with the smallest lines at their corners, hair that looked black in the shadow of the post where she stood but that frayed into a deep, burnished red where it edged into the sun.

"I happen to live here," she said. "This is my corral. And Orlando, as you call him, happens to be my horse."

"I expect Orlando's his own horse. And like I already told your husband, you cede me the corral long 's I'm here. Odd he didn't mention it."

She held his gaze a moment longer, her lips pursed. Then, with a quick jerk of her neck and shoulders, she pushed herself away from the post, out of the shadow, never uncrossing her arms. Her hair leapt into flame as the sun struck it. Without a word she turned away, opened the gate, walked through it, slammed it with a flick of her left wrist. Carson watched her back, her hair bobbing with the stiffness of her step, the heels of her brand-new riding boots hard on the gravel.

He turned back to Orlando. The horse had moved closer to him. A good sign. He felt the faint warmth of the animal's breath through the weave of his shirt.

"You handled that real good," he said. "Don't worry. She ain't about a ride you till she learns some manners."

MAGNUS CAME TO THE CORRAL THE NEXT DAY. He stood outside the fence, watching Carson work. Orlando did well at ignoring him.

"Could I talk to you?"

Magnus's voice was louder than it had to be.

"In a sec." Carson responded to Magnus and Orlando both, sensing the sudden start in the horse, keeping his own voice quiet in response. He passed his hands over the animal's flanks and withers, then wrapped the bridle around a far corral post and walked across the dust to the gate, opened it, stepped out.

"I didn't appreciate you kicking my wife out of the corral yesterday."

Magnus's words had the clipped, careful quality of a man trying to cover belligerence. Carson noted his neck thrust forward, his jutting jaw. He shut the gate quietly and turned to Magnus, who was standing with one hand on the fence, leaning his weight into his shoulder, looking down on Carson.

"Don't know as I kicked her out," Carson said. "She was where she didn't belong."

"You could be polite to her."

"She say I wasn't?"

"She was disturbed."

"No cause to be."

"She thought there was."

"She stepped into the corral. I asked her to stay outside the fence. I had a ask twice."

"And you don't like to ask twice."

"Ain't a matter a me. Orlando didn't want her in the corral."

"Orlando."

"I got to call him somethin. Seemed like an Orlando to me."

"It's a horse."

"That's right."

Magnus shook his head. "The point is you need to get along with my wife."

"I need a get along with the horses."

"You forget you're teaching her to ride?"

"Means she needs a get along with me. She ain't a horse. She'll learn to ride if she listens and does what I tell her. Don't matter if I get along with her or not."

Magnus stared at Orlando standing quietly in the corral. Then he turned stubborn eyes on Carson, his whole body swinging forward slightly off the fulcrum of his arm, intruding. "This isn't some 425-dollar horse you're buying," he said. "If you're looking for a way to leave this job and get paid for it, it's not going to work."

In spite of his tone of voice, the statement was so absurd that Carson looked up, smiling. But he saw no humor in Magnus's face. His eyes had a cold, ball bearing look.

"Is that what you think?" Carson asked. "Because if it is, you can have the last three days' work, an I'll go back to my own place. I won't work with someone thinks I'm tryin a rip him off."

Magnus's eyes wavered. He didn't like that wavering, and he tried to prevent it but finally looked away.

"I been clear about this from the start," Carson said. "I never said I wanted a be here. But I agreed, and how I feel about it ain't goin a change the work I do. I don't hafta like bein here to get along with the horses. Your wife don't hafta like me to learn to ride. I'll teach her to ride, but if she needs someone a make her happy, too, you need a be lookin for someone else."

Magnus turned back to him. Bloodless lips, an edge of teeth between them, pale eyes, the suggestion of a smile. He dropped his hand off the post.

"You're working *for* me," he said. "Not with me."

He turned away before Carson could respond.

SHE CAME BACK THE NEXT DAY. She stood outside the fence for a long time, watching Carson and Orlando work.

"Am I allowed to talk?" she finally asked.

Carson led the horse in a figure eight, teaching it the tug of a bridle. He wasn't sure whether or not her politeness was meant as sarcasm.

"No rules against talkin," he said.

"Are you allowed to stop work to answer?"

"Depends on Orlando."

"He makes the rules?"

"Most of 'em."

"So what's he say about your stopping work to talk?"

"In another minute he won't mind a bit."

Carson finished the exercise and loosely tied the reins. He came out of the corral, picked up his water jug, took a long drink. Holding the jug in both hands, the ice water cold against his brain, he looked at Rebecca Yarborough. She leaned against a windrower one of the hired men had parked near the barn a few days before. She wore blue jeans and a blue chambray shirt with a red rose sewn over the left pocket. Her hair was pinned on the back of her head. The new riding boots she'd worn two days earlier were missing. She wore white running shoes instead.

"I was out of line the other day," she said.

"Uh huh." Carson lifted the jug to his lips but stopped, surprised, when she laughed.

"That was an apology," she said. "You're not supposed to just agree."

He looked at her over the half-raised jug, flustered at her laughter, at how easily it came.

"Oh," was all he managed to say.

"You're supposed to recognize an apology without making someone put a sign on it."

He nodded, drank, swallowed, lowered the jug, shut his eyes for a moment against the rush of cold.

"Guess I need some work on that," he said.

She was taking delight in his confusion, and he felt embarrassed by it. The sun brought out faint gold flecks in her eyes.

"I don't know a thing about horses," she said. "I should have done what you asked when you asked it."

"Is that 'n apology, too?"

She moved her head loosely, a nod-shake, yes-no. "More just the truth."

He set the jug on the ground. "So why'd you go get your husband down here to give me a hard time about it?"

Her smile disappeared.

"He came down here?"

Carson nodded.

She gazed into the corral, absorbing this. "I guess I owe you another apology," she said. "I just mentioned you kept me out of the corral. I knew I'd made a fool of myself. I never thought he'd come down here."

"Maybe I shouldn' a told you."

"He likes to throw his weight around."

When Carson didn't reply, she said, "You're a diplomatic man."

"He had an opinion. I had another. We worked it out."

"I bet you did. So why didn't he inform me I could go into the corral if I wanted?"

"I suppose because you can't."

Everything that had lit up in her before lit up again, and she laughed out loud, delighted.

"You mean he didn't get his way? I wish I could have heard that conversation."

"He's used to gettin his way, is he?"

She rolled her eyes. "Oh, God."

"Well, he got me here. Wasn' my idea."

With the toe of her shoe, she touched the side of the water jug he'd set down. It wobbled, regained its balance. "He got me here, too," she said.

Carson could think of no reply. He watched the jug wobble. "Well, Orlando's waiting," he finally said.

"How's that work—Orlando telling you what to do?"

"I know where I want him to get, but he's the one knows how to get there. Every horse's a little different."

"When do I get to learn? To ride?"

A subdued, hopeful tone entered her voice, and Carson felt a sudden pang, remembering the riding boots she'd worn, their newness. It hadn't occurred to him that learning to ride actually meant something to her and that she'd come to the corral two days ago with a yearning, however small. That her entering the corral had been a mistake of hope. He'd missed that.

"I got to get a horse ready first," he said. "Orlando's comin along. Maybe another two weeks. Just confuse 'm, I put you on 'm too soon."

"He's the first priority, huh?"

"Make a mistake with a person, you can explain. With 'n animal, you got to live with it. Or start over, if you can."

She looked past him, at the distance out there, then met his eyes. The sun went deep into hers. Green pools, swimming flecks of gold.

"And what if you can't explain or live with it or start over, none of them?"

"I don' know," Carson said. "I ain't never been where one a three didn't work."

FOUR DAYS IN A ROW she asked when she was going to learn to ride.

"Patience is at a real premium on this place, isn't it?" Carson finally asked her.

He was on Orlando, getting the big bay accustomed to neck reining, shifting his weight and pressing with his heels as he laid the reins along the horse's neck to help it understand how it should turn. Orlando was confused by it. He had taken the saddle, and Carson's weight, well, but the notion of being guided, of going where another being wanted him to go, was a difficult thing for the horse to understand. Some horses wanted to be guided. Others resisted. Others had difficulty comprehending it at all.

Carson had allowed Rebecca inside the corral. Orlando had gotten used to her, seemed even to like her, and Carson was letting her help. He had her walk around the corral, and he would guide Orlando away from her, then toward and around her, to the right or left. He'd never tried this before, but it seemed to work well, and it gave Rebecca something to do. Carson didn't understand why she seemed to have so much time on her hands, but as long as she was here, she might as well be useful.

"I'm not impatient," she replied to him. "I'm just in a hurry."

"Move over to that other corner now," Carson said as he guided Orlando past her.

He took Orlando to the fence, then swung him around and started back toward Rebecca, who had walked to the corner he'd indicated.

"It's just that there's not a whole lot else to do out here," she explained.

"Don' move now. I'm goin a take him between you and the fence. See if he'll go for that. You tellin me you got a whole ranch to help work and there's nothin to do? I must look half-gullible."

"You think he lets me do anything?"

Orlando pricked his ears. "Easy," Carson said to him. "She's just makin odd sounds." The horse didn't want to go through the narrow gap between Rebecca and the fence. "C'mon," Carson urged. Orlando tossed his head. Carson saw he'd either have to pull Orlando's head hard with the reins or let him go outside Rebecca. He stopped the horse, its nose a few feet from her. Orlando was agitated, his ears moving back and forth between the rider on his back and the person in front of him.

"We're just goin a sit here a sec," Carson said. "He don' want a go through, and I don' want him to get the idea he can do whatever he wants. So while he's thinkin about it, you take a few slow steps to the side. Widen the gap. We'll accommodate him since he's such a baby about it, but he'll still be doin what he's supposed to."

She moved away from the fence, and Carson settled Orlando down, then urged him forward again. This time the horse stepped through the gap.

"We're comin back around," Carson said as he went past her. "Move a step closer to the fence. He don't let you help with things, huh?"

"Not a thing. I'm stuck."

"Good place to be stuck, I guess."

He said this as he was moving away from her. When he turned Orlando and started back toward her, she was staring at him with a face so pained she might have just stepped on a nail. Carson stopped Orlando. He looked down at her from the back of the horse.

"OK," he said. "Not a good place to be stuck."

She didn't reply. She seemed to be looking at Orlando's hooves. Carson saw that her white running shoes were smudged from the dry dirt of the corral. He saw the part in her hair, the fine line of her scalp. He nudged the horse forward until he was abreast of her. She didn't lift her head.

"Hey," he said. "That was an apology. I'm not supposed to have to put a sign on it."

Her face came up to his then.

"We gotta get you a hat," he said. "And you might want a wear them riding boots out here again tomorrow."

"You noticed that," she said.

SHE WAS ON ORLANDO, Carson on Surety, in the pasture behind the barn.

"You're doin OK," he said. "So's he. I want you to run 'm."

Her hair flowed in a delayed wave across her neck as she swung her head to stare at him. The wave parted, he saw a small emerald earring, then the wave closed again, and he saw that her eyes were the same emerald as the jewel. Or the jewel the same emerald as her eyes.

"Run him? You mean gallop? Really go?"

"You're not tryin a be a rocket. But yeah, gallop him."

"I don't know if I'm ready for that."

"You're ready. You just ain't ever done it before."

"What are you going to do?"

"Bring Surety along nice and slow."

"You want me to run Orlando out there by myself?"

"He's needin it. You, too. You don't want a just walk the rest a your life."

She lifted her chin and looked at him sideways. Carson had the impression that her eyes actually stirred deep down. Clear and mineral water.

"No, I don't," she said.

She clucked to Orlando and jabbed him with her heels the way Carson had told her, and the horse's haunches bunched, tensing under the shining coat, and already the horse was moving. Rebecca's hair flew back from her head, lifted on the created wind, so that it resembled the sheen that floated on the very surface of a blackbird's neck, color that was all light, all diffraction, without material or substance.

Carson restrained Surety, teaching her it was the rider on her back she obeyed and not the horse beside her. He watched Rebecca's back recede and Orlando's swift feet striking the earth and curling back up. Prairie dogs in their distant holes dropped their paws to the ground and disappeared.

Orlando swept to the left as Rebecca turned him, and the horse's
tail and her hair were hung on the wind, outlined against a low, distant cloud. Then they were growing toward him again, the sound
of the hoofbeats coming just behind their striking, that pleasurable
syncopation of eye and ear.

"Whoo-o-o-o!" she cried. She was shining. Alight. She flew toward him, having found the rhythm, so that she floated above Orlando
without moving, the animal a platform for her flight. Nostrils flar-
ing, mane atangle—both of them. Then she took up the reins, but
not hard, as he'd told her, and Orlando rushed to a stop beside
Surety as he had rushed away. He obeyed so well in fact that Rebecca
was thrown a little off balance and fell forward slightly over his
neck. Carson reached out and clasped her shoulder to steady her.

"God!" she cried. "God that was fun! I did it, didn't I?"

"You did it." Carson laughed himself.

"That was great!" She threw back her head—then stopped
laughing. Her eyes clouded. He saw she was looking at something
behind him. Carson turned. Magnus Yarborough's pickup was
parked near the barn, and Magnus was watching them, his elbow
sticking out the open window. He was too far away for Carson to
see his expression. Then Magnus drew his arm into the cab and
turned the wheel, and the pickup rolled forward and disappeared
around the corner of the barn.

"Well, looks like he saw you riding," Carson said.

She nodded.

"Oughta make him happy. Seein how good you got already."

She watched the point where the pickup had disappeared and
didn't reply. Surety reached down and ripped up a mouthful of
grass. Carson leaned forward, patted the horse's neck.

"He's upset," she said finally.

Carson considered this. "You got good eyes," he said, "seein that
from here."

She flicked her reins playfully at him. But her voice was serious.
"He is," she said.

"Why'd he be upset? He wants you to learn to ride."

"Wants? He agreed to it. But it wasn't easy."

Carson looked where the pickup had been, as if the empty space it had left might clarify something that he could read imprinted on the air.

"I don' get it," he said. "He doesn't want you ridin horses? This 's a ranch."

"You don't want to get it."

Carson glanced at her. She'd said the words almost as if she'd been talking to herself. As if *she* didn't wanted to get it. He saw how the shadow of her hat brim cut a curving line across her torso and upper arm. How she balanced herself when Orlando moved. He wondered if he should ask a question about what he didn't want to get. Or if he should agree to silence.

Before he could decide, she looked at him and said, "Forget him. Let's ride."

TWO DAYS LATER she suggested they load the horses into a trailer and drive to another part of the ranch. "I want to see different country," she said.

"You can learn to ride here just fine."

"You sound like him."

She said it jokingly, but the words disturbed Carson. Magnus, even when he wasn't watching, seemed suddenly present, shouldering his way into everything she thought. And Carson knew who she meant by "him." How had it happened that the word needed no clarification? And he was troubled knowing her desire to ride someplace else involved Magnus, not just riding. This was the very sort of thing Carson's grandfather had in mind when he demanded horses be brought to him. The horses and their training shouldn't be entangled in these kinds of human affairs. "Pollution," Ves had called it once. "Horses ain't askin to be trained, so if you're goin a do it, they at least deserve some purity out've it."

But seeing Magnus watching them had been a little creepy, and the thought of getting away from this ranch and into open country appealed to Carson. He just didn't want the decision to be anything but a decision about horses: where to ride them, where they liked to be rode.

"Reb," he said, looking for neutral ground. "I'm gettin paid quite a bit. But goin clear—"

"You called me Reb," she interrupted.

"I called you Reb," he repeated.

"No one's ever called me Reb."

"Rebecca, Reb. Saves me the trouble a pronouncin a couple syllables, I guess."

"That's a lot of work, is it?"

"No one's payin me four times what they're worth to say 'em."

They were standing near the corral, half-facing each other. She reached out and punched him lightly on the shoulder.

"I wouldn't pay you two cents to say them," she said.

He lost track of his thinking, got woven into the knot himself, and agreed to take the horses where she wanted.

IT BECAME THE PATTERN—loading the horses into a small trailer, driving to one of Magnus's many pieces of land, working on the things the horses needed while she learned the finer points of riding. Away from the ranch she rode better—weightless, airborne.

In July heat they walked the horses along Red Medicine Creek, five miles from the ranch buildings. She was riding Surety now, Carson Jesse. Purple and yellow coneflowers bloomed, their petals drooping in the heat, their knobby brown heads thrust to the sun. Meadowlarks sang from invisible nests. In the high center of the sky, a hawk circled and circled.

"You didn't like me when you first met me, did you?" Rebecca asked.

Out of nowhere they had a history—a first meeting they could talk about. And that she wanted to talk about. Carson looked off at the land. Good land. Good empty land, not even the telltale lines of electrical wires running anywhere. He looked at the land and was quietly pleased that she'd asked the question.

"Wasn't a matter a liking or not," he said. "Just couldn't have you in the corral. Outside the corral, I liked you just fine."

She laughed. "Outside the corral you liked me just fine," she repeated. "You sure have a way of making a woman feel good."

"That's why I got 'em hangin all over me."

She reined Surety in and gazed at the water flowing in the creek, which was diminished and muddy in the heat. Carson, on Jesse, moved on a few steps before turning and looking back at her. She sat the horse, lost in thought. Finally she brought her head up. He questioned with his eyes, but she shook her head.

"Just thinking about corrals," she said.

THEN SHE ASKED TO GO to the White River country.

"Good Lord, Reb," he said. "You want to go clear over there?"

"I've never been. I want to see it."

"You considered drivin over and havin a look?"

"Can we?"

He turned back to Jesse and rubbed the animal's shining hair. *Would the horse like the White River country?* he wondered. But he knew it was a false wonder. He was trying to deceive himself. He thought of his grandfather. "Yup," the old man would say, "that's why horses make such damn good real estate agents, they're so god-damn intristed in country."

"What do you think?"

Her voice behind him was light, teasing. Maybe too light. Too teasing. But Jesus!—what was he supposed to do? Go ask Magnus if it was OK? As if Magnus had the right to tell her where she could ride?

Several times, riding pastures, he'd seen Magnus's pickup parked on the top of a hill. Once he'd even thought—though it was too far away to be sure—that Magnus was standing outside the pickup using a rifle scope to watch them. Well, Carson had told himself, it was Magnus's land. No reason for him not to be on it. Nevertheless, he resented the man's presence. His shadow on the periphery. The truth was, if Magnus wanted to watch, the best thing was to make it easy for him. Invite it. Even ask him how he thought things were going. But Carson had the feeling that Magnus would interpret any invitation as a reason to come crowding in, to take control. Carson was too jealous of what he did with the horses to allow that.

And he was enjoying Rebecca's company. He found himself try-ing to make her laugh just to hear it. To watch the little jerk of her jaw upward just before the laughter came, her hair changing as the sun changed on it, and the surprise of the different earrings she wore, glinting through the parting wave of it. Carson imagined her holding earrings up to a mirror, dangling from her fingertips, her head tilted aside, one hand holding her hair back, her ear, its lobe and convolutions, the studied quiet on her face as she regarded herself. He imagined how she saw herself in her mind's eye with the sun in her eyes and the stone she had chosen, of one light and yet varied. He tried to remember when he had first imagined her in front of a mirror, but couldn't—just as he didn't know when they had come to a point where they had a history they could talk about, could look back and say that then things were different. When had *then* appeared?

He felt slightly out of control. Whatever was going on between Rebecca and Magnus, he couldn't keep the horses out of it. Any answer he gave to her question about the White River was freighted one way or the other. Every step he took, his foot came down in a different place than he expected. He should have insisted the horses be brought to him, where he controlled the conditions. Here, escaping Magnus's eye meant deception. Carson was drawn in, no matter what he did. It was a spinning drum, like the one he'd entered at the Central States Fair in Rapid City one year when he was a kid—a big, wooden spinning drum tipped on its side, and you had to walk through from one end to the other, and if you tried to walk it straight, you'd actually be walking it crooked, and you'd trip and fall. Carson had had the feeling the first time he fell that he'd be caught up on the sides of the thing, tumbled around like clothes in a dryer, mangled. That hadn't happened. He'd just slid on the polished wood and scrambled back up and figured out how to walk the angle of spin. But it had meant placing his feet down not in relation to the world he saw outside the drum but only in relation to the drum itself, its large, round, silent spinning. Now he had that feeling again—that he'd entered a tunnel where his landmarks had to be not in the world he knew but in the tunnel itself.

THEY WENT. HE AGREED TO IT. Was teased into it, or talked into it. By her or by himself. When the White River came into view, Rebecca let out a cry and nudged Orlando, and the big bay was gone. Carson watched them go. He watched her perfect back, gliding toward the gleaming and sandbarred river above the swing and torsion of the horse's striding, so that the river seemed to move toward them upward, as if a single horse and rider could change the configuration of the world and unroll its rivers uphill. He watched them approach the river, still running, and he was startled to see Orlando plunge down the sloping bank and pound into the water. A curtain of light rose into the air, obscuring and hiding Rebecca. Carson had the sense that when that curtain fell she would be gone and Orlando would be standing alone in the chalky water.

Then Orlando did stop, and the curtain of light descended into the river's surface, and the river flowed on, and Rebecca sat the horse's back. Orlando dropped his muzzle and drank. Carson walked Jesse on, having never yet urged the horse to any other pace, restraining him because that was what he needed to learn. Rebecca turned in the saddle and watched him come, then turned her back to him. Drops of water fell from her hat brim and hair. She waited for Orlando to finish drinking, then reined him around and walked him back to dry land. By the time Carson arrived, she had dismounted and was standing, holding the reins. Her shirt hung soaked and limp from her shoulders. Carson thought at first her face was just wet, then was surprised to see tears.

"What's goin on?" he asked.

"Why didn't you come after me?"

"Didn' want Jesse runnin yet."

"So you'd just let Orlando take me into the river? Let me fall in a hole and disappear? And just bring Jesse along slow and easy? Because you don't want him running yet?"

She lifted a palm to her face. He swung his leg over Jesse's back, stepped to the ground, and stood near the horse. He looked at her, then at the river, its slow current, the sandbars visible just under the surface of the water, then at her again.

"Wasn't Orlando takin you anywhere, Reb," he said. "You were ridin him."

"And how would you know that?"

The river shone in the sun, forced small whirlpools out of its surface, smoothed them over, flowed on.

"You sayin that ain't how it was? Sayin Orlando really was out a control?"

"I'm not saying anything. I'm just asking how *you* know how it was. How can you be so damn sure you know? Just walk along like that so smug and not even think of hurrying?"

"Smug?"

"Smug. My horse is running into the river, and you're just walking along, enjoying the damn scenery. What would you call it? What if I had fallen off? What if I'd drowned?"

He looked at her angry eyes, the hard flecks of gold in them, and the tight, straight line of her mouth. Then he looked at the river again, finally nodded at it.

"That's the White," he said. "In July. Ain't a hole deep enough to drown a cat 'n it from here to the Missouri."

But her gaze was unrelenting.

"I don' know what's goin on here, Reb," he said. "It sure don't seem to be about drownin. You really want a know, you never lost your balance. You want a fake losin control've a horse, you gotta fake losin your balance. Sway around some. Flap your arms. Slip down the saddle an grab the horn. You can't keep your back nice an straight like that. We maybe could practice it some, you really want me to break Jesse's trainin to come chasin after you next time."

For just a moment her eyes turned fierce. Even in the shadow of her hat they blazed, and he had no idea where things were going to go now. She opened her mouth—then turned her face aside, and he saw she couldn't keep a smile from beginning.

"You're a real jerk," she said. "You know that?"

"I didn't," he said.

Then he said, "Even if you'd faked it good, I probably would a trusted Orlando. Not likely a horse that smart is goin a run into a river without someone made him."

"A real jerk."

"Someone half crazy."

FRIDAY, THE SECOND WEEK OF AUGUST. They'd unsaddled Jesse and Surety and were hanging up the tack when she asked, "You want to have a picnic? I could make some sandwiches, and we could take the horses out and watch the sun set."

Carson let his hand slip down the reins he was hanging on a hook, then released them. The reins swung against the post, clacked, swished. He turned around. Rebecca was hanging her own bridle up, not looking at him. As if the question were one she asked routinely: picnic or not tonight, what do you think? Carson thought of the pound of hamburger in his refrigerator, the browning lettuce, his grandfather's small, warped table. Or he could go eat with his parents, talk about how poorly the wheat was doing, how shriveled, and how the milo might not make a crop at all. Or maybe there'd be talk of a grass fire somewhere, or doings in Twisted Tree: someone's marriage breaking up, someone's kid going in for drug rehab, or another churchgoing high schooler pregnant.

"I think I better go on home," he said.

"I'll bring beer, too."

Talk that was all circumference. All surface.

"I need a get home."

"You have other work to do."

They looked at each other across five feet of space, each of them standing by the reins they'd just hung up. Carson couldn't affirm or deny her statement. She reached up and adjusted the bridle on the hook where she'd hung it. He watched her hands: the tendons and the hollow spaces between them, her long fingers.

"He left this afternoon," she said. "A stock growers' meeting in Sioux Falls. He won't be back until Monday."

Her face uplifted to the bridle, the hook on which it hung. Her hands adjusting it as if, working carefully enough, she could make it hang straighter, truer, more plumb. That understood "he." Silence, and Carson feeling his heart thud four distinct double-beats inside his chest, against the cage of his ribs, until she dropped her hands and turned and faced him. Eyes wide, defiant, worried, but a little triumphant.

"Why'nt you go with him?"

"Four hours in a pickup cab," she said. "Waylon Jennings tapes. Daytime motel rooms. The Empire Mall."

"The Empire Mall's one a my favorite shopping places."

She smiled, but only briefly.

"Reb," he said. "I . . ."

"He didn't ask me to go," she said. "Didn't even ask."

He held her eyes a moment longer, then dropped his gaze to the concrete floor. He walked to the open barn door, stood in the rhombus of light created by the descending sun. A duck rose from the stock pond below the pasture, circled the pond twice, changed its mind for some duckish reason, and angled back, braced its feet, splashed into the water precisely where it had left. Wagner Cecil, working late, banged up the driveway from the county road in Magnus's old black pickup with the metal grill welded to the front. He got out near the second machine shed and nodded across the yard at Carson, who nodded back. Carson waited for Wagner to disappear inside the machine shed before he spoke out the door.

"What kind a sandwiches?"

"Roast beef?"

"You got horseradish?"

"I do."

He turned and looked back at her, for a moment couldn't find her, his eyes stunned by the outdoor light. Then she emerged from the shadow.

"And beer, you said."

"Beer, too."

THEY SAT NEAR THE TOP OF A HILL, the sun's angle so low it shone under the grass blades, so that the grass seemed to glow upward, emitting light. Shadows of hills cut sharp edges across swaths of gold and purple vegetation, texturing the distance. On a far hillside a herd of pronghorn antelope grazed, their rumps and sides like white rocks set into the hills, their brown bodies otherwise invisible. White rocks that shifted positions slowly against a landscape without sign of human touch, except for, a half-mile away, four parallel silver electrical lines along a county road. They ate sandwiches and drank beer.

"The way that light's in the grass," Carson pointed out, "it looks like the world's hollow and lit from inside, don't it? Shining straight up."

"It does," she said. And she told how as a girl she had thought the world was hollow and that her father could fly around inside it. He had worked as a contract miner at Homestake Mine in Lead, in the Black Hills, and every day he'd gone a mile into the earth and returned. She couldn't imagine the network of shafts and runs and winzes that constituted the mine. Instead she imagined a hollow world into which he descended: a whole world, a round world, with its own interior sky, and the gold he found like coins in the ground down there, or in iron pots behind trees. She imagined her father down there, seeking, and always triumphant in discovery. It was a world, she said, she had borrowed from picture books, from fairy tales. And she put her father in it. She would sit at her desk in the elementary school in Deadwood, and if the lesson was boring she would think of her father underneath her, walking around, his head down, looking.

"He died down there," she said. "He had a heart attack and died almost instantly. I was eleven at the time. They put him on the elevator in the Yates shaft and sent him up. Six thousand feet. By that time I was old enough to understand what the mine was. But I had dreams for years afterwards of him flying through the earth, coming up. Sometimes in those dreams he'd be swimming. Even now, when I think of it, unless I catch myself, I think of it that way. Swimming or flying. I have to tell myself he was put in the cage, and they hauled his body up on cables. But what I see is the earth all hollow and him flying up through it. Maybe, when you get far enough from something, it's easier to replace what it was with what you wanted it to be."

She broke a corner off her sandwich, looked at it in her hand. "A mile up," she said. "It's a long way to come up, just to be buried."

"Were you close to 'm?"

She lifted the corner of bread and meat to her mouth, chewed for a few moments, nodded, swallowed. "I missed him terribly," she said. "When I was little, he found out I thought he went into some fairy tale world. And he let me think it. He'd tell me stories about meeting elves down there. Bargaining for gold. Striking deals. Outwitting them. I loved it. And I loved him for it even after I knew he was lying. He never did it to make fun of me. He just wanted me to have those dreams."

She paused, smiled. "Sometimes I think I've been looking for someone to lie to me well ever since."

Carson tilted a beer back, gazed for a while at the white rumps and sides of the antelope fading in the diminishing light, that shining that had started the conversation already gone and the sun itself gone. A little distance away the horses grazed.

"I don't think I could do that—go into a mine every day."

"It was a job. I think he liked it. Liked getting into that cage with his friends. Liked that drop. And then stepping out underground, everything self-contained down there. It's a complete world—not like I thought as a girl, but complete in a different way. Cut off from everything else. And then he got to come back up at the end of the shift and step out of the cage. Into this."

She nodded at the land, the world they sat in.

"Dividing his days," she said. "It was like having two lives for him, I think."

"So you're a miner's daughter. How'd you get out here?"

"Got married."

"A dumb question."

"No. A dumb answer."

So here was Magnus again. Carson wasn't sure he wanted to know the full answer. He imagined her as a small girl sitting in a desk dressed in what?—a yellow dress? blue jeans and a T-shirt decorated with glittering stars? straight hair? a pony tail?—thinking of her father flitting around in a world far beneath her feet. Her eyes staring at the front of the room. Pretending attention, but seeing something only she saw. He wondered how many people she'd shared that vision with. And if he should be one of them. Or if he should know anything at all about her marriage. But she was telling him, and he wasn't stopping her. Vega and Arcturus had emerged from the darkness of the sky above them, the first stars, and the horses were fast becoming indistinct shadows, and as she talked darkness deepened and the animals disappeared altogether, became no more than the sound of their cropping, the ripping grass, their teeth working, until the darkness swam with stars, and Carson felt pinned to the skin of the planet, and part of what pinned him was her voice.

She'd been married before. Young. It hadn't worked. She'd met her first husband when a Frisbee he threw hit a picnic table she was sitting at near Sheridan Lake and overturned her Pepsi into her lap. Apologies, embarrassment, dismissals, forgiveness, so on and so forth until marriage. She waved her fingers in the darkness talking about this. "Who needs a crystal ball?" she asked. "I marry a man who can't even throw a Frisbee well. How long is that going to last?"

"Maybe he did it on purpose."

"Not him. He was probably stoned when he threw it."

"I thought I could change him," she went on. "Or that he'd change for me. Marriage as a project. I suppose it's dumb to be hurt when someone stays the way he was when you met him, but I was. When it was all over, I didn't know what to do. I took a job at a gambling hall in Deadwood. The Golden Spike—how do you like that name? They told me it was supposed to refer to the railroad."

She ran change and served drinks and wore a frilly Old West costume and fended off passes. She was part of the décor, part of the promise, part of the distraction, to keep people from realizing they were losing. Another bell. Another light. Another cherry that almost but didn't quite line up.

"I did it for two years," she said. "I kept thinking I'd get promoted or that things would change. That's me. Always thinking something is going to change just because I'm involved. And then I quit thinking and just hated it. And then . . ."

"Then what?" Carson asked when she didn't go on.

She shrugged. He couldn't see her shoulders move, but he heard cloth rustle, and the slightest change in the warmth coming from her, the slightest current of air.

"Then," she said, "hating the job became the reason for keeping it. I didn't have anything else, so hating that job told me I was at least alive. I guess I got afraid that if I lost the job I'd lose the hate, and then there'd be nothing."

"Sounds like a quality life."

"I think it happens to a lot of people."

"Does it?"

"You've never hated something enough to hang onto it?"

"Got an old Case tractor I hate about as much as anything. But I'd just like to get rid of it, if I could afford a different one. It'd be goin some to hate it enough to go right through wantin to get rid of it to wantin to keep it again."

Her hand came out of the darkness and touched his knee, just the knuckles grazing him, a little rap. "You're a dope. It's not the same thing."

"Didn't say it was. So what happened then?"

Then she'd met Magnus Yarborough.

"Just another gambler," she said. "Except he looked at me."

"Looked at you?"

Carson heard her hair rustle, knew she was shaking her head. "Not like that. He took his eyes off the reels when I asked him if he wanted a drink. You know how unusual that is? He spun them, and then looked away from them. Never watched them stop. Just looked at me and answered my question. I was impressed."

"That's quite a trick, is it?"

"You don't know."

"Of course I'll have a drink," Magnus had said. "This machine takes my money, but the establishment allows me to pay for a drink so that I don't care. How can I resist a deal like that?"

But he'd said it so cheerfully that she'd asked him, "Why do you come here if you know you're not going to win?"

"I have a strong feeling I could ask you the same thing."

She'd been startled. The statement was like a dart that went to her soul, penetrated a secret she thought she held private.

"Who knows?" she asked Carson. "He might have been just waiting to use that line. I wouldn't put it past him. But I'd gotten so out of touch with myself. Everything there was fake. Fake promises. Fake smiles. You know why they have mirrors all over those places? To make you forget what a little hole you're in. And to remind you to smile about it. I'd become a fake. But I thought no one else noticed. I thought my fakiness had turned into some kind of mystery. It just took one person to notice it, and I toppled. I thought he'd gone right to the core, some deep part of me. I didn't know myself any better than that."

She was both explaining and apologizing. There was no sign on the apology, but that's what it was. Another thing he couldn't place: When had it happened that she thought she had to apologize for anything in her life to him?

But he didn't have time to think about it. She went on talking. She'd stood there, gazing at Magnus, feeling exposed and thrilled. Across the gambling floor, bells clanged, and a woman screamed. A girl, barely old enough to gamble, stood in front of a slot machine that poured out coins in an endless stream. A waterfall of money. The coins spilled over the cup the girl placed under them and sprayed to the floor and rolled across the carpet in diminishing circles, hundreds of them. A casino employee rushed up with another cup, and it filled, and still the quarters chugged from the machine. The girl stood paralyzed, charmed, watching the cascade of metal, while her companions knelt on the floor and began to scoop up the money in handfuls.

"She's destroyed," Magnus said.

"Destroyed?" Rebecca asked.

"Now she thinks she's a winner. She'll spend the rest of her life trying to prove it. Feed ten times that amount back into those machines, trying to do it again. Poor girl. Nothing worse than letting someone convince you you're a winner."

"I think he enjoyed it," Rebecca said, turning in the dark to look at Carson. He knew she was looking at him, but he didn't turn his head. "He liked the irony. The way he could point it out. Stand above it all and notice."

She shifted her balance, bumped against Carson, reached up and wrapped her elbows around her knees. From out of the dark came the horses' quiet cropping of the grass. They both listened to it for a while. Carson reached down to the beer bottle he'd emptied before, picked it up by the neck, twirled it in his fingers. Then Rebecca told how Magnus had put another quarter into his machine and spun the reels and ignored them and looked at her instead and asked, "So?"

She didn't know what he meant.

"So why do you stay in this place if you know you're not going to win?"

It never occurred to her that she'd asked him the question first and he should answer first.

"It's a living," she replied.

"That's why you work. Not why you work here."

The palest light was seeping into the world, the moon rising behind them. Carson thought that in another half-hour it would be light enough to ride home. There was nothing to do until then but talk. No need to suggest they leave.

"You know," Rebecca said, staring over her knees. "I'd never thought of quitting that job until he said that. I thought every day of doing something that would get me fired. But it was all just dreaming. Never once occurred to me to just quit. So the first person who suggests to me there's life after a lousy job, I marry. You'd think I could've thought of something else, huh?"

"Guess you thought it was the best thing." He spun the bottle between his fingers and thumb, feeling the smooth glass rotate.

"Maybe. Or I didn't think at all."

Then she said, "I think we all do that, don't you? A new idea comes along, and it shows us a new life, or a new way of doing things, or whatever. And it shuts us down. It's like having that idea is enough, and we don't follow through to other ideas. We stop with that one. Let our lives end. Do you think that happens, Carson?"

"Your life's not ended, Reb."

She let go her knees with one hand and reached across his body and stopped the twirling beer bottle. It seemed as if that small thing had been turning the gears of the world, and suddenly everything stopped. Sound quit moving in the air, and the breeze eddied to stillness, and Carson was looking into her face, so close, her eyes wide, her lips half-parted, skin gleaming on the moon side, the other side enshadowed. There was grief and yearning on that face, but nothing even close to tears, and her grip on the bottle had been so sudden and strong that his fingers and thumb slipped on the neck in their turning. She stared at him, some expectation on her face that he couldn't at first decipher, and her face was so soft in the light and so lovely it hurt. She didn't speak, but he read meaning there.

"OK," he said. "It ain't mine to say if your life's ended or not."

For another moment she gazed at him, searching his face. Then she let go the bottle, and he let it go too, and they heard it roll an inch or two in the grass, and she turned her face away and wrapped her knees again, and for a while they sat like that while sound and breeze resumed.

"He wouldn't let me wait," she said after a while. "Everything was right now. My manager came out. He used to stand by these pillars in the building and watch *his girls*. That's what he called us. He came around one of the pillars and leaned against it, and Magnus saw me look at him. He's an observant man. Maybe not for the best reasons, but he is observant. Never try to work a deal on him. He'll see everything you're trying to do. He doesn't care about money, really. For him, money's just a way to not be beat. Losing it or gaining it doesn't matter, as long as he isn't beat. He saw me look at my manager, and before I even knew I was looking, he said, 'Why don't you go tell your manager there that you're quitting your job because the distinguished gentleman you're talking to has asked you to dinner?'"

"That's smooth," Carson said.

"He always has words."

"So what'd you do?"

"It was like a dare. Throw away the life I had for a dinner. Even if the life wasn't worth as much as the dinner. Still, I felt this relief.

This freedom. I had to wear a stupid, girly apron for making change. I reached back and untied it and turned around and walked to my manager with that apron and all its money swinging from my hand. I thought about whirling it around a couple of times and whacking him with it. But I just held it out. He had no idea what I was doing."

She leaned back, put her hands flat on the grass behind her, tilted her head back, turned her face to the stars, remembering.

"I was totally in charge," she said. "It was wonderful. And you know what he did? He looked at that apron like it was a dead animal I was trying to hand him, and he said, 'Is it broke?'"

"Broke?" Carson laughed—both at the word and because of her pleasure in remembering it.

"His exact words. 'Take it,' I told him. And he did. I think I could've told the President what to do that night and he'd've done it. My manager took that apron and stood there rubbing it between his fingers, trying to figure out why he had it. Then I said what Magnus had told me to say—I was quitting because I'd been asked to dinner. And I walked away."

The moon was high enough Carson could see silver whorls in the horses' hair, and individual blades of grass etched out of the dark. Rebecca's hand came out of the grass behind her, moved through her hair, went back down. She turned her face to the dark horizon, her legs stretched in front of her, crossed at the ankles, the toes of her riding boots pointed at the sky.

"I should have walked right out of that casino," she said. "Instead I walked back to Magnus. Three pillars and a dozen slot machines. The time it took to walk past them. That's how long my freedom lasted. And you know what? It was all because he made me think I was a winner."

"It's that bad?"

"You don't know."

"I can't figure a guy who'd hate his wife riding horses."

"It was good at first. Romantic. Money. Travel. Things I'd never done. Never seen. But once I married him and he got me here, it all ended. He's a jealous, jealous man, Carson. Everyone's trying to take what he has."

"He told a good lie, huh?"

"He did. And I wanted it bad."

"People seem to think he's a decent guy."

"You know what I've learned? The rich just have better lies. Better ways of keeping secrets. If you're poor, your walls are thin, and your neighbor's on the other side. I've been there. Cry in your bathroom, and somebody knows it. Rich?" She shook her head. "I could scream in that house, and no one'd know. And if someone did know, they'd never let themselves believe anything was wrong. That, too: If you're rich, you can buy belief. He doesn't like me to go anywhere or do anything. That place is like a prison. With nice bathroom fixtures."

"You ever hadda scream?"

He asked the question quietly, and it took her a moment to understand. Then she shook her head. "It's never come to that. But sometimes I think it could."

Then she said, "He doesn't like these horses, Carson. Doesn't like that I'm riding. He agreed to it because he thought I'd just ride around the house. A little pony circuit kind of thing. Cute, you know? But gees!—once I got going! And what really bothers him is that he can't find a reason for me not to ride where I want. He's lost control of it."

"That worry you?"

She lifted her chin and laughed. "I think it's great. There's nothing he can say."

Carson remembered that no one had ever seen Magnus's first wife around town. No one knew anything about her. She had only appeared in public with him and was otherwise invisible. As far as he knew, she had no friends. Then there'd been talk that she and Magnus were divorcing, and sometime after that there were reports of a new, young wife. Rebecca.

"What now?" he asked.

"Hmmm?"

"You just ride horses for the rest of your life? That enough? Ride horses and let 'm stew?"

"I don't know. It's a start. I married him. I'd like to make it work. Maybe he'll see it's OK. Loosen up eventually."

I doubt it, Carson thought. But because he wanted to put his arm around her and couldn't trust the source of his thought, he didn't say it. He sat without moving, afraid that any movement would turn into the wrong one. That any movement would change its shape once he started it and turn into the wrong one, no matter what he intended. And he had no idea what he might intend. He sat paralyzed. Bound. She lifted her hand from the ground again and ran it through her hair. He wanted to read on the topography of the muscles and tendons there some map to release. But couldn't.

THE NEXT MORNING he drove the fifteen miles to Magnus's ranch again. He told himself that he'd worked the horses on Saturdays before. He caught Surety, saddled and bridled her, led her out of the corral and into the pasture, rode away from the house. Just training. But fifteen minutes later he heard a pickup heaving over the rough pasture ground and, turning, saw Rebecca's face through the windshield. He reined Surety in and stood the horse, and the horse did well, shying away from the vehicle only at the last second, as Rebecca pulled up.

"I didn't think you were working them today," she said.

"We got hay to move back home pretty soon. Thought I'd work Surety a bit more while I can."

"Only Surety?"

"Jesse could use riding."

"Away?"

"Yeah. We could leave."

"Twenty minutes."

She turned the pickup and headed back to the house. Twenty minutes later they were loading Jesse and Surety into the horse trailer. They drove to a piece of land ten miles away, roughly in the direction of Twisted Tree. Carson knew the place. It had once been the Elmer Johannssen ranch. Elmer had been one of Ves Fielding's friends, though Carson had never met him. Ves Fielding used to tell stories of Elmer's stinginess, his absolute inability to buy anything new. "Wasn't just a dislike of new things," Ves would chuckle. "It was Elmer *couldn't* buy anything new. No more 'n a cat can play the fiddle. Wasn't possible in his nature."

When Elmer died, his wife lived on the ranch alone for a year, then sold it to Magnus Yarborough and moved to California to live with her sister. Carson was curious to see the ranch, to locate some of the stories his grandfather used to tell about helping Elmer brand his cattle or repair his fences, and how every time, no matter what they were doing, some tool or machine would break, and Elmer would stare at the broken thing with a stupefied look on his face—"like he couldn't believe it could happen," Ves Fielding said. "Like the world had a conspiracy against him, and he needed a figure it out. Spent more damn time, Elmer did, tryin a work out the nature a broken things. He coulda wrote a book. Coulda classified all things broke. If a hammer handle broke, this'd be Elmer: first he'd stare at the damn thing for a good minute or so, hold it in his hand and just look at it, tryin a see it from all angles and sides. Then he'd swear. A good, long streak a cuss words to get his mind workin on the problem. Then he'd get to discussin it. He'd say, 'Now just two days ago I had a bearing on a auger go out right in the middle a movin grain, and now this here happens right in the middle a buildin fence. Ain't that the strangest damn thing? I swear it proves the existence a the devil. It ain't temptation the devil brings to the world. No it ain't. It's broke.'

"An I'd say, 'Elmer, things break when you're usin 'em. They don't break when they ain't bein used. That's why things break in the middle a somethin. It ain't the devil brings broke into the world. It's usin things does.'

"'No, no,' he'd say. 'That's what the devil wants you to think. Wants you to think there's a simple way a lookin at broke. But it's more complicated. Two days ago that auger and today this hammer. What are the chances?'

"And then, hell, I might as well plan on sittin an listenin for a half-hour and doin nothin else, 'cause Elmer'd get off on these connections between things that'd broke for him in the past month and even the past year. Or more. Elmer'd sometimes go back ten years. I once heard 'm connect a flat tire on a bale rack with a broke axle on a homemade wagon he'd had as a kid. He'd trace 'em all out, these connections. Find all sortsa mysteries. It was the meaning of Elmer's life, damn near. The Religion of Broke. I tried a tell 'm if he'd just once buy somethin new, it might last through a job or two. But I don't think Elmer wanted a believe that. Woulda ruined his faith. Taken away his main reason for livin. A pair a slip joint pliers slippin a joint would be enough to make Elmer sorrowful, and God! Elmer loved bein sorrowful. Nothin he loved more. And then he'd get goin on the difference between the way things were supposed to work and the way they did, the difference between the theory a things an the practice, an if I didn't get 'm stopped, he'd start talkin about the spirit a things versus their goddamn materiality. He'd actually use them words. The places Elmer could go from a pair a slipped slip joint pliers! Go further 'n anyone else I ever knew."

Riding the empty ranch with Rebecca, Carson remembered his grandfather's stories. Walking the horses side by side, he told them to her, imitating his grandfather and his imitation of Elmer. She laughed at it, and Carson felt a bittersweet longing for the old man. It was good to tell her about him and to hear his stories new because of how she heard them. It was the first time since his grandfather had died that long-ago morning that Carson had ever talked about him with anyone else, the first time he'd revoiced him, let him speak again. He'd preserved the old man in a quiet area of his heart, his deepest privacy, and let no one know it. But Rebecca revived the old man. Carson hadn't thought it possible. In her laughter and understanding, she made him even more alive in some ways than he'd been when he was alive. And Elmer Johannssen, whom Carson had never known, lived again, and his Religion of Broke, with its codified laws and relationships in all their complexities. Carson understood the world through it as he rode, though it seemed, with Rebecca, a serene arrangement and a verdant philosophy, capable of explaining how he felt and how a man dead could be alive, and how time past and present could coexist in the telling of a story and its hearing.

They rode for two hours. Once a five-point mule deer crashed through the cattails in the spillway of a stock dam as they watered the horses. They heard the noise first, an ominous thrashing, but couldn't see anything. Then Carson saw the antlers floating over the rushes and under them the ears and the brown eyes, so like the color of the dry cattails that it seemed for a moment that the cattails had changed their form and that the whole marsh was converting itself into a single deer, until the animal separated itself and became a deer distinct and heaved itself up the bank and bounded away.

They rode again, in much silence, thinking their own thoughts, and they came at last to a homestead: a once white, now gray house, a barn with a caved-in roof, a windmill with a broken blade creaking in the moving air but completing no revolution. These structures stood at the end of a driveway still visible and weed-free, though potholed. Carson and Rebecca approached from over the rolling land behind the house, so that they looked down through the hole in the barn roof and over it to the driveway leading away from the house, long and thin toward the county road. Elmer had built far back from the road, coveting his privacy, and coveting, Ves Fielding claimed, "the privilege of complainin every winter how his snowplow broke down in the middle a plowin himself out, so he and Helen were stranded, even though the sonofabitch never wanted a go to town unless he couldn't make it there."

Carson had told this story to Rebecca, and when they came over the hill, she said, "There's the famous driveway, then."

They stopped the horses and looked at that driveway, imagined Elmer in the middle of a blizzard, plowing away and breaking down, staring mutely at the unfaithful machine and then softly cursing into the storm, to get his mind working, and then putting this new fact into his system of all things broke, and turning around to go home and tell his wife, reaffirming in this new betrayal of the material world his confidence in sorrow and mutability. *A strange old guy,* Carson thought. He nudged Surety and descended the hill, and Rebecca followed.

They dismounted the horses near the barn and tied them to a rusted running gear, and as Carson came around Surety's head, he found Rebecca coming the other way, and they ran into each other and were in each other's arms, falling wordless there so that Carson would never be able to remember whether he had first reached for her or she for him. It was all rush and fall and merging and not knowing what had happened. And when they finally separated and looked into each other's eyes, he took her hand and they went to the house, all without words.

Carson reached for the doorknob—the screen door only shards of wood, having long ago been ruined by the wind—but the door was open and moved inward at his touch, and for a moment he and Rebecca stood frozen in the door frame, holding each other, ready to fall like water flowing through the frame and into the house.

But from within the house there was a resistance of moving air. There was a sound of muted thunder, the sound of a world disturbed, the air in turmoil. Carson, slightly ahead, saw a blur of movement, amber eyes and ivory beaks, a confusion of wings that changed the interior space of the house and made it sway and lurch. His eyes focused, and he saw two hawks beating the air within the room, their energy so great that the room descended in Carson's eyes, tipped downward and sideways as the hawks rose up. An eye, a living agate, gazed straight into his—piercing, ancient, superior, merciless. Then the hawks tipped their bodies and timed their wing beats one after the other and burst through the broken window, the space within the shards of dirty glass like a blue flower made of sky, and they hung for onetwothree wing beats in that skybloom and were gone, sweeping upward at an angle so steep they seemed to be pushed by a wind rising from the ground.

Their wing beats still filled the room, and air rushed against Carson's face, and Rebecca's, and she gasped and let him go and stepped backward from the threshold, out of the shadows of the house and into the sun. When Carson turned, feeling only air against him where her body had been pressed, he saw her like a lost child, eyes wide, hurt, troubled. He saw how green those eyes were, and how her hair sprayed in a flame of red around her face, wild and untamed, and he was strangely puzzled, a clear, still moment of puzzlement and rationality, wondering when she had lost her hat.

He looked past her to the horses and saw the hat beneath Jesse's neck, upside down, the crown dusty, and he thought, *She must a lost it then. I must a knocked it off.*

Then confusion and emptiness returned. "Reb?" he asked.

She stood looking into the room past his shoulder, mute.

"Those were just hawks," he said. "They're gone. Just hawks."

But she shook her head and turned away from the door, and he saw her as he remembered her the first day, walking away from him, her back erect, her hair moving up and down on her shoulders, shining in the sun, her boot heels hard on the gravel. But then he'd understood the anger and hurt on her face before she turned away. In his own clarity he understood her, though she was a stranger. Now, intimacy had only confused him. He'd been about to fall into that room with her, though it might be a spinning drum that would turn them both upside down and bruise them. He didn't know why they hadn't.

He called her name again, but she didn't waver. She walked to the horses, bent down, and picked her hat from the ground. He saw her hands move on it, brushing dust from inside and out. Then she placed it on her head. He saw dust she'd missed powder the back of her hair. She walked to Jesse and untied the reins and put her foot in the stirrup, and he watched her do what he'd taught her to do and swing into the saddle, a rider, and settle herself and look at him. Across the distance they looked at each other.

Then Carson looked back into the room. Before, his eyes trained for living things, he'd seen only the hawks, and they had reversed the movement of the world, so that the room had been a blur whirling downward, sucking itself away from the birds. Now he saw the stable and still world within the walls: an oak table covered in dust, with dusty magazines sitting on it, a piano along the wall, two chairs cocked at angles along the table, with cups along the table's edge, as if a conversation had been interrupted and the people having it had gone outside to investigate a noise and had never returned, and the coffee had dried to those faint brown stains in the bottoms of the cups, grayed with years of dust and with the mundane activities of wild things: mouse droppings scattered over the table top and in the cups and saucers, the tangled, twiggy confusion of the hawks' nest in a corner of the floor, a pile of coyote scat dried to a brown-white powder, tracks of comings and goings so numerous that all was obscured and lost, and nothing could be traced.

It was as if Helen Johannssen had simply walked away from her entire life and taken nothing of it with her, so that her life and her husband's life, so recently alive in the stories Carson had been telling, had crystallized and solidified into this brittle tableau. Dead. Gone. Desiccated. The rich and living play of relationship turned to powder dry as droppings. Bone-white.

Broke. Broke. Broke. All things broke. All used, and broken in their using and left now to his stupefied gazing, who could not comprehend how they had broken or how he and Reb, so fused for that moment, so much of one mind, had broken, too, so that now she sat Jesse while he gazed into this fargone room with its stilled imprint of fargone lives. *What are the chances?* Elmer Johannssen's voice in his grandfather's voice in Carson's voice, imitation upon imitation, seemed to say. *What are the chances?*

Carson was tempted to walk across the mouse droppings scattered on the floor and touch a key on the piano, but he had the feeling that if he played a note it would be a music to shatter things. The more he looked, the more the whole house seemed made of nothing but dust, as if the dust had covered things and then the structures beneath the dust that had given the dust shape had decayed and turned to dust themselves, but the dust maintained their shapes, and everything now trembled on the border of illusion. A place suspended. If he touched a note on the piano, it would be a music suspended, too, a note that continued a song that, like the conversation over the dried-up coffee, had not ended—a song that someone else had been playing, a finger lifted that had never come down upon the key over which it hovered, so that the song was here yet, like the place itself neither real nor gone. And if Carson played that note it would be more than the place could bear—a music brought out of the past that would reveal to the house its own suspension, its own illusion. Carson imagined himself touching the piano and thought that even before the vibration from the wire reached his ear, the place would be gone, and he would find himself in the open prairie with his hand stretched before him.

He stepped back, pulled shut the door. He walked out of the shadow of the house and felt the sun strike his neck, walked to Surety, mounted.

"What the hell was that all about?" he asked. He wouldn't look at Rebecca, though they were sitting the horses side by side.

"I don't know," she said.

"You don' know? What do you mean, you don' know?"

"People lived there."

"I guess we knew that when we came here."

"Not that way."

"What's that mean? What way?"

"The table. The plates. I felt like they were going to walk in. Like we owed them something. Their privacy. Or ours. I don't know, Carson. I'm sorry. I just couldn't. And those hawks. Did you see their eyes?"

He did turn and look at her now. "That's what hawks' eyes look like, Reb."

He laid the reins along Surety's neck and ticked his tongue so quietly only the horse could hear, and he turned it away from Rebecca and started back toward the hills, the empty ranch, the horse trailer parked far away on the section line road. But Surety hadn't gone more than five steps when Rebecca spoke again, without raising her voice.

"If you don't know what I mean, lie to me, Carson. Make it all different. Make it everything I want to believe. Make me believe you believe it."

He had not, at sixteen, been able to see his grandfather alive when he was dead. Even then he would not tell himself otherwise, would not wait for a professional to pronounce the truth before he would believe it. And he hadn't known how to tell his mother anything but the fact of it, and the only concession he had thought to make to her was to remove the box of Christmas ornaments from her hands so she wouldn't suffer the confusion of dropping them. He could think of no concession to make to Rebecca at all, and no way to start a lie. He rode. He looked once to the sky, but the hawks had gone so high into the blue they'd disappeared, or they'd already circled back to occupy what was theirs.

Then he remembered the piano, the story his grandfather had told about it. It was the only new thing, Ves said, that Elmer Johannssen had ever owned, and then only because his wife had gone to Plummer's Music in Rapid City one weekend and picked it out and brought it home in the back of a pickup. Elmer had a fit, Ves said, but she wouldn't let him return it. Ves had helped unload it. In the presence of this new thing, Elmer had been unable to find a single word.

"You play?" Ves asked Helen.

She shook her head, gazing at the piano.

"Elmer play?"

She shook her head again.

They were past having children. "Why'd you get it, then?"

She sighed. "Oh," she said, "doesn't it look good there? And just think: Neither of us play, so it'll always work."

If Carson had remembered this story, he would have told it to Rebecca before they arrived at the house. Would she have laughed at it or been saddened? He'd never know. He had no desire to tell it now.

He walked Surety, hearing Jesse's hooves behind him. He didn't turn, and Rebecca didn't catch up to him. In this way they rode up and down hills across the section to the trailer. Carson wanted to explain to Rebecca how he felt and what he needed, or have her explain to him in a way that would make them both understand, but he didn't see how it was possible, and he felt too weak to even think. He wanted to start over somewhere, find the point where all could be made well and begin again, but he didn't know what point that would be or how to get back to it. And he didn't know if he could live with things the way they were: this steady, maintained distance, this silence, and all else dust and trembling.

SUNDAY CARSON SAT IN THE OLD HOUSE. He felt as if he'd vacated his life during that ride: talked it out and lived it out, and now there was nothing left. He wondered how it could be that only a few weeks ago, or days, things had felt sufficient to him, either in the present or in his hopes for the future. He looked at the bare walls around him and at the few pieces of furniture his grandfather had kept, and he thought how little it was. Everything seemed so little, and he couldn't stop remembering her lips, her body pressed against his, his hand in her hair, the small weight of her earring for a moment in his palm.

He thought of the hawk's eye. He'd felt pushed out of the room by that eye. Felt himself invasive. Felt, in the purity of that amber stare, that the hawks hadn't merely appropriated a human dwelling. They had changed it. Made it so much their own it had disappeared. In their flight through it, they had turned it to something only sinking away, a vain thing going or already gone, while those fierce eyes accused Carson—that he had brought his needs and wants to a place they were unwanted and surely unneeded. Rebecca had felt she was invading some human privacy. Carson had felt something different: He'd seen the hawks and felt himself not of them and what he carried in his heart not of them either.

Though it was, he thought. Fierce and wild. It was.

"Never shoulda happened," he told himself. But it didn't help. A bitterness he didn't understand worked within him: that she laughed as she laughed and had eyes so green; that she could startle him with the suddenness and ferocity of her grip on a bottle he was absently twirling; that she had walked with him to that doorway—and then stopped. And he was bitter against himself, too, that he'd made her laugh and imagined her before a mirror, matching stones to her eyes. But twined into these things was another and troubling bitterness, against his grandfather.

"There's nothin here," he said aloud to himself, staring at the barren walls.

After Carson's grandmother, Lucy, died, Ves had moved all the furniture out of the old house. Piece by piece, two or three pieces a day, he carried tables and chairs and settees, extra mattresses and bed frames, lamps, cushions, nightstands, out of the house and put them in the back of the Quonset shed, covering them with a blue polyethylene tarp. Charles said nothing for several days, then finally asked his father what he was doing.

"Just takes up room in the house," Ves said. "I don't need a be stumblin over a goddamn flowered chair every time I turn around."

"I suppose it takes up room in the Quonset, too," Charles observed, gazing over the irregular expanse of tarp, with the outlines of ladder-back chairs and the flat surfaces of tables discernible underneath it.

Ves had reduced himself to a small pine table, an old leather recliner, a twin bed, and three kitchen chairs. One evening Marie and Charles were sitting at supper, talking about it.

"He's getting strange," Charles said. "When Ma was alive, she kept him half-sane. What am I supposed to do with the machinery with all that stuff in the Quonset?"

"I looked at that house today," Marie said. "It feels like the barren end of memory."

The phrase surprised them all, including Marie. She and Charles and Carson all looked at each other, as if they'd heard a foreign sound, like bagpipe music on the road, or the call of swans, and they were wondering if the others had heard it, too.

"The barren end a memory?" Charles asked.

Marie shrugged. "I guess that's what it feels like to me. It's not space he's trying to gain, it's memory he's trying to lose."

"Memory a what?"

"Her. Lucy."

"Doesn't make sense. They got along."

"Got along? He's realizing he's still in love with her."

"So why'd he want a get rid've her memory?"

Marie shook her head. She wondered how her husband could sometimes be so obtuse. Or was it simply that he couldn't ever understand his father?

That had been when Carson was ten. Lucy had died of melanoma. She had come home one day from visiting the doctor in Pierre and pronounced that word with its watery syllables. For several days Carson went around pronouncing it to himself, and when he finally understood that it named the thing that kept his grandmother in bed and weakened her, he couldn't fit the loveliness of the word to what it signified, and he felt betrayed, angry at having said the word so often, angry that it was so tempting to say, and he feared his saying it had given it power.

Now he sat in the old house made barren by his grandfather's hands, and he recalled his mother's phrase and thought that he, too, had arrived there. "The barren end a memory," he murmured. It was another phrase unmatched in sound and ease of speaking with what it meant.

He looked around the room. So little. So spare. What would he do if he had the chance to show Rebecca this place? As if there were something to show. Walls and old furniture.

"You coulda left me more than this," he murmured.

But the moment he said it, he knew: He was bitter not because his grandfather had left him so little, but because he'd thought it was enough.

And it had been. His grandfather had given him more than this house. He'd given him a way to see the world. And yesterday, on that ride, Carson had seen that world with Rebecca. She had taken it gladly and rightly, and it had been a sure, good thing. But now it seemed that in taking it she'd left him nothing.

Carson remembered sitting at the truck stop in Twisted Tree a couple of years before when a sad-looking woman, a stranger, had passed his booth and he had nodded to her. That one friendly thing, and before he knew it she was sitting in his booth, telling him first that she was going to the powwow on the reservation—and from there he heard about her husband's affairs, and her affairs, and their divorce and her loneliness and troubles: all the sad, self-pitying, private things that she could unburden precisely because telling stories to a stranger implied no promise or relationship.

But if you told private stories to someone not a stranger, they became a journey taken together, steps cut into a hillside. He'd let himself believe that journey had a destination, though he'd never recognized that believing. Now, nothing had come of it. After all these years, he had finally spoken of his grandfather, and the speaking had turned out to have no power. Rebecca was as far away from him as that woman who had trapped him in the truck stop booth. Maybe further.

And he was left with this. These walls.

He repeated his mother's phrase again, and it seemed like a bell tolling, fitting perfectly where he was. "The barren end of memory," he said. "How the hell'd I get here?"

HE WENT BACK ON WEDNESDAY. To finish the job—to wrap up what he had to do with the horses and get away from the place. Still, he glanced at the house when he drove into the driveway, and he listened for her footsteps as he gathered tack from the hooks where they'd hung it Saturday afternoon, when they'd returned from Elmer and Helen Johannssen's empty house. Wagner Cecil had been doing chores when they'd arrived back and had said hello to them, but Carson could barely bring himself to reply. Carson had backed the horse trailer up to the corral gate, and Rebecca had climbed out of the pickup to open the gate, and they'd released the horses, and Carson was relatching the horse trailer gate when she said, "Can we talk?"

"What's there to say?" He knocked down the latch.

"It wasn't supposed to go this far."

"It did."

"I'm married, Carson."

"I best be goin."

"That's it? That's all you're going to say?"

He looked at his hand on the latch, paused, then turned and faced her. "What, Reb? You goin a ask me if we can just be friends? You just said it: You're married, an it wasn't supposed a go this far."

"I need time."

He lifted his hand from the latch.

"Are you coming back?"

"You turned into a hell of a rider. Horses are about trained. I'll wrap things up. I got my own ranch to work."

Four days later, he listened for her steps, but she didn't come from the house. Truth was, he'd stretched the training beyond any need. He knew it. Even the horses didn't require him here. He'd give them a good-bye ride. That was it. That was all that was left to do.

He was saddling Surety when Burt Ramsay drove up to the fence in his pickup and shut the engine off. He rolled the pickup window down.

"Howdy, Carson."

"Burt."

"Trainin goin OK?"

"About done."

"Magnus is wonderin, maybe you could give us some help."

"How's that?"

"Movin a herd. Could use another hand. Lonny's sick. Hung over, more like."

Carson just wanted to be done with this place. But if they needed help, they needed help.

"All right."

"He'll pay you extra."

"No need. I'm here."

Burt shrugged. "Up to you. Far as I'm concerned, pay's pay."

"You got a horse for me?"

"A few. Mainly four-wheelers."

Carson released Surety, carried the saddle to the barn, and climbed into Burt's pickup. As they drove past the house, he thought he might see her, a glimpse through a pane, but didn't. Burt drove a mile north on the county road, then turned off into a pasture. Dust rose from behind a hill, and the wind blew it gritty against Carson's teeth, and he could hear the cattle lowing.

It was an odd time to be moving cattle, and Carson questioned Burt about it.

"I didn't ask."

"That how it works? He says something, you do it?"

"It's his money. Don't needa make sense for me to get paid."

They bumped over a hill and saw the herd spread out below them. Burt swung wide to avoid them and circled around to where a few horses were standing saddled near an ATV.

"I'm 'na let you out here. You go ahead and grab that four-wheeler there and follow me. Got a few slipped through we need a bring in."

"Think I'll take a horse."

CARSON AND BURT GATHERED THE STRAGGLERS and brought them back to the main herd, then Carson helped push the cattle through the gate into the next pasture. He noticed Magnus driving the black Chevy pickup with the metal grill welded to the front. The herd was going through the gate well when an old cow broke away. Carson didn't see how it happened. By the time he noticed it, the cow, a black baldy, had already evaded Magnus's pickup and was running high-rumped, her back legs kicking out sideways, her tail swinging, up the rise and into the open pasture, angling in Carson's direction. He yelled at Wagner Cecil, riding a four-wheeler near him, to watch the space he was vacating, then drew the horse around.

He was closing the gap between himself and the fleeing cow when he heard an engine behind him, and then the black pickup loomed in his peripheral vision, heaving at reckless speed over the rough ground of the pasture. It startled the horse, and Carson slowed to reassure the animal.

Magnus yelled out the window, pacing Carson. "Forget the horse. We'll get her with this."

His voice was so loud and the pickup so near—edging closer as Carson guided the horse away from it—that the animal started again, and Carson brought it to a complete halt. Anyone ought to know better than to bring a pickup with a bad muffler close to a running horse. Magnus skidded to a stop, tearing into the ground, pushing dust up. The cow kept going.

"Hop in." Magnus jerked his head at the passenger seat.

"Don't need two of us to get a single cow. Might 's well one of us keep with the herd."

"Get in. We'll have the whore corralled before anyone even knows she's gone."

Carson hesitated.

"It's my cow," Magnus said, smiling. "Guess I oughta be allowed to retrieve it any way I want. Now hurry up and hop in here."

It made no sense for Carson to get off the horse and become a passenger in the pickup. He could have the cow back in minutes if he just went after it. But Magnus's smiling face disarmed him, and the man was right: He was in charge here. Carson felt the presence of the weekend. He didn't know how to behave around Magnus, couldn't discern what he would normally do. He looked at the cow disappearing over a hill. *What the hell*, he thought. *I'm just helping out. Do it his way and get out of here.* He could mention he was done with the horses and so wrap everything up. He dismounted, let the reins trail, walked around the front of the pickup, and got in.

He was pulling the door shut when Magnus punched the accelerator. The engine roared, grass and dry soil spewed from the tires, and the pickup shot forward. Carson, barely seated, lost his grip on the door handle. It slammed against his groping fingers, jamming them, and a crystalline pain, like a thread of ice, snicked up his arm. He wedged his knees against the dashboard to keep from hitting the roof on the bumps, his hand burning and limp. Magnus squatted on the seat, gripping the steering wheel with both hands. On his right ring finger he wore a heavy Black Hills Gold ring, rose and green, which he clacked against the hard plastic of the wheel, a sound barely audible over the racketing and exploding muffler and the bad shocks banging. In Carson's ear a rifle behind the seat clattered in its wooden cradle.

"Great you could help out," Magnus shouted, not turning his head.

Carson squeezed his right hand, working movement back into it, and tried to anticipate the pickup's bucking. It heaved over the rise where the cow had disappeared, sky filling the windshield for a moment, a few high, white clouds that rushed upward as the pickup nosed violently down and the cow hove into view, moving toward the blue stock pond below. She had slowed to a walk. She swung her head around and looked past her belly at the approaching pickup, her white face a triangle of wonder. Then she turned and began her clumsy gallop again.

"The bitch," Magnus shouted over the roar of the engine.

His friendly tone was gone, his voice now grim and angry.

"She's just bein a cow," Carson shouted back.

Magnus said nothing. He swung the pickup in a large circle around and in front of the running animal. The metal grating welded to the bumper rose and fell against the sky. On the stock pond, circles of feeding bass appeared and faded in intersecting patterns.

"I'll show you something about herding these ornery bitches."

Carson looked sideways at Magnus, puzzled. This is what cattle did—they ran if they had a chance. You tried to keep them in the herd, but if they got away you caught them and brought them back. That was all. There was no sense taking it personally. But Magnus emanated a palpable antagonism. The dust of the cab seemed tainted with it. Before Carson could say anything, Magnus made a sharp and high-speed turn, throwing Carson against the passenger door. When he straightened up, the pickup was heading straight toward the cow, which had stopped and was watching them walleyed, as if unable to comprehend how the pickup had gotten in front of her. She stood with legs outspread, a knock-kneed and splay-hooved upside-down V, her head lowered. A string of slobber stretched from her mouth to the ground, like a tether on one of those big, ridiculous balloons Carson had seen in parades on television he'd watched as a kid with his mother. The cow looked like it might rise on that tether, its butt end up, anchored by its jaw, astounded at its own emptiness.

"All right, you stupid whore," Magnus said. "We'll see how far you can run."

"She's just a cow," Carson said again.

"A stupidass cow."

Magnus turned and grinned at Carson, a stiff, fleeting grin of tightened lips over his teeth. The cow had turned back toward the herd, and they were pushing it along, the engine quieter now. Carson would have trailed further behind, letting the animal find her own way and correcting her direction only if she needed it. He noticed her hard, agitated trot, her back jarring up and down. A clot of manure on the end of her tail swung like a misshapen pendulum, and specks of dirt thrown from her hooves hit the windshield in a staccato of hard, dark snow. Carson looked down on the animal's spine, patches of sweat staining its back. The cow shat, green and scoury. The smell compressed the air inside the pickup cab.

"You're stressin her," Carson said.

Magnus ignored him. He inched the pickup even closer. Trotting now, stiff and limberless, the cow ran through a patch of dried Canada thistle. Magnus followed, the tops of the thistles bending before the onrush of the pickup, thumping against the bumper, then whipping under it and running in a rush and clatter along the oil pan and chassis. White seeds sprayed in a fragmented cloud that was sucked into the open windows and became individual seeds again, dark, hard knobs floating aimlessly in the cab, held aloft on lacy white architectures of filament and vein.

"Stressing her?" Magnus asked. He grinned again. "Nice you're so concerned. But she isn't your cow. And you aren't driving."

Carson's scalp prickled. At that moment he breathed a thistle seed in. He coughed, his eyes watered. Magnus hit the accelerator, and the pickup surged forward, knocking Carson back against the seat, and then the metal grill bumped the cow on the haunches, and Magnus braked, and Carson, his hand lifted to his mouth, still coughing, barely kept his head from striking the dashboard. The cow stumbled and almost fell, and a bleat of dismay whoofed out of her. She recovered and broke into her awkward gallop, tail swaying. The pickup rushed from the patch of thistles after her.

"Jesus Christ!" Carson managed to clear his throat. He spat the thistle seed, a damp brown lump, on the floor. "Give her some room."

"A little stress is good for her. Maybe she'll think the corral's not a bad place to be when I'm finished with her."

At that moment the cow broke left, and Magnus, following too closely, couldn't adjust. He shot past her, swore, braked, rammed the transmission into reverse, and backed in a circle away from the panicked animal, then forward again, cutting troughs from the sod with the tires. The high-lift jack in the bed of the pickup banged up and down, adding its metal racket to all the other noise. As they passed the cow, she had her head down, the whites of her eyes half-moons—too white: glazed, pure—and sweat was draped over her back like a dark, ugly blanket.

Magnus swung in front of her again, tires slicing the soil. Carson tried to anticipate his movements but couldn't and again was thrown against the door. The cow bellowed in dismay and wonder when the pickup appeared before her again. She put her head low to the ground, and for a moment threatened to charge but then swung around and turned toward the herd again.

"We got a slow learner here."

"She'll go on her own if you just stay back."

But Carson hadn't even finished the sentence when Magnus hit the accelerator, and the pickup closed the narrow gap between grill and haunch with unbelievable speed, slamming space shut. Magnus hit the cow and braked at once, flinging Carson forward and striking the animal on its haunches, knocking it to its knees with a sound like a sack of grain hitting a wooden floor. The cow's jaw plowed through the grass before she stumbled to her feet again.

"Christ!"

"Didn't hurt her a bit. Knocked some sense into her is all."

Magnus steered with his left hand, resting his right on the gearshift knob, the gold ring tapping, pretending nonchalance. But his face, as he stared through the windshield, had a gray look, like old concrete. In front of the pickup, the cow was swinging its head from side to side, white foam gathered on her muzzle.

"You stay this close," Carson shouted, "she's just going to break again. She'll never go in without you let her."

"We'll see about that."

Magnus took his eyes from the cow and looked at Carson, that tight, stretched grin on his face, that ball bearing look to his eyes. But at that moment, in spite of her exhaustion, the cow broke to their right, then came almost straight at the pickup, far inside its turning radius. She lumbered past Carson's window in a haze of sweat and heated air. Carson turned away from Magnus's gaze and murmured, "Go, girl."

Magnus slammed on the brakes. "The bitch!"

Carson turned his head out the window and watched the cow gallop downslope toward the stock pond, above which clouds on the western horizon were breeding white and bright.

Magnus took off downhill. For some reason Carson thought maybe he'd learned that what he was doing wasn't working and would give the cow some room. Even when he saw Magnus making no attempt to circle the animal, running the pickup right toward her, even when he saw the gap narrowing at a speed too fast for control as the V-8 roared out its bad muffler, even when he saw the cow's flailing rear legs coming up and going down, closer and closer, the clot of manure on the end of her tail growing in his vision like an ugly tumor—even then, somehow, Carson thought Magnus would turn aside and head the animal.

Then he saw what was going to happen, but it was too late. "Hey! Hey! Hey!" he cried. He had only time to grip the dashboard to brace and steady himself. He never thought to grab the steering wheel from Magnus and turn it. His realization was too slow. That step in the turning drum that tumbles you. That mistake of keeping your eyes on the world you know instead of the world you're in.

There was a moment of almost cartoon lightness, the faraway clouds rising up and up and the metal grill bearing down on the swinging tail and rising and falling flanks as if the pickup were merely going to boot the animal, and her body, soft and pliable, would compress momentarily and then loft high into the soft white bed of clouds.

Then Magnus quit swearing the streak he'd been swearing, and all was silent, the only sound a sound of rushing, and from another place and time a meadowlark's song, note by note dropping like individual bits of a distilled world through the window. Then the grill collapsed space, and the pickup ran right over the cow's rear legs, and the animal barked like a huge, hoarse dog amidst a sound of splintering.

THAT STUPID BITCH won't run away again."

Out of the silence, those words.

Magnus backed the pickup away. The cow lay with its rear legs skewed like a child's crude drawing, bone erupted and glistening out of the muscle and hide. A tuft of hair and gore clung to the jagged end of a femur and fluttered in the wind. The cow tried to rise, its front hooves tapping the ground almost gently, as if to sound it, the legs gathering for a moment under the animal, knee joints knobbed and straining before collapsing. Then the animal lay still except for a deep trembling, its neck stretched forward, ears back, eyes crazed.

Magnus stared at the trembling animal, his face as gray as the clipped hair around his head. His ring tapped the gearshift knob once, the sound startling in the confines of the cab.

"You bastard," Carson said quietly. "You ran right into her. You son of a bitch."

Magnus lifted his hand off the gearshift lever, reached up, turned off the ignition key. The gold ring splashed rose and green light across the dusty dashboard. The meadowlark sang again. Wind roamed the grass.

"You best not call me a son of a bitch," he said.

"You son of a bitch. If you'd backed off, she'd a never bolted."

Beyond the windshield the cow quivered seismically.

"I don't back off. And I sure don't listen to someone like you. You and your goddamn horse breaking. You think you can come onto my place and just take over?"

Carson stepped out of the pickup. When he shut the door, the cow groaned—long, shuddering—the voice of everything broken and sad in the world. He spoke through the open window. "You invited me onto this goddamn place. And what the hell's my horse training got to do with that pathetic thing?"

But just as he turned away, he knew. He stumbled under the realization, caught himself, veered off, dazed. What did Magnus know? And how could Rebecca have told him?

He was fifty yards away, plodding through the grass, his joints weak, feeling betrayed, confused, and totally alone, when he heard the pickup start, the ball joints knocking as it neared. He glanced back, saw it looming, a menacing thing, the sun striking the wind-

shield in a hard glaze of light, fresh blood shining on an edge of the
grill. But at the last instant it turned and came alongside him, so
close the mirror nearly hit him, and he could smell oil burning on
the manifold.

Then he saw the rifle pointed at his chest.

Magnus held the steering wheel with his left hand, the rifle with
his right, across his chest, the barrel resting on the window frame.
The green and rose ring peeked from under the synthetic stock.
Carson was too sick at heart to be frightened. He stopped walking
and stared at Magnus over the black barrel of the rifle. In one of
Magnus's thick, gray eyebrows, a thistle seed had caught.

"What?" Carson asked. "You're goin a shoot me? Like that don't
mean you're a bastard?"

Whatever Magnus believed, it didn't justify what he'd done.
Even if Carson and Rebecca hadn't stopped in the doorway, that
ruin of flesh back there could not be excused. This conviction fu-
eled Carson's anger. But for a moment he thought he'd gone too
far. Magnus's eyes receded into themselves, swallowing light, and
he tensed, and tendons stood out on the hand wrapped around the
rifle's stock. The thistle seed fluttered.

Then he smiled briefly, his teeth square and precise under his
shaved upper lip. "Herding cows with horses," he said. "Shooting
people. You are a believer in the old ways, aren't you?"

The wind freed the seed. It floated away. Carson's eyes followed
it momentarily, then returned to Magnus, and when he saw those
flat eyes again, he sensed that explanation would only make things
worse. Magnus was determined to believe what he believed, and in
running over the cow, he had created a need to believe it. He might
believe Carson and Rebecca were physically intimate, or that they
were only emotionally so, or that they were merely friends—but all
these in his view overstepped a boundary. Facts and the order of
events, what had happened or not happened, were irrelevant. Anything Carson might say would only confirm Magnus's convictions.
Denial would confirm them. Or admission. Or silence. He'd run over
the cow in rage. If he now allowed his rage to be corrected, he would
have to face that cruelty for what it was, and that he couldn't afford.

Carson turned away. He wasn't sure whether he was guilty of a wrong against this man. He probably was. But he wouldn't seek forgiveness or understanding. Not after what had just happened. Not after that.

"What makes you think you can walk away?" Magnus asked quietly behind him.

Carson kept walking.

"You're still in my employ. And you've got a job to finish."

Carson turned back.

"I ain't never been in your employ."

"I say you are. And I say that cow back there needs finishing."

"You hit it. You finish it."

Magnus let the pickup roll forward until it was next to Carson again. Over the rifle they stared at each other. Magnus jabbed the rifle at Carson's chest. Carson didn't move. The barrel touched him, a round, cold imprint through his wet shirt.

"Take it. Take the rifle."

Carson turned his back. A shadow of cloud ran over the land, darkening the dust over the hill where the other men were pushing the cattle into the adjoining pasture. Such a brief time: They were still herding them. It had been only a few minutes since Carson had turned his horse back to chase the runaway cow. The lowing of the cattle and the indistinct shouts of the men reached him. Behind him the pickup door opened and shut. Tires crushed the grass, and again the pickup slid into his peripheral vision. He didn't turn his head. Magnus paced him.

"You want to quit, let's see if you can." Magnus spoke just loud enough to be heard over the racket of the muffler and the crackle of the tires. "I left that rifle back there. I'm going home, have a beer. You want to quit, I'll give you a ride. Hop in."

Carson kept walking.

"I thought so. Goddamn horse breaker. It ain't so goddamn easy to just walk away from things."

The muffler roared, the pickup spun dust out of the grass, and grasshoppers sprayed before it over the land as it fled. Carson stood stock-still watching it, until it crested the hill in front of him and disappeared, and only the dust of its leaving remained.

He turned around. The bright clouds in the west covered half the sky, billowed and broken. He looked at them. Thought of what lay back there.

"This is no goddamn time to be proud," he murmured to himself.

The rifle was lying on the ground. Under its stock, paper-clipped together, was a wad of hundred-dollar bills. Carson stared at it, unable to comprehend what it meant. He squatted down, picked it up, fingered it. Then he realized it was the money Magnus had agreed to pay him to train the horses. Plus a fourth. He could see it was all there. The deal complete. The transaction finished. The bargain kept.

He bowed his head. He wanted to throw the entire wad away. But he couldn't. The only reason he'd taken the job was because his father had agreed to it, to help out the ranch. He felt beaten, exhausted.

He stood. He pushed the wad of money into his pants pocket, hating the feel of it, the pressure and bulge. He stared at the rifle at his feet. Then he bent down and picked up the weapon and turned back toward the wounded cow.

Part Three

ROBBING
and
STEALING

Mining Blame

∧∧∧∧∧

ORMAN WALKS ALONE heaved himself up from his lawn chair. His braid, streaked with gray, rippled against his shirt. He walked to the fire and stood for a few seconds staring into the washtub set on a ring of stones. The flames wrapped around the bottom of the tub, licked away. Earl had the impression his uncle was looking for an answer in the way the water boiled or the way the flies swarmed and swirled above the steam. Then Norm lifted the stick in his hand and stirred. Flies fled, returned. The sweetish smell of brain rose from the stirring. Norm turned from the fire and tub and sat back down in his lawn chair, the aluminum creaking under his weight. He adjusted the stick across his legs.

"Tell me more," he said.

"He said they were being starved. He said there were marks on them where someone had cut them. He couldn't say with what. He said it looked like someone was trying to kill them. Slow, you know?"

Norm said nothing. The fire's heat warped the air above the tub, and the trunk of the cottonwood tree behind it shifted, blurred, floated. The cloud of flies moved strangely in that warped air. A meadowlark sang from the distance, and a near one answered, and then the far one sang again. Norm seemed to listen to the birds.

Earl knew to wait for his uncle, but he had to say a little more. He interrupted the silence. "He was so sure," he said. "But it was dark, and all we had was the moon, you know? And that big flashlight he'd brought."

"You weren't convinced."

Earl didn't know how to answer. He had been convinced. He'd been convinced even before he and Willi had walked with Carson over the hill to the horses. Been convinced the moment he'd looked back at Tower Hill and its lights flashing among the constellations and known that he'd seen a thing intended to be hidden. Or unrecognized. But he'd resisted Carson's confirming it.

"How can you be so sure?" he'd asked.

Carson had flicked on the flashlight and run it along the horses' bodies. He'd shown Earl hair growing thin and discolored, and he'd placed Earl's fingers on long, running scars that felt like giant, scaly caterpillars. He'd knelt down and said, "An look't this," and invited Earl to kneel too, and Earl had done so and felt with Carson the thin ridge along a fetlock where a bone had cracked. Or, as Carson had put it, "Been cracked. Don' know how the hell you'd do somethin like that. Hit it with a hammer, maybe."

Then he'd clicked the flashlight off. And out of the new darkness said, "An now he's starvin 'em. Ain't enough to hurt 'em. Looks like he plans to leave 'em here till they die. If you hadn't a seen 'em, they'd a just turned inna bone out here."

Against his fingertips Earl could still feel, like a residue, the thick, coarse scabs and the way the horses' skin had quivered when he touched them. His fingertips wanted to curl into a fist, press themselves into his palm. Or rub themselves on his blue jeans, or on a rock. Something. Scrape away the memory of that scarred and quivering flesh.

"But a lot of things could cause those scars, you know?" he said. "Maybe they hurt themselves, and they're penned up until they heal. Maybe we're the ones making a problem here."

And it almost made sense when he said it. His fingertips weren't convinced, but his mind almost was. Goat Man could be found anywhere, Earl thought. Those who hunted him could smell him in smoke from a fire, find his track in the way a grass blade bent. Their eyesight could be too good, their hearing too acute.

"Look 't this pen," Carson said. He flicked the flashlight back on and ran it all the way around the barbwire fence surrounding them. Earl's eyes followed it, a faint circle of light hitting the barbs and gleaming in the wire, and touching the grass beyond the fence in a dim oval. When the light returned to where Carson had started it, he flicked it off again. "What makes this different from any pen you've ever seen?" he asked.

Earl wasn't in the mood for a riddle. "It looks like a fence to me," he said.

Willi, who'd been silent, spoke. "I see what you are seeing. There is no way to leave."

It was true. The strands of barbwire went corner to corner without a gate.

"Whoever built this fence," Carson said, "must a built it around these animals. An he didn't intend they'd be walkin out. Not unless he tore the fence down."

"That," Norm said, when Earl had finished telling this, "is a spooky thing, nephew."

That's what Earl had felt, too. He'd thought of someone bringing the horses to that spot of ground, staking them, then methodically building this fence around them, digging the holes for the wooden corner posts, pounding the steel posts into the ground, stretching and clipping the wire, all while the horses watched. Then walking away. He'd thought of that person walking away. Carrying his tools.

Norm pushed down on the stick he held in both hands, drove it into the ground and rose up from his chair on it. He went to the fire, stared into the washtub again. After a while Earl rose and stood beside him. They listened to the buzz of flies.

"You told your mother about this?"

"No."

"Why not?"

"I didn't want. She would . . ."

Norm leaned his entire weight into the stick, his huge hands around its top. He put his chin in the hollow of his thumb.

"My sister-in-law," he said. "She would have asked you what you were doing in that pasture. Hanh? That would have been her first question."

Earl said nothing, and Norm twisted the stick back and forth, its end digging into the ashy ground at his feet.

"And I guess," he said, "it's my third or fourth."

"What?"

"Question. It's not my first, but I am asking it."

"I was on top of Tower Hill," Earl said. "I saw the horses from up there. I went down to look at them."

"Not much happens on Tower Hill but parties."

"There was a party. But I wasn't drinking."

Earl watched small bubbles rise and burst in the solution. A whitish foam gathered along the rim of the tub. The calling meadowlarks called again.

"Mom," Earl said. "Sometimes I can't. Something like this. I can't."

"Your mother is a fine woman, nephew. Never forget that."

"She won't even let you in the house. You're family. That isn't the way it should be."

Norm returned to his chair, sat, laid the stick across his knees again. Earl waited a few moments, then returned to his own chair, and they gazed at the fire from their different places. Norm was silent for so long that if Earl hadn't known him, he would have thought he'd gone to sleep. The meadowlarks went through a half-dozen calls and answers, and the thousands of grasshoppers in the prairie around the motor home without wheels that served as Norm's house chewed on the vegetation.

"Those two meadowlarks," Norm finally said. "They've returned from last year."

"The same ones? How do you know?"

"Their songs."

Norm was about to talk. But first he had to direct Earl's attention to something else. As if he wanted their talk to be part of a larger conversation. Or wanted the meadowlarks' conversation to be part of their talk. And wanted Earl to listen to the entire thing. Out of respect for his uncle, Earl listened to the meadowlarks call and call. Then he said, "They both sound the same to me."

"If you sat here long enough, you would hear the difference."

Earl listened again. The birds sounded identical. *The Deaf Indian*, Earl thought, *listens intently*.

But Norm interrupted Earl's interior documentary. "Sometimes I think I'll listen well enough," he said, "that I'll know individual grasshoppers by the sound of their wings. That would be a good thing."

"Why?"

Norm chuckled. "I'm not sure," he said.

Then he said, "Your dad was a sweet guy, Earl."

Earl shifted in the chair's webbing. He'd come to ask his uncle about the duty Carson and Willi had laid in his lap. He wanted to know if Norm thought it was his duty. If he had to accept it. But asking his uncle anything often involved long journeys to the answers. Even to the questions. That was all right. For a while Earl could forget the horses and Willi's repetitive insistence that they had to do something about them and Carson's strange, disturbing presence— the steady, unwavering, impassive way he regarded Earl, in his eyes some mystery Earl couldn't decipher. When Earl couldn't detect the tiny ridge of bone that Carson said was a crack in Orlando's fetlock, Carson had taken Earl's fingers in his own and guided them to the ridge, rubbed them lightly over it. It had been the oddest gesture Earl could have imagined. They had squatted, touching at the shoulders, and Carson had reached out with Earl's fingers and rubbed them as if they were his own against Orlando's skin.

"Feel that?" he'd asked.

Earl watched his fingers, moved by someone else. "Yeah," he said. "I feel it now."

"That's what I'm talkin about."

But now Norm was talking, and Earl could forget that tiny crack in the bone, and his fingers moved over it by someone else's hand.

"A sweet guy," Norm repeated. "My little brother, the Sweet Guy. That's what we need, hanh?—an Indian comic book hero. The Sweet Guy. Your mother ever tell you about those trees?"

Those trees: Earl had been hearing about those trees all his life. He didn't reply.

"They're a marriage proposal," Norm said.

Earl didn't know that part of it, but he wasn't sure he wanted to. "Mom says she can hear my father's voice when the wind blows in those trees," he said. "But, you know, they just sound like trees to me. Trees and wind."

"And meadowlarks sound like meadowlarks to you. You pay attention to your mother."

Then, periodically rising to stir the tub's contents with his stick, Norm told how he'd gone to the nursery in Pierre with his little brother, Cyrus, to get trees. The people at the nursery couldn't figure out why an Indian would be planting trees. They glanced at Norm and Cy, who stood near the bags of fertilizer, waiting for assistance, then glanced away again and attended to someone else.

"I'm not sure how long Cy would've stood there," Norm said. "But I got impatient. I was drinking in those days, and I wasn't that far out of Vietnam, and drinking and Nam both had a powerful effect on my manners. I was, you might say, engaging the clerk in a discussion when Cy walked between us and asked, 'Could you figure how much twenty of those trees over there would cost?' He points to some little saplings stacked against the wall. The clerk is so glad to have something to do not involving me that he whips out a pencil and comes up with a figure I could see when he looked at Cy he thought was a number no Indian would be willing to pay, for it didn't matter how many trees.

"But your dad just smiled. He reached into his pocket and pulled out five hundred-dollar bills and fanned them out like he wasn't sure it was enough, and says, 'Looks like I can handle that. Make it twenty-five.'

"The clerk strained his eyeballs staring at that wad of bills, nephew. But he got more helpful then. We all three loaded trees into the back of Cy's pickup and then went inside to pay for them. The clerk punched numbers into the register and tallied up the bill and announced it, tax and all. And what does Cy do? He reaches into his back pocket and pulls out a checkbook. He slaps it down on the counter and writes out a check and rips it out and hands it over. I tell you, nephew, I had to go over and lean on those fertilizer bags and read the hazard warnings on them and imagine getting cancer just to keep from laughing out loud. The clerk was just staring at Cy's hand writing out that check, like he didn't believe an Indian could use a pen. The last thing he wanted was a check from an Indian, but he'd just helped that Indian load twenty-five trees. Cy ripped that check out and held it out, and the clerk looked like he thought it was going to give him herpes, so Cy laid it on the counter and said, 'You've been very helpful. I'll tell my friends to come here and buy trees, too. If I have any questions, I'll be sure to call you.'

"Then we go out the door. As soon as it shuts, I bust out laughing. But Cy's quiet and serious. Sweet, hanh? He just climbs into the pickup and starts it and heads out of the parking lot. He looks up and down the street for traffic, then pulls out nice and easy, not to bump those trees around, and says, 'The real lesson for that guy's gonna be when that check turns out to be good. That'll upset his whole world. He won't sleep for days.'

"That was the way your dad was, Earl. It'd been me, I'd a had that clerk by the neck, and he'd a had me in jail. But Cy saw right to the heart of things. He figured out how to make things work so even a guy like that clerk didn't know what was happening to him."

They'd rolled the windows down and headed south down Highway 79, away from Lake Oahe and the Missouri breaks until they were traveling over rolling prairie. "Ain't it crazy," Norm had said to Cyrus, "a prejudiced little white guy has to tell a couple of Indians how to plant trees?"

"Not so crazy," Cy had replied. "Indians didn't plant trees."

Outside the windshield the land rolled away like a sheet on a line billowed horizontally by a strong wind, snapped into hills.

"Indians burned things," Cy said. "Indians and lightning. The prairie did its own planting."

"So us Indians got lightning knowledge."

"That's it, brother." Cy grinned at Norm.

"So why are you planting trees?"

"You use lightning knowledge and start setting fires, you got to be able to move. That's why the old-time Indians lived in tipis. One reason. Even the lightning goes back into the sky. It doesn't build a house and settle down in the middle of a fire."

Norm could see that this was true.

"White people have a funny way of doing things, enit?" Cy said. "They find a forest, they cut it down so they can settle there. They find a prairie, they plant trees so they can settle there. Find a swamp, they drain it, but if they find a desert, they make a lake to irrigate it. Backwards thinking."

"They just want everything to be the same."

"Know what a modern-day tipi is? A motor home. Used to be us Indians lived in tipis so we could get away from fires and chase buffalo. Now the white guys live in motor homes so they can get away from all the places they ruined and chase golf balls. They stick us on the rez because they can't handle all that roaming we did. Then they build roads to make roaming easier and put wheels on the tipis. What is the lesson from this, big brother? To be an Indian now, you must buy a motor home and learn to golf."

They laughed, and Norm, telling the story, laughed again, and Earl laughed, too.

"When things get that crazy," Cyrus said, "you have to do something different. So I'm planting trees. Besides, Lorna likes trees."

He smiled across the pickup at his older brother.

"So we got us a marriage proposal in the back of this pickup?"

"We do, brother."

"Used to be a man would bring horses."

"Lorna would rather have trees."

"So," Norm said to Earl, "we spent the whole day, me and Cy, planting trees around your mother's house. Lorna'd bought it when she came back from her big-city life in Denver. I was drinking back then, but I spent that whole day sober, helping my little brother propose to your mother. Hadn't worked that hard since I left Vietnam—digging those holes, putting little sticks in, packing the dirt back, watering. Hanh—it was good work."

Then—Cyrus told Norm about it later—Cy sat in the house and waited for Lorna to return from work. By the time she did, it was dark, and Cy had moved to a chair outside. He let Lorna drive up, and then he rose and moved toward her, flashlight in his hand. When she stepped from the car, he clicked it on to pool light at her feet.

"I thought you might be late tonight," he said. "So I got new batteries." He wiggled the light at her feet, lapped her toes with it.

"I want to show you something," he said.

"I'm awfully tired, Cy."

"Won't take no time."

"It can't wait until morning?"

Cy clicked the flashlight off, then on, then off, then stood in the dark.

"It can," he said. "But I can't."

So she let herself be led across the patchy ground to each of the twenty-five trees. He clicked them individually into the flashlight's beam: the yellow pools of light, the clawed shadows on the ground. After all twenty-five, they stood side by side in the dark.

"So you planted trees on my place for me," Lorna said. "That's good, Cy. They'll look real nice some day."

"I wanted you to see them, you know?"

"My feet are killing me. Let's go in. How about some light?"

He gave her light for her feet. They started toward the house.

"They need to be watered every other day," he said.

"How long will it take for them to grow?"

He snapped off the light. She stopped moving and turned back to him. "I'm wearing dress shoes, Cy. You want me to break an ankle?"

"No. But I was wondering. Those trees—how long it takes for them to grow. Do you think we could find that out together?"

By the time Norm finished telling all this, the sun had moved lower in the sky, and he had risen several times to add wood to the fire. The meadowlarks had stopped their calling. Norm rose from his chair yet again to peer into the washtub. Earl sat without moving. When he was young, he'd hated those trees. At times his mother had seemed to care more about them than she had about him. She had made him spend so much time watering them, holding a garden hose or hauling water in pails where the hose wouldn't reach. In dry summers when their shallow well ran dry, she had even bought water. The trees had seemed nothing but a burden to Earl, and he had wished they would all shrivel and die, and on those hot summer days, when he'd seen the pickup with the green fiberglass water tank on the back turn off the county road, bringing them water, he had complained bitterly to his mother of the waste of it, water being poured into the ground and the money that might have bought something else just sinking away. Useless. Just so those weak and fragile trees would live. Earl had hated their weakness and fragility.

He had never heard the story as Norm had just told it. His mother and father never had found out together how long it took those trees to grow. So much of the world suddenly seemed to Earl weak and fragile. Everything vulnerable. Everything in need of care. Whenever his mother had told him to be careful, all Earl had ever heard was to be cautious. He'd never heard *careful* mean *full of care*. To avoid contempt for those things that needed care. Voices in the wind: such wind, such wind.

To take his mind away from it all, his childishness and regret, he asked, "Do you live in a motor home because of what my father said about them being tipis?"

Norm turned and stared at his home, considering the question. "Maybe," he finally said. "You could be right, nephew. Hanh. Maybe that is why I got it. I never thought of that. Maybe I should get myself a set of golf clubs, too. I could practice my driving and putting right here."

He gazed around at the prairie spreading in all directions. "Plenty of prairie dog holes," he said. "Just stick some pointy flags in them."

He nodded, thinking of it. "My home," he said. "My little, personal piece of New Jersey."

Then he got talking again and told how he'd acquired the motor home. He'd been working at Brad Monk's Service along I-90, and a retired couple had blown the engine on their motor home a mile from the station. By the time they had walked in ninety-degree heat along the shoulder of the freeway, semis blasting past them, ripping at their clothes with the force of their slipstreams, the husband had learned more about his wife than he had in the previous forty years of marriage. He confided much of it to Norm in the cab of the wrecker Norm drove out to the derelict motor home. The wife had never wanted to buy the motor home in the first place, and she'd loved the home they'd sold to purchase it. "I had no idea," the husband told Norm glumly. "I thought this was fun for her. An adventure." During that ninety-degree walk, she'd told him she was going back to New Jersey whether he came or not, and she didn't give a damn about the sonofabitching motor home—"I didn't even know she could swear"—and didn't give a damn if they lost the whole damn forty-thousand dollars the thing had cost them, they could make that up by traveling only to see their grandchildren and doing that by car—that is, if they stayed married that long, and that was up to him, and she damn well wouldn't try to influence him one way or the other.

"This was a man," Norm told Earl, "seriously out of touch."

Norm towed the motor home back to Monk's Service, while the man talked of his hopes of at least seeing Mount Rushmore. For a half hour, between the candy bars and the aspirin in the service station store, he talked in whispers with his wife. Then he bought a plastic model of Mount Rushmore for $7.95. Norm thought anyone was better off not seeing Mount Rushmore, but he couldn't watch as the man accepted his nickel in change from Brad. Holding the model against his chest, he walked out to the motor home while his wife stayed in the air-conditioned store. He patted the motor home's windshield. His wife watched him for a second or two, then turned and glared around the store at Norm and Brad, who, under her stare, remembered they had work to do. When the man returned to the store, he bargained listlessly with Brad for the sale of the motor home, the plastic presidents presiding over the transaction. Then Norm drove the couple down to Jim Reed's Chevrolet where, he heard later, they bought a used Celebrity.

But Brad never got around to fixing the motor home. Its dereliction made the entire station seem derelict. Weeds grew around it. The pavement underneath it cracked. Paint faded. The windshield grew so dusty it looked like a fallow field. Bird manure ran in dirty white streaks down its panels, obscuring the painting of mountains and a lake. Two of the tires lost air while the other two retained it, so that it listed to one side, making the station appear to list the other way. Brad began to hate the thing. It squatted there in silent accusation, a piece of junk out of which he'd hoped to profit, for which he'd taken advantage of another human being's small, shattered dream. Every morning when he arrived at the station, he cursed the motor home's ugliness. When he began taking breaks from working on engines to stand in the door of the station, wiping his hands on a greasy red towel and staring at the thing, Norm, seeing how the motor home's soul was beginning to possess him, suggested he take it off Brad's hands. Brad agreed, relieved. Norm borrowed the tow truck, pumped the bad tires up, hauled the motor home down to the reservation, returned the truck, and, having thus become the owner of a paid-for house, quit his job.

"My tipi," he said to Earl. "Some day I'm gonna dig a basement, hanh? I'll be the only Indian on the rez who has a tipi with a basement. Only Indian in history."

"You could make The *Guiness Book of World Records*."

They laughed together. Then Norm grew quiet. The fire was dying down, but he didn't rise to add wood.

"Your mother and me," he said, having not forgotten what Earl had said earlier. "It's true. She is not friendly toward me. But there are things you must understand, nephew. I came back from Vietnam screwed up. I volunteered for Nam. The warrior tradition. The Indians in Nam, we were all in some kind of special unit. Tougher than tough. Being a warrior is something to be proud of, and I was. But to be a warrior you have to know who your enemies are. That's real important. And Vietnam."

He stopped talking. The sun touched the top of the cottonwood west of the motor home.

"Vietnam," Norm repeated. He nodded at the washtub. "Tanning hides is an odd thing for a warrior to do, hanh? It is a slow and quiet thing. That is why I do it. The US government says to our grandfathers: 'We got a deal for you. You can give us your land and go on the rez, or we can shoot you. Take your pick.' Then, with Vietnam, the government comes back and says: 'We got another hot deal. How'd you like to go across the ocean and do the same thing to some other people who think they should rule themselves and live on their own land?' And a whole bunch of us on the rez perk right up. 'Now we can go be warriors like our grandfathers,' we say. And we were some warriors, nephew. But the best warrior isn't the one who fights the best. It's the one who knows the best who his real enemy is. With our grandfathers, that was pretty clear. In Vietnam, it wasn't.

"When I volunteered, I was young. I thought I was gonna be Crazy Horse swooping down on Custer. Hanh. But there wasn't any swooping in Vietnam. There was just leaves. You couldn't generally see ten feet over there, not where I was fighting. And it's still the same. Even now nobody can see what happened over there. You try to form a picture of it, you can't. You think of The Battle of the Greasy Grass, you can picture the river and the hills and the horses, even if you've never been to Montana. You can see Custer looking up and saying to his lieutenant, 'I wonder if this is going to affect my chances of becoming President.'

"It is this way, nephew: Not everyone is going to form the right picture of The Battle of the Greasy Grass. But they will form one. They will make some sense of it, even if it is the wrong sense. Hanh? But when people think about Vietnam, they don't see anything. Everything is still just a bunch of leaves."

Norm paused again, adjusted the stick on his knees. Earl waited. The fire had turned to coals, a flame low down among them, but talk had taken over, had become the thing that mattered in the world, and neither of them thought to build the fire back up or to remove the tub from over it.

"There are many reasons Vietnam is hard to talk about," Norm finally said. "The leaves are one of them. If you try to talk about it, you have no picture you can make people see. It is a blank. A nothing. Words fall into that nothing and disappear. I got back here to the rez and found that out. That's when I decided to get drunk. And when I make a decision, nephew, I stick to it. I stayed drunk for ten years."

A grasshopper landed on the arm of Earl's chair: round obsidian eyes and glittering wings. It seemed a mineral animal, made of stone and mica. It crouched, the delicate joints in its legs bending tighter, and then it was gone, a blur of body and air. A prairie falcon flew low overhead in its peculiar striding flight, its long, rectangular tail carving the air behind it.

"Your dad never drank," Norm said. He pushed the stick into the ground and traced some marking there which he then traced out. "And isn't that something, nephew? Me an alcoholic, him not touching it, and we're brothers. And he's the one gets hit by a drunk driver in the wrong lane. I made it through bullets and rockets and grenades and alcohol, and my sweet little brother, who plants trees and stays on his side of the road, comes over a hill one night and sees nothing but lights. And the other guy survives. When they found him, he was a quarter mile away, wandering around, so drunk he didn't even know he'd been in an accident.

"But that guy wasn't the only one drunk on the rez that night, nephew. I was at a party when I heard about my brother. When I finally got it through my head what'd happened, I got in my car—what else would a drunk who's just heard his brother was killed by a drunk driver do, hanh?—and drove to see your mother. Stumbling in her door. Think about that, nephew. She's just found out her husband's been killed by a guy so drunk he can't see the road. And who shows up to comfort her? That guy."

Earl thought of it: his mother weeping, lost, his uncle stinking drunk, offering his arms. The dance of avoidance that must have followed. His mother's horror and anger, and Norm's shambling, stubborn insistence that he could help. The moment when Earl's life had changed, when all its forms had set. He had slept. Two years old. How did his mother ever get Norm out of the house? It hurt—hurt to think of it. Hurt to think of Norm reeking, trying to put his useless arms around Lorna. Trying to pat her. Mumbling drunken condolences or seeking them. Hurt to think of Lorna pushing him away. Tears streaming. Hair tangled. And finally, finally, finally, closing the door against her husband's brother. Finally closing the door.

It hurt too much. Earl was glad when Norm spoke again. "Your mother won't tell you these things," he said. "But you should know. Don't you blame her. She's got good reason not to see me."

"It was a long time ago," Earl said.

"It was and wasn't. Some things take longer to be a long time ago."

"You're family. *Tiospaye.*"

"I am."

"You don't drink any more."

"I don't."

"But she still won't see you."

"And I still won't blame her, nephew. You never saw me drunk. She did. And she loved my little brother."

How odd, Earl thought, that he'd come to Norm to speak of the three horses, but instead this conversation had sparked and grown. These things he'd never known, that had lain hidden. Now here they were. Why not before? Why now?

"How did you quit?" he asked.

"That is a story, nephew."

And Norm told of sitting above the cemetery in the dark with a sack of long necks and drinking them while staring down at his brother's new grave. "Or at least where I thought it was," he said. "It was dark, hanh? But, of course, the more I drank, the better my vision got. I got to seeing so well my eyes bored a hole right through the dirt, and I could see my little brother in the grave. And I had a good, clear thought: The only way I was gonna be with him again was to be with him. There, in the grave. Understand, nephew, I wasn't exactly a wise man back then. I didn't have people following me around asking me the meaning of life. But I sat on that hill getting drunker and wiser by the minute, hanh? Until I knew what to do. Of course, I finished the beer first. For a drunk, being certain about ending your life is no good reason to waste Budweiser.

"When I finished the last bottle, I thought, *Now there's not even that to live for.* I got up and started down the hill. Don't know how I made it home, but when I got there I went right to the drawer where I kept my .38, which I'd bought when I got back from Nam. There were many things in my drawer, nephew—wire and paper and pliers and some old bottles of cologne this white girl I once dated thought were perfect gifts and didn't work too bad for starting fires. But I couldn't find my .38. Someone'd stole it.

"You believe that? Hanh? Walked right through that door there"—Norm jerked his head toward the door of his motor home—"and found my .38 and walked right back out with it. And nothing else. Just the pistol. I looked around to be sure. My clock radio that same girl'd give me was still sitting there next to the mattress. The clock part of that radio hadn't worked for two years, and then the radio part quit working when I got mad at the clock part for not working and gave it an uppercut one day. But what thief's gonna notice that? What thief's gonna walk into a house and check to make sure everything works before he stuffs it in his gunny sack?

"This was a question I was seriously thinking about when I remembered the reason I still had that clock radio, and the reason was that when I'd taken it to a pawn shop in Rapid to get money to buy beer, the pawn shop owner plugged it in and fiddled with the knobs and noticed how perfectly silent that radio was and how stubborn it was about insisting that the time was exactly seven oh two.

"I guess there's nothing worse than a clock radio that's both too quiet and too sure of itself. The guy pushed it back across the counter and said, 'Get outta my shop.' Now that is something, nephew. I was kicked out of a pawn shop. Hanh. How many people have accomplished that?"

"That could be on *Ripley's Believe It Or Not*."

"It could, nephew. You are right. So I was standing in my bedroom remembering it. I still had my hand in that drawer where I thought my .38 should be. And then I remembered that it *had* worked, and I had pawned *it* for beer. So there I was, so low, nephew, I couldn't even kill myself. That's even lower than getting kicked out of a pawn shop!"

Norm laughed. All the grasshoppers silenced. "Funniest thing that'd ever happened to me. I couldn't even kill myself! Where do you go but up from there, hanh?"

Earl stared at his uncle for a moment, then burst out laughing, too, while Norm gave up trying to talk, and his laughter came out of him in great exhalations, and he wiped tears from his face with the palms of his hands.

"Oh, Lord," he wheezed, "when I realized my situation, I just fell on the floor, laughing so hard. There I was, I couldn't even kill myself!"

They were both howling with laughter now. Norm's chair was shaking under his weight. They laughed until they were exhausted and couldn't laugh any more.

"That was it," Norm finally said. "When I finally got off that floor, I figured if I couldn't kill myself I might as well live. I quit drinking right then. I didn't just decide to quit. I quit. Of course I needed help to stay quit. I got into AA, and that helped some, but it was the traditional religion, the sweats and the healing ceremonies and then the Sun Dances that really helped. Kept me on the Red Road. Still, nephew, I know the exact moment I quit drinking. The exact moment."

He paused, nodded at the coals of the fire, wiped more tears from his face. "The exact moment," he said again, solemnly. "Seven oh two."

Earl thought how much his mother would like Norm if she knew him now. And how his grandmother, more than liking him, would be delighted by him. She would giggle like a girl just being in his presence. How much they were missing by Lorna's refusal to relent. And it wasn't even Norm who had hurt her. He'd merely been visible. Merely shown himself, while the man who had killed Earl's father remained unseen. The police, when they came to her, offered only loss. They did not show her cause or blame. Then, minutes after they left, Norm in all his drunken heaviness, an imitation of the man who'd killed her husband, appeared. With grief like hers, any substitute would do.

By why so long? Earl thought. Sometimes it tore him apart, this rift between his uncle and his mother. The guilt he had to conquer every time he came to talk to Norm. A year after Cyrus died, Lorna had had a Wiping of the Tears Ceremony, to let him go. But Earl didn't know. Perhaps his father's spirit had been released, but he wasn't sure his mother's heart had been. Why couldn't she honor Cyrus without blaming Norm? Why mix the two things up? Sometimes it left Earl breathless, with a panic in his chest—that nothing would ever change, and he would be trapped forever between his mother and his uncle. Or torn apart completely. Only the thought of leaving, or the cool world of equations, could override that feeling.

He realized Norm had asked him something. He looked up from the last coals of the fire, glowing now through the dusk, and saw that Norm was waiting for an answer. Then he realized that Norm had just asked him to go on with what had happened on the hillside the other night. It took Earl several seconds to surface from the stories Norm had told him and find again the one he'd come here with. For a moment they all got mixed up in his head—his father planting trees, his mother turning her face toward a door through which a body bumbled, his uncle laughing at his inability to kill himself, the three horses standing on the hill. Then he separated them and told Norm what had happened.

"We have to do something," Willi had insisted. "We must tell someone about this."

"Tell someone?" Carson's voice was bleak.

"The police will stop this. They will arrest this Magnus."

"The police," Carson said, his voice even bleaker. "That's Greggy Longwell."

Earl was standing to the side, letting them talk. But he knew what Carson meant.

"We don't have a 'they' when it comes to police," Carson said to Willi.

"You do not have a 'they'?"

Carson seemed about to explain to Willi, but he changed his mind. He looked at the three horses behind Willi and said, "This ain't either a yours problem. It's mine. I'll have to deal with it."

"Why do you say that?" Earl asked quietly.

He'd been silent so long his own voice surprised him. *That was a stupid move,* he thought to himself as Carson turned and stared at him. Earl stared back.

"Just the way it is," Carson said.

"Just the way what is?"

Carson shut his eyes, and his face went slack, and Earl heard his intake of breath, as if he were seeing the answer to the question inside him but were sucking it back in, keeping it. When he opened his eyes again his voice was tight.

"I ain't had a big impression you want much to do with this all," he said. "So what's it matter? I'm sayin it's my problem. So why 'nt you leave it be?"

Good question, Earl thought.

But what he said was, "I don't know. Maybe it's because I found these animals, you know?"

"And I'm sayin they're my concern. For reasons of my own. I'll take you home, and you can forget this place. That ought a make you happy."

"Happiness is not the thing to look for here," Willi said.

"Then I'll take you home and you can be unhappy," Carson said tersely.

In the silence that followed, Earl thought, *Take the door. He's holding it open.* He remembered the math problems he'd been trying to work before Carson and Willi picked him up. He could return to them, and tell his mother and grandmother something neither lie nor truth about where he'd been, something vague about driving around with a couple of friends, and if his mother asked who, he'd mention Willi, say the German kid had gotten attached to him and was always asking questions about Lakota traditions. That would divert them, and Earl could return to equations and differentials and the green lines of the graphing calculator his mother had bought for him, spending money she didn't have so that he could follow those lines right out of Twisted Tree. Those elegant lines. Those mapped solutions.

There was the Red Road of the good life, Earl thought, and there was the Black Road of the bad life, and there was the Green Road of the math life—not good and not bad, but pure, with such neat intersections.

And there was where he was standing right now, which seemed to be no road at all.

The Wire Road, maybe, Earl thought. The wire road, with its cutting barbs, that went nowhere even if, like a tightrope walker, you could balance on it. Dance and jump. Even then you just returned.

Take the door, he thought. *Walk away. Be the Careful Indian now. Take any road, as long as it leads somewhere.*

But he couldn't. Maybe it was Carson—the way that, underneath his confident mask, Earl sensed this other thing. This other being. Earl didn't know whether he was angry at Carson for his secrecy or if he felt sorry for him and wanted to help him. Or both. He didn't have time to sort it out.

"I don't think so," he said.

"You don't think so what?"

"That I'll go home."

Carson's stare was bleak, antagonistic. Then Willi said, "What are you going to do, Carson? This problem that is yours. How will you solve it?"

"Cut the wire," Carson said, still staring at Earl, his voice tight. "In fact, I'll do it right now."

He reached into his back pocket and pulled out a pair of pliers, started toward the fence. But Earl reached out and grabbed his wrist as Carson tried to pass him—not hard, but enough to stop him.

"That won't solve anything," Earl said. "How far do you think they'll go, you know?"

Carson looked around. Earl went on. "They're gonna start grazing right away. They'll stay right here. Be real hard to find again."

Earl let go of Carson's wrist. Carson gazed around a moment, then put the pliers back in his pocket. "I'll take 'em to my place, then," he said. "Hide 'em there. Anyway, what's it matter to you?"

"Did you train these horses?"

Earl wasn't quite sure where the question came from. He just asked it, and he saw Carson's head jerk back, his eyes glint, and that strange possession surge to the surface of his face. And suddenly he knew why he recognized it so well. It was his mother's expression when he'd seen her in unguarded moments, times when the work she was studying would fall into her lap and she would stare at the wall, or in the middle of a discussion about some injustice when she'd seem to slip away, forget what she was talking about, and go silent. Had he seen that face bending over his bed the night his father died? Had he woken to it, swimming upward out of sleep toward it? Confused it with his dreams?

For a moment Earl thought Carson would refuse to answer. He struggled with whatever was inside him. Then he got it under control. "Yeah," he said. "I trained 'em."

"You got an idea why Yarborough's doing this?"

"I might."

Earl waited. Carson said nothing more.

"But we don't need to know, is that it?"

"There're people involved. Who don't need things gettin around."

"That is what happens," Willi said. "There is a secret. People agree to keep it. For all different reasons. And then more secrets come. And more. It grows."

He intoned this so somberly that both Earl and Carson turned to him, wondering what he was talking about, but Willi didn't explain.

"I don't care about secrets, you know?" Earl said. "You can keep them. I'm talking about something practical. If you trained these horses and you know anything about them and they disappear here, it's not too hard to solve for x. Your ranch is going to be the first place Magnus looks. Then he'll be the one bringing in Greggy Longwell."

Carson didn't reply, but Earl saw he'd reached him.

"Willi's right," he said. "We need to let the law take care of this. Even if it is Greggy Longwell."

Carson shook his head. "Longwell and Yarborough are like this," he said. He wrapped his middle finger around his index finger. "I say something to Longwell, he'll call Yarborough. An he'll make up some story. Turn it against me. It'll turn out I abused these animals when I trained 'em. Who knows? Even if Greggy don't believe it, the whole thing'll go places I don't want it to go."

"Still," Earl began, but Carson shook his head.

"I can't talk to Longwell," he said. "So if someone's gonna do it, it's gonna be one a you. Longwell'd get a real kick outta Willi here. A foreigner comin in an reportin this. He'd take that real serious. So who's that leave?"

Both he and Willi stared at Earl.

"How do you like that?" Carson said. "Three guys standin on a hill, and the best candidate they have for talkin to Greggy Long-well's an Indian."

Earl's defenses shot up. He felt the blood rush to his head. Then he saw the beginning of a grin appear on Carson's face.

Norm went beyond a smile to laughter when Earl told him. "That cowboy's got it right," he said. It was dark now, crickets rocking the world, and the coals of the fire the faintest glow, far away.

"He does," Earl said.

"Too bad those horses aren't on the rez. You could talk to the police here."

"Just like that it was decided, you know? Without even deciding anything. I didn't even have a say in it."

Norm's chair creaked. "I see," he said. "So you're thinking maybe you should just forget it."

"Greggy Longwell won't listen to me."

"Probably not."

"Should I just forget it, then?"

"What do you think your mother would say if you asked her?"

"She'd tell me to be careful. She'd say this is nothing but trouble and stay away from it. I know she would. She'd tell me not to step into someone else's trouble."

"You got it right, I think," Norm said. "That sounds like Lorna to me."

Earl felt relieved. His mother was rescuing him. "So you think that's what I should do?" he asked. "Stay away from it?"

"If your mother would tell you to leave it be, why are you talking to me and not her?"

Earl sat stock-still in his lawn chair, trying to take in this sudden reversal. His gut twisted at the thought of Greggy Longwell's suspicious eyes turned on him.

"I don't know," he finally said.

"You oughta be getting back. Your mother is probably waiting."

"She is."

Time passed.

"I suppose I have to talk to him, don't I?"

"I suppose you do. If you think so."

More time passed.

"It wasn't you, uncle."

"Wasn't me?"

"I know. Even if Mom doesn't. It wasn't you."

Earl did not look, but he heard his uncle draw in his breath. The fire had diminished into darkness. The silence coming from where Norm sat was long and deep. Out of the corner of his eye Earl saw his uncle lift a hand to his face. The silence went on.

Finally, in a voice high with restraint, Norm said, "Thank you, nephew."

Earl waited a little longer. He was about to say good-bye when Norm spoke again. "There's so much blame around here. Our biggest resource, nephew. If we could mine blame on the rez, we'd all be rich."

The Lights of Koblenz

∧∧∧∧

WILLI WATCHED THE TUNA CASSEROLE slide across the table toward him. It came like a boat, riding over the double warp in the Druseman's table and then down again, until it anchored in front of him, a square, white ceramic bowl filled with noodles and chunks of tuna with melted cheese and crumbs on top. A hot dish: Willi heard it as two words. He'd expected Indian tacos to be good. At the powwows he'd attended in Germany with his *Indianer* club, where everyone lived in tipis for a week and dressed in traditional Indian clothes and talked of some day going to Pine Ridge, Willi had eaten Indian tacos and anticipated eating them in South Dakota. But he'd never heard of Tuna Hot Dish, and when his American mother first served it, he'd been overcome with pleasure and surprise.

But this time he looked up at Kathy Druseman, whose hands had pushed the bowl toward him. *"Nein, danke,"* he said, speaking German because she wanted to learn the language.

She caught something in his expression or tone, and her own face changed to worry. Her hand fluttered at her collar.

"Bist du . . . ?" She fumbled for the word. "Sick?" she finished.

Willi smiled for her. "I am fine," he said. "I am full. Even for Tuna Hot Dish."

"Hotdish," she corrected him, saying it as one word.

She smiled, plucked the bowl from the table, took it to the counter, and scooped the contents into a plastic bowl she called Tupperware. "Is everything all right?" she asked.

"Everything is fine."

"Things are all right at school?"

"They are fine."

She scraped the last of the Hot Dish into the Tupperware and pressed a lid on. Willi heard air whoosh out.

"You're not having trouble with any of the teachers?"

"No. They are good."

"Do you miss home?"

She turned and faced him, holding the sealed bowl in front of her.

"Miss?" It was a usage he wasn't familiar with.

"Are you lonely? Would you like to see your parents?"

"A little. Maybe."

"If you want to call them, you know you can."

Willi's program had guidelines about calls to home. They were supposed to be limited, to allow students to adjust to their new culture. But Willi had called home so seldom that Kathy Druseman was constantly urging him to. He felt a small surge of tenderness for her and a small surge of guilt for misleading her. He went out of the kitchen and made a show of taking the phone off the hook at the top of the stairs so she would hear it. He carried the handset to his room, shut the door, threw it on the bed, watched it bounce. He went to the window. He could see the Badlands scraping the sky to the west, the sun nearly touching their tops. The Drusemans had taken him to the Black Hills and Mount Rushmore, to the Nebraska Sand Hills and the Niobrara River, to Denver and the Rocky Mountains, to Minneapolis and its lakes and the Mall of America, but for some reason they'd bypassed the Badlands.

He could walk to them, he thought. He imagined doing it—going downstairs, out the door, down the highway toward the sun, until the land changed around him. He thought of getting lost in that big, unpeopled country. From here, from this window, it appealed to him—to be where no one was. Where nothing had been spoiled by people, nothing touched or changed. He imagined himself out there, small and alone. But he knew he wouldn't do it. He turned from the window and looked at the phone again.

He thought of calling Earl. He wanted to know if Earl had talked to the sheriff yet. But if he hadn't, calling would only irritate him. Until that night on Tower Hill, Earl had ignored Willi, and Willi felt that even now Earl wished he could ignore him, but the horses prevented that. Willi was the stranger here. Why did he feel more involved in what was happening than Earl seemed to be? He half-envied Earl his disengagement, his mistrust of what seemed obvious to Willi. Willi couldn't strike from his mind the way the horses stood with bowed heads, ribs beginning to show.

Obsessed: yes. He was obsessed. He thought of his grandmother. "Of course," she would say. "What nobler thing than to be a savior?"

Her prunelike lips would crinkle, and derision would light her raisin eyes.

WILLI PICKED THE PHONE OFF THE BED, looked at the numbers, let his eyes follow the sequence that would connect him home. He calculated the eight-hour difference. His father might be up already in the early morning, drinking coffee and looking out at the dark Rhine below him, and the lights of Koblenz. The sound of the morning trains from the tracks along the river would be rising up the hill to him, coming through the glass of the large window, shaking it a little. If the phone rang, his father would turn to it until it rang a second time, then set his cup down on the coffee table, bending at the waist, and go to the phone and wait for the third ring—always—and then with his right hand pick the handset up, transfer it to his left, put it to his ear, speak.

Willi thought of how he used to rise in the early morning, too, and come out of his bedroom, to stand in silence, watching the lights of Koblenz with his father, listening to the trains rattling the windows, booming down the tracks along the Rhine, father and son standing like two sentries, not speaking. As still, as silent, as the bronze statue of Kaiser Wilhelm on his horse where the Rhine and Mosel Rivers met. They could see it from their window. A monstrosity, his father called that statue. A waste of money and a waste upon the eyes. Brass and water. Horse and rider. The lights of the city reflected in the river—deepdown lights that came up from the bottom and shone through the water. And he and his father standing there, as mute as the three horses now, in a suffering they could not name any more than the horses could fashion names for theirs.

Willi thought of the biblical Isaac. Had that Isaac spoken to his children? How silent could a man become, having stared at the blank, blue sky, and then seen the knife in it, and his father's face, set and determined, all self-horror willed away? How did Isaac make sense of his own children? They must have seemed strange to him. Improbable. A future not his. No wonder he was confused between his ear and his hand, unable to know Jacob by his voice—a father deceived by a future he had relinquished when he saw his own father's God-crazed, obedient, merciless eyes above the rocky altar. In his old-age blindness, did that face still appear before him, to steal from his other senses? And what did Willi's father see out there in the early-morning lights? What pattern did those lights make, shifting in the river's running, standing out against the sky? Did his father see a private constellation—an uplifted arm, the knife sharp as light itself, a child on a bed of sticks?

WHEN HE WAS SIXTEEN YEARS OLD, Willi sought out his grandmother. He stood on the steps of an old house in the western part of Koblenz. Through a gap in the buildings, he could see the vineyards rising up the Mosel valley. He'd found his grandmother's name in the telephone directory. So easy. So close. He might have met his grandparents strolling a path along the Rhine from bridge to bridge. He might have passed them in a shop or on a street.

He left the bus two stops from the address he'd found and walked the remaining distance. He needed to approach gradually, to see the houses appear, their numbers progressing toward the one he sought. As he walked, he allowed himself to think that the address would be nonexistent—a house number that turned out to be, after all, a number only: a possible house but one that didn't exist. A hole in the sequence: 41, 43, 45, 49—but where was 47? He would stop, find 45 crowded against 49 with no space or empty lot between. Forty-seven would be simply not there: gone from space, time, memory, history. Not, and never been.

But 47 was there: a white door in the gray stone façade that ran from one corner of the block to the other. Willi stopped before it. He gathered it in.

He thought he could walk away. He didn't know that information has its own power. He thought that if he knew enough, he could batter down walls and obstacles. He did not think he might himself be battered.

The Silent Indian

~~~~~

GREGGY LONGWELL'S WRIST FLICKED UPWARD, and the pen he was holding left his fingers, slid, hit his coffee cup, and spun three times. Greggy laid his notepad down on the edge of the desk, then leaned far back in his chair, a spring in the pivot squeaking, and gazed at Earl across the dusty metal desktop. The window air conditioner in the small office wheezed and rattled, spewing out a moldy air, not cold enough to keep Earl from sweating but enough to make him clammy. He stared at the pen Greggy had flicked, JIM'S WESTERN FEEDS written in red letters across its barrel. On Greggy's notepad he could see Greggy had scrawled his name, EARL WALKS ALONE, in square letters, pressed hard into the paper.

Greggy laced his fingers across his stomach and turned his gaze away from Earl to look at the window, even though the air conditioner filled it completely. He sucked his teeth, then shook his head, turned his small, hard eyes back to Earl. In his exhaled breath, the ends of his sandy mustache briefly moved. Greggy was in his thirties, just starting to bald, just starting to turn soft. The ceiling light reflected off his forehead.

"Let me get this straight," he said. "You found some horses on Magnus Yarborough's land that're being hurt and starved."

Earl felt a drop of sweat start coldly down his side. He wanted to reach over and rub it, make it soak into his shirt, but he didn't, and it slid down, infinitely slow. He nodded, leaned back a little in the steel folding chair Greggy had pointed him to, and let his arm fall against his side, obtaining some relief.

"Yes," he said. "That's right."

Greggy looked down at his hands, and Earl couldn't help but follow his gaze: the pudgy fingers, black hair curling out of the knuckles, the wrinkled uniform over the fleshy belly into which those hands were pressed.

"So," Greggy said, meditatively, to his hands, "you're accusing Magnus Yarborough of abusing horses."

"I think they're hurt, you know? I think you should go look at them."

"You think I should go look at them," Greggy repeated.

He stared at his hands a moment longer, then looked at the air conditioner, then reached across the desk. His thumb and index finger hovered over the pen, then came down around it. He spun it, watched it circle, waited for it to stop, spun it again.

Still watching it, he said, "There's a reason you're on that side a the desk and I'm on this side. Reason is, on that side a the desk, you report things. On this side, I decide what to do about them. So I think maybe we should stick to that, don't you, Mr. . . ."—he leaned away from the pen, glanced down at his notepad—"Walks Alone? I got that right? Earl Walks Alone?"

Earl nodded, staring at the pen, which had stopped, pointing right at him.

Greggy picked it up, circled Earl's name on the pad.

"I thought I got it right," he said. "You got a job, Earl?"

"I'm a student."

"A student." Greggy sounded as if he'd never heard of such a thing.

"At the high school. I'll graduate this year. I'm—"

He stopped himself. He was about to tell Greggy he had plans to attend college, maybe Harvard or Princeton. But Greggy might consider an Ivy Leaguer worse than an Indian. And an Ivy League Indian? The humor of it overcame Earl's anger. *The Ivy League Indian in the sheriff's office,* he narrated to himself. *Note how the sheriff is impressed with the Ivy League Indian's theories on things.*

"Something funny here, Earl?"

Earl looked at his hands on his knees and composed his features. "No."

"I don't think so, either. So why don't you tell me what's going on?"

"I don't know. That's why I came to you. So you could find out."

Greggy tapped the pen on the desk and stared at Earl. "That ain't what I mean, Earl, and I think you know it. But let me be clearer. You got something personal against Magnus Yarborough? Or is this some kind of AIM thing?"

"Aim thing?"

"Russell Means. Dennis Banks. You gonna tell me you ain't never heard a the American Indian Movement?"

"Oh. AIM. No, this isn't like that, you know? I found three starving horses, and—"

Greggy lifted his hand. "You already said. Just so I'm clear, this is something you're doing on your own, then?"

"Doing? I'm just reporting that . . ."

He stopped, seeing the uncompromising look on Greggy's face. A terrible, helpless feeling filled him, overwhelming and complete— as if all along he'd been empty and this feeling had been waiting to blow in and fill that emptiness. He could find nothing to say, and his hands on his knees seemed far away, and he seemed far away from himself. Greggy had reversed everything and was accusing Earl. Earl couldn't find his thoughts. Within the helplessness he felt a hideous and useless shame. He knew it was unjustified and hated himself for feeling it but couldn't expel it.

"Uh huh," Greggy said. "You're just reporting something. Well, Earl Walks Alone"—he peered at his notepad again—"let's just consider your report. You say you saw these horses from up by the TV towers. That right?"

"Yes." Earl despised himself for mumbling—and then despised the fact that he despised himself. It all circled inside him, and he couldn't get control.

"On a Friday night."

He forced himself to look up, to meet Greggy's gaze, to speak clearly. "That's right."

Greggy laughed dryly, unimpressed, little pilot light expulsions of sound. "Well, Earl, you must think I'm some kind a idiot."

Greggy's mouth stood half-open in a patronizing sneer, his left canine tooth jutting over his lower lip, showing through his untrimmed mustache. He balanced the pen straight up on the notepad, his index finger resting on the clicker.

"I know damn well what goes on up on Tower Hill on a Friday night," he said. "A bunch a—" his mouth twisted, he bit off the words. "If you think I'm going to disturb Magnus Yarborough because some—*teen*ager who probably couldn't see ten yards claims to've seen horses a half-mile away in the dark—well, shit, Earl, you better start thinking different. The world don't work that way, and it's time you found out how it does work."

There was nothing funny here. There was no voice Earl could find to lift himself away from what was happening, no interior camera crew, no narrator to explain and get things wrong. But rising out of the helplessness he felt, Earl felt anger growing, stronger than the shame, pushing the shame aside.

"You don't have to disturb Magnus Yarborough," he said. "All you have to do is go up behind Lostman's Lake and see for yourself."

"Simple as that, is it?"

"It's as simple as that."

He held the sheriff's eyes, challenging him.

Greggy lifted his index finger, let the pen drop onto the notepad, watched it fall off the edge of the pad onto the desk, then leaned back in his chair again. "Simple as that," he said to the air conditioner.

He nodded to himself, then turned back to Earl. "Well, then, let me go over the sequence of events, make sure I got things clear. You saw these horses from the top of the hill, and then you said you went down there. And that's when you suspected they were being starved?"

His voice was friendlier now. Earl thought he might have a chance after all. "Yes," he said. "I went down there, and one of them was limping. And they were penned up in this small pen. Without a gate." He didn't mention Willi—that would only make Greggy more suspicious—and Carson had made it clear he thought his own involvement would create problems.

"Uh huh, then." Greggy picked up the pen again and wrote on the pad, murmuring, "Lame horses in small pasture," as he wrote. Then he looked back up at Earl. "That's very interesting, Earl. You musta been pretty close to them horses to observe them so well. Is that right?"

"Yes. I saw them real well. You can go up and look yourself, make up your own mind."

Earl felt he was getting somewhere now.

"I will make up my own mind, Earl," Greggy said mildly. "That's my job. But before I do, I need to get some other things clear. You can't see those horses from the lake. Is that right?"

"That's right. They were behind a hill."

"So how close were you to them? A hundred yards? Fifty?"

"I was right up next to them."

"Hmmm."

The sheriff seemed to be seriously considering what Earl was saying now.

"You were right up next to them," Greggy mused. "That is interesting, I must say." He reached up and ran his hand over his forehead, pushing strands of thin hair back. His balding forehead gleamed.

"I was," Earl said. "I wouldn't have come to you if I wasn't close enough to know something wrong was going on up there."

Greggy nodded. "And they were inside a small pen. And that pen was on Magnus Yarborough's land?"

"That's right."

"And you couldn't see this pen from the lake."

Earl was confused that Greggy would return to the question of seeing the pen from the lake. "Yes," he said. "I mean, no."

"Which is it, Earl?"

"No, you can't see it from the lake."

"So where can you see this pen from? That's what I'm tryin a get clear here. You were standin right next to this pen, you say. If I wanted a go check this out, where would I have to go?"

Greggy leaned forward in his chair, confidential, intent on Earl's answer.

"You've got to go over a hill," Earl said. "On the north side of the lake. The horses are hidden behind that hill. Out of sight of anything, you know?"

"Uh huh. I see. And at that lake public property goes what?— maybe fifty, seventy-five yards up? That about right?"

"I guess."

"I just want to be sure, you see. It seems pretty clear from what you're saying, I mean there ain't much doubt is there, that you were on Magnus Yarborough's land when you examined these horses?"

Earl stared at Greggy. The sheriff's tone was suddenly cold, all trace of friendliness gone. Earl realized he'd let himself be caught. He'd let himself believe the sheriff wanted justice. Earl's thoughts abandoned him, helplessness and shame returned, and the silence went on and on.

"Seems you don't have an answer," Greggy said coldly. "Well, Mr. Earl Walks Alone, I'd say you were trespassing. And it ain't like you wouldn't know. I remember right, there's NO TRESPASSING signs all over that fence up there. And since you're in high school, I assume you can read. So if you saw those horses like you say, it ain't all that clear who's breaking the law, is it? Things ain't so simple like you think, are they?"

Earl had no answer. He wanted to be angry again, but the overwhelming power of the sheriff and his position were palpable in the room, stifling even Earl's anger, turning him into exactly what the sheriff wanted to see—a troublemaking Indian who thought he could get away with something. Earl felt dirtied inside and out. He wished he were someplace else. Anywhere else.

"And you think I can just go walking up there and have a look," Greggy went on. "Ever occur to you police have to obey the law? I can't go traipsing up there without I get Magnus Yarborough's permission. Or a warrant. And I gotta say, Earl, you being as quiet as you just somehow got, I ain't about to embarrass myself in front of a DA by askin for a warrant."

Earl wanted to say something. Anything. But couldn't.

"Suppose I could ask Magnus," Greggy said. "'Course if I do that, he might decide he's the one oughta be pressing charges. So what do you think I oughta do, Earl? You want I should ask him?"

The air conditioner rattled and wheezed.

"Funny how silent you got, Earl," Greggy said. "Let me give you some advice. You get outta that chair and walk out that door without sayin another word, and you leave Magnus Yarborough alone. If you do that, I may just consider this whole thing not worth pursuing. And you have no idea, Earl, how much trouble that'll save both of us. You have no idea at all."

Substitutes for Speech

~~~~~

<span style="font-variant: small-caps;">C</span>ARSON WAS ALONE IN THE OLD HOUSE after supper, sitting in the dimming light filtering through the heavy drapes his grandmother had put on the windows years ago. The phone rang. Earl had said he'd let Carson and Willi know when he'd talked to Greggy Longwell. Carson rose, expecting no good news.

Rebecca's voice in his ear jarred him. He hadn't expected to hear from her again. She'd told Magnus about their relationship. In having spoken, she'd made a choice more lasting than the choice she'd made in the doorway of that abandoned house. Carson could not deny, in spite of his loss, that the first choice was hers to make. But why the second? Why speak to Magnus? She should have known him better. She'd told Carson of realizing the foolishness of trying to change her first husband. How could she be so ignorant of the man she was now married to? Or so ignorant of herself? Carson had seen himself compressed within the round, wet eye of the wounded cow, and in that eye he was holding a rifle while behind him white clouds moved. Those clouds seemed to form themselves from the albumen around the eye, move across the dark pupil, fade into the white again. A merry-go-round of cloud. And a tiny, warped, misshapen man in the middle of it, holding something that looked like a stick.

Carson had seen that stick enlarge within the eye and wind itself around the pupil. He'd seen the little man's hand grow larger than his head within the curved distortion. A mushroom of lumpy knuckles. The sound, when it came, seemed to come from the world of the eye, bursting from it into the world where Carson stood. The last thing that small world produced. Then there was only Carson in the world he was in, with the high, white clouds above him streaming horizon to horizon, and he a little man watching a mass of flesh quiver and then still and that other, tiny world dry out and fade.

He wouldn't allow himself the luxury of regret for doing a necessary thing. But that day he'd seen much needless suffering. Seen suffering substituted for speech. Suffering as a message. He knew it was Magnus's message. Knew it had its source from some constricted place inside the man. Yet he laid the rifle down next to the cow and said—to himself, to the world that was not listening except, in the aftermath of the rifle's report, to know that ordinary sound could begin again—"Jesus, Reb. Why?"

"Carson? Are you there?"

"Yeah. I'm here."

It was too good to hear her. But she'd made that choice. She'd spoken to Magnus. Carson did not allow his voice to express more than the words it shaped. She heard. For a while they were connected by nothing but silence, by the fact that each of them held a plastic handset in different places, unknowingly imitating each other's posture, connected by nothing but potential: If either of them spoke, the other would hear.

"He's outside," she said. "I don't know how long. I may not have much time."

That "he" that needed no clarification. Magnus at the periphery, his movements framing this conversation.

"The horses, Carson," she said. "They're gone."

He heard strange, faraway sounds. It took him a few seconds to realize she was crying but trying to hide it from him. Then she gave up trying to hide it and sobbed, "I don't know what he did with them. All three of them, Carson. I don't know how long they've been gone. I couldn't call until now. I never had a chance."

Her weeping cut through Carson's desire to reserve himself. Or preserve. Cut through his anger. He'd been so caught up in his own sorrow, his own coming to grips with everything, that he'd never imagined hers. Never imagined what she might be going through in that house that, even before Magnus knew anything, she'd called a prison with nice fixtures. What was it like now? What emptiness and sorrow, what anger, did it harbor? Rebecca had said the rich have better ways of keeping secrets. Better lies. And now she was afraid to use the phone.

Carson closed his eyes. It was hard to for him to believe Magnus exerted that kind of control over her. Yet he himself had been lured into the black pickup with the man, been trapped there to witness that grill crashing into the running cow's back legs, turning them to bloody straw. And Carson had found himself paralyzed, unable to move. He thought of Magnus's words: *That bitch won't run away again.*

He suddenly knew, like a gray mold exposed and flaking in his chest, that she wasn't crying only for the horses.

"What'd he do to you, Reb?" he asked. Even in his own ear, his voice was grainy—bits and pieces of voice patched together. Barely holding.

He could tell she had the receiver away from her mouth. Strangled sounds, very far away. He pictured her—couldn't help it—with her face turned aside, tears falling. That hair.

"Rebecca," he said. Was aware he'd used her full name, pronouncing every syllable. "I'm just goin a wait. And then you're goin a tell me. OK?"

Another few seconds of silence. Then her voice came back, stronger, closer, still broken.

"Oh, God," she said. "You derail me."

That he didn't expect. "Derail you?"

"I thought you'd be worried about the horses. I didn't think you'd . . ." She stopped.

"I know about the horses."

"You know?"

"What'd he do to you?"

She didn't answer.

"Did he hit you?"

Silence. The son of a bitch.

"How bad, Reb?"

"He slapped me. No fists. But it was hard. I'm bruised. My face."

She choked. Couldn't tell him about her face.

Spinning, spinning. How had it gone this far?

Or had it always been there, a spiral, a spring, wound tightly inside Magnus? And they had just released it?

Carson tried to stay right here. With her. Tried to stay calm, impassive. "He ever done that before?" he asked.

"No. Not that. I shouldn't have pushed him so far."

"You know what that is, Reb? Bullshit."

The force of the word stopped her crying. Then she said, "It is, isn't it?"

"It is. This is him, not you."

"I don't know him, Carson."

But you knew that, he thought. *You told me that.*

What he said was, "What do you want me to do?"

"Nothing. Anything you do will make it worse. Promise me, don't do anything."

"I ain't about a make a promise I might not keep."

"There's nothing you can do."

She was right. He knew it.

"You're alone right now?"

"He's just outside. Don't come over here."

"I'm not thinkin that. Get out of there."

"I just wanted you to know about the horses. That's all."

"Leave the sonofabitch."

"Where would I go?"

"Figure it out later. Just leave. Get in a car and drive."

"It's over. He's still angry, but—"

"Shit like that ain't ever over, Reb. This ain't no time to kid yourself."

"Do you know where the horses are?"

"They're alive. It ain't the horses I'm worried about right now."

"Oh, Jesus. I'm going to cry again if you keep doing that."

"I trained you, too. I got a right to be as concerned for you as the horses."

She laughed—a painful laugh, but a laugh. Good, in its small and painful way, to hear.

"Goddamn, Carson," she said. "I wish—"

He wanted to hear what she wished, but he wouldn't let her go there. "This ain't a time for wishing, either," he said. "Another kind a bullshit. Just slows you down. Take the first chance you get and leave."

"He's coming. I've got to go."

Just like that the line was dead.

Well of Life

~~~~~~

WILLI WATCHED EARL'S MOUTH MOVING, and he heard the words, but Earl had to say them twice—"He's not going to do anything"—before Willi comprehended them. He felt stupid, as if he no longer understood the language here. And even when he did comprehend what Earl was saying, it seemed impossible.

"He is the sheriff," Willi said. "He is the law. How can he not anything do at all?"

He caught the way he reversed the sentence, felt even stupider. Earl lifted a shoulder. "Like you say, he's the law."

"But if he will not anything do"—there it was again, that reversal; he had to pay attention, had to be alert—"what do we do? Is there someone else we can tell?"

They were standing near a corner of the school. Earl had stopped by Willi's locker just before school ended. He hadn't spoken to Willi but to the locker, as if he were merely stopping to look at a Magic Marker drawing above the lockers, of a football helmet and a player's name—BEST OF LUCK, LANCE!!—one of dozens of such drawings made by the cheerleaders in preparation for the weekend game. Earl stood near Willi, gazed at the drawing, and quietly said, "See you outside." Then he walked away. The girl next to Willi's locker looked at him, but he didn't know whether she'd heard what Earl said or not.

Now Willi waited for Earl's response. The shadow of the school building cut across Earl's face from left eye to chin. Dust drifted across the parking lot from where students were spinning their tires when they hit the gravel at its edge. Shining in the sun, this dust obscured with its brightness the right side of Earl's face, but in the shadow of the building it disappeared, leaving the air clear, and out of that dark clarity Earl's left eye gazed at Willi.

"We can tell anyone we want, you know?" Earl said.

Willi shifted position to get out of the sun and could see Earl's face tight, his jaw set hard. He'd never seen Earl's face that way, and he could hear only pure, acid sarcasm, with no joking, in Earl's voice.

"But there is no one who can do anything?"

"It all goes back to Longwell. Maybe we screwed up, you know? If we'd told a veterinarian, say, and convinced him, he might've convinced Longwell. But now anyone we tell would go to Longwell. And he's not believing anything."

"What did he say?"

Earl shook his head.

"Is not there anything we can do, then?" Willi asked.

"There must be something. I don't know what. But I'm not letting this go."

Willi had never heard Earl so determined. He remembered how Earl had walked away from the pasture the first night, left him standing there. Remembered how he hadn't wanted to see anything wrong. Earl seemed to know what he was thinking. "I don't like being called a liar, you know?" he said.

Another student spun his tires at the edge of the parking lot, and dust rolled toward them. They watched it approach, let it engulf them.

"If I were you," Earl said when the air cleared, "I'd try to have a good time here. Talk your family into taking you someplace you haven't seen."

"I haven't seen the Badlands. But what do you mean?"

"You don't live here. You're wandering through, you know? Like, you're taking pictures. This horse one didn't turn out. That's all."

Willi felt his face flush. "I am not just wandering through," he said hotly.

Earl looked at him with those angry, determined eyes. "Well, that's something," he said. "You going to become an Indian, then? Become a true-blood Lakota? Stay here and live on the rez?"

Willi didn't know how to defend himself. He knew Earl was not really angry at him but was angry at everything, and mostly at whatever had happened with the sheriff. But he didn't know how to tell Earl that this was not a question of blood. Or even a question of home. That some things pushed you into wherever you were. They put you there. Or maybe it was your home that followed you. Home and family and blood. Followed you. And you found them—in the night, under the stars, with steaming water pouring from the ground. And horses dying.

Willi hadn't thought the old woman could come to haunt him here, in the heart of this continent, on a Lakota reservation, among the people of Crazy Horse and Sitting Bull. He was thinking about her more now than he had in Germany, though he'd come here partly to escape thinking of her. It was almost as if she'd ridden in the plane with him, a whisper of pale skin and lavender scent. She inhabited his dreams here, and when he woke in the mornings, she emerged out of the whorled patterns in the ceiling above him: the wisps of her hair, the wrinkles of her dry and velvet skin.

For a while she'd been unable to follow him here. The confusion of new things had overwhelmed her: the powwows, the singing, the dancing, the speech patterns, the land itself, the ceremonies—all the things Willi had hoped for. He'd had a sense the world could be new again, revived. Had a sense the Lakota people had an older knowledge, and that knowledge could frighten her away, a wind blowing her like dust off the floor of his mind.

It seemed to Willi, almost, that she had prompted him to follow Earl away from that party and off that hill to that white, steaming spring. He imagined her pale hand, ghostly even when she was alive, hovering over that pasture, her finger pointing. "See them. Cages are everywhere."

Everywhere. Everywhere. Willi tried to shut his ears against the chant of it. He had to sing nursery rhymes sometimes, children's songs, songs his mother used to sing before he went to bed, to keep his grandmother's refrain of cages from his mind. Everywhere.

And the irony of that hot, artesian spring—letting the horses live just so they could die.

HE'D STOOD BEFORE HER HOUSE. A triangle of vineyard was visible in the distance between buildings—the vines marching up the Mosel valley slopes against the dark soil. Willi had thought of people out there, walking the vineyards in the sun, the Mosel flowing wide and swift below them. It would be good to be one of them. He played with the possibility—avoiding this encounter, letting his life be what it had been, what his parents had made it for him. He raised his finger to the bell and let it fall, raised it again. He imagined the freedom of the Mosel valley, its space.

But he pushed the bell. And heard the sound of steps beyond the door, then the sound of bolts sliding backwards through their journals. The door swung open. A musty smell of interior space washed over Willi, and an old woman looked out at him. Fine white hair. Skin age-spotted. Nothing in her eyes spoke recognition.

Then her expression changed: the slightest opening of her eyelid, sliding like dry, almost translucent paper over her pupil, the smallest forward movement of her jaw. She settled back into a standing repose. Her index finger at her side twitched. From within the house something shrieked.

"So," she said, her voice a sparrow's. "You came."

She turned and walked into her house. She didn't invite him in, but she left the door open. From within came the smell of carpet cleaner, room freshener, bleach, bird droppings, an old woman's sweat and age. Willi hesitated, then stepped into that smell. Standing on the carpet, he held the door for a moment, looked back at the bright afternoon street. Then he pushed it shut, heard the latch precisely click.

She was already sitting in a stuffed chair too large for her. Her elbows seemed to rise up to meet the chair arms. Frail bird wings. She stared at Willi, unblinking. He felt she might spring from the chair and flap toward him, crying a hoarse bird cry. Then one of her fingers moved. Only that. He saw the half-moon cuticle, the soft, wrinkled flesh around the knuckle.

"You may sit," she said.

The finger indicated a high-back chair, maroon leather, brass tacks. Willi looked at it. She'd allowed him into her house, but did she really know who he was? She showed no wonder, no welcome—just this dusty expectation, this failure of surprise. But she waited for him to sit, so he sat, looked around the room.

"You may look at me. It's why you came."

He looked: a small woman, in pale green slacks and a gray cardigan. Thin, a frail neck. Her hair straggled in loose white whorls around her head, a dark mole visible through it just above her forehead. But other than the hair, she had a preened look. Willi was aware of her joints: the sharp elbows on the arms of the chair, the knees bent inside the slacks, the brittle wrists—a body of breakable angles.

"I'm Willi," he said. "Hermann's son. Your son, Hermann. I'm . . ."

He let his voice drop off. She stared at him without expression. Was he in the wrong house? What if this woman was not his grandmother but someone deluded, who mistook him for someone she'd been waiting for?

"Do you think I don't recognize my own blood?"

Her voice was faded, weary, with a tinge of cynical humor—not unfriendly but not inviting, either. For a moment Willi didn't understand what she meant. That strange term: blood.

"I came," he said. "I've never met you. I came because . . ."

Her finger on the chair arm lifted. Just that. "I suspect you don't know why you came or what you want," she said. "No more than your father."

So: just like that, the heart of things.

A shriek. Willi started. Behind him a white bird clawed its cage. She ignored it. Two of her fingers moved on the chair arm, coming together. Shears.

"How could he know?" she asked. "Cut off from his blood."

Again that jarring, dissonant term: not mother, not family, not even relationship—but blood. Willi had imagined some moments of awkwardness, the protocols of greeting, exclamations of delight, perhaps even tears, all perhaps embarrassing, but nevertheless welcome. Wanted. But she had not even said his name.

"I came for a reason," he said. If she would not be surprised at his presence, he would stick to business. "I need to ask you something."

But she shook her head. Only once, a jerk more than a shake. Almost a spasm. But it stopped his words. "You came to find yourself," she said. "Whatever else you think."

Behind Willi, the white bird fluttered. Its wings battered the silver wires. Willi turned from his grandmother to watch it. It was a medium-sized bird with a powerful, curved beak. A cockatoo, he thought. Perfectly round eyes. It fluttered for a while, then stopped, seemed exhausted, its wings drooping, one eye staring at him. Something about the bird's dark eye reminded Willi of how his own father stared out the window every morning, and he realized that his father was staring in the direction of this house. Staring at a place he'd canceled from his life.

"I think I've made a mistake," he said.

"Of course you have."

He'd begun to rise, but her words confused him, and he sank down again. She sighed. "All right," she said. "Hello. I'm your grandmother. And you're Willi. It's so good to finally meet you. I've been waiting years and years. Is that better?"

She smiled, her lips velvety, stretched across her teeth, erasing for a moment the wrinkles around her mouth. She lifted her chin, raised her hands, linked her fingers, regarded him. The bird fluttered again, and Willi cast his eyes to it.

"Do you like the bird?" she asked.

Willi didn't know. He shrugged. He didn't know what to look at here.

"It lives in that cage," she said. "Sometimes I let it out. It flies around the room, then returns to its cage and flaps around like that, trying to get out. What do you think of that?"

He couldn't think at all. The conversation was an escalator he'd stepped on, changing speed and direction, tripping him every time he matched its momentum.

"Is it foolish to return to its cage?" she prodded. She lifted her chin. The thin, loose skin under her neck stretched tight, then sagged again.

Willi sensed it was somehow an important question. That, in spite of her tone, there was gravity here. That she'd been waiting years to ask this question. Imagining it. Playing out the possible answers in her mind.

"I suppose so," he said. The bird's wings drooped at its sides, its body so limp he thought it might fall off its perch. "If it lets itself be caged when it could be free."

"I see. So your father would say, too."

A shiver of alarm ran through Willi—that she was speaking not with him but with his father, whose name she would not speak. Arguing with him. And Willi was only a substitute in an argument she had to have. An argument she needed to win more than she needed anything—but which, all these years, she'd been prevented from having.

"Its food is in that cage," she said. "Its perch and water. Is it foolish to return to those?"

Willi was somewhat calmed. He felt a responsibility to speak well in his father's place. "It would learn to find food and water on its own," he said.

"I suppose it might. If it lived long enough. But suppose it angered me by not returning to its cage, and I locked the cage with the food and water inside and shut the windows and put all other food into cupboards and left the house so as not to hear its chattering—and when I returned, suppose I found it clinging to the outside of the cage, dead, trying to get the food and water there. Would you say then it was a wise and happy bird?"

Willi was astonished that she would even imagine such a scene—this bird, this pet of hers that he supposed assuaged her loneliness. "That would be cruel," he cried.

She was unmoved. "Of course it would be cruel. We are not discussing cruelty. We're discussing the wisdom of birds. The nature of cages."

"But if you're determined to kill it, it doesn't matter if it's foolish or wise. It has no choice."

"Choices," she said. She gazed at him, her eyes unblinking. "Of course. Your father again. You chose to come to my door, I suppose?"

"Yes, I did."

"No doubt." She looked around the room. "Cages," she said. "They're everywhere. There." She unknotted her hands and her finger flicked, indicating the bird cage. "There." It flicked again, and Willi felt the walls around him, the door with its bolts. "Out there." She lifted her forearm off the chair and swept the air with an abrupt, backhand movement that shrank the world and condensed the sky.

"The cages just get bigger," she said. "Until people forget they exist. Our cages make us happy. That's why we return to them. We want only to be allowed to think they don't exist."

"That isn't true."

She laughed, a dry twitter. "And so he makes my point for me," she said to the bird.

Then she lifted her hand slowly off the chair arm, and one finger grazed a withered breast. "And some cages are in here," she said. "The important ones. That's why you're here. In spite of your father, you've returned to your blood."

Somewhere in the house a clock ticked and tocked and ticked and tocked.

The old woman's white hair moved in separate strands above her head, as if caught in small, individual currents of air. She placed one fragile, loosely wired knee over the other, rearranging her bones, and she looked at Willi with eyes no more reflective of light than raisins.

"Whatever your father told you," she said. "It was not the truth."

"He didn't tell me anything. I didn't even know you were alive until . . . Until the funeral. And then my mother told me about you."

"As bad. She knows only what he told her."

"There were things she didn't know," Willi admitted.

"So you've come to me. As I said—to know yourself. You've returned. Choice?" She smiled, lifted weightless shoulders. "Cages. Blood. Fulfillment. There is no difference."

Willi felt he'd come to a place where time whirled slowly around itself, forcing conversation into circles, spiraling constantly toward a single idea. He could think of nothing to say.

"You pity me, don't you?" she said. "An old woman, alone. No husband. No son. You thought perhaps you'd give me a gift. That you'd reunite the family. That I'd be grateful."

Willi flushed, embarrassed. Exposed. It was true. He'd imagined her gratitude. He felt childish, naïve.

"I have only one regret in my life," she said. "And that is that he did not win the war."

"He?" The word came out even as he tried to clamp his mouth shut on it, already knowing.

"A great man with a great vision," she said. "Brought down by betrayal. And then made small by lies. Diminished by them."

She stopped. Her finger on the arm of the chair jerked involuntarily. She stilled it by lacing her hands together again in front of her. She looked as if she were praying, or performing a magic act—bringing from those hands some enormous and wonderful thing. Then she dropped them, empty, into her lap. Willi felt again that she was having an old argument, that she'd said all these things before. It was almost as if he'd walked into the house and happened upon it.

"An old woman's dream," she said. "Is there anything more pathetic?"

THE HOUSE SWALLOWED AND MIXED all order. He would be unable to remember when she rose from the chair, but she must have, for he drank tea from a cup she handed him and ate pastry that must have been shaped by her blue-veined hands. He lifted his cup from the saucer and set it down, lifted his pastry from a plate of the same pattern that he held under his chin to catch crumbs, and he wondered what he was doing there. He had thought it might be a quick visit: He would ask her what he couldn't ask his father, and she would answer or refuse to answer—but he had thought those could be the only possible responses. He hadn't envisioned the sun moving slowly across the sky outside while he remained in the house, hadn't imagined the endless echo of the endless clock. He drank tea, ate pastry, caught his crumbs, let his cup be refilled, accepted a second pastry so as not to offend.

"I was in the cathedral of light," she told him. "At Nuremberg. I heard him speak. He showed us, those who were there. He built with light. An architect of light. A genius. Other architects had built to shield us from rain and wind, but he girded light against darkness itself. Welded light together. Riveted light to itself. We knew the world would never be the same."

But Willi had learned of this in school, and he had asked his father about it, and he spoke for his father now, confident. "Spotlights," he said. "That's all it was."

"What can you know? You think because you've been a boy and played with flashlights in the dark, you know."

But Willi did know. He'd read about it, and his father had spoken of it: Speer's cathedral, made of spotlights pointing into the sky, beams meeting like rafters ten thousand feet up, and a hundred thousand people gathered under those insubstantial filaments, imagining a structure that was all illusion, a structure that wasn't there.

"Yes," he said. "It was nothing but big flashlights. And brutal boys."

Her finger jerked. She tried to disguise the movement by lifting her hand, waving it as if shooing a fly. "You weren't there," she said. "You don't know lie from truth. It was a cathedral, the greatest ever built. Those of us there were baptized that night inside it. We were baptized in light. And reborn into our own, true blood."

She picked up her teacup, sipped, set it down, following with her eyes the meticulous movement of her hand, the cup placed precisely and almost soundlessly in the center of the saucer. The bird fluttered, scraped its claws upon the wire cage with a sound like fingernails against a chalkboard.

"You think you know the truth," she said. "But history has lied to you." She spoke toward the cup, as if it were a narrow receiver to funnel the words to Willi's ears. "It is just another cage you don't see. If he'd won, we'd have a different history. And so a different truth. You would not be sitting here with your questions. Or your judgment. Had he won, all his ideas would be justified. Even your father would know. History is no guide to the truth, as he thinks it is. It is merely stubborn. Or stupid."

She looked up from the cup to Willi, alone in the maroon chair, framed by bright brass tacks, then let her eyes skip to the bird. She clicked her tongue. "Fly, little bird," she said. "No?"

"He didn't win," Willi said.

She smiled, imperturbable. He'd hoped to anger her, but she seemed beyond anger or irritation, a heart so ravaged by its dream it was like a leaf dried to vein and stem alone, through which the wind could blow and never move it. "So I've noticed. About that no one disagrees."

"History doesn't prove his ideas rotten. His losing does."

For the first time since he'd entered the house, he surprised himself. And her. In this argument she was having with herself, or with Willi's father, this argument in which Willi was a cipher, she had manipulated every answer and response, but not this one. Willi had said something new. Her eyes moved back and forth for a frantic second, dark spots dancing without rhythm in their hollows, before she adjusted, smiled.

"And how is that?" she asked. Amused. Condescending. A little weary. An adult entertaining the notions of a child. She picked up her tea, sipped, set it down. But the cup rattled against the saucer when she picked it up, a tiny, shrill, fantastic bell.

Willi had blurted out the statement—the sort of thing his father might have said. Now she was asking why. But he'd had history drummed into him in school, had learned history as a warning, had had teachers, ashamed themselves, teach history to make their students ashamed. He'd resented it, grown bored with it, but now that knowledge aided him, gave him a way to think.

"Master races don't lose," he said.

Four fingers lifted from the chair arm in easy dismissal. She'd heard it from herself before, had waited sixteen years to respond aloud: "He was betrayed."

"He was? Who betrayed him?"

She thought he was ignorant. She saw a chance to teach. "His generals did," she said. "In Russia especially. And others, too. Speer. Goering. Many used him for their own gain. Or simply did not follow his orders."

"So he could have destroyed inferior races if his own race had been loyal. And history would now show how right he was."

"Yes," she said. She allowed herself a small triumphant tone: He'd seen the truth, as all along she'd known he would, having for sixteen years won this point with his father. "You see it now. Your blood knows it. You can't deny it."

But she'd fallen into Willi's trap. "So," he said. "Master races betray themselves. Some mastery."

For a moment her face was hung on wire mesh being crushed. It elongated, and her cheeks fell into the spaces between her gums. She swallowed, the movement a wave in the loose skin of her throat. Even the bird seemed to know that something had changed in the house, for it caught itself by beak and claws on the wire and beat the air with feathers. Then Willi's grandmother regained the structure of her face and managed a thin and bitter smile.

"Bird, be still," she said, her eyes on Willi.

Astonishingly, the bird went still. The old woman's mouth twisted. She seemed to be fighting to force her lips to cover it. "They've taught you well," she said. "Built your cage so well you've learned to maintain it yourself."

But she avoided answering the challenge his statement posed. And he thought, in the few moments of clarity her confusion gave him, that perhaps all bad ideas destroy themselves. Bad intentions, no. But maybe bad ideas all rotted from the inside out, swelling and bloating with their own incoherence, and time was a sieve in which they caught and through which they could not flow.

Yet he knew he would not change her. He'd heard there were people like her, though he'd never thought he'd find his grandmother one of them. Her own insight into why he'd come was true: He'd hoped to reunite the family. And not just the family—reunite the past and the present. But within that house, where the present had ceased to exist and the future never emerged, Willi began to understand his own alienation. The metallic, ammonia smell of the caged bird seemed, as he sat there, the underlying taste of his life: a bitterness he lived with, unrecognized till now. He had thought he might find a grandmother once capable of causing her son to leave her—but no longer so. She would instead be lonely, hurt, eager to ask forgiveness, waiting for her son to know her again—as she now was, not as she had been. And such a grandmother would justify Willi's anger at his father for those wasted years of not knowing who he was or whom he came from.

He hadn't prepared himself to find his father right. To find his grandmother locked within the past and himself substituted for his father, while the clock in the distant room refused to move time forward but thumped again and again the same identical beat.

"Would you like more tea?" she asked.

He shook his head.

"What is your question, then?"

"My question?"

"You came here with a question. Have you forgotten?"

Dread as cold and swift as the Rhine filled him. For he realized this was her final weapon. She'd saved the question he'd come to ask until she needed it. Now, when he'd achieved his little victory, his little play on logic and words, she would demand his question. She knew he would have to ask it. Would have to hand it over to her. Would have to let her fondle it. Stroke it. Examine it, turn it over. And then answer.

He was caught within her grip. It made him a coward. It made his tongue thick. But he asked, as she knew he would. She listened patiently, primly, as he heard his voice say, "When I was a baby, my father tried to kill himself. Why? You know. I know you do."

"I see," she said. She looked at her lap, reached down, finger and thumb like soft, white pincers, and picked a crumb from her thigh, held it over her saucer, rubbed finger and thumb together with precise, papery rustles.

"I did not know he tried to kill himself," she said, looking at her saucer where the crumb had fallen. "Marti never said anything. And your father himself. Well, you know."

Willi stared at her.

"You expect me to be shocked," she said. "Maybe guilty. In sixteen years he hasn't visited me. His choice, not mine. He didn't even come to his father's funeral. He's been dead to me as much as if he had been dead. Why should this news shock me now?"

There was something self-pitying in her tone, though she pretended to be brusque, unmoved. Willi knew she was talking to him now, not his father. And that he was in a battle. He refused to acknowledge her self-pity. "Why did he do it?" he asked.

"Ask him. As I said, I didn't even know he tried."

"But you know why he did it. And I'm asking you."

"Why would I know why he did anything?"

As he'd thought: She was toying with the question, a bauble he'd given her, a charm for her old age, a bright thing to make the time in this house pass even more slowly, to drug and paralyze it. Willi stood. He'd been sitting so long he almost fainted, the room swam, and he put back his hand to steady himself. "All right," he said. "If you don't know, I'll go. I've met you now."

Her eyes glittered with a strange, eerie fear. Willi's hackles rose. A devouring hunger played in her face. His standing and offering to leave was, he saw, a deprivation. She needed him. Was ravenous for him. But why? He shivered, turned away, was halfway to the door, when she said,

"I doubt you want to know."

He stopped, breathed deeply, turned back. Her cunning face. She gestured to the maroon chair again. He returned to it, her prey. But he had to know.

"There," she said when he sat down. "That's better. I find it amusing, I must say, when people claim they want to know things without knowing what they want to know."

She tittered, little-girlish. But Willi was tired of her digressions. He had only emptiness inside him, futility. A kind of awful, numbing calm. He didn't respond.

"You could seek ignorance," she said, her voice light now, cheerful. "Why do people always seek knowledge? You, for instance: Why are you really here? You could spend your life pretending you're someone other than you are. Your father could have, too. He would be happier. He wasn't ready for the truth. Yet he poured his life into finding it. And then tried to kill himself when he did. Wouldn't he have been better off seeking ignorance? Letting other people decide how he should live? Without the strength to sustain knowledge, one is a fool to seek it."

Willi stared at her. With no emotion whatsoever, he imagined shaking her: her raisin eyes falling from their sockets, her teeth loosened in her jaw and scattered on the floor like hard, fossil rain.

She saw something in his gaze. "It would be easy to silence me, wouldn't it?" she said. "And then you would remain in your happy cage. Where you know nothing of your life. Fed and watered."

"Tell me." He just wanted it over.

"It's not me who's against you, Willi," she said, her voice intimate now, conspiratorial. "You're my grandson. I've kept track of you. Marti has informed me. I'd be proud of you if you'd let me be."

"I don't even know you."

"That isn't my fault."

"It might be."

"You're certainly stubborn."

A small triangle of sunlight leaking through the shades had crept up the wall opposite Willi. In its illumination he could see the tinge of an older layer of paint, a thin discoloration, under the current one. A sickening suspicion struck him, born of things he'd learned in school and perhaps not true at all here—that a Jewish family perhaps once lived in this house, and the Nazis had taken it from them and given it to his grandparents. He didn't know it was true, but the chair he sat in suddenly seemed a vile thing, the possession of someone starved and turned to smoke. He had all he could do to stay seated. This place had infected his imagination. Everything around him seemed unreal, a museum of death, occupied by ghosts, and his grandmother one of them. This house seemed a place where cruelty and stupidity and idealism and rigidity and hypocrisy and self-loathing and accusation and justification had mingled to form a glue that gummed up time. The triangle of light might extinguish itself, and darkness might fill the room, but he and his grandmother would sit here forever facing each other, with real or imagined other families who had lived here, too, and only his grandmother's papery breathing to fix and hold awareness, while the bird slept and the clock clanged on in its timeless night.

"Stubborn as your father," his grandmother said. Willi stared at her, horrified—that she could go on talking. Go on breathing. Go on pretending to live. "Well—I'll tell you what you claim you want to know. Have you ever heard of *Lebensborn?*"

Willi started. *Lebensborn:* Fountain of Life, Source of Life, Well of Life. His father's words to Marti echoed in his ears: *Your mother. My well of life.*

His grandmother was watching him. "Ah," she said. "You recognize it. Perhaps you know of the National Socialist Welfare Organization, too. Your grandfather and I met in the cathedral of light. He was already married, but our love was instantaneous. Unstoppable. Unquenchable. In that structure, at that time, we saw the country's future, and we saw our future, and we bound ourselves together to create those futures."

She paused, and her hand went to her hair. She brushed it lightly, caught up in the memory. Then she saw Willi watching her, and her hand dropped back to the arm of the chair.

"It horrifies you, doesn't it," she said, "to discover the passions of the old? As if you grew from seed and invented passion on your own. We asked each other what we could give to the *Führer.* It was, of course, difficult for us to see each other. He had his marriage. And his other responsibilities. We saw each other when we could, and for a long time that was all. A secret thing. But those days were glorious. So much was new. You will never know."

A reverent tone had come into her voice—reminiscent, sad, longing. Willi was listening to the old woman voice the meaning of her life. Her burning bush. He listened, fascinated and horrified, knowing that everything she said was a story of betrayal that she had twisted into a story of faith and loyalty. It was the first time in his life that he'd even vaguely understood that betrayal could look like loyalty, death like life, hatred like love, darkness like light. It all could be turned, and this old woman, fervent and elegiac, was speaking of her holiness.

"Then the Party gave us our answer. They gave us *Lebensborn.*" She pronounced the word as someone else might pronounce the name of God, almost unspeakable. "We loved each other, and we saw a Reich lasting a thousand years. Such a Reich needed children—young men to fight its battles. We could not be married, but we could give the *Führer* and the Reich children. This was *Lebensborn.* And so we did."

She looked at Willi, and on her face, mixed within its confused, sad radiance, glittered that hunger he'd seen earlier, a greedy hope: that he would believe. This was why she needed him. This was why she was speaking, why she'd opened up, made herself so vulnerable—not because she wanted to answer his question for him, but because, after sixteen years of silence and waiting, she was investing her entire life in what she told him, in the hope that he would understand, approve, and validate her. Willi wondered if she had already devoured him. And if she hadn't, had he left a trail by which he could find his way back to wherever he'd come from, to whoever he had been?

"My father," he said.

She nodded. "Yes. It was for the future, don't you see?" She was breaking down, disintegrating. Willi had the sense she could turn to a pile of bones in the chair, quilted in silken skin. She was desperate, pleading with him to understand.

"It was for a glorious future. A son for the Reich. For Germany. For the *Führer*."

She stopped, watching him. He stared at her, stricken. How long he didn't know. A shadow passed across her face. A finger twitched on the arm of the chair. She jerked her head, pulling the loose skin under her chin temporarily taut. Then she composed herself.

"Your grandfather returned to his work," she said. "And to his wife. I went to live, as we had planned, in one of the houses provided by the National Socialist Welfare Organization for women in the *Lebensborn* program. Everything was for the child. The best care. The best food. All for the child. For health and strength. And when he was born, it was a celebration. He entered a community. Do you understand? He was not alone. There was even a naming ceremony for him."

Still Willi didn't respond. He tried to imagine his father as a baby in the arms of black-jacketed SS men performing some ritual perversion of naming, but his mind rejected the image. *A community?* he thought. *Not alone?*

His grandmother, facing the weakness of his response, resembled a melting candle, its flame guttering, without energy, shedding a light so small and wavering that it served only to deepen the darkness beyond it. She seemed to have to talk, to finish the story, though she had lost all hope it might affect him as she needed. Her voice was almost a whisper now.

"Then everything came to an end," she said. "He lost the war. We lost everything. Except our love for each other. With the war lost, your grandfather saw no reason to remain married to his wife. He divorced her, married me. And our son. Our son." Her voice broke when she said the word, the slightest catch, like a thin, damp cracker breaking, only that. "We were able to get him back. He'd been given to a family to raise, but without the *Lebensborn* support and money, they were happy to return him."

"And my father found this out," Willi stated. He'd been silent so long his grandmother's voice had come to seem the only voice in existence and his own voice sounded foreign and otherworldly.

"He did. He kept searching. He had to know. Why did he have to know? Tell me that, if you can? He was our son. We loved him. We raised him. Isn't that enough?"

Her voice still guttered, still whispered, but it had the force of plea. Her last one. But Willi shook his head. She'd not given birth to a son. She'd given birth to a sacrifice. To a weapon. A rifle or bullet or bomb. A soldier for the Reich. And she couldn't repent, because she would first have to admit the wrong, and it was a wrong too grievous to name. For protection against what she'd done, she'd turned herself into this dried and desiccated thing, hoarding her memories of passion, nursing her sense of wrong.

Since he'd found out about his grandfather's role in the SS, Willi had felt some shame at being the grandson of a man who had supervised death and suffering. Now he understood a different shame—the shame his father must have felt when he'd taken that pistol and pressed it to his forehead, before the lights of the car containing his wailing child—that future different from the one his parents had planned for him—struck and filled the room. That shame was the shame of being born already sacrificed to a dream. Already abdicated. Given up.

Willi stood. In the room darkness had thickened. His grand-mother's face was a white shape only, featureless. He turned away from it. If she could not repent, how could he forgive her? He felt a great cruelty—to destroy her illusion, even if it destroyed her. But even his cruelty was futile; there was nothing he could do.

His hand was on the door when she spoke again.

"Well. I am sorry I could not make you see. It would have been a glorious future."

Willi looked at his hand on the knob. He spoke to it. "The future's now," he said. "A future that would have been isn't a future at all."

He opened the door and walked into the night. Left her with her ghosts. He looked up, but the streetlights blinded him. He couldn't see the stars. He couldn't see the vineyards on the hills above the Mosel. But he looked anyway. They were there.

Stacking Hay

~~~~~~

CARSON SPUN THE CASE TRACTOR in a tight circle, straightened it out, shoved in the clutch, slammed the transmission into reverse, and let the clutch back out, all in one continuing motion. As the tractor backed up, he lowered the bale prongs on the three-point hitch until they were sweeping through the stubble two inches off the ground. He backed up to a big round bale of hay, slid the prongs under it endwise, shoved in the clutch, pushed the three-point hitch lever up to lift the bale off the ground, shifted the transmission into fourth, and carried the bale forward to the stack he was building. There he repeated the whole process in reverse, backing into the stack, dropping the hitch, and driving forward, leaving the bale. Then he set off for another one.

His father was using a Farmhand fork on an old International M to build the second and third layers of the stacks, Carson establishing the base and his father finishing. Carson was a couple of stacks ahead, a quarter mile separating the two tractors in the field. He shoved the last bale into place on the stack he was building, then slipped the Case into neutral and let it idle, watching the M move across the field, a bale nearly as large as the tractor itself hoisted in front of it. The image he'd been seeing again and again interposed itself before his eyes: Magnus's hand striking Rebecca's face, thick fingers coming from nowhere, her head jerking sideways.

That image had been in his mind when Earl called about Greggy Longwell. Carson had listened to Earl's perfunctory description of what had happened, but he found it hard to pay attention.

"Guess that's what we expected," he said when Earl finished.

"You guess that's what we expected?"

"Never was much of a chance Longwell'd take it seriously."

"So things are going according to plan? Is that what you're saying?"

"I need to think about things some more."

"I guess we do. I got to go think right now, you know?"

Carson didn't know what Earl expected from him. Was he supposed to apologize for Greggy? Tell Earl how bad he felt? Greggy was a bigot, and he'd behaved like they thought he would. Carson had never wanted to go to him in the first place. Or was Earl just responding to Carson's listlessness? Carson tried to recall the anger he'd felt when he first recognized what was being done to the horses. But the image of a hand striking Rebecca's face—her startled, hurt expression, her hair swirling in chaos under the blow—kept interposing, and he couldn't recapture his former concern for the horses. This other despair overwhelmed it.

He'd left the house after Earl's call and found his father replacing one of the hydraulic rams on the Farmhand parked near the Quonset shed.

"You got anything goin on tomorrow?" Charles asked.

"What're you thinkin?"

"Hay needs stacked."

It was the job he'd told Rebecca needed doing the Saturday he'd gone to work Surety, hoping she'd ride with him. And she had, and they'd gone to the Elmer Johannssen ranch. A sharp regret struck through Carson. "Yeah," he said. "Guess we oughta get that done."

His father glanced at him. Carson didn't meet his eyes. He didn't know whether his parents suspected anything or not. The day he'd come home from shooting the cow, Carson had entered the new house and walked up the half-flight of steps into the upper level, where his parents were eating. He'd reached into his pocket for the ugly bundle of bills and placed it down in front of his father's plate. All three of them looked at the crumpled wad as if it were some soggy thing he'd found in a culvert.

"Job's done," Carson said.

"He paid you in cash?"

"Appears so."

"Man's got 'n odd way a doin things."

Carson started to turn away.

"It's your money," his father said.

"It's the ranch's money." Carson felt the tightness in his voice.

"Put it in your own account."

"I don't want it 'n my account."

There was a hitch in the conversation, a hiccup of silence. Then the conversation skewed off in a different direction, avoiding recognition.

"All right. Those horses train OK?"

"They trained fine."

"Rebecca," his mother asked. "She's done learning, too?"

"She can ride. I'm finished with Magnus Yarborough." He turned away again.

"Carson?" his mother said.

"Yeah?"

"Eat with us."

"I gotta clean up. I'll eat over there."

"This money'll help," his father said.

"Only reason I took the job."

Now, standing next to the Quonset shed, Carson felt his father's gaze on him and saw his father's gloved hand, wrapped around a pair of blue-handled channel lock pliers, stop working the spring pin out of the hydraulic ram.

"Things OK?" his father asked.

"Fine. The Case ready?"

Charles nodded. He gripped the pliers and pulled, but the pin was tight and didn't budge.

"You could tap that out with a hammer," Carson told him.

"Could. Didn't have a hammer handy. Had a pair a pliers."

Carson started toward the toolbox on the M to see if there was a hammer in it.

"I'll get it," Charles said. "Just need a yank a bit harder."

Carson reached the toolbox, found an old wooden-handled hammer, blackened with embedded grease and dirt. He was about to hand it to his father when Charles grunted and twisted, and the pin slid out of its hole. Charles held the pin up, and they both looked at it as if it were a trophy they'd been competing for.

"Hammer woulda worked, too," Charles said, almost apologetically.

"What's wrong with that ram?"

"Leaking. Have to buy a new one, maybe. Never ain't something breaking down."

"Ain't that the truth."

"Guess that money from them horses'll buy a ram, huh?"

His father might have whipped him with thorns. Is that what everything added up to? A new hydraulic ram? He couldn't even sit in the old house any more without feeling its sparseness. Had he sold his stories for a ram? Learned to feel a paucity in his grandfather's legacy, and an emptiness in the air at his own side—for a ram? Had Rebecca's face been bruised for a ram?

His father was just making talk. Carson stood, letting the sting of the words pass, then said, "Guess I'll put this hammer back."

Standing behind the seat of the tractor where his father couldn't see him, Carson leaned forward, palms on the tractor's cast-iron platform, and stared at the ground, the scattered and meaningless stones. When he came back around the lugged tire, his father had the ram out and was carrying a different, smaller one from the pickup. He set it down on the Farmhand's frame.

"What'd you think a Magnus Yarborough, anyway?" he asked.

"Didn't like him much," Carson answered.

"Why's that?"

Because he runs over animals and breaks their legs, Carson thought. *Because he hits his wife.*

"He thinks everything's his," he said. "Thinks everything oughta be his. Doesn't just like getting his way. He hates not getting it."

"Big difference," Charles agreed. He picked the ram up and set it in the frame, pushed the hardened steel shaft through the holes in its end, picked up the pliers again, and pushed the spring pin through the hole in the shaft to hold everything in place. "He interfere?"

"That's why I didn't want a go over there in the first place."

He heard the accusation in his voice. "Anyway, I got 'em trained," he said, trying to dismiss and correct himself. "It's over. What time you want a start tomorrow?"

His father seemed for a moment about to say something else, but then just answered the question. "Right after chores, I guess."

Charles reached out his gloved hand and grasped the stainless steel shaft of the ram and wiggled it. The metal clunked against the pin.

"Think that ram's big enough?" Carson asked.

"It's gonna hafta be. Till we get another one."

This talk of steel and the limitations of hydraulics. The strength of seals and the pressure against them.

"It gets old, don' it—this always fixin things?" Charles asked.

NOW, TWO STACKS AHEAD OF HIS FATHER, Carson let the Case idle, the diesel engine drumming, and watched the fork on the Farmhand open. The bale in its tines rolled ponderously onto the stack, then settled. That smaller ram seemed to be holding up. Carson thought again of all that had happened, and for nothing but money. A deep sadness settled in him. He was worried about Rebecca and wondered if she would leave Magnus, and if she didn't, what would happen to her? There was nothing he could do for her. She'd said it, and it was true. But what was he doing stacking hay?

"Shit or get off the pot," his grandfather would say. "You can mope all you want, but that won't do any good. So do what you can."

Carson had to let Rebecca deal with Magnus, and do what he could. The horses needed help. But he was unable to think of anything he could do. He laid his forehead on the Case's steering wheel and stared at the dirty platform between his feet, felt the pound of the cylinders in his skull. The engine seemed to be racketing inside his brain. He lifted his head and stared at the land again, its rolling emptiness, with the M moving slowly in the distance, picking up scattered bales. He turned his head, looked in the direction of Lostman's Lake, and thought of the horses out there. He remembered the feel of Orlando's cracked bone beneath his fingers.

His former rage over the horses' mistreatment stirred within him. He'd almost acted on that rage, almost cut the wire and let them go. But Earl had stopped him. Carson remembered how the Indian kid had reached out and grabbed his wrist when Carson headed toward the fence with his pliers. Earl's grip had been so soft it was almost not a grip at all. But it hadn't loosened, either, when Carson tried to withdraw his hand. It had been that consistency that had stopped Carson, a sense that Earl would follow him right to the fence, not resisting him but not letting go either, his fingers as soft as butterfly wings on Carson's wrist, but completely unwavering.

"How far do you think they'll go?" Earl had asked—his voice close and quiet, lilting the way so many Indian voices did. He'd seen the consequences of Carson's action so clearly. Earl had been so quiet and reserved that night, and his voice seemed to be always asking questions, as if he were afraid to commit to anything—but when it came down to it, he'd had the clearest vision of anyone that night, the most dispassionate and disinterested, and he'd been, maybe, the most committed of all. Carson regretted he hadn't paid more attention and asked for more information when Earl had told him about Greggy Longwell. Greggy probably put the kid through hell. Thinking all this, Carson felt the need to talk to Earl again.

He smiled ruefully. "Crazy," he said to himself.

He wasn't accustomed to finding himself needing help from anyone, but to find himself needing help from an Indian teenager—this was rare. He watched his father slip the Farmhand's tines under another bale and hoist it off the ground. Then he looked away, in the direction of the reservation. *Time for a visit,* he thought. How odd. The rez was only a few miles away, but he hadn't been on it since high school, when he'd visited a few Indian friends. But he'd lost touch with them. The rez was its own world. He didn't have much to do with it. Well, he did now. Far off, at the edge of the horizon to the west, the spires of the Badlands pierced the sky.

Conversion

∧∧∧∧∧

ARL OFTEN WALKED THE TWO MILES home from school. The bus went out of town in a different direction and traveled thirty miles before reaching his house. He usually preferred to walk, clearing his mind of the haze of school, the sexual tensions and posturing, the constant maintenance of the pecking order that often, by the end of the day, left him feeling exhausted and numb. The walk home helped restore him. He walked on the left shoulder of the road to discourage offers of rides, but it didn't always work. For people on the rez who didn't have cars, mass transportation meant walking down the highway in the direction of their destinations until someone stopped and gave them a ride. Earl sometimes had to refuse four or five offers in the two-mile stretch to his house.

He was just stepping over the blown retread that had been lying on the shoulder for several weeks, its cords protruding from the rubber like distended veins, when he heard a vehicle slow down behind him. He swept his arm forward to indicate it should go by, but it didn't. It appeared in his peripheral vision and stopped. Earl turned and saw Carson Fielding leaning out the window.

"Headin home?" Carson asked.

Earl nodded.

"I'm goin up to Lostman's Lake."

A fall chill was in the air, and the wind whipped Earl's shirt sleeves in a frenzy around his elbows. He stuck his hands in his pockets, pressed his elbows against his sides to silence them, and wondered what this cowboy was up to. Carson hadn't seemed to care at all when Earl told him about Greggy Longwell. Not that Earl was expecting sympathy—or not too much, at least. Some. A little. At least

a word or two directed against Greggy Longwell. Instead Carson
had acted as if Greggy's behavior, being expected, was also accept-
able. But it wasn't, and Earl's meeting with the sheriff had turned
the problem with the horses into something personal. It wasn't just
about saving them any more; it was redeeming himself, compensat-
ing for the humiliation Greggy had put him through. But he'd been
unable to come up with anything he could do.

"You want a go up there?" Carson asked.

Earl looked down the highway in the direction of town. When
they'd been up to see the horses before, Carson had as much as told
Earl to stay out of his business. Now he was inviting him to go back?
Earl suspected a trick. He imagined himself reaching for the door
handle on Carson's pickup only to have Carson speed away, laughing, muttering something about a dumb Indian.

"Why?" Earl asked.

Carson stared blankly at him, puzzled. "To look at them horses,"
he said.

A horn seared the air, and an eighteen-wheeler rocketed between them, sending Earl back a step with the battering ram of hard
air it pushed. Straw and dead leaves swirled high behind it and descended in slow, chaotic circles as the semi's square rear end diminished down the highway, a doorway growing smaller and smaller
toward oblivion. The smell of the cattle it carried remained for
a few seconds, thick as soup, before the wind diluted and swept
it away.

"I don't think those horses have changed much, you know?" Earl
said. "I don't need to look at them again."

Carson stared through his windshield, watching the semi recede. "It ain't just lookin," he said. "I need some advice."

This surprised Earl. "About those horses?"

"Not a whole lot else we got in common, is there?"

The statement was so direct, and so true, and so totally without
animosity or irony, that it struck Earl as funny. He walked around
the pickup's hood, opened the door, got in. *Notice that the vehicle,* he
thought as he reached for the door handle, *does not move away as the
Suspicious Indian approaches it.*

"We ought to go get Willi," he said as he sat down.

"Willi? Why?"

Earl didn't have an answer. Funny how things happened: Walk off a hill, and someone follows you, and just like that you feel he ought to be involved.

"We just should," he said.

"You're the one I wanted a talk to."

"He's just back in town. Not far to pick him up."

"I suppose."

"You said you wanted my advice."

"Wasn't what I wanted your advice on."

Earl lifted a shoulder, let it drop. "You start asking for advice, you get more 'n you bargained for, you know?"

"I guess so." Carson put the pickup into gear, glanced in his mirror, and heaved the steering wheel around in a U-turn, the right wheel going over into the ditch on the opposite side, so that Earl was hanging in space before Carson completed the turn. They headed back to town. Willi answered the door when Earl knocked. He glanced over Earl's shoulder and saw Carson's pickup at the curb. Before Earl could say anything, he asked, "Are we going?"

Earl heard other people in the house and was struck by the familiarity of Willi's question, the truncated code talk of it. Willi's words were almost like the symbols of calculus, a language all its own, and Earl felt an odd fondness for Willi, hearing it—a question only Earl and Carson would understand, embedded in a specific sequence of events, meaningless on its face, yet immediately conveying to Earl an image of the night and the depression behind Lostman's Lake, and the mute suffering of the horses. That image bound them together, and out of it a language was born. A fleeting moment of intimacy bloomed and faded between Earl and Willi as Willi asked the question and Earl nodded.

A plastic grocery bag, pregnant with wind, floated high over the Drusemans' roof as Earl and Willi walked down the sidewalk to the pickup. Earl watched it, shining whitely in the high sun. Somewhere beyond town, perhaps, the wind would desert it, and it would deflate and descend, and a sagebrush bush or Canada thistle or cone-

flower would blossom with plastic. Earl opened the door to the
pickup and got in, working his left knee over the gearshift lever.
Willi followed and slammed the door. Carson reached over Earl's
knee, his shoulder bumping against Earl's, and put the pickup in
gear. They waited silently at the intersection for the stoplight to
change to green, then left town, past the blown retread, its tenta-
cled cords waving in the wind. They were a quarter-mile past Earl's
house before Carson spoke.

"I've always wondered somethin," he said. "About those trees
around your house."

"What about them?"

"How'd you get 'em to grow like that?"

Earl leaned forward and looked in the right side mirror, saw the
trees in diminished reflection, a round oasis of green against the
distorted sky and land of the convex-mirror world. So many possible answers, he thought. *Love*, his mother would say. *Love and spirit.
My love. Your father's love. Love and memory and their persistence. Rooted,
knotted, fibered, twined. Things that go and things that stay. Love remains,
Earl. Your father whispers to us yet. He speaks in the leaves.*

And Norm had once said, "It's spirit. The spirit in things. The
thing about spirit, nephew, is that it won't appear unless you pay attention. And you and your mother paid attention to those trees. You
can't get the spirit world to answer unless you ask it in the proper
way. And make a way for it. That's what you did there—made a way."

Carson waited for an answer. Earl thought of the hours he'd
spent holding a hose. Even a little watering takes a long time when
it's twenty-five trees. Every other day, the little guy with the glasses
at the nursery in Pierre had told Cyrus—and Cyrus had told Lorna,
and Lorna had insisted upon it to Earl, so that every other day Earl
had stood, summer after summer, watering. Their place didn't have
a deep well. The main water table, with its hot artesian currents,
was so far down at their place that Lorna couldn't afford one. She
had bought cheap water from a rancher's stock pond, and Earl had
gotten to know the rancher well and had become familiar with the
sound of his pickup on the highway, turning into the driveway with
the green fiberglass water tank in back. When Earl complained, and

he did often, Lorna said, "Your father planted those trees. We're going to make sure they grow."

Norman planted them, too, Earl often thought. *Why do you forget that?* But he never voiced this thought.

"We just watered them a lot," he finally answered Carson.

"That right?" Carson asked. He seemed genuinely interested in the trees. "My mother's tried a get trees to grow for years. Waters all the time, but they ain't never amounted to much. Half the time she gets 'em growing, an a wind knocks 'em over or the cattle get out and trample 'em. She's about give up. I think you got more than water working there."

"Like what?" Earl asked.

"Thought maybe you knew."

Earl stared out the windshield. He didn't know. He had only guesses, conjectures, mysteries, statements of reverence. Carson Fielding had from the first unsettled him, he wasn't sure why—and now he was touching on the core of Earl's life, apparently willing to believe things about that life that Earl himself doubted and that caused Earl to lie awake at night, listening to the wind in the trees outside his window and hearing only wind and leaves, a great loneliness. A great aloneness. Earl was tempted to tell Carson what his mother said about the trees. Tempted to tell him what Norm said. But if he opened that door, he would find himself, before he finished talking, a baby with a newly widowed mother weeping over him and all the stories about the reservation that Carson might have heard— its dangerous highways, its alcoholism—confirmed by Earl himself. So much of Earl's life had been set toward resisting such stories. And now to admit to Carson, whom he didn't even know, that his life was grounded in that kind of thing? Admit he'd been shaped by that kind of thing from a time before he was even self-aware? Earl's stomach twisted into a knot. He didn't want to admit it even to himself.

And he couldn't tell Carson what Norm said—that it was spirits. Trust, again: Carson might just laugh at that. Or, if not laugh, he might hear it wrong—think of the spirits as some kind of magical way to manipulate the world. To get what you wanted. An Indian substitute for technology. Or else a way to leave the world entirely, float in dreams and visions. Earl didn't want Carson to conjure up the Drunken Indian, but he didn't want him to conjure up the Noble Indian either. Earl hadn't waved a wand over the trees. He'd waved a water hose. And if he'd done it in the proper manner, he hadn't known it.

"I don't know what else there could be," he said. Both lying and telling the truth. Or neither. "We put a lot of water on those trees."

On a hill an abandoned white church lifted its steeple against the sky in the midst of a junkyard of cars lying like a miniature, decrepit city around it—rusted, broken, hulking, random—a city of coyotes and fox and badger, mice and snakes, grasshoppers, ants, beetles, rust and broken glass. Dissonant psalms, sermons of wind. "I have been wondering since I got here," Willi said as they passed it, "why does that church have all those cars around it? Are even the cars religious here?"

Earl was glad for the distraction. He looked at the junkyard. It had always been there, and he'd never thought much of it. Just part of the landscape, part of the place. But Willi's question brought it into relief. As long as the place was just there, it was normal. Only when you thought about how it might have gotten there did it seem odd. The church, once painted white, had a molted appearance, portions of paint still gleaming in the sun amid patches of gray, weathered wood, lifting its steeple above its congregation of cars.

"Just happened," Carson said. "They built a church in town and quit usin this one. Were goin a tear it down but never got around to it. Then a member a the congregation's car broke down on the highway. Wasn't worth fixin, didn't want a pay a wrecker to take it. So he took his pickup and towed it himself up by the church just to get it off the road. Then someone else decided he had a good idea. Got to be a half-dozen cars up there. By the time people thought there was a problem, it was too many for anyone to keep after. And there were more appearin. They'd grow overnight. Might still be happenin. So many up there now you wouldn't know if there was a new convert to that church or not."

"Where'd you hear all that?" Earl asked.

"My grampa. Spent a whole afternoon up there with him when I was a kid. He knew every car, who'd owned it, everything. Told all these stories about 'em. Had two up there himself."

"He sounds like an interesting grandfather," Earl said.

"He was. He's the one taught me to train horses."

Then Carson looked out the side window and went silent.

Around a curve they saw the blue waters of the lake come and go between hills, and then they approached the turnoff, and Carson pulled up along the boat ramp. As usual there was no one at the lake. The horses stood with their heads to the wind, but when Carson spoke their names they turned, and the wind blew their manes and tails forward like old rags they wore. In the cool air the artesian spring sent up clouds of steam. The horses moved gaunt and emaciated through it. Horses of vapor, rising weightless from the earth. Their physical presence seemed leached away, and they came with heads down, responding to Carson's voice without heart or curiosity. Mere movement. The ground they walked was dust.

Earl and Carson and Willi stood rooted, watching the animals materialize from the steam. The horses reached their heads over the barbs. On their breath Earl smelled not the grassy, fermented smell he knew from horses but something sour and corrupt, metallic, and he thought it was the smell of death. Their coats under his fingers were stiff as thorns. Touching Surety, he thought for a moment he'd been cut.

"The bastard," Carson said. But Willi left the fence and ripped out grass until he had an armful. He brought it over, dumped it in front of the horses. They crowded greedily around it, snuffing, devouring it.

"We gotta get 'em outta here," Carson said.

"They are not interested in sometime in the future getting out," Willi said. "They are interested in eating right now."

"You got a point."

The three of them set to work, ripping the dry fall grass out of the ground in a widening circle around the pen and carrying it to the horses, throwing it in heaps at their feet. As fast as they could carry it, the horses devoured it. Finally Carson stopped it. "Feed 'em too much," he said, "we could kill 'em."

Willi threw a last armful of grass into the enclosure, then leaned on a post and watched.

"Keep this up, we'll be pulling grass a quarter mile away," Carson said. "We need a move 'em."

"Move 'em?"

"One word for 't. I don't suppose either a you's had a lot've experience stealin horses."

"You're asking for our help?"

"Guess I am."

"That's new."

"Things change."

Earl's dark eyes gazed into Carson's pale ones.

"This will look good on a scholarship application, you know?" Earl said.

"If you can't, you can't."

"I'll help. That sheriff . . ." Earl shrugged, didn't finish. Then he thought to himself, *You just said you'd help steal horses. You just said you'd become a criminal.*

"Willi?"

"I told my sponsors I was coming to South Dakota for the culture. They would be happy, I think, to know I tried everything you do here."

"Guess that settles it, then. We'll all three get 'em out. But like I said before, I need some advice. We need someplace big to take 'em. Where they can get lost. Far from roads. They're branded, and even without that, they're the kind a animals stick out from average horses. So we need a place they're not likely to be seen by someone just drivin around."

"In other words, the rez," Earl said.

"You got it."

"It's not that easy," Earl said. "We can't just let them go in the middle of the rez. A lot've land is family land. If they wandered onto someone's family land, and he didn't know about them, he might be looking for the owner. So we'd need to find someone willing to keep stolen horses on their land, you know?"

The horses stamped the dust, grinding the last of the grass between their molars. The wind freshened, the barbwire hummed.

"I was hopin we could just find a big, empty space on the map."

"That's the rez—just a big empty space."

"Sorry. Didn't mean it that way."

Then Willi, who'd been leaning with his chin on the back of his hands, watching the horses, turned to Earl and Carson.

"I think I know someone on the reservation who might be willing to have on his land stolen horses."

"You know someone?" Earl felt a little defensive. What was Willi doing, making claims to knowing the reservation better than he did? "How would you know someone?"

"Parties."

"Parties?"

"I go to them when I am invited."

"And you met someone at a party who'll take stolen horses?"

"It is the best place to meet someone like that."

"That's a point," Carson said.

"Who?" Earl asked.

"Ted Kills Many. I think you know him, too."

Manifold

~~~~~

STEAL THEM?"

Norm had his head under the hood of his Dodge Polaris, bent far over the engine, his right arm submerged to the elbow in iron, tightening a manifold bolt with a socket and ratchet. His voice echoed off the raised hood with a tinny sound. Earl saw his shoulders stop moving, and the clicking of the ratchet ceased along with the heavier thunks of the handle against the manifold and engine block. Norm didn't raise his head, just went still, looking down into the engine like he did when he dropped a nut and couldn't find it.

"We can't see another way, you know?" Earl said.

"Hanh," Norm grunted. He clicked the ratchet a couple of times back and forth, then stopped again. "I suppose you've told your mother about this plan, and she's given it her highest approval?"

When Earl didn't reply, Norm said, "I'll take that for a yes. And if your mother approves, who am I to discourage you?" He clicked and thunked for a while.

"What do you really think?" Earl asked.

"I think if I don't think you have such a hot idea, you wouldn't want to hear me anyway. Especially since your mother's such a fan of it."

He leaned further into the engine and turned his head sideways to get a better angle for his arm. His braid slipped off his back and onto the valve cover. Earl looked up from his uncle's sideways face over the hood of the car. The prairie falcon that seemed a permanent occupant of the space above Norm's place ran down a plane of air in a line so straight it looked like it was running on tightened wire. Then, as Earl watched, it suddenly veered, rose in a looping half-circle, turned into a bundle of feathered chaos as it thrashed its wings, then straightened out to become bird again, the clean rectangle of its tail guiding it in a new direction.

"Hand me another bolt, would you?"

Earl plucked a rusty manifold bolt off the fender and held it out. Norm withdrew from the engine, stood, arched his spine, then took the bolt and went in again. He concentrated on the task, the bolt clinking in the depths of the engine as he sought to fit it. He found the hole, and the sounds changed to the scrape and hush of threads meshing. Then Norm stood and picked up the ratchet again. He looked at it in his hands. "Well," he said. "It's an honorable Lakota tradition."

"What is?"

"Horse stealing."

He bent into the engine again, and the ratchet knocked around until he found the bolt head. His voice came out of the metal, echoed off the hood. "Those old traditions. It's hard to keep them alive in the modern world. I'm happy you're willing to work at it, nephew."

Earl stared at his uncle's bent back. Sometimes he couldn't tell when Norm was joking.

Norm unbent again. "This car," he said. "It's going to put me and my back in the VA hospital. Tighten a few of these bolts for me, nephew."

Earl took the ratchet, exchanged places with his uncle, leaned over the engine, found the bolt Norm had been tightening, fitted the socket over it. He began to work the ratchet, his wrist twisted at an uncomfortable angle. Norm's voice came from behind him: "Just make sure you steal those horses. You don't want to be a robber. You want to be a horse *thief.*"

"A thief?" The socket slipped off the bolt head. Earl fumbled around to find it again.

"Like Iktomi."

"Iktomi?" Earl found the bolt head, slipped the socket over it, ratcheted away.

"Iktomi is a trickster, nephew. And being a thief is the biggest trick there is. Robbing, though—that is serious business. Real grim."

Earl felt the bolt begin to tighten. He strained against the ratchet handle, finished the job, turned around to face his uncle. "I don't see the difference, you know?" he said.

"Let's say you got something I want," Norm said. "Like, for instance, a million acres of land, hanh? So I ask you, 'How about you give me some of that land?' You're not sure that's a wonderful idea, so I get a big gun and point it at your head and say, 'What I said was, how about you give me that land?' So this time you say, 'I've reconsidered. You have yourself a deal.' So we both agree, and there's no secret how the deal was reached. Everything's clear and in the open. Aboveboard, you might say. That's robbing, nephew."

"What's stealing, then?"

"Stealing is an art, hanh? A thief has to carry whatever he takes. He's got to be able to hide it. A thief could never take a whole continent. Robbers go armed. Thieves don't have to. And thieves are always laughing. But you don't want to joke with a robber, hanh? Custer did not have a sense of humor."

Earl laid the ratchet on the air cleaner, leaned against the bumper of the car. Norm was looking at the landscape, collecting thoughts.

"The old-time Lakota horse thieves were magicians," he said. "If you commit a good thievery against someone, they will believe everything except what actually happened. They will believe they misplaced what you took. They will believe their memory is bad. Or that their eyes do not work or that their minds are loco. A good thief creates disbelief, nephew. Makes people believe the world is different than they thought."

Then Norm began to speak of their ancestors thieving horses, how they would sneak into the enemy camp, where everything was ordered, known, secure, and they would take the one thing it would seem impossible to take—the living beasts that might give warning—so that the men of the afflicted tribe went out to the horse herd in the morning and for a while only sensed something wrong without knowing what it was—the borders of their world blurring as they gazed at the remaining horses, an absence there they could not identify.

They blame their slight unease on the light or the weather or their residual dreaming, and they look to the east for clouds and sniff the air and wonder, without speaking of it to each other, about their quiet foreboding. They make small jokes to hold the feeling off, but the sense of something wrong and troubled in the world will not leave them. They look to the morning clouds again, bright white on their eastern edges but gray-blue, darkened by their own shadows, on the west, scudding in the high morning winds like a herd of horses galloping and brindled.

Then one of the men, thinking of how the clouds are like horses far away in the regions of light and thunder, drops his gaze to the real animals before him, and only then does the sense of something wrong find a center. He stares at the horses, saying nothing yet to his companions for fear of being laughed at should his sense prove wrong. The horses mill. They shift positions. Accounting for them all, even to a man who knows them well, is difficult. The other men, alerted by his concentration, turn their eyes to the herd, too, and a moment of complete and utter human silence grows and crescendos, a silence of the kind that can only occur when the world is shifting shape and the shape it is assuming has not yet been identified.

Then the joke descends. The world cracks. Someone manages to count the horses or notices a particular animal missing and states his discovery. But how, how, how? In that moment, when the discovery is made but belief in it has not solidified, anything is possible. In that moment the thievery descends to the foundations of the world and shakes them. The turtle rolls over, the earth slides off its back.

The men cannot believe the horses are gone. Yet the horses are gone. And because they cannot believe what is before their eyes, indisputable, all possibility opens up, the possible and the impossible switch places, and all their sureties fly apart and combine in new, exotic ways. And far away, across the rolling plains, their trail gone cold, the Lakota warriors are leading the missing horses, relaxed and laughing. They tell each other the story of how they did it, and in telling push each other beyond the boundaries of the world: They had, they say, stretched the possibilities of silence, gone beyond the silence of owls or the silence of the grass they crept through, beyond the silence of silent things. It didn't matter whether the sentries were awake or asleep, they tell each other—they had come into the herd of horses like the grass growing among the myriad hooves, so unstartling that the animals bowed their heads to the strange bridles held up to them as if the earth itself upheld them and followed the warriors out of the herd at a pace no faster than the pace of a night-grazing animal, until darkness had swallowed them wholly and the warriors had mounted what was now theirs.

"The point of all this, though, nephew, was not having the horses," Norm said. "The point was the magic. It was the joke. The best horse thieves took horses staked right outside a tipi. It is as if the horses vanish, hanh? A man stakes his finest horse outside his tipi and goes to sleep with his ear a few feet from it. When he wakes and it is gone, he will not believe his eyes. Do you see? He will have to gather other evidence before he is sure that what is before him is before him. He will have to know if other horses are also gone. He will have to find tracks. He will have to talk this over with his family. All to convince himself that his horse, which he can't see, is gone."

Norm laughed. "That's the point of thieving, nephew. To make someone believe nothing and everything. A good thief makes a man believe—for just a moment—that horses can fly."

He picked up another rusty manifold bolt and handed it to Earl. "Suppose we ought to finish this job," he said. "See if that one will go."

Earl took the bolt and leaned into the engine again, feeling with his fingers until he found an empty bolt hole.

"Indians honored stealing and thieves," Norm said. "But white people honor robbing. It is hard for robbers and thieves to understand each other. For one thing, a robber doesn't want to see the world any way but the way he sees it. He has to know the value of what he's robbing. The point of thieving isn't having the thing, but the point of robbing is. So if you're a robber, you're going to rob as much of the world as you can. It is the only way to make sure it stays the way you see it. But a thief"—Norm paused—"he's not trying to control anything."

Earl had been working the ratchet. He felt the bolt tighten, gave the handle two more pushes, withdrew his arm. "That one's good," he said.

"One more to go." Norm handed him the last of the bolts. He seemed to be done talking, and Earl worked in silence, thinking. He wasn't sure how Norm's distinction between thieving and robbing applied to taking the horses. He had more urgent and practical matters to be worried about. He finished with the bolt, pulled the socket and extension off the ratchet, and replaced them in his uncle's toolbox.

"What's bothering me, you know," he said, "is where we're planning to take them once we get them out."

"Hanh?"

Norm was inspecting the manifold, pulling on it with both hands to see that it was tight. Under his efforts the Polaris rocked on its springs.

"We plan to take them to Ted Kills Many's."

Norm stopped rocking the car. Earl tried to read his expression, but his uncle was looking at the engine, almost as if he hadn't heard Earl.

"It looks like a good job," Norm said. "It will be different, not breathing carbon monoxide."

"What do you think of him?"

Norm gazed at the air cleaner of the car. "I think," he finally said, "these horses are beings of great spirit. It is like the old stories, nephew. In the old stories there is always danger when you cross into the spirit world. It doesn't matter where the stories come from. In all of them it is hard to find your way back. Birds eat the trail of crumbs you leave. Or you begin to think you are a bear and forget you were ever human. Memory is a hard thing to maintain when you cross."

Norm took an old white sock from the fender of the car and wiped his hands, wrapping each individual finger in the sock, rubbing off rust and grease. Then he tossed it to Earl and reached up and slammed the Polaris's hood. The clanging boom momentarily silenced the grasshoppers, and the sparrows in the cottonwoods.

"In the old stories, you have to be careful. You have to obey everything you are told to do. But sometimes not. That is the thing. Sometimes you have to behave crazy. You have to suspect trickery everywhere and do the opposite of what you are told. It depends on who's telling you. You have to know who to trust. But you have no way to know that. And you can't just cross back, nephew. There is a task to perform first. Always. You might be ignorant of what it is, but that is no excuse for not performing it."

When he was younger, Earl's grandmother had told him such stories while she beaded—people rising for reasons they didn't understand and going off to join the bear or buffalo people and coming to think of themselves as buffalo or bear until they couldn't recognize their own family. These people were always endangered, both their old and their new kin likely to mistake them, and confused by their own identity. But Earl knew the horses were real. They might be beings of great spirit, but they were also animals that smelled, right now, of death.

"In those old stories," Norm went on, "people do not realize they have crossed a boundary. This is so. They do not feel special. They do not feel blessed, and they do not feel cursed. Mostly, they just feel confused. They just think their lives have gotten a little strange. They lose their direction. That is all, they think. They are not sure which signs point the right way. They are not sure which stars to follow. It is like Goat Man, nephew. He is always out there. Leaving tracks. But when you see him, he is gone. This does not mean you did not see him. But you will think maybe you didn't. That is Goat Man's trick—to be more real when you don't see him than when you do. People can get so confused they believe they are not confused at all. That is when they are really in trouble."

"You're confusing me, you know?"

Norm laughed. "Confusion is a funny thing," he said. "It makes it harder to do anything, but it makes it more likely you will do the right thing when you do. And it can go even further. In the old stories, sometimes, feeling confused can be part of the confusion. Everything might actually make sense. And usually does. But I think it's time to start this car and see how it sounds."

"What about Ted Kills Many, though? What do you think of him?"

"You're confusing me now, nephew. I thought I answered that."

"It's just they're dying, you know? I'm not sure I have time to figure your answer out."

"So you think I should, hanh?"

Earl gave a little shrug. Norm gazed over the roof of the car at the prairie undulating away from the cinder blocks that served as steps to his home. "It's different," he said, "the guy who gives an answer interpreting it, too. But near as I can figure out what I said, if you don't trust Ted Kills Many, he may be someone you should trust. Trouble is, you trust me, so maybe you shouldn't."

"That helps a lot, you know?"

Norm opened the door of the Polaris. "I only have the stories, nephew. And I know when people walk into those other realms, they sometimes need the strangest kinds of help. Half the time the trick is recognizing the help that is there instead of waiting for the help they recognize."

Earl shoved his hands in his pockets and stared at the ground. His uncle seemed unwilling to be clear. Or maybe he couldn't be clear. "OK," he said. He had to respect what Norm had said and try to make sense of it.

Norm started to get in the car, then stopped, looked at Earl over the open door.

"I do know this," he said. "Ted Kills Many, what I know of him, he reminds me of a guy I once knew I would not have trusted with anything."

Earl almost felt relieved. At last an answer, a reason to avoid Ted. "Who's that?" he asked.

"Guy named Norman Walks Alone."

How to Seduce White Girls

~~~~~

EARL KNEW WHERE TED'S PLACE WAS supposed to be, but twice he took the wrong gravel roads, which started out in the right direction but serpentined around and turned into dirt tracks with grass growing between them, and then into nothing but ruts, and then into nothing at all. The second time this happened, Earl got out of the car, walked to the front of it, leaned against the hood, and stared at the prairie before him. He had the vague idea that maybe if he looked hard enough, he'd see the road reappear out there in the distance, emerging from the grass, winding its way up a hillside.

He wanted to kick something, but there was nothing to kick but the car, and it was his mother's. What were these roads doing out here if they didn't go anywhere? Probably someone lived out there—or had—someone who came into Twisted Tree every two weeks or less for supplies and who used the ruts that had just disappeared to get there. The thought made Earl both envious and angry—that someone might have a life so secure and confident that these ruts were all the connection he needed to the rest of the world. Or on the other hand it might be a life just ground down, poverty-stricken, hopeless.

There were people who knew every road on the rez and knew who lived on those roads and who had lived on them for the past many generations since the roads had been built and before even that. There were people who wouldn't be lost if they were thrown into the trunk of a car and driven around for an hour. Released, they would climb out of the trunk and take a look around and find a hill or a tree they knew, the slightest odd configuration, and from that hill or tree they would turn and point their lips in the direction of their nearest relative's dwelling and start walking. And Earl couldn't even find a place he'd gotten directions to. The peaks of the Badlands erupted from the prairie in the distance. Ted lived somewhere in that direction. But the only way for Earl to get there was to turn around and retrace his route and figure out where he'd gone wrong.

He got back in the car. Willi looked at him. "Are we lost?" he asked.

"Not lost. I just don't know where we are."

"I am glad we are not lost."

Earl backed the car in a circle and turned around. The grass between the ruts rushed along the chassis. Gradually the ruts became a kind of road again, and a mile after that they came to the dirt road they had turned off earlier. Earl stopped the car. In both directions the road ran through the brown prairie, featureless, nondescript, without suggestion or promise.

"Right or left, do you think?" Earl asked.

"I do not know. What is it you say?—I am just along for the ride? I am clueless?"

Earl pulled onto the dirt road and went back in the direction he'd come. He couldn't remember any other road leading off it, but if his directions were right, he'd already gone too far. The dried gumbo of the prairie, a powder fine as flour, rose in a cloud behind him, filling his mirrors with gray commotion. It leaked into the car, visible in the air, even though he had the fan going full blast so the air pressure would force it out. About a mile and a half down the road, he found the intersection he'd been looking for. From the direction he'd first come, it had been obscured by a few scraggly bushes, their leaves gray with dust. The stop sign that a reservation official had decided the intersection needed had been knocked over and was lying in the bushes, its metal pole bent, its letters pocked with .22 fire and shotgun pellets, so that the s was gone and the sign, facing the sky, said TOP in leprous-looking letters.

"Someone should fix that sign," Willi noted as Earl turned.

"Why? Maybe two cars a day go by on that road. And they raise so much dust they're visible two days before they get there, you know? Anyone who needs a stop sign there is too drunk to obey it anyway."

The Kills Many trailer house sat in a dry draw connected to Red Medicine Creek. Five cars squatted on cinder blocks and two-by-fours outside the trailer, their wheels removed. They had an ancient look about them, a sense of dignified and ceremonial purpose, and they were arrayed about the trailer like spokes emanating from a central hub. Pathways ran between them. They gave to the place a mysterious sense of quiet, of an order that might be ascertained if one were dedicated enough and thought long enough about it— that perhaps the sun rose between those cars at the solstices and that they traced like sensitive feelers the wobble of the orbiting earth. Earl and Willi coasted down the dirt track in silence, as if they were approaching an old shrine or set of ruins.

They were thirty yards from the trailer when dogs erupted from the cars—lean greyhounds that shot like living arrows out of the open windows, flew through the air, touched the ground, and flew again, arcing in and out of the grass, their ears back, in full run before they touched the ground, as if they knew no other way of moving. After them a wave of other dogs scrambled less gracefully out of the cars—blue heeler and pit bull mutts that scrabbled at the windows and fell down into the grass, their claws raking the paint. They bounded back up and followed the silent greyhounds, howling and barking, all of them headed straight toward Earl's car. In a moment he was driving through a sea of dog flesh, which parted before the car and closed behind it, the dogs in front of his windshield looking back to check the car's pace, the ones alongside threatening the tires with bared teeth. Earl gripped the steering wheel, afraid that if he changed speed or turned he'd hear the thump of tire against flesh. Like every other teenager in Twisted Tree, he'd played chicken with Bambi dozens of times, but he'd never had this many dogs surrounding his vehicle at once, and he wasn't sure any of them could get out of the way if he swerved. They'd run into another dog before they could avoid being struck.

Willi gaped. "I have never seen so many dogs," he said.

"A family's got to eat," Earl replied. "There's nothing like dog stew for protein. And nothing like old cars for raising those dogs in."

Willi's mouth gaped even wider before he realized Earl was joking. Earl stopped the car in front of the trailer house. The dogs gathered outside the doors of the car, milling, their rear ends moving back and forth so violently their feet slipped in the grass and dirt. The trailer looked abandoned, as if it had been placed here centuries ago, until it had weathered into the land and become a natural thing.

Earl opened his door a crack. The dogs closest to it backed away, their heads up, instead of coming closer and low to the ground—a good sign. He opened it further, and one of the mutts, whining insanely with desire, pressed its muzzle into the opening and, using its head as a wedge, forced the door open even though Earl pulled with all his strength to keep it shut. Scraping its neck and ribs against the door frame, its back feet kicking up spurts of grass and dirt while its front ones clawed badger-like at the floor mats, the dog forced its way onto Earl's lap, squeezing against the steering wheel, filling the car with its unadulterated dogginess, the old-cave smell of its breath. It stuck its face against Earl's as he swung his head to avoid it, and its claws dug into his thigh. The whole animal squirmed with pleasure.

"It is good that is a friendly dog," Willi said. "Or it would be eating you, I think."

Earl opened the door all the way, pushed the dog out, and stood up before it could crawl back onto his lap. He shut the door and started toward the trailer house, but dogs pushed against his legs and leapt up to put their paws on his chest. It was like trying to walk in a fast stream with boulders bumping in the current.

Then the door to the trailer house opened, and Ted Kills Many stepped out. He said nothing, just stood on the pallet propped on cinder blocks that served as a stoop and gazed at Earl, his black eyes expressionless, his mouth a straight line. Earl stopped moving, and at that moment one of the pit bull mutts leapt against his chest. He stumbled back, tripped over a dog behind him, flailed, and fell into the swarm of animals. For a frightening moment he thought his falling might become a signal for the entire pack to attack him.

Instead, the dogs were delighted. They licked him, thrust their muzzles into his crotch, raked him with their claws. When Earl tried to stand up, they knocked him down again, ignoring his cries that they stay down.

Then he heard what sounded at first like thunder, a deep guttural noise building to a crescendo and suddenly cracking at the end. Earl realized it was Ted.

"Baaaaack!" The sound rolled over the pack of dogs, stilling them. Every dog stopped moving, every head turned to the trailer house. Earl got to his feet in a world eerily still. The dogs didn't seem frightened or intimidated but merely attentive to the sound of Ted's voice, waiting to know what that voice wished them to do.

Ted lifted his hand to chest level, flicked his fingers backwards.

"Gwan now," he said in that same deep voice. The dogs waited a moment to be sure he meant it, then lifted their tails and trotted away, a few of them looking longingly back at Earl. In a few moments they'd all disappeared back into the cars or the tall grass around the trailer or the shade of the trees in the draw.

Willi got out of the car. "How did you do that?" he asked Ted.

From the pallet Ted looked at them without answering. Finally he said, "You two must be seriously lost."

"We came to talk to you," Earl replied.

"You came to talk to me." A sardonic smile lifted the corners of Ted's mouth. "You become Christers? Gonna save me from the error of my ways?"

Earl shook his head. "Nothing like that."

"Not? Too bad. Woulda been entertaining. 'Course you've been that already."

Ted leaned his shoulders against the door jamb of the trailer and crossed his arms. The wind blew a thick strand of his neck-length hair across his face. "I'm waiting," he said.

"We want to talk to only you, you know?" Earl said. "Is anyone else home?"

"A couple cousins. They're asleep."

Earl knew that Ted's parents were serious alcoholics. They drifted from bar to bar, city to city—Sioux Falls, Lincoln, Omaha, Pierre, Rapid City—staying with friends or relatives a few weeks or months, then moving on to another city, another set of drinking friends. They returned to the reservation only sporadically, after making one of their periodic joint resolutions to dry out, resolutions that lasted two or three months, after which they would find themselves going by a bar at Interior or Ruination or White River, and the urge to drink would come upon them both like a visitation, and whichever one of them was driving would pull into the parking lot, and they would climb from the car without a word, guilty and terribly relieved both, looking at each other with an understanding that passed for love. Later, after the fourth or fifth beer, they would speak of it with a kind of religious fervor to whomever would listen, how it had struck both of them at once and how each had known what the other was thinking. They would be awestruck by their compatibility, the attunement of their minds. "Of course," one or the other would always then say, "if we didn't think that way, maybe neither of us would be sitting here right now." And the other would lift a glass and reply, "I'll drink to that," and they would, and smear beery kisses across each other's faces, thankful they had each other to despise. It was the gift they gave each other—someone else besides themselves to despise—and it made them inseparable and gave to their relationship all the appearances and accouterments of love.

In the vacuum created by their absence, the upkeep and care of the family land had fallen to Ted. For two years after he was conceived, his parents had quit drinking, but when they started again they took their child with them, enrolling him in schools in whatever city they happened to find themselves—until, when Ted was twelve, he'd stood in the doorway of the trailer house and refused to go with them. He'd seen enough of the world. His parents, already in the car, looked at each other and, with their perfect, mutual understanding, decided without words that if he was old enough to refuse to come with them, he was old enough. Ted's father turned the ignition key. His mother lifted a hand just above the window frame, and they left Ted in the doorway of the house.

Ted had scavenged, or he had lived with his grandmother, or he had lived alone and with his grandmother alternately, or he had hunted for food. It depended on who was telling the story. In any case, he'd survived, developing an intermittent relationship with his parents and with the school system. At sixteen he'd dropped out of school altogether, at seventeen kicked his parents out of the house when they were drunk and told them not to return unless they were sober.

After claiming the house by the simple act of establishing rules of conduct in it, Ted decided to begin drinking himself. Having put it off for seventeen years, seeing in his parents all the reasons not to, he gave in finally to a sense of fatalism: If this was who he was, he might as well get on with it. He had the house and land; he might as well have the identity, too. He drank himself into unconsciousness the first time he drank and woke the next day to a sun too hot and a world too loud, and only one thing to do to seek coolness and silence.

Always, though, Ted kept the rule he'd made for the house. He wouldn't allow himself or anyone else to bring alcohol into the house or to stay there when drunk. Since he refused to travel, having seen as much of the world as he cared to before he was twelve, this rule served to limit how much and how often he drank. For within Ted, as strong as the need to drink, was the need to walk the family land, to sit in the shade of its trees, to see the deer that grazed its grasses and the moon rising over it.

Through gossip and conjecture, Earl was vaguely aware of all this. He thought of those cousins asleep inside Ted's house. The house was known as a place where anyone who wasn't drinking could come for a roof and for whatever food they could find. Even the reservation's numerous abandoned dogs seemed to know that Ted refused no guest.

"How about coming down by the car," Earl said. "In case your cousins aren't sleeping."

Ted snorted. "You playin some game with me?"

"We just have some serious stuff we want to ask you."

Ted's eyes glinted with derision and suspicion, though he remained leaning against the doorway, appearing nonchalant and indifferent.

"I got lost two times trying to find this place, you know?" Earl said. "All we have is one question for you. If you say no, we'll leave. We just don't want anyone else hearing the question."

Ted pushed himself away from the door jamb with a heave of his shoulders and stepped off the pallet, loose-limbed as if he were stepping off a dock into water. He came across the dog-trammeled yard, his tennis shoes leaving neat, oval imprints in the rakeage of claws. Leaves from some distant cottonwood blew past, yellow swirls in the air. Earl moved to the rear of the car, and Willi joined him there. Ted stopped four feet from them, hands in his pockets.

"You remember that party?" Earl asked. "Those horses I saw?"

"I might."

"We went down and looked at them. They're Magnus Yarborough's. They're being starved. We're going to steal them. We need a place to take them. Can we bring them here? That's all we want to know."

Earl said all this in a rush, not stopping and not explaining anything, and when he was done, Ted stared at him for several seconds, unmoving, his face impassive, unable to believe or quite disbelieve something so outrageous and direct.

"You're gonna steal Magnus Yarborough's horses," he finally said. "And you want to bring them here?"

Earl nodded.

"No one would look for them here, we think," Willi said. "And if they did, you could say you did not know anything. That they just appeared."

"You two are gonna steal horses."

"And Carson Fielding."

Earl shot Willi a warning glance. The less said the better. But it was too late. Ted saw the glance. "Carson Fielding," he said. "That horse trainer, enit?"

"Yeah. That horse trainer."

Earl's glance at Willi had convinced Ted he was being told the truth. His derisive air remained, but he couldn't keep genuine curiosity from his voice. "How'd he get involved with you two?"

Willi seemed willing to answer any question put to him. "I know him," he said. "I have from him some riding lessons taken. When we found the horses, we asked him what to do. Then we found out he had trained them."

Ted tilted his head and regarded Earl and Willi through narrowed eyes. "Stealing horses," he said. "You two remembering that's the kind of thing people go to prison for?"

"We don't plan to get caught."

"I bet you don't. This don't make sense. Why're you doin this?"

"They're starving, you know? Like I said."

"Lots a things starving. All over the world. You gonna save 'em all?"

"Just these horses."

"Yeah. Everybody wants to save something. Might as well be a Christer comin out here, giving me this shit. Save these horses and then go off to college and tell those white girls what a warrior you are."

Earl shriveled under the attack. His mind went blank. He felt himself growing hot as Ted's black eyes bored into him.

Then he heard Willi say, "Yes, the only reason I want to steal these horses is so I can go back to Germany and get the girls in bed. I have always thought stealing horses is the best way to do that. In Germany I can never any action with the girls get because there are not any horses to steal. But here is nothing but steal horses, hop in bed, steal horses, hop in bed. But if you will not help us with those girls, we will have to find another way. Maybe we will try lying to them. Let's go, Earl."

Willi walked to the passenger door of the car, opened it, got in, slammed the door. Earl and Ted were both so surprised they stared at him, then at each other.

"He's right, you know?" Earl said. "We'll have to lie."

He turned to go. But Ted's voice, quieter now behind him, stopped him. "Walks Alone. Wait."

Earl turned back to him. Ted turned both hands outward at his sides, briefly lifting and dropping them. "You really ain't shittin me, are you?" he said.

Earl just looked at him. *The Aintshittin Indian,* he thought, *pauses on his way back to his vehicle.* "We just want to hide them for a while," he finally said. "Until we can think of something else. You've got land. And not too many tourists out here, you know?"

Willi opened the car door and stood up out of it, listening. A greyhound, thin as a snake, wandered out of the grass, thrust its nose into Ted's hand hanging at his side, then flopped down, emitting a small grunt of satisfaction.

"We figure with the land out here being trust land, all cut up, if someone did happen to find them out here, you could just say they must've come from somewhere else. That you didn't even know they were on your land, you know? But there could still be trouble for you. So if you don't want to do it, we'll think of something else, I guess."

"Trouble? I don't know—you and me might be cell mates."

Ted smiled, a lock of hair falling over one of his eyes. He jerked his head to clear his vision, then looked back to Earl, still smiling.

"That would make the time just fly," Earl said.

"They're Magnus Yarborough's horses?"

Earl nodded.

"Rich sonofabitch. Yeah, you can bring 'em here."

Earl and Willi exchanged glances over the hood of the car.

"Quite an outlaw gang you got, enit?" Ted said. "The Apple, the Kraut, and the Cowboy."

But he grinned so widely that Earl couldn't take offense, and Willi was merely baffled. At that moment a commotion began at the abandoned car furthest from them. The door creaked slowly open, and a bare foot emerged, followed by a foot wearing a dirty white tennis shoe. These two feet found the ground, patted it tentatively, settled themselves. Then from the dark interior of the car, a figure unfolded itself, standing on those feet—a tall Indian, gaunt and raggedy, wearing a tattered, red Western shirt and blue jeans.

He hunched himself up from the open door, stood, wavered a moment, then reached back inside the door and emerged with a misshapen felt cowboy hat which he placed carefully on his head, adjusting the hat several times until it sat at the proper angle. Then he dropped his hands and fumbled with his fly.

Glancing around while finding his zipper, the tall Indian saw Ted and Earl and Willi watching. He nodded in their direction, unperturbed. Ted nodded back. The tall Indian leaned back against the car and peed into the grass. In the bright sun the stream of urine looked like a curved, golden wire attached to his groin.

"There you go," Ted said. "The reservation Golden Arches. All we need 's a marketing campaign."

The man finished his business, zipped himself up, then fished in his shirt pocket, pulled out a pack of cigarettes, shook one out, stuck it in his mouth, replaced the pack, snapped shut the pearl snap on the Western shirt, reached into his pants pocket, pulled out a lighter, lit the cigarette, dragged deeply, exhaled a cloud of smoke, replaced the lighter, leaned back more comfortably against the car, lifted the cigarette to his mouth again. A dog crawled out of the car door he'd opened, sniffed the grass where he'd urinated, lifted its leg in the same spot, then trotted away.

"Uncle Johnny," Ted said. "He don't like sleeping in the house."

"Why is that?" Willi asked.

"Too far to the bathroom."

Willi and Earl stared at him, then laughed.

"S' truth," Ted said.

Then he said, "Tell you what. Some of this land"—he nodded backwards—"ain't visible from any road. No one'd ever find those horses on it. You can bring 'em here. But I got one condition."

"What's that?"

"You let me help steal 'em."

Earl flashed a warning look to Willi. The more people involved, the more likely something would go wrong. And he wasn't sure he trusted Ted in something like what they were planning. Ted was sober right now, but would he be sober when the time came? Earl imagined how difficult Ted could make things if he came along drunk.

Ted saw the look Earl gave Willi, and when Earl looked back at Ted, those dark, sardonic eyes were gazing at him.

"Don't worry, Walks Alone," he said. "I got this belief. Drinking and stealing don't mix. Don't you think if I'm gonna risk getting arrested for stealing horses, I at least got the right to steal 'em?"

Earl glanced at Willi again. Willi shrugged. "That is a point," he said.

Goat Man Forms

~~~~~~

THEY CAME BY THEIR SEPARATE WAYS to the Donaldson's Foods parking lot when light was waning. They stood in silent contemplation of that waning. At first they stood apart from each other, as if they had just happened to come here for individual and private reasons, but Willi gathered them together, speaking first to Earl, then walking with Earl to where Carson stood, and the three of them finally nodding to Ted, who pretended at first not to see them, flipping his hair out of his eyes with a jerk of his head and staring out of the parking lot at two stray dogs trotting down the street. But when the dogs disappeared, Ted stuck his hands in his pockets and ambled over to the group. He stopped a little apart from the others, as if he were content in his own isolated business, which just happened to bring him near. But Willi thought to introduce him to Carson, and Ted stepped forward to shake hands, and then no one could think of anything to say. Shadows crept up the yellowed stucco wall of the grocery store, and light from inside began to form faint rectangles on the asphalt.

They'd thought it would be too obvious if they all drove to the lake and parked. If someone recognized their vehicles and connected it to the horses' disappearance, it would make, as Earl had said, "Greggy Longwell's job a bit too easy, you know?" But now they felt conspicuous, standing in a parking lot, two Indians and two white guys in a group, doing nothing. Luckily, no one was there to see them. So they were dismayed when Mrs. Germain's ancient Continental heaved off the street, shocks banging and springs creaking as it swung over the slope into the parking lot. It coughed past them, missing on one cylinder. They watched as the door swung slowly open and Mrs. Germain's immense form emerged, rising ponderously and blowing hard from the effort. She smoothed her dress and shut the door and walked toward the store, her skirt immediately hiking up her large butt, defying gravity and all the grasping efforts of her hands to control it. They watched as the automatic door hesitated when she reached it, as if deciding whether or not to allow her passage, and then jerked and hissed and opened. They saw her, through the plate glass windows, seek and find a cart, place her purse in the upper cage, and disappear into the lighted aisles.

From where they loitered they could see the last light glowing on the tan tops of the hills above Lostman's Lake, and they could see, in contrast, the deep shadows of draws angling down those hills. To the southwest the earth turned into what looked against the darkening sky like high and ancient pueblos sheared off and sharpened by wind and rain: the Badlands, where stone skeletons rose from the land year after year, a rebirth by erosion, an alphabet of bone that, read rightly, told a story stretching back to the endless water of the Bearpaw Sea. In the Badlands the earth became an organ moaning musically and incessantly when the wind was right, a music that Norm had told Earl was a music of spirits and of the earth singing to itself.

The shadows of the hills crept into the streets of Twisted Tree, into the parking lot, struck the toes of their boots, and the sun was gone. The streetlight at the edge of the parking lot began a hesitant, static flickering, buzzing with a sound like angry insects. Mrs. Germain reappeared in the windows of the store. Then again the doors started and struggled, and she emerged, pushing a grocery cart before her. The cart, like her skirt, had a mind of its own, breaking from her line of travel. She tacked her way back and forth to the rusted Continental, the cart shooting right or left every time she reached back a hand to pull her skirt down over her thick thighs. She talked quietly to herself and glanced up once at the group of young men standing near Carson's pickup, then immediately looked away, her eyes veering off to erase and cancel the vision. She whoaed the cart near the trunk of her car, hauling back on the red plastic bar with all her tremendous weight. Then she reached back with both hands to tug her skirt firmly and evenly down. She bent at the waist, and the skirt hiked back up. She inserted a key in the trunk lid, opened it, reached into the cart, and methodically, one by one, transposed the white plastic bags from it into the gaping maw of the trunk. Finished, she shut the lid and turned and stared at the cart corral with its red sign and white letters asking customers to please place their carts within it. Mrs. Germain read this request, then bowed her head toward it, repentant and respectful, and gave the cart a little shove in its direction. The cart careened and wobbled and stopped in the middle of a driving lane. Mrs. Germain gazed at it reproachfully, as if she would stare it into movement. Then she got in her car and drove away. The abandoned cart glowed palely blue in the new, artificial light, listing on a bad wheel.

"There's a sad thing," Carson said.

It was the first any of them had spoken since Ted and Carson had said hello.

"What's that?" Earl asked.

"A grocery cart like that sitting in the middle of a parking lot. 'Bout the saddest sight in the world."

Darkness deepened. The wires of the cart glowed more intensely in the bluish light until it seemed a cage of light, alone in emptiness, with no thing it could hold.

"When do we go, then?" Willi finally asked.

They all looked at him as if they didn't understand the question, as if they'd gathered here merely to watch the strange equation between light and dark work itself out.

But Carson replied, "Any time. It's dark enough."

Then they milled for a moment like baffled animals, or like dancers seeking the beat, hesitant in their first stepping.

"Who's driving?" Earl asked.

"I gotta take the pickup," Carson said.

"We're gonna end up at my place anyway," Ted said. "I might as well drive, too."

Then it was a matter of deciding who would go with whom, more shuffling and hesitancy, until Carson said, "I need someone to hook up the horse trailer for me. Earl, why 'n't you come with me?"

It was a relief that the question of pairing could be decided on lines of competency, all of them assuming Willi knew nothing of trailers and ball hitches.

CARSON AND EARL LEFT, and Willi followed Ted across the parking lot to his car. In spite of what he'd told Earl, he didn't actually know Ted very well and wasn't sure what to say to him. At the parties he'd attended, he'd heard things about Ted from various people but had spoken little with him personally. Ted seemed to regard Willi as he regarded most people, as an object of sardonic humor. Willi settled into the passenger seat of Ted's car, trying to think of something to break the silence. His seat belt was stuck. He jerked on it several times, then gave up. Ted didn't even reach for his. Ted started the engine and flicked on the headlights. A static sizzling, like an angry insect, came and went under the dashboard, and a flickering bluish light illuminated the upholstery and sculpted weird shadows out of the dark interior. Ted's car was a mess—an Italian's car, Willi thought, not a German's—full of cans and bottles, various tools and automotive belts, scraps of paper. Willi put his feet down carefully, guiding them by the intermittent flashes from under the dashboard.

"What is that flashing?" he asked as Ted pulled out of the parking lot.

Ted glanced down. "Oh, that," he said. "Got a bad connection."

"Is it something you can fix?"

"I suppose. The car runs."

As Ted left town and headed down the highway into the moonless prairie, Willi noticed that the headlights dimmed when the spark sizzled and brightened when it stopped, so that the car moved forward toward a darkness that would suddenly suck itself into the windshield, then be pushed weakly back again. The darkness was so thick it seemed to Willi as solid as a wall they were constantly on the verge of running into, but Ted never changed speed or seemed to notice. Glancing at him, Willi saw his face in profile, chiseled from shadow by the small arc and suspended against the black, opaque plane of the window. The car creaked and rattled, and the muffler banged. Willi thought of a comment an Indian friend had made outside the school one afternoon, when a student with a bad muffler had rent the air, gunning his engine. Willi had jumped, and the friend had laughed. "On the rez," he'd said, "even the mufflers are secondhand."

"You have your own personal lightning," he said to Ted.

Ted's face turned to him, eyes all dark hollowness, skin along his cheekbones glowing, his hair, in the faint electric light, a sheen of blue, like those odd birds with the odd names here, grackles, who strutted on lawns in the summer, stiff and jerky, bending their necks so that the sun changed the black there into green and blue.

"Lightning?" Ted asked.

"The Thunder Beings are in your car. The Wakinyan."

"The Wakinyan," Ted said. "In my car."

"Maybe."

"Hell. I thought I had a bad wire."

The connection sizzled, the headlights dimmed to almost nothing, the wall of darkness outside rushed toward them. Willi braced himself for a collision, even though he knew it was only darkness. Then the headlights sputtered, glowed, forced the darkness back again.

"Makes driving more interesting," Ted said.

Willi was a bit embarrassed by his reaction. He removed his hand from the dashboard, but he wished the car had a seat belt. "Yes," he said. "It is boring to always see where you are going."

Ted smiled, the first time that evening. "Ain't it, though," he said.

In front of them Carson signaled a left turn. He'd parked his horse trailer up the hill behind The Church of Cars, as Willi thought of it.

"Think we oughta follow him?" Ted asked.

"I think we should go on. They will meet us at the lake."

Ted drove past the gravel driveway to the church. Carson's taillights were weaving slowly up the hill. Then he shut his lights off and vanished. Willi craned his neck as Ted drove on, imagining Carson creeping up the road in the dark. They had chosen this night because there was no moon, and Willi could see nothing at all of Carson's pickup.

"So," Ted said, "what do you think of reservation life?"

Willi was surprised to find Ted initiating conversation. "I have learned a lot," he said. "It has been interesting."

"Lot a Germans interested in Indians." Ted made the comment as a statement, not a question.

"Yes. There are *Indianer* clubs."

Willi stopped, unsure how much he should say, but it was too late. Ted glanced at him, curious. "*Indianer* clubs? What's that?"

"People live like Indians. They get together and have powwows. They live in tipis. They sing Indian music. There are people who belong to drum groups. And do beadwork and tan hides. They try to live like Indians."

"That right? A bunch of Germans whose hobby is bein Indian?"

"Sort of. But it is not just a hobby. It is how they live, too. Even when they are not at a powwow, they try to live like the Indians lived. With respect for the earth and . . ." Willi stopped, unsure how Ted would take all this. "Even their religion," he finished.

"You belong to one a them clubs?"

Willi was uncertain about admitting that he did, but he couldn't lie. "Yes," he said. "I have learned to speak Lakota, and . . ."

He stopped again. Ted was gazing at him, a small smile on his face, the kind of smile Willi had seen him direct at people right before he made a sardonic comment. Willi's pride in his knowledge of Lakota culture dwindled under Ted's gaze. Ted finally turned back to the road without saying anything. The headlights dimmed and brightened, counterpoint to the blue and garish brightening and dimming inside the car. Ted pulled into the gravel drive to Antelope Park. Small stones cast long shadows down the headlights' beams, then sucked those shadows back into themselves as the car moved on. Ted parked the car under the cottonwoods, far back from the road. It was the middle of the week. The park was abandoned. They walked back up the track toward the highway and the lake on the other side of it.

"Those *Indianer* clubs," Ted said. "I never heard of them before. I belong to a secret Lakota society that is something like that."

Willi's curiosity was piqued. He knew of many Lakota societies and groups but couldn't think which one Ted was referring to. "You do? What is it?"

"Not many people know about it. It's one of the most secret and powerful societies on the rez."

"What do you do?"

Ted flipped hair out of his eyes. "I don't know. Maybe I shouldn't be tellin you this stuff."

Willi said nothing. He was intensely curious but knew better than to press. They started to climb the slope up to the highway. "Ah, hell," Ted said. "I guess you can know. We get together and dance polkas. We got accordions. We wear those leather pants and drink beer out've those big glasses, what're they called, steins? It's called the Germaner Society. We're hobby Germans."

He grinned at Willi. Willi was abashed and fell a few steps back, but Ted called back from the middle of the highway, "You oughta see what the Frencher Club does!"

CARSON'S PICKUP, PULLING THE HORSE TRAILER, passed by on the highway. He parked it further down the road, pulling into a field approach and hiding it behind a hill. They would have to walk the horses down from the lake and across the highway and load them behind the hill. They couldn't be sure someone might not chance by if they loaded them on public land, either at the lake or in Antelope Park. Willi and Ted stood near the lake and waited, and five minutes later they heard footsteps, and then Carson and Earl appeared out of the darkness. Without a word all four of them turned up the hill toward Magnus Yarborough's land.

ORLANDO HAD TRIED TO ESCAPE. He stood apart from the other two horses, his head bowed far down. In the darkness, it wasn't until they were right next to him that they saw the gashes across his neck and withers, the dark blood soaked into his hair, running down his legs, staining the ground. "Oh, shit," Carson said when he realized what had happened. "Goddamn. Goddamn." He knelt before the horse and reached out and touched the wounds. The other three were muted by his sorrow, and they stood in a close group, watching him.

"You've always been a stupid sonofabitch," he said quietly. "But I never thought you was this stupid and ornery. Jesus Christ, horse, just because you're starving don' mean you got to be a idiot. That's barbwire you was tryin a go through. You know what barbwire is?"

The words were a quiet chant, while Carson's hands touched every wound and came away bloody. Earl had never heard a speech more full of grief.

Carson finally stood. "He's gonna be OK," he said. "He's cut pretty bad, but nothin to the bone. I swear, though, he'd kill himself. Let's get them out of here."

He reached into his back pocket, pulled out a pair of pliers, and opened and closed it once. The metallic sound was sharp as breaking ice. He strode to the fence, reached for the top wire, and put the cutting jaws of the pliers on it. At that moment Earl understood what Norm meant by the difference between stealing and robbing.

"Wait," he called. "Don't cut it yet."

Carson's shoulders slumped. He dropped the pliers to his side and turned slowly to face Earl. "You got somethin against cuttin wire?" he asked. "What is it this time?"

Earl was so excited he could hardly talk. "No," he said. "I mean, yes. I mean, we got to make them fly, you know? We got to give them wings."

The other three stared at him. "Jesus," Carson said. "First time I decide to be a crook, I choose a loony for a partner. What the hell are you talkin about?"

But Earl could see it. He could map the trajectory and the angle, and in his mind he saw the horses rising up in curving lines, leaving green, phosphorescent traces in the air, nearing the fence as if it were a y-axis, rising and nearing and rising and nearing. He could almost find the equation. Except that in calculus it was always an infinite nearing. The lines never touched. They just became infinitely closer forever. For a moment Earl was transfixed, thinking about it.

They were going to steal these horses. Make them fly away. Break the rules of physics, even the rules of math.

"We'll pull the staples, you know?" he said. "Take the fence apart. Then we'll cover all the tracks and put the fence back together. Just like it was. So no one can even see it was taken down. That's what we gotta do."

"What's the point a that?" Carson asked. "All we want a do is get 'em outta here. We don't care if anyone knows they been taken. Long 's they don't know it was us did it."

As Earl talked, a slow smile had started on Ted's face, and he was looking at Earl now with disbelief and admiration.

"Damn, Walks Alone," he said. "That's a damn good idea. That's just what we gotta do."

"How is that a good idea?" Carson asked. "The longer we're up here, the more likely someone's gonna spot us. We do what you're talkin about, we'll have to go back to my pickup and get tools. An a tarp to wipe away tracks. And then take time puttin the fence back together. And for what? It sounds like a pisspoor idea to me."

But Earl imagined Greggy Longwell coming up here and staring at the empty pen, its gateless configuration, its smooth and trackless surface. Earl imagined Greggy's moment of doubt, when in spite of his rank confidence in himself and his view of things, he wouldn't be quite sure the horses had been taken by human hands. That tiny flame of panic, too low to be acknowledged. He would pretend to himself that he just had a crime to solve, and he would pretend that he even had an idea who had committed it. But—he might not even know it—as his eyes darted around this empty place, he would be looking for evidence that might indicate not *who* had taken the horses, but *what*. Evidence of a natural disappearance. And he would find none. Would find nothing at all to fulfill his need that the world be as he believed it to be. That's what Norm had been talking about: that need. Greggy would walk from this pen troubled, unfulfilled, and discontent, with nothing here to suggest that humans rather than aliens took the animals. Nothing to suggest that horses can't grow wings. And his sleep would be disturbed by dreams of an empty pen that cannot by any means be empty. He would wake troubled and insecure and looking to see that the things of the world operated as he thought they did, and even the rising of the sun would become suspect to him.

Ted was grinning at Carson and shaking his head over his objections. "No, man," he said. "It's what we gotta do. It is. We do it, old Magnus Yarborough won't know if his head or his ass is sittin on his shoulders."

"Willi," Carson said, "you got 'n opinion here? You gonna help me out?"

Willi thought of the Karl May books he'd read, how he'd occupied his youth with them—all those scenes where Old Shatterhand and Winnetou had covered their tracks to avoid being followed, and how baffled their enemies had always been. Willi had delighted in those scenes, and though he knew better than to think those books were real, something of their excitement and silliness captivated him now. He had read those books before he had learned of his grandfather and grandmother, when tragedy in his life was so light a thing as death on the autobahn—not serious enough for a child to even think about. Back then, Old Shatterhand's exploits and cunning, and Winnetou's wisdom, had been enough to explain and clarify the world.

For a moment Willi wanted to laugh, delighted at the idea that he'd come to America, as Karl May's fictional Old Shatterhand had, and that he could do in real life what Old Shatterhand had only done on the page. But the moment he thought this, a deep grief filled him, for he remembered his grandmother again. He thought of her white cockatoo. He thought of the bird escaping its cage in the night, some birdish cunning his grandmother had never anticipated working in its brain. He thought of it flying away through the windows she in her confidence had left open, so that she rose in the morning to a house made lonely by the absence of shrieking, the absence of claws scraping metal. A house changed. A radical transformation.

Willi imagined his grandmother standing before that empty cage, and it seemed to him it would be fitting if there she wept. If there, at last, she sorrowed. And he thought she might. The cockatoo was the last thing she had thought to fix to herself. The last thing she had thought to make dream her dream. And if it fled that dream and left her, at last, alone with it?

She was already dead. She had died before Willi came to America. He had attended her funeral. Yet it seemed unreal to him. It seemed that the bird might, in fact, have flown, and that she might yet weep, her heart might yet break if that final cage of her invention stood empty. More than anything, Willi wanted that weeping. Wanted that heart's breaking. Cruelty and retribution and kindness: all of them. He wanted all of them.

Carson was waiting for an answer.

"I think we need our tracks to cover anyway," Willi said. "This Mr. Longwell could match our shoes, I think, with all this dust. So we have to get a cloth from the pickup anyway for that. And then I suppose we could get tools, too. To do what Earl says."

"All three a you want a take this fence apart?" Carson asked.

"Think about it," Earl said. "If we do it and Longwell comes up here, the more he looks, the more it's gonna raise some questions, you know? Like why did Magnus Yarborough build a pen without a gate in the first place? If it's obvious how they got out, Longwell might not even notice that."

"Hadn't thought a that. Hell. Let's climb back over this sonfoabitch and get those tools."

They turned toward the lake and the parked pickup. Over the prairie, in the direction of the Badlands, in a dark draw, leaves stirred in a wind, in a place where no wind should find its way. Stirred and stirred. Whirled. The wind grew stronger, whirled harder. Rose. A shape formed out of the whirl and emerged from the draw and stood on the prairie. Starlight glittered on horn. Or something like it. Goatish nostrils, or something like them, nostrils made of wind and air, sniffed the air and wind.

Part Four

GOAT MAN

^^^^^^

Sightings

~~~~~

T RACKS EVERYWHERE. A swarm of stories.

A half-dozen people drinking beer around a campfire on a table of land near the Badlands hear a sound of wind approaching. Out of the darkness and into the edge of light comes a rushing thing, tall as a dust devil, darker than night itself, a blackness inside the blackness, with footsteps like thunder and breath like burning grass. The telltale glittering horns. Obsidian eyes. Even the campfire is cowed, bows down its flames, sinks into its coals. Then the thing veers off and is heard whoofing and grunting away. After drinking two more bottles of courage, two men fumble to their feet with a flashlight. They find deep indentations in the hard-baked clay, like cloven hooves the size of hubcaps.

Two men are poaching deer, waiting at the top of a draw for the animals to make their way to a spot where the draw widens and brush thins. One of the men is lifting a beer to his lips when he stops. The other, seeing his widened eyes, looks into the draw and meets the eyes of Goat Man, golden eyes this time, gazing up at him, horns swept back over a woolly head, legs thick and corded as tree trunks, mossy hair tufted around the hooves. The legs bend, the muscles bunch beneath the hair like wet rope twisted tight. Then up the hill Goat Man bounds. *Like he's on the moon, man. Like he don't even* know *what gravity is.* The man with the rifle raises it and presses the trigger, but forgets to take the safety off. Such silence. And in it, the clicking sound of hard hooves striking rock. And then nothing. A cedar tree. A boulder. An ordinary draw. The men wait a half hour, finishing their beer. They descend the draw, find a tuft of dirty hair, strands as long as a young girl's, caught in the needles of a cedar. And the imprint of a foot depressed into a platform of solid rock.

The stories sweep back and forth across the reservation. They leave the reservation and return. Arling Frederickson, having coffee at the Windmill Truck Stop in Rapid, brings back to Twisted Tree the tale of horses that have disappeared from a pasture where there was no break in the fence, no wires cut, no broken or bent fence posts, no tracks of tire or human or horse.

"Aliens," one man said.

"Some government thing," said another.

"Who knows?" a third concluded.

In Twisted Tree the hearers of Arling's tale say, "Goat Man."

And "Goat Man" say the hearers of all the tales in all the double-wides and single-wides and project houses and stick-builts and traditional tipis and abandoned cars throughout the reservation.

And "Bo*shit*," says Greggy Longwell. Fingering his coffee cup. Staring at the steam.

Trying to Go Blind

~~~~~

THROUGH THE DARK GLASS of the welding helmet, the arc was a far-off, irregular sun sputtering alone in blackness. Carson ran the bead along the Farmhand's cracked brace, pushing the rod into the metal as the arc melted it away, spraying comets of slag. As the rod shortened, the arc rose toward Carson's gloves until there were only a couple of inches remaining. Carson jerked the rod up. The arc gasped hollowly, spreading for a moment like a corona in the gap between metal and rod. Carson flipped up the helmet, gazed at the red heat in the metal slowly turning to orange and then a dull gray, the slag ridged like some ancient shell. Still kneeling on the gravel outside the Quonset, he turned around to snap the welder off and found a pair of black boots behind him, rising into sharply creased tan pants.

Startled, he paused with his hand on the welder's switch. *So,* he thought. *He knows they're gone.*

He clunked the switch down and stood, laying the wand on top of the welder. "Howdy, Greggy," he said. He removed the helmet and set it down next to the wand.

Greggy nodded. "Carson."

Carson pulled off the heavy gloves, laid them next to the helmet. "How long you been standin here?"

"Just a minute."

"You been watchin that arc? You tryin a go blind?"

"Yep. Gonna start a new career. Reffing high school basketball games."

"You lose someone?"

A few years back the county commissioners had decided to save money by making Greggy wash his own car. In response to this insult to his professional dignity, Greggy refused to chase suspects onto gravel roads where he would dirty his vehicle, unless the suspect had insulted him more than the commissioners had. Anyone committing a minor traffic violation—speeding, crossing the center line—who saw Greggy's lights in his rearview mirror and who made it to a gravel road before Greggy identified him was probably safe from pursuit, as long as he made it to the gravel politely. He had to pretend not to have noticed the flashing rack in his mirror, keep his speed consistent and use his turn signal, give the impression of actually having a destination somewhere down that gravel. If he betrayed in the least his intention to lose Greggy, he was done for. Greggy would dog to hell anyone who indicated he thought he could drive faster or better, and Greggy, when challenged, was inescapable, a driver, for all his seeming lethargy, of prodigious skill and tenacity, and absolutely fearless. The sight of his flashing lights flying over a hill in the darkness, skewed at some impossible angle to his direction of travel, was something almost everyone who lived in the county had seen.

"Nah," Greggy answered Carson. "Didn't lose nobody."

"Thought maybe someone you was chasin turned inna our place."

It had been a week and a half since they'd taken the horses out of the small pasture behind the lake, repaired the fence, dragged a tarp through the dust to hide all tracks, and then walked the horses down in the moonless dark to the waiting trailer parked across the highway. Ted had gone back to Antelope Park for his car, and then Carson had followed him, taking deserted gravel roads, passing only two vehicles during the trip out to Ted's place. Out of sight of the trailer house, they had unloaded the horses. The animals had immediately begun grazing, their front legs scissored far apart to keep their muzzles low, their heads never rising from the grass.

"Seems too easy, you know?" Earl said.

"Easy so far, maybe."

"Worst of it's over.

"Who knows?"

"Hey, what's likely to happen now?"

"It is what is not likely that always makes the trouble."

Now Carson wondered what Greggy had discovered. If he was here because Magnus had found the horses gone and called him, what had Magnus told him? How had Magnus explained that pen behind the lake?

"I'm lookin for some horses," Greggy said.

"You takin up ridin? Or you mean you're lookin for some particular horses?"

"Stole horses."

"Stole horses. So why're you here?"

"Shit, Carson. It ain't my idea. Magnus Yarborough got some horses stole. He says I need a talk to you about it."

"Talk to me? I'm a horse trainer, not a horse detective."

Greggy took off his hat, brushed back his hair, put the hat back on. "Like I say, it ain't my idea. Just doin my job. Trackin down leads, even if in my opinion they ain't worth shit. Magnus seems to got a bur up his butt about you. I ain't here askin for advice. I'm here seein if them horses are on your ranch."

"Magnus thinks I stole his horses?"

Greggy tipped one shoulder up, spread his hands. "Says there's bad blood between him and you. Says you trained them horses and got to thinkin they was yours an not his. Says you threatened to do somethin about it. Says he thinks what you did was take 'em."

"I don't like Magnus Yarborough none. That's true. But I ain't in the habit a stealin horses I train. Hard on my reputation."

"Look." Greggy gazed around at the ranch site. "I know damn well you didn't take no horses. What you and Magnus got against each other, I don't need a know unless I got more suspicions than I got right now. I just gotta do what I gotta do."

"Magnus tell you how to do your job?"

Greggy's jaw hardened. He sucked his teeth, a single, quick, fish-like sound, the corner of his mouth jerking upward.

"No, he don't. But I ain't a idiot. Guy like that can make trouble for me. There's doin my job, an there's appearin to do my job. Right now, I'm appearin to do it."

"Well, hell then. You wanta appear to look around here, go ahead. Just shut the gates behind you."

"I appreciate that. I'll peek into a pasture or two, just so I can say I did."

"Where was I supposed to have stole these horses from, anyway?"

"Says they were in a pasture about a half-mile from his house."

It took Carson a moment to absorb this. Lostman's Lake was nowhere near Magnus's house. So Magnus had found the horses gone and then invented a lie. Hoping Greggy would find them on Carson's ranch, he'd misdirected Greggy. If Greggy found them, Magnus could dismantle the fence above the lake before Greggy got a warrant to prove or disprove Carson's story, and when Greggy went up behind Lostman's Lake, he'd find nothing but a patch of trampled grass, or maybe not even that. Magnus might take a disc harrow up there, claim he was going to seed it, and so hide all evidence. Pretty shrewd, Carson thought. There was no reason for Magnus to believe Carson had a hand in taking the horses, but he'd gambled on the possibility while manipulating the story to protect himself. Pulling levers, hoping for the reels to align.

Greggy took several steps toward his car, then stopped and turned back. "Mind if I ask you something?"

"Go ahead."

"You have a problem with the way Magnus treated them animals you was training?"

Interesting, Carson thought. New territory now. Something going on that Magnus hadn't thought about and didn't control. Greggy doing his job while appearing to do his job. Why would Greggy ask the question? And how to answer it? Magnus hadn't mistreated the horses while Carson had worked with them.

"I don't like the way Yarborough treats a lot of things," he said. "Including them horses."

Greggy gazed at him. "That right?"

Carson thought he might have revealed more than he wanted to. As Greggy had just said himself, he was no idiot.

"Why you asking?" Carson wanted to make the sheriff talk. He wasn't sure what question might emerge from Greggy's mouth right now if he were allowed to ask one. Odd, though: Was he protecting Rebecca or endangering her by directing the sheriff away from Magnus's treatment of her? He didn't know. For the moment he had to take her at her word.

Greggy sucked his teeth again, jerked his head in a small, dismissive gesture.

"I got my own suspect I think stole them horses," he said. "Indian kid. Talked to me a while back. Claimed some horses was bein harmed. Claimed they was on Yarborough's land, but not where Yarborough says they was. Kid says they was bein starved. You think Yarborough'd starve horses?"

Carson felt himself on slippery ground. By being too sure in his answer, he could give away his own involvement, reveal too much. At the same time, it wouldn't hurt to reinforce any suspicions Greggy might have about Magnus Yarborough.

"Yarborough's a curious one," Carson said. "You don't know what he'd do."

"That right?" Again, that gaze.

Carson shrugged.

"A funny thing," Greggy said. "You been hearin them stories about some horses lifted right out've a pasture? Goat Man shit? How you suppose that kind a thing gets started? And then I get this report about stole horses. Don't know what to make a that."

"Guess I ain't heard them stories."

"You ain't, huh? You need a get out more. Anyway, I guess I done enough lookin to satisfy appearances here. I need a go talk to the real suspect. Maybe he has an idea."

Beadwork

∧∧∧∧∧

CARSON WATCHED GREGGY LEAVE, then called Earl and warned him. "He's fishin," he said. "He don' know a thing. If he did, he wouldna come out and seen me, no matter what Yarborough told him. He's got suspicions, but that don' mean nothin."

"But what if he asks where I was that night? He could find out I wasn't home, you know?"

"What night? It's been a week an a half. He don't know when them horses disappeared. It ain't like Yarborough's been up there every day checkin on 'em."

"I suppose."

"Look, Longwell don't even know where those horses disappeared from. Yarborough told him someplace different."

"But I told him right."

"None a that's gonna matter. Longwell don't know anything unless we tell him. All you gotta do is, if he asks you a question, you ask one back. Make him be specific. He won't be able to be. Long 's you do that, you'll be OK."

"How do you think Magnus Yarborough found out? Maybe he does know when they disappeared."

"He doesn't. Wouldna taken Longwell this much time to get goin if he'd got a report right away. Truth is, I can't see Yarborough visiting them horses at all. Unless he went up to see if they'd died yet. Could be just bad luck anyone found out at all."

"I hope so."

"Longwell said somethin odd. You been hearin stories about some Goat Man stealin horses?"

There was a pause on the line. Then Earl said, "Some."

"Who the hell's Goat Man?"

"We talk about him, you know? He's, I don't know. Not real, really. Or maybe he is, kind of. It's hard to explain. He's like half-goat and half-man."

"Somethin like Bigfoot?"

"Kind of. But not, too."

"How'd that get started? Weren't no wild goats out here. Why would the rez have a goat man? Seems like a deer man or a buffalo man'd make more sense."

"Maybe he doesn't want to make sense."

"Well, it's another strange thing. Longwell was wonderin how them stories got started before he ever got a report on these horses. You think that's coincidence?"

"Maybe. Or maybe Goat Man saw us taking those horses and started the stories himself."

"Maybe we should ask him next time we see him."

"He doesn't like being asked questions."

GREGGY VISITED EARL just as Carson said he would—came within an hour of Carson's call, and Earl was thankful for that call when he saw Greggy's police cruiser pull off the highway and come down the driveway, through the intersecting shadow web of the fall trees, yellow leaves rising behind Greggy's car or loping alongside the wheels for a moment, then settling. Earl had been waiting outside and met him in the driveway. They stood in the leaves, and Greggy demanded to know where Earl had been on the night the horses were taken, but Earl followed Carson's advice and asked what night Greggy meant. Greggy tried to intimidate him as he had in his office, but Earl was on his own land now and prepared, and he refused to give the sheriff anything. A wind arose. Leaves swirled past their feet in a yellow current, coming out from the trees and sweeping over the ground, a stream of leaves rustling and scraping, so many and so loud that Earl had to raise his voice when he talked. Greggy switched tactics and asked Earl to say again where he had found the horses he had reported. Earl told him he had nothing new to add to the report he'd given, that it had been complete and the answers to Greggy's questions were in it. The wind blew harder, and the stream of leaves became a river rising up from the ground, sweeping over their shoes, then clutching at their pants cuffs, beating against their shirts. Shouting. Raving. Howling and chattering. Earl was standing with his back to the wind and didn't pay much attention, but Greggy became restless. The leaves rose higher, in gusts and starts, rushed past Earl's head and at Greggy's face, brittle claws scraping at his eyes until he could no longer stare Earl down, and as Greggy's glance shifted to the ground, Earl felt himself growing taller, more confident, buoyed by the wind at his back, his voice rising above the commotion, until he became certain that Greggy would get nothing useful out of him.

"Damn!" Greggy finally exclaimed. "You got ignorance down to a art, don't you? Don't know why I bothered to come out here. And don't you ever rake this place?"

"No," Earl said. "We don't."

Greggy turned his back on the wind and went to his car and slammed the door against it. Leaves pulverized themselves against his window like water breaking into bright droplets, a mist of leaves streaming past the car, and Greggy staring for a moment out of it until he started the engine and left. Earl watched him out the driveway.

The Ignorant Indian, he thought, *doesn't even know what a rake is.* Then he noticed how suddenly quiet it was.

AND THEN HIS MOTHER FOUND OUT.

"A policeman?" Her eyes widened, and under the strands of her shining black hair, Earl saw the silver feather of an earring quiver. She stood stock-still, except for the tiny glint of that changing light. "A policeman was here? What was a policeman doing here?"

Earl gave his grandmother a look of betrayal and dismay. He'd shut the curtains to the house after Carson called, claiming there was too much sun through the windows, and he'd waited outside, hoping the noise of the television would hide the sound of Greggy's

car. But even if his grandmother did hear the car and get up and
peek through the curtains, Earl thought she would keep it a secret.
She might ask him what was going on, but he never thought she
would go straight to his mother. His grandmother had often been
his confidante when he was younger, and though he spoke more
with Norm now, he knew that his grandmother, in her quiet way,
understood much that he didn't reveal. Sitting in her corner, watching television, beading, she seemed the center of the world, taking
everything in. She was the fulcrum of the family. Though she seldom got directly involved in disagreements between Earl and his
mother, she understood both of them, and their knowledge of that
understanding, their confidence in it, quieted them, allowed them a
kind of balance. Simply because they knew that she understood,
she served to dampen any mood swings and bring them into balance, sometimes without saying a word.

But she'd never done this kind of thing. Never, like a little child,
tattled. True, cops didn't come to the door every day, but his grandmother hadn't even asked him what it was about. She had spied
through the curtains, then kept silent for several hours, pretending ignorance, and the moment his mother came home, told her.
Earl was sent reeling by it. And his mother was looking at him,
waiting for a reply. And when he didn't reply, his grandmother did.
Calmly lifting more beads onto her needle and sliding them down
the thread, she ignored Earl's stricken gaze and answered Lorna's
question.

"He was talking to Earl," she said. She pulled the needle upward
and away, locking the beads onto the moccasin. On the television a
narrator was describing the habits of hippopotami, how they graze
on the bottoms of rivers.

"Earl?" His mother's tone made it clear he had better explain.

Earl had never lied outright to his mother. He couldn't start
now. The thought of doing so ran through his head, but no lie
would form in his brain. He couldn't disrespect her by telling her
what wasn't true.

"Some horses were stolen," he said. He shot an accusatory
glance at his grandmother again, but her needle swung in its little

dance through the air without missing a beat, dipped into the tray, clucked contentedly among the beads.

"And?" Lorna demanded.

Earl returned his attention to his mother. "He thought I might know something about it."

Lorna raised her hand, bent at the elbow, to chest level and waved it, as if she were tentatively trying to stop traffic, or waving to someone she wasn't sure she recognized. "Wait," she said. "I've heard about these stolen horses. You mean that isn't just talk?"

"I don't think so," Earl's grandmother said calmly. "Otherwise a policeman wouldn't have come here to talk to Earl."

Earl couldn't believe what was happening. He stared at the floor. A few wind-driven leaves struck the windows. The trees, thinned of their foliage, made a sound half-whistle, half-moan. A crow cawed.

"We're going to start this whole conversation over," Lorna said. "And both of you, I want Earl to do the talking. All right?"

Both Earl and his grandmother thought it best to keep silent.

"All right," Lorna said. "Earl, did a policeman come here to talk to you about some stolen horses?"

Earl nodded.

"*Why* did he want to talk to you?"

"He thought I knew something about it."

"And do you?"

Earl nodded again.

Lorna took a deep breath. "Whose horses were stolen?"

"Magnus Yarborough's."

"Magnus Yarborough's. And why would you know anything about horses stolen from Magnus Yarborough?"

Earl hesitated. For a moment his mother waited. Then her body seemed to lose its internal supports, as if her bones were made of crystal sugar, and water had been poured on them. She staggered, put out her hand, then collapsed into the nearest chair. Her coat, which she hadn't taken off—Earl's grandmother had told her about Greggy Longwell the moment she stepped in the house—puffed up from the floor, settled on her knees momentarily, then dropped, to hang forlornly off the chair cushion.

"Earl," she said. "You actually had something to do with this?"

Earl looked to his grandmother, not accusing her any more but hoping for support, hoping that since she'd gotten him into this, she might help him out. But his grandmother merely smiled at him, a brief, fleeting smile that Earl couldn't interpret—as if she thought there was nothing the matter, everything just as it should be. Within her black-rimmed glasses, reflecting for a moment the television's light, Earl saw two identical herds of tiny hippos filling the frames. Then she turned back to her beads, and the herds disappeared, and the narrator said something about how docile hippos looked but how dangerous they could become.

Earl's mother picked up the hem of her coat and laid it across her knees. She straightened her shoulders. "You'd better tell me, Earl," she said. "Did you have something to do with stealing horses?"

He nodded, still unable to find his voice.

Lorna stared at the floor. Her hands lay together in her lap, like someone else's hands she'd merely borrowed. "Oh, Earl," she finally said.

The words more sad than angry. Earl had the impression that, more than blaming him, his mother felt he'd given into something all around him, that what had happened was just too bad and too sad for words, but, in the end and ultimately and after all, not that surprising. As if she'd been expecting something like this all along and now here it was.

But Earl had given into nothing. He'd chosen what he'd done. There had been nothing passive about it. He hadn't been acted upon. He'd acted. And it bothered him that she could think otherwise.

"They were being starved," he said. He heard the edge in his own voice. From the corner of his eye, he saw his grandmother raise her head. He saw her needle suspended and stilled in the air, and the eight beads on their thread hanging in a small parabola, stilled, too. Never had he seen the beads stilled. Always, in the fluidity of his grandmother's movement, the beads were moving, too. But he didn't have time to think about this. It was just a fleeting moment of strangeness. Of something changed and different.

"Stealing horses," his mother said. "That's a crime." She seemed not to have heard what he'd said.

"So we took them, you know?" he said. He felt anger growing inside him, rising into his voice, and he was afraid he wouldn't be able to control it. "Because they were going to die, Mom."

"This place," she said. "Is there anyone it leaves alone?"

Earl had the feeling of being in a circling wind—of moving and moving but never going anywhere. Returning always to the same spot. Leaves in a tornado. A hollow center which he couldn't escape, circling around it forever. The only clear thought he had—clear and startling and unexpected—was that he was actually glad his mother knew about the horses but that she couldn't be allowed to think this way about what he'd done.

"It's not this place," he said. Voice of the wind. Hollow and distant: voice of the wind. "It's me."

But still his mother seemed not to hear him. "I'll just bet Norman had something to do with this, too," she said.

"Damnit, Mom!"

Norm had often told Earl there were no obscenities in Lakota, and in that respect Earl tried to speak his native language. Not once that he could remember had he ever sworn. To use such language now, against his mother—the entire room went silent. He was shocked. His mother was shocked. Hippos overturned a boat, and the dispassionate narrator noted that, though hippos look sleepy and lethargic, and even comical, they can be more dangerous than crocodiles if enraged. Leaves swirled outside on the gravel, making a soothing, chuckling sound. Earl and his mother stared at each other, eyes as wide as if they'd never seen each other before.

Then Earl raised his hands toward her. He didn't know whether he was holding them out to her for understanding or to keep her at bay: a gesture of suspension—that nothing, for a few moments, happen or change. He should apologize immediately, he thought. Try to erase the words, though words could never be erased. Only repented and forgiven. But he didn't want to apologize, and he realized he wasn't repentant. Shocked, yes, but not repentant. And he didn't need forgiveness. He needed understanding. This was not a time to say the right thing. It was a time to say the needed thing. He'd been spending too much time with Carson and Ted, that their language would come out of his mouth like that. But it had come out, and now it was Earl's language, too—his word, at least.

"You're not listening to me, Mom," he said, all anger gone from his voice now. Merely stating things. Merely saying what was true. "I chose to steal those horses, you know? Nobody forced me. It's not because I live here. It's not because you couldn't ever get me away from bad influences. It's because I decided to steal them. That's all."

His mother's stricken face went on staring at him, and for a desperate second Earl thought she still wasn't hearing him, and never would, thought that her eyes were looking past and through him to the old tragedy. Blinded by lights. Pupils hardened by them, unable to focus on anything else. Then there was the smallest dilation of her eyes, and Earl realized she was hearing him. Seeing him. That something had changed.

He went on, quietly. "And Norm. Yes, I talked to him. He knows about it. But you want to know how much he had to do with it? You really want to know, Mom? About as much as he had to do with Dad's dying. I would've done it whether I talked to him or not, you know? You can't go on blaming Norm. No more, Mom. He's my uncle. *Tiospaye.* He's what I've got. All my life you've wanted me to have Dad. But I don't have him. I have Norm. And Grandmother. And you. That's the way it is. I wish you'd let it be that way."

His mother didn't move, but everything had changed. She was transfixed, but not from shock. She was absorbing every word. Taking it all in. Almost overwhelmed by what Earl said. When Earl mentioned his grandmother, he half-turned to her and saw that she sat motionless, too, with the moccasin in her lap and both hands resting beside it, the beads on their thread curled like a tiny, brilliant, sleeping snake in her palm, and on her face a look of peace. A little smile. And he thought she nodded at him. As if to say, *Yes. This is how it is, and this is how to speak of it.*

"I'm not on the Black Road, Mom," he said. "Maybe it's not the Red Road, either. Maybe I don't know what road I'm on. But I do know what one I'm not on. It's not all that out there"—he swayed his head in a circle—"that made me take those horses. It's inside me. I took them because it had to be done. You raised me, Mom. Why do you keep thinking it didn't take?"

When he stopped speaking, Earl noticed that the wind had come up again. He heard the trees his father and Norm had planted moving but staying put in it. His mother stared at him with a face like brown and brittle pottery, even the earring that before had quivered now hanging motionless. Absolutely stilled. As if sunlight on water could freeze. Or the beat of a heart could quit shaking the body. Earl knew that his mother was hurt, and he was sorry. And yet not. Sorry that she was hurt, but not that he was hurting her. They were different things. They were different things.

When his mother did speak, Earl realized that she was hurting for all the reasons he knew, but one he hadn't even considered. There was sorrow in her voice when she spoke, but no tears—sorrow without weeping, trees bending to the ground in rain, long prairie grass before the gray onslaught of storm.

"Oh, Earl," she said. "You sound just like your father. You sound like Cy."

For just a moment Earl was surprised and pleased, before he realized that his mother might be seeing and hearing a ghost. He had to be sure she was seeing and hearing him. Only then could he take what she said with pride.

"But I'm not," he said.

His mother's eyes narrowed. The silver earring quivered. She raised her hand to her shining hair and smoothed it back. Tucked it behind an ear.

"No," she said. "You're not."

"I'm sorry I swore."

"It woke me up," she said. She pursed her lips in a self-deprecating smile. "I just don't want . . ."

She didn't finish, but Earl knew what she didn't want. She didn't want loss. Didn't want grief. Didn't want needless holes appearing at random in her life. Didn't want the structure she'd managed to build crumbling around her. But preventing all that could not be his sole purpose in life. Or hers. He realized that he would go to college—take the Green Road, if that's what it was. But it was his road. He would go because it was his road, not because it was the road that would take him to safety or preserve him from the ravages he'd always felt his mother feared for him. And realizing this, he felt a new longing for the things he'd only faintly known here—the dancing and the traditional religions. They could be part of his road, too. Going away and staying did not have to be opposites. He'd never realized that.

He noticed a new silence in the room and turning saw that his grandmother had turned off the television. She was beading again, the needle rising and falling, dipping and diving in its three-dimensional dance. Earl didn't know if he'd ever seen his grandmother beading without the TV on. Lorna realized the silence at the same time Earl did.

"Mom," she said. "The TV."

Earl's grandmother shrugged. She looked at her daughter and grandson, her eyes bright through the lenses of her glasses. "Who cares about a bunch of crazy hippos?" She tightened the string of beads. Earl saw the pattern on the moccasin. It was somehow familiar, but he didn't recognize it as a traditional pattern. Before he could ask what it was, his grandmother said, "At least we have another horse thief in the family. Your great-grandfather, Earl, was one of the best."

Lorna had forgotten the horses and the fact that Earl had helped steal them. She turned to Earl. "Those horses. What's going to happen? What if they find out?"

"We hid them good," Earl said. "I don't think anyone will find them. And if they do, I don't think they could connect it to us. We were careful, you know? Like you always want."

Lorna smiled. "Yes. Like I always want."

Then she asked, "Why didn't you tell me?"

Earl didn't know what to say. Before he could try to answer, she said, "No. You're right. I would have stopped you. But Norm. You told him?"

"I made up my own mind, Mom. He just let me make it up, you know?"

Lorna considered this.

"I ought to invite him over for a meal sometime," she said. "Do you think he'd come?"

"It's about time," Earl's grandmother said.

She lifted her needle, caught more beads, swung them into the air. When she turned the moccasin to attach them, Earl saw the pattern, partially finished, that he couldn't make out before: blue water, a red horse, running.

Gradations of Intimacy

∿∿∿∿∿

CARSON SWUNG THE CASE'S steering wheel around, and the tractor circled ponderously, and there was Rebecca walking across the stubble toward him, wind blowing her hair across her face so that she looked as if she were walking slantwise, coming with careful steps over the stiff stems of the cut wheat straw. So unexpected and familiar. His heart tumbled. He knocked the tractor out of gear and shut it off. The diesel engine trembled and died, the cast metal shuddered. He didn't know whether to leave the cab or stay inside it. She was obscured for a moment by a streak of grease on the windshield, and he moved his head to keep her in view.

He rose, opened the door, stepped onto the ladder, stood on the ground. On the abandoned section line road at the edge of the field, he saw her car. She must have driven there, pushed down the rusted wire of the fence and straddled it while he was turned the other way. And then come toward him. He waited. When she was about ten yards away, she reached up and brushed her hair off her face and held it in her fist long enough to meet his eyes. She didn't smile—just held his eyes and continued walking toward him, and he couldn't tell if she was troubled or glad to see him. Then she unclenched her fist and let the wind have her hair again and came the last few steps to where he stood near the rock box on the front of the tractor, feeling the heat of the radiator against his back.

She was so near and still coming. For a moment too much memory returned, and he thought she would walk right into him as she had in the abandonment of Elmer Johannssen's place. His muscles tensed to step toward her, and his arms began to lift, but before the motion could leave his shoulders, she stopped with three feet of

stubble between them. He didn't know whether she stopped because she saw him about to lift his arms, or if she stopped because
he hadn't.

"Hi, Carson," she said.

It struck him as a strange greeting—too simple and familiar, in-
adequate to the task of breaking silence between them or of touching upon who they were to each other. She had driven here and
crossed a fence and walked through wind to stop before him while
a tractor's engine cooled, and his heart had missed a beat when he
saw her, yet she said "Hi, Carson" as if they were merely old friends
who had met in an expected setting, on a street in town or in the
aisle of a store.

"Rebecca," he said, restraining his voice to match hers.

Yet he was stretched wire. The slightest wind could make it groan.

"It's good to see you," she said.

"Good to see you, too."

He wanted to say, "It's good to hear your voice." He didn't, yet
thinking it, he realized how much more it would mean to say it than
to merely say, "Good to see you." He thought of the other senses.
"It's good to smell you," he might say: perfume and sweat and the
shampoo she used. "It would be good to touch you. Taste you." Intimacy could be marked by such gradations, and he might, without
embarrassment, say any of those things to her. But other things restrained him.

"I should have kept going," she said. "But I had to see you."

"Going where?"

"I'm leaving. Like you told me."

It was what he had told her. But that didn't mean he could actually imagine her gone.

She took her hair in her fist again. "I did what you said. I got in
the car and left. I'm on my way to Rapid City."

"Just like that? He know?"

Her eyes clouded. "He left. I saw my chance."

"What do you mean, left?"

She looked to the ground, still holding her hair in her fist.
There was something small about the way she held it. Small and

endearing. That clenching. That restraining the wind's wildness. He wanted to reach out and enclose the hand that enclosed her hair.

When she looked back up at him, her eyes were swimming. "The sheriff came over," she said. "He went with him again. To show him where the horses were again. You took them, didn't you, Carson? You've got them somewhere safe."

He lifted his arm, rested his elbow on the rock box behind him. He wanted to reach out and touch her eyelids. Squeeze the tears from them, then put his hand behind her head and pull her into him.

"They're OK, Reb," he said.

"I knew it."

She lifted both hands to her face, covered her mouth and nose, her hands a triangular mask, the tips of her middle fingers in the corners of her eyes and her eyes wide and large and her hair tangled in front of them. Then she moved her fingers outward, wiping away the traces of tears.

She touched her fingertips to her jeans. Small, dark stains drying instantly in the wind.

"It's why I was able to leave," she said. "Because I knew you'd taken them. I knew they were safe. And if you could do that, I could at least have the courage to leave."

He nodded. "Yeah. You need a leave him."

"He told the sheriff you were involved."

"Longwell came and talked to me."

"He didn't . . . ?"

Carson shook his head. "They're nowhere near my place. And Longwell never believed I took 'em in the first place. He wasn't exactly pushin me hard."

"I never thought it could go this far."

She meant the horses, but the moment she said it they both heard the reference to their relationship, and their eyes met before she looked away.

"Why would he go after the animals?" he asked, salvaging her thought.

"What happened with them?"

He told her briefly—the pen, the scars, the apparent intent to let the horses starve, and how he and the others had taken them into the reservation. When he was finished, Rebecca seemed shaken.

"I don't know him," she said. "He never wanted me to have those horses. It's like he's blaming them. Them and me and you and everything. You know, he can be really generous when things are going his way. That's all I saw. Even when he wouldn't let me go anywhere or do anything, I thought it wasn't so bad. It didn't seem possible it *could* be bad."

"Long as he had control, it was just a fairy tale, huh?"

"Maybe it still is. Just not one for kids."

"How's that?"

"In the originals, the wolf eats Grandma and Red Riding Hood and even the woodcutter."

"That right? Some wolf."

"Some wolf."

"Hell, though. Even the wolf don't hate Grandma. He's just got 'n appetite."

"I know."

They were both silent for a moment. Then she said, "He doesn't stop, Carson."

"Meaning?" He heard some warning in the words.

"If he thinks he's been wronged. He isn't able to let things go. I've seen it before. Smaller things. He'll throw a thousand dollars away a night, gambling, and consider it entertainment, but if he thinks a car salesman took him for a hundred, he'll never forget it. And this."

This: They let the word lie between them. But Carson wasn't sure what "this" was. "All we did was ride horses," he wanted to say. But it would be both true and false and would come out as an accusation, disguised as an excuse.

Rebecca spoke again. "He's so jealous. Just filled with it. When he first took the horses, I thought he'd sold them to punish me. And that could have been what he intended. But once he started, he had to punish them, too. He can't stop. And you. He blames you even more than he blames me."

He heard her concern. "Don't worry," he reassured her. "What can he do to me?" He didn't tell her about the cow. Remembering it, though, stirred up an anger in him, that it had happened at all, that he'd been ambushed like that because she'd told Magnus whatever she'd told him and not warned Carson. If he'd at least been prepared.

To take his mind off it, he asked, "When he found out them horses were gone, what'd he do, anyway?"

"He was awfully angry. He wouldn't say anything to me, of course. But I knew something was going on. He got a call from Longwell, and—"

"Longwell called him?"

She nodded.

"You tellin me he didn' report it to Longwell?"

"No. He was angry Longwell was involved. That anyone knew. That he'd lost control of it. He didn't want to deal with Longwell at all."

"This don' make sense. How the hell'd Longwell find out, then? The only people knew about them horses was us."

The wind gusted even stronger, and her hair went wild. She couldn't contain it. Carson reached across the space separating them and with his index and middle finger gathered several strands that had sprayed across her eyes. When she realized what he was doing, she stood completely still. Didn't move toward him. Or away. She might have quit breathing. Might have been a statue. Except she shut her eyes, and his fingertips brushed her eyelashes. When she opened her eyes, he had her hair between his fingers. He moved the strands to the side of her face. Offered them to her. Her fingers opened, closed. He dropped his hand to his side.

"Can we get out of this wind?" she asked.

She moved past him, into the lee of the tractor. He rotated his body against the rock box, around it, stood near the engine. She turned at the tractor's lugged tire and faced him again. Her eyes so green.

"What was that all about?" he asked.

She shook her head, sorrowing. In the shadow of the tractor's cab, her hair was dark, and it fell now, out of the wind, straight along the sides of her face, moving with the shake of her head.

"I'm married," she said.

"You're leaving."

"Even leaving."

"You seeing a lawyer in Rapid?"

"I haven't seen one yet."

"In my book, Reb, when he hit you, your marriage ended. Don' matter what a court says. Or a church."

"It isn't as clear in my book."

The tractor's radiator gave a final, loud tick, and wind thrummed in the fan belt. Rebecca reached out and fingered the hexagonal head of a bolt, distractedly running her finger around its angled edges. Carson watched that finger go around and around.

"What he did to me can't be a reason for anything we do," she said quietly. "You and me. I don't want him involved that way."

"He is involved."

She didn't answer. In her silence, Carson didn't know whether anything he and Rebecca had was purely theirs. Even now, alone in the middle of this field, they were discussing Magnus. Had she been simply drawn toward Carson? Or pushed toward him because he was unlike Magnus? And he himself: Was his attraction to her mixed up somehow with his dislike of Magnus? Some opposing pole against which he reacted?

But he didn't care. He wanted to touch her right now. Right now he didn't believe in purity. Didn't believe in things unadulterated, distilled. Didn't care if her eyes seemed deeper, greener because something he didn't know in himself saw them as precious stones stolen from a man he disliked. And Carson didn't want her walking out of his life with some notion that by doing so she was keeping their relationship pure. By not keeping it at all. If that's what it took, he wanted no part of it. That was a dream not worth having. Just a way to justify emptiness. To tell yourself it had to be.

"Why'd you tell him, Reb?" He asked the question almost without out knowing he was asking it. He felt the dull grip of his anger. Remembered how the cow had lain there, waiting. White clouds in the high blue. Circling in that eye. Was all of that because Rebecca needed some purity?

But she looked at him without comprehension. "Tell him what?"

He found it hard to speak. "About what happened. Between us. That day."

"I didn't tell him."

"You didn' tell him?"

"No. Why would I tell him?"

Her puzzlement was so genuine, so obvious, that Carson felt displaced. He'd never assumed anything but that she had told Magnus. He couldn't get his bearings. "Jesus," he said.

"What are you talking about?"

More to himself than her, he said, "How the hell'd he know, then?"

"Carson, talk to me."

"It don't make sense, Reb. He was gone that weekend. He might've been suspicious, but things changed that weekend. He came back, an he knew somethin. I thought you'd told him. Thought you were feelin guilty or—I don't know. Just thought you'd told him. But if you didn't tell 'm, how'd he know?"

Her eyes narrowed. "How do you know he knew something right after that weekend?"

"Huh? You told me what he did to you."

"That was later. I never said when he found out."

Carson realized his mistake. Her eyes were expectant, probing, curious.

"I don't know," he said. "He fired me the next day. Guess I assumed."

She shook her head. "Unh uh. I don't believe it. What happened? What'd he do, Carson?"

But he couldn't tell her. Perhaps because he'd been blaming her for it. Perhaps because he felt residual shame for having been victimized by Magnus, falling into his trap. Or perhaps it was something else entirely—a thing private and close to sacred, not to be violated, of which to speak would be to desecrate the animal more than it had already been desecrated. And the only way to undo that desecration at all, to redeem it at all, was to hold its dying to himself, that round globe of eye and cloud and warped, sticklike, wrenched human being compressed in memory and sealed off forever from other ears. Or maybe that was entirely the wrong thing to do. Maybe he had to tell her. But he couldn't.

Still, he couldn't mislead her, either. "I can't say," he said.

"You can't say? You mean you won't say?"

"I mean I can't."

"Damnit, Carson. This is me. I'm in this, too. I have a right . . ."

He lifted his hand off the frame of the tractor. "Reb," he said. "I can't."

She was angry—her jaw forward, lips compressed. She tossed her head. "You can frustrate the hell out of me, you know that?"

"Guess I can't help that. I ain't tryin to."

She looked at the horizon. A long time. He looked at her. Saw that she was wearing her riding boots. Without turning back to him, speaking to the horizon, she quietly said, "I love you."

It was the last thing he expected to hear. She'd never said those words. He'd never said them. And now? To say them now? She'd come to tell him she was leaving. There was no place words like that could take either one of them. It hurt to hear them. Hurt to the core. He went on staring at her boots, even when he knew she'd turned to him and was watching him.

"You're wearing those boots," he said.

"Carson."

"Why say it, Reb? Why say it now?"

"Then you do?"

"Why say it?"

"Then you do."

She had no doubt. Why did the knowledge give her relief and cause him such grief? Or did it grieve her, too, but less than if he didn't love her? She had moved further into the gap between the tractor's tire and the cab. Barricaded by metal and rubber. She seemed further from him now than she'd ever been.

"You best be goin," he said. "It's a good ways to Rapid."

Ruination

∧∧∧∧∧

THE TIN QUONSET HUT was all that was left of the town of
Ruination, other than the abandoned hulks of wood-frame
stores surrounding it, their paint peeled off, their insides exposed through great gaps in the siding where drunks had rammed
their pickups or scavenged firewood for parties on the plains, so that
the buildings now stood in silent testament to the prophetic wisdom of those who had named the town, when more foolish and
hopeful men had envisioned their children's children happily scurrying here and not the mice and raccoons and coyotes and feral cats
that now prowled, oblivious to history or walls, happy to make of a
drunk's mistake a shelter from the elements or a hunting ground.
The painted words that had once identified the buildings' purposes
were worn away by wind-driven dust until the letters had become
so faint they looked like a message leaching outward through a
transparency in the wood rather than something applied over it.
Carson sat in the darkness, near an alley between two of these buildings. The alley was choked with tumbleweeds driven there year after
year by hard winds, a tangled rage of stalk and stem, bone-white in
the moon.

He dozed a little and woke and watched the door of the Quonset,
a rusted galvanized-steel building that looked like a huge beer can
half-buried sideways in the ground. No letters proclaimed the building's name, but it was known as the Ruination Bar, and its sole purpose was to maintain the fiction of the Municipality of Ruination.
The fiction's sole purpose was to maintain a city council to meet
once a year and reapprove the Ruination Bar's municipal liquor license and approve also the spending of the money the bar earned.

The Municipality of Ruination, in spite of the fact that it no longer existed except in memory and on paper, funded, through the proceeds from its bar, road improvements miles away from its tumbleweed-choked alleys, and cancer benefits, hospital stays, economic-development schemes that never worked—a mix of philanthropy and ill-advised dreaming all watched over by city council members who believed not in the town itself—for there was nothing to believe in—but in the fiction that allowed the disposal of so much real money.

A half hour past the bar's closing time, with Carson barely awake in the pickup cab he had appropriated, the door to the bar opened, and a pallid rectangle of yellow-red light draped itself over the edge of the dirty cement slab and stained the gravel beyond. Shadows of men formed in the doorway, adjusting their hats, hitching up their pants. They emerged one by one, black and one-dimensional against the light, but disappearing at the edge of the rectangle, then reappearing again several steps further out, having gained dimension in the darkness while losing their edges: soft, clothed, calling to each other, wandering to their vehicles.

Burt Ramsay didn't see Carson until he had his hand on the door of his pickup. He froze. His jaw opened slowly. He stared through the side window slack-jawed. Then he stuck his tongue against the corner of his mouth and pushed his cheek outward, then bowed his head, hiding his face a moment, then looked back up, shrugged, opened the door. He climbed in, settled himself behind the steering wheel, filling the cab with the smells of cigarette smoke and alcohol, and stared at the graveyard of tumbleweeds outside the windshield.

"Scared the shit outta me," he said. "Thought for a sec there you was my ex come back to collect more money."

"How you doin, Burt?"

Burt unsnapped the flap on his shirt pocket and fished out a can of chewing tobacco. He removed the lid, lifted a wad of tobacco with his thumb and forefinger, and stuffed it between his gum and lower lip.

"I look up and there's this face," he said.

"You drunk bad?"

"You was wantin to talk to me, you coulda come inside."

"How bad?"

"Some."

"I got some questions. You gonna be able to answer 'em?"

"Didn't figure you was sittin in my pickup cause you was lackin a chair at home."

"I am lackin a chair."

"Sorry to hear that."

"What I wanta know is, he payin Wagner Cecil more 'n he pays you?"

Burt paused a moment.

"Wagner Cecil," he finally said. "Now there's a subject. Wagner Cecil is not my idea of a outstanding young man. Can't hardly stand to be around the sonofabitch. Don't hardly know his pecker from a fence post."

"That right?"

Burt nodded, the brim of his cowboy hat describing small arcs, rising and falling.

"He have some different responsibilities than you, maybe?"

"Maybe."

"Like what?"

"You gettin at somethin?"

"He talk to Magnus more 'n seems necessary, for instance? He go off on errands you got no idea what they are?"

Burt put both hands on the steering wheel and gazed into the pile of tumbleweeds, a picture of suicidal intent to ram the pickup into the vast and brittle mess.

"Appears you got things figured about the way I do," he said.

Andrew Pettijohn, the bartender, appeared black in the door of the bar, reached out with a thin arm and pulled the door shut, leaving nothing but night. Then the flash and commotion of headlights and brake lights began, the sound of engines rumbling, tires spewing stones and gravel, squealing on pavement as the pickups hit the highway. Headlights splashed over the windshield, illuminated the dirty interior of Burt's pickup where Carson and Burt sat: Burt's

creased face, the slip joint pliers on the dashboard, the dirty foam
erupting from the cracked vinyl.

"Tell you the truth," Burt said, "if I hanta knowed you better, I
might a wondered myself about you an her. Ridin all over the country like you was."

"It look that bad?"

"I'm just sayin a guy coulda wondered, he was inclined to."

"He hired me to teach her to ride."

Burt raised both hands off the steering wheel, turned them
palms up, dropped them again. "Like I said, I knowed better."

"He was suspecting us from the start. Felt like he hired me just
so he could have suspicions. She was just tryin a get away from it."

"I don't need a know any a that," Burt said. "He's a controlling
sonofabitch, ain't no doubt."

Carson wondered again how he had gotten tangled in this
thicket of circumstance and uncertainties. Even as he sat here and
explained how Magnus had made his own suspicions come alive and
nurtured them, he remembered in shattering counterpoint that
long day's ride on Elmer Johannssen's ranch and how his grandfather had risen up from the past on the swell of Rebecca's laughter
and how she had been there when he came around Surety's head, as
unavoidable as the day. How much did Magnus have to do with that?

"The man don't make any sense to me," he said.

Burt rolled his window down, spat, his breath an explosive white
plume thrust into the night. "Goddamn gettin cold out there," he
said. He rolled the window up. "Magnus makes sense all right," he
said. "He wants things his way. Clear as a bell. An he has the money
to have 'em his way. So there you are."

"I don't know. Seems too simple, Burt."

"It is simple. Shit. It's the rest've us don't make sense. We want
things our way, but then we ain't so sure we oughta have 'em. So
we back off. Fits 'n starts. Zigs 'n zags. That's how most've us live.
Confusin what we want with what we oughta want. Till we don't
know either one."

"Ain't that called growin up?"

"You got enough money, you don't gotta grow up. You just go on wantin what you want an gettin it. There ain't no particular complexity to that. Ain't like you gotta go to college an major in Magnus to figure out how goddamn deep he is. Break your neck divin into that. You will."

"You sure you're drunk?"

"Oh, hell, I ain't nearly this smart when I'm sober."

Burt contemplated the night.

"You an me," he said. "We're the deep sonsabitches. Sittin here in a goddamn pickup in the middle a nowhere. Neither one've us got a cent to our name. Shit. I sold a ranch to Magnus an lost a wife and went to work for the bastard. An I'm probably pissed off as hell about it all, but I'm a reasonably happy man anyway. Would be at least if I weren't such a pathetic, forlorn sonofabitch. Don't know what the hell I want or how the hell to get it or what the hell I'd do with 't if I got it. An I'd feel guilty as hell if I did. That is, if I knew I had it. Which I wouldn't. An you can't figure Magnus Yarborough out? You shouldn't even be talkin a me."

"You think he's got what he wants?"

Burt spat out the window again. The smell of sagebrush and grass, the smell of fall, of cold, of high, desolate, imminent winter winds, filled the pickup cab.

"You mean her? Bein she's gone an all?" He shrugged. "She does complicate things for 'm. No doubt. Puts a dent in my theory, some. Women tend to do that."

He thought some more. "I guess he wanted her," he said. "Probably thought money could keep her. Then when he started a figure out it couldn't . . . Hell, I don't know. I need a drink another beer before I'm wise enough for that one. My own wife left half because I wasn't rich enough. Spite a the fact she ain't never gonna find a finer man, huh? An Magnus's got all the money in the world, an his wife leaves him because I guess money's all he gave her. She's the complex one. She's the one hard a unnerstand. Wants money, but wants somethin else, too. Who knows what? But Magnus, he's simple. Thinks the one thing oughta be enough."

"An when it ain't, he starts to spy on her."

"Yep."

"An pay someone else to spy on her."

"Wouldn't surprise me none."

"Wagner Cecil."

"Wouldn't surprise me none either."

"Jesus, Burt. He was havin Wagner spy on his own wife?"

"Spyin, now, would suggest more intelligence than Wagner has. An I ain't sayin I absolutely know any a this. Just Magnus and Wagner seemed a have more to talk about than me and Magnus ever did."

"Wagner got a pretty good imagination, you'd say?"

"I'd bet Wagner can imagine about anything he thinks he might be gettin paid to imagine."

Wagner had been working around the ranch that evening when Carson and Rebecca had returned from their picnic on the hillside, and he'd been there again the next day when they'd returned from riding the Elmer Johannssen place. Carson remembered saying hello to him. What had Wagner reported to Magnus? What could he have reported? Almost nothing, if he stuck to the facts—that Carson and Rebecca had ridden out twice, returned late Friday evening, and spent much of Saturday gone. That was all. Even if Wagner had somehow followed them, watched them with binoculars, all he would have seen was sitting and talking and riding. Except for that one single moment at Elmer Johannssen's place—and that was in the middle of a section of land. Carson had never seen Wagner ride a horse, and if he had followed them with a four-wheeler or a pickup, they would have noticed. Wouldn't they? Carson wondered if he could have possibly been so wrapped up in Rebecca and in the stories he told her about Elmer and his grandfather that he would have failed to notice the sound of an engine in the distance, pacing them.

All of it chilled him—to think that Wagner might have been out there, over a hill somewhere, watching. Magnus's eyes. But it wasn't much better, though more likely, if Wagner—lazy, deceitful, cowardly—had made up for Magnus whatever he thought Magnus wanted to hear, elaborated on the facts he had, and then given his boss the story he thought he was being paid to give. Earning his wages. Working overtime. In either case, Wagner was suddenly a malevolent presence added to Carson's sense of what had happened, and he couldn't fit him in, couldn't picture him or place him. It was as if part of Carson's memory was incomplete. Somewhere within it Wagner Cecil stalked, but Carson could not find him. Where had he been? In all that growing intimacy between himself and Rebecca, all that assumed privacy, where had Wagner Cecil been? How much had his movements intersected theirs, how much had his invisible story blended into theirs, how much of what he told Magnus had he actually seen, how much made up?

And the horses themselves. Rebecca had said that Magnus hadn't called the sheriff and had instead been surprised when Longwell called him. Had Wagner Cecil been visiting the horses? Ever the minion, ever the sycophant, had he taken upon himself the perverse role of watching the animals starve? Had he enjoyed it? And, finding them gone, had he reported immediately to Magnus? Or had he perhaps talked it around over too many beers, spooked out of his wits by the way the horses had disappeared without sign, from an ungated pasture, afraid to tell Magnus but afraid to keep it to himself, too—and had that been the origin of the Goat Man stories? Or had Goat Man, as Earl said, started those stories himself?

Far away in the night, in the hills beyond Ruination, a coyote howled—a sound old, familiar, comforting. A few moments later another one answered, and the two calls demarcated a vast space, measureless by any other means. Carson wanted to open the pickup door and walk away. Walk into that big darkness. That great aloneness. Walk and walk between the calls of coyotes, and never meet them, and be soothed by that endless recession. Be alone and alive out there.

"Damn coyotes," Burt said.

He opened the window and spat again. Before he could roll it shut, the first coyote repeated its call, and the sound through the open window had the clarity and force of music. Animal and land together. The loneliest music Carson knew. When he was young— he couldn't recall his age—his grandfather had taken him out one night to a hillside and sat him down, against his mother's protests, which Carson faintly remembered as a sound of birds protesting a strong wind, a sound which only claims the wind and notes it without any faith in stopping it. He could remember the night and his grandfather's hand, and his mother's voice coming out from the open kitchen door and then stopping, and then the silence of the darkness, and then, just as he'd heard it now, the burst of a coyote's howl: the night ruptured, torn apart. He'd spun like a top into his grandfather's legs and clung there, and the old man, laughing, had hoisted him from the ground and into his tobacco-smelling arms, his tobacco-laden breath, and without breaking stride had gone on walking, marching to the top of a hill amid the brief, bright yips and the eternal, drawn-out howls of the coyotes all around them. He had sat Carson down in his lap until he quit trembling, and then Carson had felt himself open up, the coyotesound tumbling into him from all around, a weird and—though he was too young to know it then—sensual, akin-to-sexual, delight.

After a long time in which he and his grandfather only listened, the old man said, "Ain't that a sound, now? If you had a be eaten alive, wouldn't they be the ones to do it?"

Carson wasn't quite sure what he meant, but he agreed they would be.

"Useta be wolves," the old man said. "Shoulda heard them. Pity you can't."

"Why can't I?"

"They're all gone."

"Why?"

"Shot."

"Who shot 'em?"

Carson vaguely remembered his own concern and dismay at the question. Yet he knew his grandfather, should any coyote actually decide to eat them alive, would shoot it without regret and without even considering its music.

"My father," the old man said. "Me. Just a couple. When I was a kid."

There had been sorrowing in his grandfather's voice—not complete sorrowing, not a giving over to sorrow, but a practical and everyday sorrow: that he'd done something he believed had to be done, and he'd do it again, but he would rather it hadn't been necessary. Just as, though he took joy from the coyote's music, he would indeed shoot any of them that dared to approach.

The old man then spoke of the last wolves and told how his father knew them as numerous as insects, a scourge that had to be removed, and how men on horseback would drive them toward the center of a narrowing circle and shoot dozens at a time. He spoke of Three Toes, the last wolf in South Dakota, gone in 1925, and how the news of Three Toe's death had traveled across the state and how he'd heard it on the streets of Twisted Tree as a boy and had felt that a great thing had been accomplished, and yet on the ride home an emptiness had visited him, and he'd had to ask his father, riding on the wagon seat beside him, for reassurance that the death of Three Toes was a good thing.

Carson felt, even young as he was, that he was missing some knowledge of his grandfather, not being able to hear the howls of the wolves his grandfather had once heard, that sound lost to all history and never to be released again upon this land. It was a mystery in his grandfather's makeup he would never know. When he had walked into the night, holding his grandfather's hand, the cries of the coyotes had seemed maniacal and dreadful. They had turned ecstatic and exultant, vibrating inside him like song. Now they suddenly seemed mournful, cries of the greatest loss. He had the feeling that his grandfather, more than anything in the world, wanted to pass along to him the sound of wolves in the night, but that sound was locked inside his memory like the vision of a mute, crazed prophet, so that all he could do was take his grandson out and point him to the voices of the lesser gods and, sorrowing, suggest that once, yes once, there had been greater. A time when the world was not safe to sit so like this. A time when the world was benumbed with godkilling and men wandered in it enraged and armed and unaware that their rage would turn to sorrow. And if they had been aware, even then they would not have known regret.

Sitting in Burt Ramsay's pickup and hearing the coyotes outside the windows, Carson felt himself wrapped in things he did not know.

He did not know the sound of wolves. He did not know what his grandfather had seen or felt when, not yet a teenager, he had sighted down a barrel and pulled a trigger against a wolf. Neither did he know what the old man had felt in his later days, when he sat at his kitchen table and seemed to be listening to the world. Was he remembering the sound he'd first diminished and then destroyed? Did he hear in the night a land abandoned? Hollow? Dissonant with silence?

And Carson did not know where Rebecca slept or of what she dreamed. And if he wanted to walk alone into a world made large by the coyotes' calling, he also wanted to walk with her and sit beside her as his grandfather had sat with him, and speak of voices locked inside him. But he did not know for sure what those voices were. Unless he spoke them. Until he spoke them. Until she allowed him to speak them. Brought them forth.

And, more practically and near at hand, Carson did not know what story Wagner Cecil had told Magnus and from what basis that story had been built. Did not know what movements Wagner Cecil had performed or in what shadows he had enacted them, in what blind spots of Carson's vision he had been and out of what clouds of ignorance and half-knowledge and obsequious need he had spoken. This minor character, this blot, this cipher—just what did he have to do with that mad race across the prairie that had ended in that pile of distraught, heaving flesh and broken bone? What did he have to do with those weak and starving horses? Carson knew nothing of him. Did not want to know anything. Yet wanted to know everything.

Yet, he thought, whatever story Wagner had told Magnus, based on how much or how little evidence, and whatever story Magnus had compounded and imagined beyond what Wagner told, they had approached the truth. He had to admit it. It was the startle of hawk eyes only, those golden eyes cutting swaths of light across the dim rooms of Elmer Johannssen's house, that had kept their stories from being truth. That near. Or it was the weight of a piano only, dusty from years of never moving, the mouse tracks in the dust upon its keys, the touch of mouse feet too light to bring any music forth, that long silence. As if false stories, as if gossip, as if imagination and suspicion, as if babble and Babel all, rushed from windows, then veered upward, almost but not quite becoming what had happened. How important, Carson wondered, was the not-quite? Was it all or nothing? Or something in between?

In the face of the false story that had been built, he thought, the truth itself could never be conveyed. Even if he and Rebecca could agree on the truth, on so simple a thing as the order of events, their halting and their going forth, they could never oppose it to the false story in a way that mattered. The god of jealousy imposed a tongue not spoken by other men, and the gulf between Carson and Magnus was too great to bridge with words. The cow's death, that terrific heave and snap and sandbag leadenness, had been a wordless message, and words could not correct it or reply to it. Of all the languages human beings could not translate for each other, the gulf between the voice and the fist was surely greatest, between the voice and a pickup speeding through thistles. He could no more speak to Magnus with the hope of affecting him than he could speak to affect the course of the moon.

Carson listened to another coyote howl, listened to the sound diminish and die. "It's unbelievable, Burt," he said.

"That Magnus'd pay Wagner to spy on his wife? Or that Wagner'd do it?"

"All of it."

He meant more than Burt knew.

"Lotta things're unbelievable," Burt said ruminatively. "I don't believe half the shit that's happened to me. Least I wouldn't if it hadn't a happened."

"You know about them horses?"

"Them horses." Burt nodded slowly. "He got rid a them pretty quick after you was gone."

"Is that what he did?"

"That's what I *know* what he did. If I got any other suspicions, they was never confirmed."

"Because you didn't want a confirm 'em?"

Burt opened the window he'd shut just moments before, spat, then stared into the cold darkness for a while, while the coyotes echoed each other and his white breath blew back around his head so that he looked like an ancient prophet wrapped in smoke.

"Damn right I didn't want a confirm it," he finally said. "Workin for Magnus is a *active* ignorance. I work real hard at bein ignorant. Otherwise, shit! I know how to do anything needs doin, but I start tryin a find out *why,* there ain't no end to it. Magnus says plant that there field inna wheat, and I know damn well it oughta be planted inna milo, I just whistle 'Yankee Doodle' an planter inna wheat."

"You whistle 'Yankee Doodle.'"

"Oh, hell, you got no idea how tuneful a guy can get workin for Magnus."

"You help build a fence above Lostman's Lake, maybe?"

Burt reached into his mouth, hooked the wad of tobacco with his forefinger, lifted it out, balanced it on the crook of his finger, and flicked it into the darkness.

"You seen that fence, huh?"

"I seen it. You help build it?"

"Me an Wagner started on 't. Wagner finished on his own. I did a lotta whistlin buildin that thing. Every damn tune I knew. Whistled up a goddamn storm. Goddamn hurricane."

"Wagner do any whistlin?"

"Wagner's asshole's pulled so tight he ain't got enough skin left over to purse his lips."

"Bit curious, ain't it, Wagner finishin that fence on his own?"

"Damn curious. I hadda work up a regular sweat a ignorance on that one. I oughta get paid more, hard as I work at not knowin a damn thing."

They sat in silence for a while.

"What the hell happened the day we was movin them cattle, anyway?" Burt asked. "That old cow took off and you after her, and then Magnus goes drivin off to help. I was tryin a tell him you'd handle it, but a course I work for him so I can't tell him anything. Two a you after one cow. I never did notice when she got corralled."

"You don' wanta know."

"You're goddamn right I don't. Almost forgot myself there. I appreciate bein reminded."

"You think Magnus'd starve them horses, Burt?"

"That what he did?"

Carson didn't say anything.

"Yeah, you're right, I don' wanta know that either. An I sure as hell don' wanta know why Greggy Longwell showed up the other day. An it's a mystery to me how some horses that far as I know was sold, could also turn out to be stole. An the last thing I wanta know is who the hell stole 'em."

"Life's just full a mysteries, ain't it?"

"It is. Nothin but a wonder."

"So you think he'd starve 'em? Or you think Wagner could get that idea on his own? You know, interpret what Magnus says about 'em a little liberally?"

"If Wagner can have any idea on his own at all, it'd be that kind a idea. On the other hand, Magnus does like things to go his way. When they don't, he has a hard time distinguishin one thing from another. Magnus is a differences-disabled person."

The coyotes howled and racketed, then all at once went silent, and the world seemed to ring more loudly with that silence than with the howls.

"A woman like her," Burt said. "I wondered how long she'd put up with it. I don' know nothin, you unnerstan. But if a guy thought much about it, which a course I never, it sure could seem Magnus wanted her just because she was the type wasn't goin a be reined in like he had her reined in. Some women'd take it, I guess. Sit in that house and not go anywhere an think they was happy 'cause they could buy new drapes. But Magnus didn't want a woman like that. Not one who'd *be* happy. He wanted one he could force inna bein happy. Or force inna somethin. Screwed up as that thinkin is, he sure could also think it woulda worked, just hadn'a been for them horses."

Dogs and Spirits

~~~~~

FROST RIMED THE GRASS in the mornings, the prairie a glittering sheet of metal. At the edges of the stock ponds, ice formed in delicate tracery, clarifying the water and stilling it. And then, before they knew it, the horses were back in Magnus Yarborough's hands. Willi listened to Ted's halting, apologetic story on the phone and thought, *This is how it is. This nothing ever ends. This no thing can be finished.*

"They've never behaved that way before," Ted was saying. "You believe me?"

"It is not your fault," Willi said. "You cannot know what dogs will do."

"Something got into them," Ted said.

"Got into them?" The phrase puzzled Willi.

"It had to be, enit? Something more 'n them just taking off running."

Ted had heard the dogs milling in the night, their restless shifting outside the house, the padding of their feet along the trails they'd worn through the grass between the cars. He lay in bed listening, and a feeling of dread came over him. He couldn't rise, he told Willi, couldn't throw back the thin blanket that covered him. Maybe he was paralyzed only by the eerie chill of waking to commotion, to things moving beyond his eyelids and dreams. But he wasn't sure. It might have been something more. In the trailer house he heard the breathing of sleeping others, the various refugees who had drifted in during the day, knowing they wouldn't be refused. In the dark that lay inches from his eyes, Ted couldn't remember who they were. Someone moaned, and the moan traveled through the house and pierced someone else's dream, and that person cried out in great alarm, something unintelligible, as from a lost and ancient language. And beneath it all the dogs were gathering.

"What do you mean, though?" Willi asked. "Something more— what do you mean by something more?"

He lay on his bed in the Drusemans' house, following with his eyes the whorls on the ceiling. How they circled and started again. If he ignored them, they were just haze and texture, but if he concentrated on them, they gave him no rest. They forced his eyes to constantly trace them. Constantly start over. Constantly end.

"I mean a spirit," Ted said. "Keeping me down. The same one that got into the dogs. If I'd a got up sooner I mighta called them back. But I couldn't get up."

A feeling like a moving, cold, and slippery stone ran up Willi's back, starting at the base of his spine, constricting the muscles around his neck.

"You don't believe it, do you?" Ted said, a little bitterly.

Willi realized he hadn't responded. His eyes reached the end of a whorl, started on another. He shut them. He might go crazy. Darkness—nothing—was better than that endless repetition.

"No," he said, quietly. "I do. I think there could be spirits."

"On the rez there are," Ted said. His voice was bleak. "Nothing 'could be' about it."

Willi thought of his grandmother, dead now, a ghost dressed in pale green slacks, with her hair wispy and floating, swooping out of the darkness over Ted's place, material and insubstantial both, passing over the dogs so that they raised their muzzles to the stars, looking for what had just touched them, and then feeling in their doggy hearts a rush and longing that made them scramble to their feet out of their grassy beds or off the ripped car seats where they slept. His grandmother, the ghostly dogherd. She would do it, he thought— she would become a ghost if anyone would. She would will herself to ghostliness, carry the ghost of her living right through her death and keep living it. And then insert all her confusion and twisted logic, which she could never in her life make anyone believe through words, directly into the hearts of those mute and helpless dogs.

Willi almost asked Ted if he had felt an actual force holding him in the bed. Did it feel like a soft, white hand? Did a single index finger lift and drop upon his chest?

Before he could find the words, however, Ted said, "Goat Man."

"Goat Man?" Willi asked.

"Mighta been him. He's been back, lately. Anyway, it was something."

Willi didn't know what to make of that. In his studies of Lakota culture, he'd heard of Hinshmu, the Hairy One, a wild, apelike being, but he'd never heard of a Goat Man. What was Ted talking about? And why had Willi not heard these stories, in spite of all his questioning, all his listening? But Ted didn't give him time to ask. Ted needed to talk, and Willi understood that Ted had chosen him to listen.

Ted had finally managed to force himself to move, to creak from his bed, to slowly lift the blanket and rise, but by the time he made it to the door and into the night, where clouds high and barred and regular imprisoned the moon, the dogs were moving shadows at the edge of the clearing, disappearing into the deeper shadows of the willows and cottonwoods along the draw. Ted managed to call, in spite of his fear that it would direct the spirit's attention back toward him. He knew where the dogs were going. He knew—and he barked them back, in languages both human and canine. He saw them in the shadows turn their shadowbodies toward him, saw their eyes, hard as glass, flickering in the light of the caged moon. Then all those pairs of eyes but one turned away from him again. All those shadows but one lost their form to the deeper shadows of the trees and sculpted earth and were gone, and the single dog that stayed, at the end of the line, having not yet crossed the border where Ted's voice lost its power and the call of the night and spirit gained force— that dog sat on its haunches and howled in misery, in confusion. But the others did not answer. They were silent as cats, prowling single file along the pathways worn by cattle and deer under the trees, emerging into the intermittent moonlight of the prairie on the other side, a dozen of them, trotting through the grass slick as weasels. On the hunt.

Coyotes wouldn't have done what they did, Ted told Willi. Not even wolves would have done what they did. Coyotes and wolves could not be infected so easily by evil or stupidity. But dogs had lived with people long enough to be susceptible to the manipulations of spirits, or to have lost their instinctive common sense.

Ted hadn't seen what happened, but he knew, and as he talked, Willi listened with a wonder that bordered on disbelief—not in what had happened, but that Ted could imagine the hearts of the animals so well. The dogs had slipped through the grass, trotting at first and then loping and then all out running, the greyhounds holding back, the pit bulls and the mutts straining to keep up, the greyhounds with their heads high, scanning with their eyes, the others casting for scent. Moonlight alternated with darkness on the land. Long swaths of grass lay in silver light and long swaths lay in blackness, and the dogs ran through them heedless, and when the greyhounds saw the horses, barred with light and darkness, they raised their voices, and immediately the whole pack raised its single, multitudinous voice, and Ted, standing motionless outside his house, heard it rolling back to him.

But by then the horses had jerked their heads up, out of their standing dreams, and before they were even awake were running, heaving themselves about, leaning into the circles their bodies cut, coming fully out of sleep only after they had taken several strides, so that they woke to find the wind they made tangling their manes, the earth coming hard against their hooves, and an old equine terror of canine smell and sound residing in their hearts.

"It could've gone either way," Ted said. "They could've just stood there and kicked the shit out've them dogs. And maybe they would've in the day. But at night—they just took off. Didn't think about it. Just went."

In that race across the prairie, through light and darkness, the horses galloping over the grass, the dogs through it, the horses had all the advantage. Not weak or sick, having regained their strength, with genes of speed both evolved and bred, they widened the gap between themselves and the wall of pursuing sound. Except for the greyhounds. Relentless, poised in their running, their bodies bending and flexing like tireless springs—some of them descendants of racing greyhounds abandoned by the Rapid City greyhound track, that various people had bought and brought to the rez and then abandoned again—they came on. And on. The other dogs dropped out. Collapsed one by one. Stained the grass with their slobber, great puddles of it where they lay down to regain their breath before turning their backs on the chase and slinking home, tails down.

But the greyhounds followed the horses, and the horses, having widened the gap, slowed their pace—then with startle and new panic in their chests realized the dogs, though diminished in number, were narrowing it again. Nothing in the horses' makeup had prepared them for this. The greyhounds, of course, were nonthreatening as puppies: mild-mannered, sinewy, nearly weightless, bred for speed and not violence, they would have stopped had the horses stopped. Would have sidled off, confused, looking back over their shoulders, unsure what that frenzied chase had been about, finding only horses, familiar and domestic as themselves, standing in the moonlight.

But chasing and being chased had taken over. The whole thing was a sham. A mockery. A mask and foolishness. But once started, it was beyond the capacity of either species to stop.

"That's all a spirit's got to do sometimes," Ted said. "Just get something started. And let it go."

Willi thought how true that was. And how long something could go.

Ted first heard the yips and howls of the other dogs end, leaving only the greyhounds' weird, thin chorus, and then he heard that chorus fade as the other dogs, shadows still, appeared out of the ravine, and he knew there was nothing he could do to recover hounds or horses. They were far away and getting farther. He feared the horses would come to a barbwire fence and not see it, but barring that, the animals would run until daylight revealed to them their own stupidity, fleeing nothing and chasing nothing. Or they would run until one species or the other wore out. And neither was designed to wear out quickly.

"So they're gone," he concluded. "I don't know where they are."

Willi wanted to be hopeful. "Maybe it is OK," he said. "Maybe the dogs have taken care of our trouble."

"How's that?"

"Maybe the horses will go where no one will find them."

"Only place for that's the Badlands," Ted replied. "And they might not live too long there. They'd need to find water. That ain't a place you'd want to take a horse and drop it off."

"Why did you call me?"

Ted was puzzled. "To tell you they were gone."

"No. I mean not that. I mean, why did you call me and not Carson or Earl? Maybe they would know something to do."

The phone was silent for a while. Finally, in a voice Willi could hardly hear, Ted said, "Walks Alone's gonna blame me for this. I know he is. Fielding, I don't know what he's thinking. I said I'd take these horses. And look what happened. Goddamnit. I'd like to do something right once in my life."

Willi was unprepared for such contrition. Such vulnerability. Ted cared what Earl thought? Was bothered if Earl blamed him? Willi heard his own breathing in the handset. He'd thought Ted agreed to take the horses only because he didn't like Magnus Yarborough or rich white people in general. He'd had no sense that Ted cared what anyone else thought, and surely no sense that Ted had seen this as a right thing he could do to counterbalance the weight of his life.

Willi knew of trying to do right things and the impotence it could bring. He recalled standing outside his grandmother's house in the gathering dark and trying to see the invisible vineyards of the Mosel valley, then turning and looking across the city. One of those lights out there might be his house. Or it might be sunk in darkness. He had felt abandoned. But by whom he did not know. Himself, perhaps. He had thought that his father might be looking out the window, and here he was, looking back—as if he were looking out of a mirror, the patterns of lights reversed, but both of them invisible to each other, and neither knowing the other was looking.

Willi had begun to walk to the bus stop. His grandmother was probably still sitting in her chair, rehearsing her arguments, wishing he would come back—recalling one more thing she might have said, one final statement to convince him. Willi hadn't been convinced, but nevertheless he felt defeated. He'd discovered what he'd come to discover, but nevertheless there was no triumph in it. He'd thought that by a single visit he could crack the shell of his grandmother's dream and reveal his father's error. Had thought time would have worn her dream-made shell down so that he could crack it open and reveal to them all—himself, his father, his grandmother—who she really was: newborn, shining, receptive. He hadn't known the reverse could be true: that a shell could grow inward, could be thickened by years, until it ate into the soul it was protecting, until it devoured and replaced that soul, so that in the end there was nothing to shatter. Nothing to break. His grandmother had become the wall she'd built, the shell she'd grown. Nothing more. A shell that went to the core.

Listening to Ted's defeated voice, Willi remembered how he'd ridden a nearly empty bus back home. He'd thought to know his grandmother but instead had run up against his own history. Maybe it was the same for Ted—taking the horses to change something and finding nothing changed. Even his trusted dogs had betrayed him, succumbing to the spirits and the spooks. Maybe Ted, like Willi, felt caught in his own history. *Cages are everywhere*, Willi thought. But he chased the thought away. Refused to think it again. But for just a moment it seemed to him that history was the biggest cage of all and that it lay all around him, all around Ted, all around them all, in steel and glittering array, and everywhere they turned they bumped against its bars.

AUNT MARTI HAD BROUGHT THE NEWS of the old woman's death. She didn't weep or cry or protest this time—merely arrived and announced it, dry-eyed and shriveled, breaking no secrets, making no demands, as if one such argument was enough for a lifetime, or as if she couldn't stand to hear her brother once again refuse to attend, to pray, to acknowledge, to mourn. She might have been a piece of newspaper blown through the door. Only a bit of self-pity in her voice, only a carefully restrained look of reproach in her eyes.

When she left, Willi said, "I will go to the funeral."

His father turned from the door through which his sister had gone. Willi expected opposition, but his father said only, "If you wish."

It seemed to Willi that his family had become devoid of emotion. As if they had been fighting a thing, and each other, so long that they no longer knew how to feel. Shocking as it might be, he wished his father would celebrate the old woman's death—dance, drink, toast her absence, ask friends to celebrate with him. Or he wished his father would weep and regret that she was gone and that he had never forgiven her. But his father wouldn't even oppose himself to Willi: "If you wish."

A stubborn anger stirred in Willi. He wanted to probe his father's passivity, force his father into some response. Some reaction. Something other than words like dust.

"Will you go?" he asked.

His father looked out the picture window. It was afternoon, the city gray, only the traffic lights on the streets across the river shaping any possibility of pattern. The Rhine below them was faintly stained downriver by the reflection of the Ehrenbreitstein Fortress on the water. Such massive, built stone—it was a wonder, almost, that its reflection could float.

"No," his father said.

"Did you *ever* love her?"

It was a question. It was an accusation. Willi himself could not imagine the woman he had met being loved. He could never love her himself. Yet he cried the question out and realized that, for some reason he didn't quite comprehend, he wanted his father to have loved her. Sometime.

But he could not make his father budge. "It doesn't matter," his father said, no emotion in his voice.

"It doesn't matter if you loved her?"

"No. It doesn't. Because in my life there are two times. A time before, and a time after. I am living in the time after. And will go on doing so."

The answer made no sense to Willi. He vaguely understood his father meant a time before he knew what he knew and a time after he knew, or perhaps a time before he tried to commit suicide and a time after—but Willi didn't see how he could divide his life that way, insist on its separation, and so deny the meaning of love or hate. He remembered stories his father used to tell of swimming in the Rhine when he was young, of treading water in the powerful current, waiting for a boat to come upstream, and then angling to it, letting the current sweep him into it, and clinging to ropes the laughing deck men threw out. His hands would find a rope in the water, and he would grab it, and the current would wrench him around suddenly, the force astonishing, exhilarating, so strong he almost thought his arms could be pulled from their sockets, and he would sweep into the hull of the boat and cling with all his might, lifting his head from the rush of water to breathe, then diving down into it, pulled through the singing water like a porpoise, and above him the deck hands calling, and below the thrashing of the propeller coming from all around. And when he reached the bridge he had started from, he would let go the rope and be taken by the current again and angle across to shore and step gleaming from the river. Surely, Willi thought, he had loved his mother then. It seemed impossible for a child to walk home from such play and abandon and not love the mother he walked home to. How could he step from the Rhine's rush and not love his mother? Or how could he remember swimming in the river like that and not at the same time remember walking home, entering his house, finding his mother there—and knowing whether he loved her?

"Why don't you go to the funeral and denounce her?" he asked, his face flushing, his voice hot. "Why don't you stand up and tell everyone how terrible she was? Let everyone know. Instead of just standing here?"

Even then his father did not react or rise to the challenge. All he said was, "This is a family matter. And I won't denounce the dead."

Because he said it so calmly and so quickly, Willi realized that he had actually considered it. The idea did not shock him, because he had thought it through already, debated it within himself.

His father turned to him. "Go to her funeral if you wish," he said. "I would not ask you to stay away. She is your grandmother.

The harm she did, she did to me. She did not imagine you when she did it. She couldn't have."

Willi had never told his parents that he'd gone to see his grandmother. It seemed taboo. He couldn't bring himself to tell them. But the way his father looked at him, and the words he used, made Willi think he knew. Or suspected, at least. Because Willi had talked with his grandmother, he understood what his father meant—that his grandmother had accepted his father's death as a soldier for the Reich from the moment he'd been conceived and could therefore not have imagined a grandchild. The thought chilled Willi. He'd never considered that. When he'd opened her door, had he been an impossible ghost from the future, as she to him had been one from the past?

"I went to see her," he said suddenly. He'd always wondered if he would say it—and now there it was, already said.

"I thought perhaps you had." His father seemed not surprised at all. "Then you must understand that the time before was false. Before I knew what I know now—it was a false time. An imagined time. If I imagined I loved her then. If I imagined she loved me. It was just imagined, Willi. How can it matter? How can I let it matter?"

It was too much for Willi to take in. Too much to understand. For the first time in his life, he felt his father was actually talking to him. That they'd broken through some barrier. Freed themselves from something. But all he could think was that love had to matter. Somehow, even imagined love had to matter. And wasn't all love imagined? Wasn't that what it was? If his father's mother imagined that she loved him, even after conceiving him for the Reich, then didn't she love him? Truly? And couldn't that be enough?

SO HE LISTENED TO TED'S QUIET VOICE accept guilt for the horses' leaving, wishing he could do one right thing in his life, and he knew what Ted meant and how he felt. Though he'd never said a word to Ted—or anyone—about his grandmother, he wondered if somehow Ted had sensed a source of sympathy in him, common ground.

"Sometimes you cannot do the right thing," he said. "Sometimes even the spirits are against you."

"Yeah," Ted said. "That's sure the truth, enit?"

Yet, Willi thought, he and his father had talked.

"But not all of them," he said to Ted.

"Not all of what?"

"The spirits. They will not all be against you if you try the right thing to do."

"You think?"

"Yes, I do."

"What do we do now?"

"Maybe if this Magnus Yarborough gets the horses back, he will treat them better."

"Why 'd he change?"

"Because he knows that someone knows. He would think, maybe, that someone is watching."

"I doubt it. As much land as he's got, he can find a way to hide 'em. And do what he wants."

"We must wait and see."

"Those damn dogs."

"It is not their fault. They are just dogs."

"I shoulda kept 'em tied up."

"It is not your fault, either. I will tell Carson and Earl. They will know it is not your fault, too. Maybe, sometimes, things just happen."

Nine Hundred an Acre

∧∧∧∧

STARING AT HIS PARENTS, Carson felt caught in an immense machinery that ground on and on. He almost laughed, but his father wasn't joking. Carson set his fork down, picked it up again, looked at his mother, saw on her face the confirmation of his father's words.

"This ranch?" he asked. "Our ranch? He made an offer to buy our ranch?"

"He did." Carson's father cut off a chunk of roast, watching his knife saw through it, then lifted it to his mouth.

"That's nuts. This place isn't for sale."

His parents didn't reply. He looked from one to the other of them. His mother sat with her hands in her lap, looking down at her plate, and his father, still chewing, gazed at the uncovered bowl of mashed potatoes steaming in the center of the table. Carson had heard many silences, but never one like this.

"You aren't considering this?" he said. "You aren't even thinking about it."

He set his fork down, heard the tines ringing.

"He's offering nine hundred dollars an acre," Charles said. "That's twice what this land's worth. Twice 'n a half."

He swallowed, picked up his coffee cup, gulped the steaming liquid, set the cup back down. Carson watched these actions, his mind reeling. It had been a week since Willi had called to tell him how the horses had been chased from Ted's pasture. The following day they'd been discovered along the highway, identified, and returned to Magnus. Carson had gone up to the small pasture behind

Lostman's Lake, found the pen dismantled—Wagner Cecil must have been busy—the artesian spring spouting and vaporous amid the trampled dust where the horses had stood. But Carson didn't trust that this was the end of things. Rebecca's leaving could only have inflamed Magnus's rage. If, as Burt had said, he had blamed the horses before, he would doubly blame them now; now they were the only visible object of his jealousy, the only thing left that he could see and control and release his anger upon.

Carson stood in the middle of the trampled dust and looked at the brown hillsides rising around him, the red lights of Tower Hill blinking faintly in the afternoon sky, and he thought of Rebecca. Wondered where she was. How she was doing. He hadn't heard from her, and he didn't know what that parting in the field had meant. He'd watched her walk back across the stubble, watched her push down the wires of the fence and swing her leg over them, then climb up the road ditch to her car. The chrome surrounding her mirror flashed in the sun when she opened her door, so bright even from that distance that Carson winced, and at that moment a great doubt seized him. Had she just said a final good-bye? Was that why she'd come? So much suddenly seemed implied by the things she'd said. In saying she didn't want Magnus involved in anything she and Carson did, was she closing off any future between them? Was she saying anything they might do would always be tainted by that dark silhouette standing on a hilltop watching them? Would she give Magnus that much power, believing she was freeing herself from him? On the other hand, did she intend to return to Magnus, to try, after all, as she had with her first husband, to make her marriage work?

These doubts ran through Carson's mind in a flash as she shut the car door, and he realized how little they'd ever really talked of anything that might answer these questions. Even the fact she'd said she loved him seemed full of ambiguity—perhaps the kind of thing said only because she now felt it was safe to say. The chrome stabbed his eyes again as the door swung shut, and then a few moments later, the car already moving away, the sound reached his ears. He wanted to call out to her, but it was useless. Useless. Her car trailed dust over the rise, and the dust remained for a while, besmirching the sky. She'd left no number where he might reach her. He could only wait for her to call. If she would.

And now Magnus had the horses back. It was almost too much to think about. Thinking just returned to its beginning or meandered aimlessly. Yet Carson couldn't stop thinking about it all: her words, her hair aslant in the wind, the way she had disappeared inside the car without waving or looking back at him. And the horses: Where were they now? He lay awake nights thinking about it. Sometimes he noticed in the darkness the smell of his grandfather, still faint in the rooms, and yet so powerful that he had the feeling, if he could snap the light on fast enough, surprising even himself with the movement, he might find the old man leaning against a wall and looking out the window, or sitting at the kitchen table with his boots up on its edge, thinking of horses. Or—Carson wondered—perhaps eyes. A woman's hair.

Now, though, he stared at his parents, all other thoughts washed away by this new thing they were saying. His father had just told him that Magnus Yarborough had stopped his pickup on the road alongside a field where Charles was working and flagged Charles down and, right there, standing on the road side of the fence while Charles stood on the field side, had offered to buy the entire ranch.

"I couldn't believe it myself," Charles said now, shaking his head. He cut another piece of roast, brought it meditatively to his mouth, shook his head again while he chewed. "I told him what you'd expect. Asked him where he'd come up with the crazy notion the place was for sale. Weird guy. He doesn't bat 'n eye. Says he thinks maybe it is for sale, only I don't know it yet."

Charles swallowed, worked his tongue against his teeth, then reached over the table for the green beans, lifted a spoonful onto his plate. Carson felt his mother's eyes on him, but he couldn't look at her. He felt physically unbalanced and had to put his hands on the table to steady himself. Even then the room seemed to tilt around him.

"He says to me," Charles went on, "'How much would it take to convince you your ranch's for sale?' I don't even understand the question, and when I do, I got no answer. But he's serious. I joke with 'm, say, 'Twelve hundred dollars an acre,' kind of laughing, you know, tryin a figure out what his game is. You know what he does? He takes me serious, nods a little, an says, 'Twelve hundred's a lot. Maybe you'd consider nine.'

"Maybe I'd consider nine. Jesus." Charles glanced at Marie. He'd forgotten he didn't use the Lord's name in vain in her presence, but she gave no sign of disapproval.

"Maybe I'd consider nine," he said again. "And maybe I'd consider the sun comes up in the west. But the guy is dead serious. *Dead* serious."

He stopped. He waved his fork in a series of little vertical circles, trying to make sense of what he was saying. Then he stopped the circles but kept the fork held up and looked at Carson.

"Nine hundred, Carson. He's dead serious about nine hundred. The man is not joking. He'll give us nine hundred an acre for this place. Every goddamn acre of it."

He glanced at Marie again. This was all so unprecedented he couldn't contain himself, couldn't remember his language. But again she registered no surprise. She was observing Carson.

"Nine hundred dollars," Charles said. "You got any idea what that adds up to?"

"What'd you tell 'm?" Carson's voice echoed in his skull. By staring at a spot on the wall hard enough, he'd stopped the room's spinning, though he felt it could start again at any moment.

"Told 'm I'd think about it. Talk it over with you and Ma."

"You told him you'd think about it."

"Carson," Marie said.

Carson couldn't think. Was this what Rebecca had tried to warn him about when she'd said that Magnus never quit? Did she know something then, or was she just worried, conjecturing? And was this an attack on Carson or was it just business? Carson couldn't pin his thoughts down. The one thing he knew was that his father had already made up his mind. He felt the old inability to understand his father. He'd seen the gleam in his father's eye when he'd pronounced "nine hundred an acre," and that gleam had been replaced by a bulldog tightening in his jaw, the muscles hardening in the shadow of the overhead fluorescent light, when Carson had spoken.

Carson knew his father had already thought about it. He already knew.

He was grateful for his mother's interruption, and he turned from his father's tight face to his mother's sorrowing one. And yet hopeful, too. Sorrowing and hopeful and with a reddish blush of shame brightening her neck, the edges of her jaw.

"We haven't made a decision yet," she said. "We're just talking about it. But we can't just dismiss this." She glanced at Charles. "We'll never get an offer like this again."

"We don't want an offer like this again."

His mother looked at her hands in her lap. Her eyelids downcast, neck bowed. Something meek, prayerful, innocent, hurt, in the gesture. Carson felt sorry for her. It pierced his other feelings, and for a moment he was purely sorry for her, with nothing else inside him. She didn't want to be doing this to him. But his father was so excited. So ready.

"It's like winnin the lottery," Charles said.

"I don't want a win the lottery. I want a ranch. Far as I'm concerned, this ain't somethin we oughta even think about."

Carson tried to still his mind, to calmly consider what was happening. He'd known this land as long, nearly, as he'd known his mother's face, and the wind over it was the way he moved. This place was his heart and breath. But how could Magnus know him that well? How could Magnus know he wasn't like his father, who saw the money as opportunity and dream? Saw it as the lottery—a rare, impossible alignment of random events? It surely did not make sense that Magnus would offer to enrich the man he saw as the thief of his wife's affections—yet he had to know that Carson would share in any profits the family made selling the land. Two and a half times the ranch's value? To imagine that as an act of revenge? It felt like an act of revenge to Carson—but could Magnus have that kind of imagination? Could he possibly see that far? That deep?

Carson was as shocked by his own vulnerability as he was by the offer itself. He'd been so confident when he told Rebecca not to worry. "What can he do to me?" he'd said. He'd never imagined this. Couldn't have ever imagined this. How had Magnus managed to think of it? How could he reach this deeply into Carson's interior and pluck this forth? If Magnus truly intended to take from Carson what was most dear to him because he thought Carson had stolen Rebecca, then his was an imagination strangely large, his was a mind that, in its exercise of power, didn't recognize any boundaries. And Carson knew nothing of Magnus. The more involved he became with the man, the more he receded from understanding. It couldn't be that this was aggression and revenge. And it had to be.

Rebecca had said that money for Magnus was just a way to power and control and that otherwise he cared nothing for it. Could Magnus possibly understand that Carson, in an entirely different way, also cared nothing for money, and that therefore this offer would enrich him violently—and leave him bereft? Was that possible? Or was this just a business deal, acquisition and profit only, indifferent to love, indifferent to jealousy?

"Why 's he want this land?" Carson was almost afraid of the question.

"Says he wants a set up a game lodge. Raise pheasants 'n grouse 'n deer, even elk 'n buffalo. Charge big to hunt. He's got the old Elmer Johannssen place already, and this one runs up against it. He figures to fence around both of 'em. Needs the room, he says, for them animals to roam. An we got water. The Johannssen place's only got one decent stock pond. Man does his research—he knew we had three ponds and that artesian well. Enough water there, if you can stand to drink it, to do about anything."

"Hunting'll pay off twice what land's worth?"

"I sure don't know. He seems to have it all worked out. He's talkin corporate trips. Memberships. Safari stuff. Hell, he even talked about puttin in a golf course. Maybe that's what he'd use that well water for. Anyway, he's got the money. He can afford to wait a long time for a place like he's plannin to pay off."

Carson pictured bison and elk roaming over this place, outside the window, rubbing up against the old house, grazing around the Quonset. It was an odd vision but one he could live with, something familiar in it. But then he thought of strangers, dozens, perhaps hundreds, of them, arriving here—by plane, by car, coming from their anonymous places and claiming this land with their ironic, confident eyes: smooth-shaven, corporate types with thousand-dollar shotguns and rifles. Making their big kills. Turning the place into an arcade and pretending it was real. Toasting themselves in the evening. He thought of them on the Johannssen place, outside that abandoned and wrecked house with its never-played piano, the hawks listening within. Quivering. It seemed a defilement, and he understood suddenly that it had been an explosion of the holy that had driven Rebecca and him back from that doorway. They had intruded on the sacred, and the wind of the hawks' wings against their faces had encrypted a message of mystery and power; the amber eyes had carved it like lighted brands, suspending hieroglyphics in the air; the piano's silence had played it.

He felt how such defilement could be a private thing, a defilement of the heart itself. For he thought of those anonymous hunters opening the door of Elmer and Helen Johannssen's house and tramping in, making loud comments, clanging the keys of the piano, kicking the hawk's nest into dust. And then he thought of them on this place. He looked out the window past his mother's shoulder and saw the door to the old house out there, and he thought of them breaking down that door, the tiny whirlwinds of dust its opening would churn—and then, cocksure and curious, invading. Voyeurs. Casting their cynical eyes upon his grandmother's drapes. Laughing at the meager furniture, kicking the few chairs around, and never understanding why it was so little—because his grandfather had made those small, painful pilgrimages to the Quonset with the things that Lucy treasured, preserving them there as he preserved them in his mind. Carson imagined those anonymous men defiling the place year after year, then flying away again to their plush living rooms and air-conditioned offices, and telling their stories. Turning what they'd done into an adventure. And never understanding, or caring to understand, the real story. The real history. Never knowing they had been in the Old House.

Carson came out of these thoughts to his father's voice. Only a few seconds had passed, for his father was still talking about Magnus Yarborough. But there was something tired, wasted, slightly bitter in his father's voice that Carson hadn't noticed before. "He ain't like us," Charles was saying. "Every year here it's nothin but survival. Can't wait for nothin. Just hope to break even."

But Carson had his own thoughts churning inside. "This is Grampa's place," he said.

The reddish tinge in his mother's neck leapt into her cheeks, and though her head remained tilted downward, her eyes lifted, wide, to Carson, a moment of surprise and understanding. But Charles was unfazed.

"No," he said. "It ain't. It was. But it's ours now."

"He worked his whole life for it. Jesus. He died out there. Right out there in that corral. I was there. How's twice-and-a-half market value make up for that?"

Potatoes, beans, roast sat on all their plates now in cold disarray. The solenoid in the refrigerator clicked, and the motor hummed, and liquid trickled inside its pipes. The overhead light caught the tines of Carson's fork. They gleamed in curving lines. Then, very softly, Marie said, "Everyone dies, Carson."

She spoke to her hands, then lifted her head.

"What's that mean?"

"Only what it means. People die in places all the time. In houses or fields all over the world, all the time. And most of those places get sold. Eventually. Or people die in places that don't belong to them. Hospital rooms. Motel rooms. And when they do, they're taken away. And someone else goes into the same room. Maybe to die in the same bed. You can't make a shrine of a place because someone died there. We have to live the lives we have."

Carson was quieted by how deeply his mother understood him, how she so easily knew what he meant. Yet she had taken that meaning someplace else entirely. He knew what she meant, too. But couldn't agree.

"But this ain't a motel room," he said. "It ain't a hospital. Grampa didn't die in any a those places. He died here. Where he belonged. If it's a shrine, it's his livin here makes it that. Not just his dyin. And as far as livin the lives we have, the one I got wouldn' be the same without this place."

Mother and son held each other's eyes, each saddened and made momentarily mute by their understanding and differences.

Then Charles spoke, from outside their conversation, with a tone still slightly weary and bitter, and without raising his voice, as if he were speaking to himself, saying things he'd never allowed himself to say aloud, "I been workin this ranch all my life. Been workin it since I was born. I ain't never been away from it. But I ain't like you an Dad. You ever notice that?"

It was a real question. Something was being spoken here that had never been spoken. Perhaps never been completely thought. It subdued Carson, and he turned to his father and answered the question asked of him. "Yeah," he said. "I guess I have."

His father nodded. "Half-obvious, ain't it? This place"—he moved his head backwards vaguely, indicating the window behind him—"I can't say I ever enjoyed workin it all that much. This business ain't never come natural to me. Just I got started with it and kept goin. Never got away from it."

He stopped and stared at the glossy surface of the table, the aimless reflection of the light in it. Carson had the impression he was looking at his whole life there. He'd never seen his father like this.

"I even quit thinkin about gettin away," Charles said. "Decided that was somethin best forgot." He looked at Marie, and a long history passed between them. "No point thinkin it or rememberin it. Then out a the blue."

Charles lifted his big right hand, turned it palm up in a gesture of helplessness and amazement, let it drop to the table again.

"All of a sudden," he said, "some things've gotten kinda clear to me. Your ma and me been talkin about it. All of a sudden I'm just pretty sure about some things. Pretty damn sure, Carson. Like pretty damn sure I never did like stickin my hand up inside a cow. Never did care for brandin calves. Or castratin 'em. I never did like gettin up in the middle of a blizzard to check livestock. Hell, I never liked drivin tractor much. Or ridin horse. None a that stuff. Just there wasn't no point in realizin all that. Just make me unhappy, realizin it would. Make your ma unhappy, too. So I went on. Not much else to do."

Carson stared at his father as if he'd never seen him before. And he hadn't. Not this man. Carson had always thought of Ves as the stoic one, taking all hardship as part of life: loss and gain, failure and success all met with the same appreciation, the same humor, and the same suspicion. Charles, on the other hand, took crop failure and low prices hard and could be depressed for days and even weeks over them, and he was apt to fly into quick, explosive rages over the smallest things gone wrong: a broken belt, a rock knocking out a sickle blade, a burst hydraulic hose. Carson had thought these things spoke of his father's excitability and moodiness, an instability about his character. He'd had no idea that underneath that moodiness was a strain of stoicism so deep and perhaps dark, so inherently a part of his life, that it defined everything he did, defined even his moodiness: a man who had looked at his fate when he was young and hadn't liked it but had decided it was his. Period. End of story. The way things were. So get on with it. And make sure you don't trouble others with it. Make sure you don't hurt those you love with your own dissatisfactions. So submerge not just your dreams but even your awareness of them. Do it for someone else. Do it so your wife isn't hurt. So she can stand to live with you.

It had never occurred to Carson that a person could live this life of ranching without loving it, could do it the way people did other jobs—because he'd fallen into it and could not see a way out. And it had surely never occurred to him that his father had within him such reserves of philosophy, such impartial, cool distance on his life.

"This ranch ain't nothin," Charles went on. "Scrub land. Kind a land you spend your life fighting. Which I done. I swear when God told Adam he was gonna work by the sweat of his brow, He didn't have land this hard in mind. You fight it hard enough, it'll let you live off it, but it grudges every second. One thing I wanted was you'd get some distance on this place. See it truer. Decide if you really wanted a stay here or not. You don't know what it's like to be older an lookin at what you got and seein it ain't much more 'n you had when you started. Some ways less."

He paused again. The refrigerator shut off with a clunk of machinery. In that new silence all three of them could hear each other's breathing. Charles looked down at his plate, considered the piece of meat there, then reached out absentmindedly and picked up the salt shaker. Tiny crystals rang against the porcelain. Charles set the shaker back down, picked up his knife and fork, set them back down, looked at his son.

"The one thing I managed," he said, "was to save up some money so you'd have a chance to go to college. Wasn't much. But it was some. You know where that money is now?"

Carson was too benumbed and dazzled by the man speaking to him to even guess, to even shake his head. Charles waited a moment, then jerked his head backwards toward the window.

"Out there," he said. "Place just ate it up. When you decided you didn't want a go to college an moved into the old house, hell, this place sucked that money back in so fast we didn't hardly know it happened. Like plantin bad seed. Just gone. And nothin to show for it. I ain't blamin you, Carson. Just tryin a tell you. But even that, I quit thinkin about it. What's the use? Just the way things are. You ain't me, and what you want for your life maybe ain't what I'd want for it. Or for my own. But so what? It's your life. No sense me sweatin up a lot of regret. Land was gonna get that money one way or the other, probably."

He shook his head, as if he couldn't quite believe he was saying the things he was saying. Couldn't believe he was hearing them from his own mouth and wondered how it was they were coming, and from where.

"I'm just tryin a say, twice and a half—it's got me realizin some things I ain't let myself realize maybe ever. You want a hold on a your grandpa out there. Could be I want a get rid've him. I ain't sayin that in a mean way, Carson. I don't mean him, himself. But . . ."

But he'd finally hit the point where the thing to be said was greater than the rush and torrent of words that might say it, and the words curled back into themselves, leaving the backwash of implication. His right hand was lying on the table, half-closed, and he opened it, a quick movement, as if he were casting seed or shaking off water.

"Twice and a half," he said. "It's gotta get you thinkin different. It ain't just money. It's a goddamn revelation, Carson. It's . . ."

He stopped again, stilled by his own thoughts, his inability to get them said. He picked up his utensils again and began to cut the piece of roast on his plate. His knife screeched against the porcelain.

Carson was overwhelmed. He wanted to say to his father, "Jesus, Dad. I never knew." Wanted to whisper it.

But he also wanted to shout at them both that they were being used. And claim the land as his birthright: an ancient privilege beyond decision making, beyond all notions of buying and selling, something passed necessarily into the future unless the future itself refused it. And he was the future. He wanted to say he understood his father's sorrow and regret and revelation—understood it like tunnels bored into his heart—but even so it did not matter. Hollowness of heart, his or his father's, or the heart's pulverization and crumbling into dust—they were meaningless as reasons or excuses or justifications for selling the land. When he was four years old, he'd gone alone into this land and, though not lost, had been found and brought home on a horse and, half-waking, half-sleeping, had ridden onward, wrapped in his grandfather's arms. And he was still riding. The land was his, he its. Set that down against anything his parents might feel, and it would outweigh those feelings. How could they not know this? How could they mistake Magnus Yarborough's money as a substitute for his, Carson's, inheritance?

His mother spoke. "You could buy another ranch. With that much money, if you wanted to ranch, you could buy another place. Probably a better one."

Carson looked at her. It all made so much sense. And so little. So reasonable and so completely crazy and surreal.

"I don't want another ranch," he said. "This is family land. I don't see how . . ."

And here he stopped, having encountered his own stone cliff, against which words broke and curled back and were abashed. For he had been about to speak of his grandfather's death in the corral out there, on a day colder and snowier than this one and yet much the same. He was about to speak of that death, but in forming the words in his mind, the image of it returned with such clarity and

brightness that he saw it as if outside himself: snow falling against
the kitchen walls in streaking lines and his grandfather upside down
alongside the horse and the horse's hoof snaking up and the sound
of the hoof striking bone, so loud it seemed to explode in the
kitchen. He hadn't remembered until now that it had been so loud.
It had been so loud. Loud as a shotgun, or a tire popping off a rim.
And his grandfather's useless neck, unable to resist the force. A neck
as loose as rope. The head like a weight on a string. Already dead,
already empty. Blank as bleeding stone.

He'd never told anyone what he'd seen. At the table one evening
a few days after the accident, Charles reported that he'd talked to
the coroner, and the coroner could not determine whether Ves had
died of a broken neck or a fractured skull, from hoof or earth. Carson,
hearing this, bowed his head and felt muteness inside him like a
crawling thing. He knew. It was hoof. Hoof, hoof, hoof.

But he'd never known anything could be so irrelevant. So absolutely and completely and deeply and inherently meaningless.
Something only he knew—knew inward to his core and outward to
his fingertips and maybe even beyond them to the air that moved
when he moved. What a unique and useless knowledge. Yet when his
mother had said, responding to the coroner's ignorance, "It doesn't
really matter, does it?" Carson had jerked his head up and stared at
her with blazing eyes, so that she'd paled and reached out to him,
sixteen years old, and touched his forearm and said, "Oh, sweetie,
I'm sorry. I didn't mean his dying doesn't matter."

But he hadn't misunderstood her. He just didn't know why what
he knew mattered so much and didn't matter at all. Now here it all
was again, visible in this kitchen with snow falling inside it and the
horse kicking inside it and his grandfather falling inside it and the
noise exploding inside it, and none of it able to be spoken.

Words: words might say, *He didn't just die on this place. He didn't
die here like people die in hospital beds. He was getting on a horse, and he
was smoking, and the cigarette fell, and he fell, and the horse kicked him
when he was upside down. Upside down. The skin all hanging wrong. And
his head came forward. Snapped forward. Like there was nothing inside it*

suddenly. Like life can weigh something. And it was just kicked away. And nothing was left. He didn't just die here. I know. I was there.

Words could say that. But even then.

The kitchen reasserted itself. Walls, ceiling, corners. The present firmed up its boundaries, and snow from that long-ago storm quit falling in the house, and Carson found himself looking at his mother with his mouth open and she waiting for him to finish speaking. Her face seemed to swell up out of nowhere, like an animal at night swelling up into moving headlights out of a wealth of darkness, and he didn't know where she'd come from or what she was waiting for. He dropped his eyes and saw his hand lying on the table. And seeing it there like something apart from himself, he realized that he had seen someone else within that interior snowfall, someone else woven in the mix of times and spaces: Rebecca, standing in the corral when Ves fell. Hair black and hair red within the light and shadow. Green eyes watching. Golden flecks. Emerald earrings. Riding boots. Standing against the corral fence. Watching. Not astonished. Not dismayed.

He could tell her.

And would have. Could and would have: how gray his grandfather's face had suddenly been, though the morning light was bleached by the falling snow, as pure as earthly light could be. But in spite of such light, that gray and dishrag face. He would have told her. In a future different from the one that had happened, he would have: how his grandfather's cheeks, suddenly flabby, swayed backwards like a delayed wave in water, then forward again, all liquid. How lying there completely stilled, he had smiled. And not.

His mother still waited. "You don't see how what?" she finally prompted him.

He expelled his breath. Saw the ridges in his knuckles, bent his hand to erase them.

"Magnus Yarborough," he said. "Christ! The way he's going, he'll buy the entire state. We'll all be working for him. And you want to sell to him?"

He stood. He couldn't talk any more. Or listen to them talk.

"I don't want another place," he said. "I'm sorry if you never wanted a ranch, Dad. But this is our place. Grampa's, too, even if you say it ain't. I just can't see sellin it. I just . . ."

If he couldn't say what he meant, why repeat what he'd said? He left the table, walked down the half-set of steps to the entry and out the door. The wind was blowing in the dark. As always. The wind was always blowing.

A Thing Unsaid

^^^^^

MARIE FIELDING WATCHED HER REFLECTION in the kitchen window over the sink grow more and more distinct as dark thickened outside and the dishes piled up in the drain rack beside her. The sound of water in pipes filled the house. Charles was taking a shower, and Carson had gone back to the old house, and she was momentarily alone with her reflection—that sad-eyed woman, she thought, out there in the night, staring back through the window at her.

For a while her reflection put its hands into soapy water out near the old house where her son was sitting in his own silence, and when her reflection lifted a dish out of that water, it lifted it out of the earth and rinsed it in a stream that materialized in the air, and placed it down on the earth again. But the sinking sun sucked its strands of light under the curve of the earth, and gradually the old house disappeared, and the earth under it disappeared, and the sad-eyed woman continued her dish washing quietly within a slowly forming kitchen, with walls and lights and faucets—until that kitchen displaced any other world, even the darkness itself. Marie shut her eyes and washed dishes by feel alone, groping on the counter for them, listening to them clink against each other: the slick soap, the smooth contours of cups, the mild prick of forks, the detergent bubbles popping with the gentlest of sounds. With her eyes shut Marie was completely alone, not even her reflection watching her.

Water stopped running in the pipes. She kept her eyes shut until she heard Charles's steps on the living room carpet cross into the tiled kitchen. Then she opened them, and he appeared in the window. She saw his eyes rest on the curve of her reflection's hips, the small of her reflection's back. She felt a twinge of despair and gratitude both, that he could still look at her that way. He hadn't combed his hair. There wasn't all that much, anymore, to comb. What there was stuck out at various angles.

Then Charles's eyes in the window met hers. He knew she'd seen where his eyes had been. Her reflection's lips turned up in a little smile, and some of the sadness in those eyes went away.

"Nice view?" she asked his reflection.

"Always is."

She thought he might step toward her then and push his body against hers and move his hand up her stomach, and she half-desired that he would and half that he wouldn't. She'd play-protest, of course. She'd leave her hands in the water and pretend to continue with the dishes, and she'd let his hands rove and watch it all happening in the window, knowing that just letting him would increase his desire, until she would have to turn to him and put her wet hands on the back of his clean, dry shirt.

But he didn't step toward her. He let the space between them remain.

"It's tough, isn't it?" she said then.

He nodded behind her. She saw it in the window.

She knew he was silent because he was thinking, *Damn tough,* but he didn't want to say that, so he let silence speak. It was one of those little two-way nonsecrets between them. She knew he swore around other people, and he knew she knew, but there was intimacy in pretending otherwise. She'd shocked Ves that long-ago time when she'd sworn at him, and sometimes she thought it would be fun to shock Charles by doing the same thing. Cussing a blue streak over some small thing that went wrong, just to watch his reaction. To laugh at it. But whenever she thought of doing it, the desire to preserve the fragile pretense overcame her. Charles didn't think she had virgin ears, but there was something close and near and sweet in his pretending that she did. In the special speech he reserved for her, marked by the absence of those words. A speech formed by what it wasn't. She remembered how just an hour earlier Charles had sworn at the supper table, then looked at her as if to say, "It's the only way I can say it, Marie. The only way I can get it across, what this means."

But what were words, any words, going to do? Words said or unsaid: What were they going to do? Even if they got it across? Even if they said it? And she didn't know whether they had.

"I'll talk to him," she said. "I'll go out when I'm done here and try."

"All right."

It was so dark outside now that she could see the color of his eyes in the window.

"You think you can get anywhere with him?"

She let him see her lift her shoulders, drop them. She didn't tell him what she was thinking. She'd thought it before but never told him. Odd—all the things they'd talked about in their life together, but this thing she wouldn't tell. She would ask Carson, maybe, tonight, finally, but she wouldn't mention it to Charles.

"Probably not," she said.

"It's tough."

She saw his eyes linger for a moment on her hips. Then he turned and went back to the living room.

Not a time for hands, she thought to her reflection. But the expression on her reflection's face seemed to disagree.

SNOW WAS FALLING. She hadn't seen it through the window or heard it on the roof. She knew it first when she felt it striking her face—needle-fine, hard, running down the wind. Her eyes watered, and she lifted her hand to clear the tears. She had no coat on—she was only going to the old house—and was surprised at how the snow and wind together cut right into her. She felt completely exposed, even looked down to be sure she was clothed. She halted on the steps, thinking of the jacket on a hook inside the door, then wrapped her arms around herself and bowed her head and hurried.

At her knock she heard Carson's voice. She turned the knob, entered, shut the door, found herself in a thicker darkness than that outside. A pungent darkness: How long, she wondered, before the smell of Ves's cigarettes and body would leave this place? Sometimes she felt it was more than smell—that Ves still hung around, just around corners, unable or unwilling to leave. She'd once seen a television show about haunted places. She'd let it spook her and the next day had asked Carson if he ever felt anything strange in the old house.

"Like what?"

"I don't know—a feeling of someone there."

"You saw that show, too, huh?"

"You saw it?"

"Yeah. I know what you mean. I think it, too, sometimes. But he's gone. Took off for good. Least as far as I can tell."

"I suppose." But then she thought, *How would you know? How would you be able to tell yourself from Ves?* Carson was so like him in some ways, it would be like turning around fast enough to see his own nose.

"Carson?" she called.

"In here."

His voice came from the kitchen.

"Can I turn on a light?"

"Sure."

She fumbled along the wall, found a switch. The overhead light, a bulb missing from the fixture, wanly showed the familiar rooms she'd lived in when she and Charles were first married, before Lucy had come over one day and proposed that Marie and Charles move with the baby into the new house and Lucy and Ves return to the old.

"Oh, no," Marie had protested. "Ves had that house built for you."

"There's three of you now. You need the room."

"There's enough room here, Lucy. I'm not going to take your house."

"I'm not asking, Marie."

Marie was startled. She stared at her mother-in-law. Lucy, embarrassed at her own forcefulness, giggled like a girl, then grew serious again.

"Ves doesn't like the new house," she said. "He says he's afraid to put his feet on the furniture. And you and Charles would be happier in the new house. You know you would."

"But what do you want?"

Lucy reached out and covered Marie's hand with her own. Marie was young then, a young mother, and Lucy wasn't that old, but Marie remembered her hand as having that silky, dry feeling of very old hands. Warm at the palm, cool in the fingers.

"Oh," she said, "the less grumpy Ves is, the happier I'll be. And you know what? There are fewer rooms here. Less to get messed up. I'll be happy being a grandma, no matter where."

So Marie had agreed. For a long time she thought she wanted to be like her mother-in-law some day: an old woman content, satisfied with her life. After Lucy died, however, Marie had come to wonder about that conversation, whether it had expressed contentment or resignation, a lack of want or a subordination of her wants to other people's until she'd lost her wants altogether. Had even forgotten she'd ever had them. But depending on how you looked at it, maybe that was all right, too. Maybe that was how life worked, how aging worked—you learned to mold your desires into the desires of people you cared about, until caring about them defined what you wanted. But Marie didn't know. It seemed a fine line between losing yourself completely and finding yourself completed in other people. Especially if memory grew chancy and you forgot what it was you'd once hoped for. Lucy had never seemed the least bit unhappy about moving back into the old house, but Marie wished she'd known her mother-in-law better, enough to discern the roots of her calm.

Carson was sitting at the same kitchen table where Lucy and Marie had sat that day, in one of those same ladder-back chairs. His feet were up on the corner of the table when Marie came into the kitchen. Like his grandfather. The pale rectangle of light from the living room lay on the kitchen floor. It reflected upward, a strange light casting reverse shadows, so that her son's face seemed unfamiliar, darkly foreign.

"Hi, Carson," she said.

He lifted his feet off the edge of the table, stood, pulled out another chair, offered it. He waited for her to sit down, then sat down again himself.

"You OK?" she asked.

"No, I'm not."

There was no accusation in his voice. He simply wouldn't pretend, for either of them, that nothing had happened. Yet his honesty and directness put him into his own and isolate world—not far from her, in fact very near, but somehow invulnerable. She almost wished he'd lie. Wished he'd be angry, sullen, hurt, withdrawn. Then there would be something for her to crack, to break through, and if she did, they'd truly touch. She remembered fleetingly the day Ves died. Then, too, Carson had looked at loss and named it, done nothing to hide it from himself or her. And then, too, she'd felt this awe. This love. And this distance: What could she possibly do for him?

They sat in silence for a while, sideways to the table.

"Do you always sit in the dark?" she asked.

"I was sittin when the dark came. Too lazy to get up and turn on a light."

"That's pretty lazy."

"It is."

"We haven't made a decision about this, Carson. We're just talking."

"I ain't so sure."

There again, that hard, difficult clarity. His refusal to see what wasn't there or to accept proffered hope. He sat there across the table, in those strange, upcast shadows.

"What went on over there, Carson? When you trained those horses? What happened?"

He didn't move. She had thought she might startle him, but he seemed unsurprised at the question, though he didn't answer right away. Finally he said, "I shoulda stuck to horses."

"Did you get involved?"

"Was it that obvious?"

"Not obvious. But there were signs."

"Signs. Yeah, I guess I got involved."

"I wondered."

"Don't think the worst, Ma."

"I heard she left."

"Not because a me. She left because a him."

"What happened?"

"I taught her to ride. You can't do that without talkin."

"Do you love her?"

"That ain't the point."

"It's not the point?"

For a moment she thought he was being evasive. It was so un-characteristic she was startled, but also minutely and privately glad: a break in his self-containment and unflinching assessment of how things were. But when he continued, she saw that he understood what he said, and meant it.

"Point is, Yarborough thought there was somethin goin on."

"Why'd he think it?"

"He was inclined to."

"But do you love her?"

"It still ain't the point."

"I'm not asking because it's the point."

"I feel like I'm inside a spinning drum, Ma. That's just one more thing I can't quite catch and hold."

"She's married, Carson."

"I know. I ain't tellin you I feel good about any a this."

"And now this ranch thing, huh? It doesn't make things better."

"Christ!"

"Two and a half times, Carson. It's not something we can just ignore."

"I could. Would."

"Yes. You would. But your father and me."

"We're a lot different, ain't we? Me an him?"

"A lot."

"I never quite figured that out till tonight."

She felt caught between husband and son. Caught between their differences. Between their dreams and faults. And what were her own dreams? she wondered. Maybe she was like Lucy after all. Maybe she'd let the men she loved do the dreaming. And now found herself caught between their dreams, with no dreams of her own to counterbalance theirs and clarify them. Charles had stayed on the ranch while dreaming of leaving it, and because he had, he'd allowed Carson to build a dream of staying. And now, suddenly, it was too possible to leave. And here she was. What did she want? Nothing, it seemed, but for them to each have what they wanted. Then where had she gone, herself? Or was that the wrong question—to try to think of yourself as apart from anyone else, your dreams as separate?

Carson and Charles finally understood each other in a way she had always understood them both and wanted them to understand each other. And their understanding might now tear them apart. Could misunderstanding be a glue that bound people to each other? And if understanding tore them apart, whose side should she take—Charles's, who had no chance, if this dream went, to build another, or Carson's, who hadn't yet learned, maybe, how hard dreams were? Or had he?

"Hear that?" Carson suddenly asked.

His face was lifted to the ceiling, a look of rapt wonderment on it. She didn't hear anything. He scraped his chair back and disappeared into the living room. She heard the outside door open, and coming through it then the burbling, piping calls of sandhill cranes up there in the darkness. When she reached the doorway, Carson was standing on the withered grass, a statue, his face to the sky, and the descending sound of the birds made the whole near earth sound as if it were underwater. A sound that rose and fell: thin, fluting, bubbling, as if the birds carried the voices of rivers within them. Marie followed Carson's gaze. Ambient light was reflecting off the scree of snow on the ground and back into the sky, and it turned the cranes purely white. They were ghost birds in ragged formation, flying overhead through faint lines of snow. Relentless birds, vulnerable and beautiful. Onward into darkness. Marie was weakened by beauty.

When they were finally gone, pulling their music into the night with them, and the world was only the sound of snow scraping out of the air, Carson brought his face down, and she saw a reverent wildness there. Something ecstatic and to be feared.

"You see them?" he asked.

She nodded.

"Cranes. Flying at night."

She didn't know how he'd heard them from inside the kitchen. Even talking to her, even absorbed in a conversation so hard and difficult, he'd heard the barest call of cranes and run to see them. She thought of this woman they'd just been talking about, Rebecca Yarborough, whom she'd never met. This woman who might have fallen in love with her son. This married woman.

Marie thought about this woman and Carson riding horses together across this land he knew so well and loved so much, land that included, for him, the sky and wind and snow and the transient sounds of migrating birds. And Marie thought it would be easy to fall in love with him. Terribly easy. And incredibly hard. What kind of woman, she wondered, could pierce his self-containment? And live with it? That self-containment, its paradox, that included the land around him, so that in the middle of a conversation about what had to be a crucial and painful thing in his life, he could still leap to his feet and go to the door and step outside to watch great birds pass overhead on their way to another part of the planet, having heard their signature calls through roof and ceiling. Would the woman he left behind in such a conversation follow him to the door to share what he heard and saw? Or would she in time grow tired? And what if it was a crucial point in her life they were discussing? Would she begin to feel as if her life with him was a series of small but constant leavings-behind, small but constant interruptions by the world? And if she felt left behind, would he in any way at all be able to understand her feelings? And if he did, would he be able to do anything about it? Could you prevent yourself from hearing the sound of cranes? And even if you did not rise to see them, could you keep your mind on earth if your ears were open to the river of their calls?

Marie was standing in the doorway to the old house, leaning against it, watching her son. He took a last look at the dark sky into which the cranes had disappeared, then walked past her into the living room. She shifted to let him pass, and she felt again how close she was to him, and how far away. She felt a small pang of jealousy for the woman who might be closer. If that were possible. And she felt a small pang of fear, for Carson, that it might not be possible. Or that it might. Either way. She looked to the sky again. Empty. Silent. Snowing.

Back in the kitchen they sat again, each with their own thoughts for a while, and the cranes strung out far to the south already, passing whitely over sleeping land.

"Carson," Marie said. "I don't know if it matters, but there's something I want to tell you. What your father said this evening, about never wanting to run this place. He wanted to take flying lessons. Airplanes. That's what he really wanted to do."

"Dad? Dad wanted to fly planes?"

"When he was younger. Before we married. He probably wouldn't want me telling you."

"And he didn't because of this place?"

"He couldn't get your grandfather to hear him. There was a time, Carson, when Ves was a hard man. He wasn't with you. But there was a time. And there was always something unfinished here. Your father kept thinking he'd find a time when he could go. Some point when things got wrapped up enough for him to leave. But there's no such thing on a ranch. No matter when he decided to go, he'd be leaving in the middle of something. Between that and your grandfather."

"Hard for me to see Dad as a pilot."

"I suppose it is."

You become who you are, she thought, *and not who you wanted to be. And people see who you are. Especially your own children.*

"You tellin me Dad still wants to fly planes?"

"No. I'm just saying this whole thing looks a lot different to him than to you. He sees opportunity. A chance to do something he's never done. To not do what his father told him to do. Or what this place demanded. Which are the same thing, really. That's one of the reasons your father tried not to ever force his opinion on you. He didn't want to make your decisions for you, like he felt his were made for him. But I think sometimes it just made it hard for you two to understand each other."

She wasn't sure she should be saying so much. But it was said now.

"The thing is, Ma," Carson said, "I get it. I do. I can see where Dad might not want a ranch. Always wondered why me an him had a hard time makin a go of it. So maybe I know now. But it don't matter. You can get me noddin my head over everything you say, an when it comes to sellin this place, I'll still say no. An no again."

"I know. I'm just telling you. Maybe I don't know why. Maybe I don't know what I'm saying."

But he did. Deep underneath, she was talking about herself. She was apologizing. She didn't need to put a sign on it. He heard. She was telling him she had chosen Charles first and would stand by him, even against her son. She didn't hear herself saying this, but Carson did. And didn't question it. He felt neither anger nor remorse, hearing it, though he knew she was saying she would agree to sell the ranch from under him, and she only wanted him to understand why.

There was one thing he might say to sway her. He might tell her of that mad chase across the prairie in Magnus Yarborough's pickup: the panicked cow's rising and falling haunches, its wooden-jointed run, the clot of manure swinging on the end of its tail, and the gray face of the man who had offered to pay twice-and-a-half market value for this land. Carson could tell his mother how the metal grill had neared the cow's rear end, of his own hands spread on the dashboard—as if they could stop anything. Of the jolt that ran through his shoulders. And the sound of breaking bones and tearing muscle. The tuft of hair and skin that blew in the wind from the jagged end of a femur. And the words as the pickup backed away: *That bitch won't run away again.* And he could tell her how he'd stood alone, later, with the rifle, and heard the cow's labored breathing, its neck stretched on the ground and phlegm rattling in its lungs. And white clouds in its eye.

If his mother knew all that, she might change her mind. Might and might not. Carson realized he didn't know her well enough to know so subtle and fine a balance within her, and what might or might not tip it. Still, what had happened with the cow, that story, was the one thing he had to sway her.

"I should go back," she said. "We all need to think about this more."

He looked at her. He knew she would return to his father, and they would talk, and always in their talk there would be stated and unstated meanings binding them. If Charles told her the money was too good to pass up, he would mean partly he was sorry he'd never made enough to give her the comforts she might have said she wanted if she thought they were possible. And if she said she'd be happy to live somewhere else, in Rapid City or Sioux Falls, she would also mean she wanted to give him his chance to do something else. If he said he was sick of working so hard and not getting anywhere, he would also mean he was sick of seeing her drive a beat-up pickup into town for groceries, sick of seeing dust on the grocery bags by the time she got them home, sick of seeing her putting apples into the refrigerator while tiny points of silica shone in her hair. And if she said she would like a place where trees grew and shade was available, she would also mean she wouldn't mind sitting with him in that shade and seeing him cool on summer evenings instead of working late and entering the house in clothes soaked in sweat.

They would mean everything they said about themselves, but they would also mean another thing about each other. They were bound to each other as much by what they didn't say as by what they did, and it was a knot Carson could not unravel. And maybe did not care to.

They seemed to him a rich, green island split off from him, forested and thick with vegetation, an entire ecology grown from the soil of their love for each other. And they were talking to him across a strait of water, but the real talk was their own murmur to each other, like leaves in a mild breeze. He couldn't even name the trees that marched down to their shore or the birds that sang in their branches.

"Yeah," he said. "You better go. We'll all think some more."

She rose. He knew that if she walked out the door, his chance was gone. Too much of the world was going to men like Magnus—men to whom land was only acres and not a way to live. A man like

Magnus should be revealed for what he was. The story of his violence should be told. He should not be given his way.

Marie reached the door. "Ma," Carson said.

She stopped and turned back to him. "Yes?"

She knew he had something more to say. Something important. She looked at him as she used to when he was young and came with news from school—all waiting, all attentive and expectant. Eager to hear him speak. She wanted something from him, hoped for something in his words—but he did not know what. And he saw beneath the expectancy an expression worn and tired, like the time the wind had come up in the night and broken every single one of the hackberry saplings she'd planted. Snapped them off. They'd tried to come back, but the effort seemed too much for them. Only a few of them had lived. That morning, that whole day, his mother's face had had the exhausted look that lay beneath the surface now. He saw that, and it subdued him, made him gentle.

"Good night," he said.

Disappointment flickered over her face. He didn't know why, or where it came from. She looked at the floor, pushed her hair back, looked back up, compressed her lips. Nodded.

"Good night," she said. She turned and left.

An island, he thought. And if his mother walked the short distance back to the new house, to his father, that island would twine around itself tonight, and the decision would be made. He could still walk to the door. Could still call out to her. It had even seemed for a moment that she wanted him to—some hope on her face when he had spoken, some need. He could call her back, and speak, and with his words he could build a bridge across the strait to the island that was them.

But it was an ugly and misshapen bridge. He couldn't bear to speak it into existence. Couldn't bear to use Magnus Yarborough against his parents. Against their hopes.

But even more than that, he couldn't bear to use his parents against Magnus. Even if Magnus was using them against him. Even if that were so, Carson couldn't use them that way. He watched the door through which his mother had gone. Imagined her, head bent into the wind, arms wrapped around herself, going toward the new house. He let her go. He let his parents be. He put one foot, and then another, on the edge of the table. He thought of cranes, their beaks like needles stitching the hemispheres together, between the earth and moon.

A Thing Decided

~~~~~

ARL WAS LYING ON HIS BED listening to music when he heard a knock on the front door. He rose and padded stocking-footed to the front room. His grandmother, without looking up from her beading, said, "It's a cowboy."

Through the front window Earl saw Carson's rockpitted pickup squatting at the edge of the driveway, frozen bug guts smearing the windshield in greasy half-circles. He opened the door.

"You got a minute?" Carson asked before Earl even greeted him.

"Yeah. You want to come in?"

Carson glanced past Earl's shoulder at his grandmother, then said in a lowered voice, "Maybe we can talk outside."

"OK. Let me get some shoes on. Come in a sec."

Earl went back to his bedroom and slipped on his Nikes and a nylon windbreaker. His grandmother and Carson were exchanging comments on the weather when he returned to the front room. Earl excused himself and Carson, and they stepped outside. Winter was hard in the air, though the calendar claimed it was still fall, and even with the windbreaker on Earl shivered. He shoved his hands in his pockets and hunched his shoulders.

"So, what's going on?" he asked.

"It ain't over."

Burt Ramsay had called Carson. Ignorance, he said, was a vital part of his job, but when he returned to work after a weekend and found the three horses gone from the corral where they'd been kept since being found along the highway, and Wagner Cecil acting more sniveling than usual, he'd gotten curious. He asked Wagner if he'd worked that weekend, and when Wagner replied that he had, Burt

asked if maybe he knew where the horses had gotten to. Wagner
said that no, he didn't. Whereupon Burt—who was asking these
questions in the privacy of a machine shed—grabbed Wagner by
his coat and knocked him so hard against the rubber lugs of a tractor tire that Wagner went white, and while he was trying to breathe,
Burt suggested he might be lying, and if the horses were being mistreated and Burt found out later, Wagner might want to start living
very carefully and fasten his seat belt if headlights came up behind
him on a gravel road some night—a threat Wagner took seriously.
He told Burt he'd moved the horses, under Magnus's orders, to a
pasture west of Lostman's Lake, on a section of broken land out of
sight of any road or dwelling.

"They got food?" Burt asked.

"Some," Wagner replied.

"Water?"

"Kind of."

"Kind of? You got shit for brains? There ain't no *kind of* water."

"There's a draw. There's some water in it."

"You do any fence building up there?"

"Some."

"Christ! You're too damn pathetic to even beat the shit out of.
You know that?"

Wagner, breathing again, agreed. Burt slammed him into the
tractor tire again just because he couldn't stand to see the sonofabitch breathing like a normal human being, and suggested that
this conversation ought to be their secret, since Magnus might not
look favorably on Wagner telling Burt what he knew, and Burt
would look even less favorably on Wagner telling Magnus. Wagner
grunted his understanding.

"I oughta quit this job," Burt told Carson. "It's like sandpaper.
Just wears me away. Sometimes I ain't sure there's anything left a
me any more but dust. Trouble is, way Magnus's buyin land, I could
go work for someone else, but by the time I got there, that someone else'd be Magnus."

Carson winced. He told Burt Magnus had offered to buy his
place.

"Your place? The hell."

"True. Offering nine hundred."

Burt whistled into the phone. "Nine hundred."

"Claims he wants a start a huntin operation."

"Tourism with a chance a shoot somethin. Might work."

"I wouldn't sell. But Ma and Pa. I don't know."

"Anyone with two ounces a common sense is gonna take that offer an run. Even you oughta know that."

"Right now I gotta deal with these horses."

"Someone does. I was hopin you'd volunteer. I need a get back t' not knowin nothin."

As Carson told these things, Earl listened with a feeling of snow both in and against his chest, a swirling inside, cold and austere. "Did you go find them?" he asked Carson.

Behind the window he saw a shadowy movement—his grandmother risen from her chair to take a peek at them. He couldn't make her out, only a vague and indistinct shape behind the glass. She knew what was going on, Earl was pretty sure. Or had a good idea.

"Yeah," Carson said. "I found 'em."

"What did you find?"

"They maybe got a half-acre this time. Poor grass. A little muddy water in the bottom of a draw. Be freezin up soon. They'll kick through the ice for a while, till it freezes to the bottom. Then, I don't know. Eat snow till they're gone."

Earl shivered. The wind raced through the barren trees surrounding the house. They moaned thinly, and their skeletal limbs shook, and a last few leaves detached themselves and swirled away.

"I don't get it, you know?" he said. "Why's he keep going after these horses?"

Carson shook his head. "Maybe it don't even make sense to him any more," he said.

"If he hates them, why not just get rid of them, you know? Or just shoot them and have it over with?"

A wild chattering came from the top of a tree. They both looked up. A plastic grocery sack had just caught against a twig in the very top of the tallest cottonwood in the grove. It was shaking violently in the wind up there. Carson listened to the bag's vibrations for a while.

"I dunno," he said. "Maybe sometimes you do somethin so screwed up and ugly you gotta keep it invisible even to yourself."

"Maybe, huh?"

They contemplated this.

"But still," Earl said, "why's he doing it at all? They're just horses, you know?"

"Yeah. To you an me. To him? I don't know. Maybe they explain every bad thing ever happened to 'm. Bad deal, makin an animal something it ain't. And he's pissed at me—maybe he wants me to know about 'em. Way a gettin revenge. Wants me to know they're starvin, an nothin I can do. He's all caught up in this thing, just like we are. Only difference is he thinks he's the one pullin the strings. Can't see he's controllin things so much he's lost control of himself."

"He's controlling things all right. Seems like there's nothing we can do now."

"There's a thing."

"There is? What?"

"Shoot 'em. Like you said. Take 'em out an shoot 'em."

Carson might have been talking about how to repair an automobile. Earl stared at him, waiting to see if he would take back or explain the words, but he didn't. He let them stand, by themselves, for what they were.

"What do you mean?" Earl asked.

"What I said. Nothin else I could mean."

"But there's got to be something else."

"Name it."

"Maybe Longwell."

Carson's gaze was withering, and Earl was almost ashamed to have suggested the sheriff, after the way Longwell had treated him. It was just that he wasn't ready to think about what Carson was suggesting.

"Far as I know," Carson said, "Longwell's still tryin a pin somethin on you. We're lost in a goddamn maze with that. Even supposin we convince Longwell somethin's up, first thing he does is go to Yarborough an ask about it. An Yarborough stalls 'm an moves 'em. By the time Longwell gets to where they are, they're not. An we gotta find 'em again. How many times you think Longwell'll put up with that kinda cryin wolf?"

"Still, you know, it might be enough to get Yarborough to stop."

"He don't stop. Someone knows 'm well told me that, an I'm findin it out. He don't." He shrugged, fatalistic. "Don't know how to. Like I said, in control of everything but himself. Kind of a sad sonofabitchin thing, really."

A crow appeared in the blue sky above the trees, feathered its wings, and landed in the tree next to the trapped plastic bag. They both swayed high up there, white bag and black bird, one yammering incessantly, the other giving a single, loud caw, then going silent.

"If you're going to do it, I'm coming with you," Earl said.

Carson betrayed no surprise. He gazed upward at the crow.

"You think so, huh?" he asked.

"I do."

"I don't."

"And so are the others, if they want."

"Even less likely."

"We're all involved. Maybe this started between you and Magnus. But it sucked the rest of us in. So we're in. Until we're out."

"It complicates things," Carson said after a moment.

"That can't be helped. We all crossed into this. You don't cross back just by saying you did."

"That some kinda Indian philosophy?"

"Indian named Jack Bean Stalk."

"The hell?"

"Jack's just going about his business, you know? Just selling a cow. And what's he get? Seeds that will take him into the sky. And then, there's no stopping. He's got to go through until the giant's dead."

"We ain't killin no giant here."

"That's OK. We're not getting any golden eggs, either."

"We sure ain't."

"My uncle would say, if you walk into a story, you have to stay there until it's finished. And we all walked into this one."

"Maybe you're right."

"I am right."

"Uncle a yours sounds like an interesting guy."

Another Option

~~~~~

THE FOUR OF THEM LEFT TED'S CAR in the shadow of the Badlands wall, on an abandoned section line road Carson pointed out, and they followed him, crossing a fence line, then another, until they found the draw Burt Ramsay had described. They descended into it in deepening dusk. The horses came to them.

"Unbelievable," Carson said.

Where the draw widened, water had collected, and on this water ice had formed. They could see where the horses had kicked through it at the edges. Their ribs showed through patchy coats. Their eyes were stone, in hanging heads.

"They do not look so good again," Willi said.

"They look real bad. This cold weather takes a lot out of 'em. An look 't this forage."

Dried and skeletal forbs stood out raggedly in the gloom, and dark, intermittent silhouettes of sagebrush punctuated the foreground of sparse, bunched grasses.

"Anyone see another way?" Carson asked.

All bird and insect life had fled the land before the approaching winter, and the land was silent.

"It is hard to believe there is not another way," Willi said. "But we cannot let them starve."

"We tried the law and we tried breakin the law. We was kiddin ourselves thinkin they wouldn' be found. Be kiddin ourselves if we tried it again."

"We could just turn them loose out here, maybe."

Carson shook his head at Earl. "That water's gonna freeze solid before long. I don't know how far it is to other water. Long ways, I'd say."

Ted had his arm over Surety's neck. "This is one real bastard," he said.

"One word for 'm."

"It seems like there has to be something else we can do, you know?"

"I've gone around and around with 't."

"There is another thing."

Willi spoke so quietly his voice seemed to come out of the night itself. The other three all turned and looked at him. He looked back without speaking, his features obscure, his hair a pale corona wavering above his head.

"Yeah?" Carson said. "You got 'n idea, name it."

"We could Magnus Yarborough kill. Instead. We could kill him instead."

Orlando shifted his weight. Arcturus stuck its red point through the dark envelope of sky.

They couldn't look at each other. Willi's words affected their eyes, so that they stared at the spaces between shoulders, the chunks of night outlined by bodies. For a moment they stood stunned, paralyzed: a tableau of stone.

Then Ted whistled softly. "My man," he said.

"Wait," Earl said. "You can't even be meaning this."

"Can't? Why not?" Ted undraped his arm from Surety's neck.

"Because you can't. Because it's murder. That's what you're talking about."

"What do you call this?" Ted waved his hand at the horses standing around them.

"Not murder."

"I ain't sure about that. He's the one hurting things, enit? And we're sitting here talking about helping him. Willi's got it right. We oughta be going after him."

"No," Earl said. "I won't. I won't even think about it."

"You won't even think about it? Christ, Walks Alone! What kinda shit is that? We shoulda thought about it a long time ago. You can't take the easy way out just because you don't have the guts for the right way."

"It ain't about guts," Carson said quietly. "There's nothin easy about either thing."

Ted's face was shining, exultant and contemptuous. He turned to Carson. "You agree with Walks Alone?"

"Maybe my reasons ain't his. But I come up with the same answer, yeah."

"Reasons? Shit. Yarborough's hurting these animals. They ain't done nothing wrong. So why're we even talking about finishing his job? Seems pretty clear to me he's the one we need to finish."

"It'd suit me just fine if Yarborough was dead. You got no idea how many problems that'd solve for me."

"There you go."

"Which is why I can't even think about killin 'm."

Ted's face twisted in scorn. His eyes glittered. "What's that mean?"

"Means I ain't about a murder someone to solve my own problems. If it was just the horses, I don't know. Probably not then, either. But I got too many other reasons."

"That sounds like so much bullshit."

"You want a think so, fine. But I ain't murderin Yarborough."

"I can't believe this. What kind of system is it where you even gotta ask this question?"

"A screwed-up one, maybe. But that don't mean we're gonna commit murder."

"Goddamn white-man system is what it is."

They were taken aback by Ted's vehemence, and his sudden change in direction. In the silence that followed, he glared at each of them, challenging them to speak. When no one did, he went on, bitterly. "A guy starves horses and we're called murderers if we do something about it. You think that'd happen in a traditional culture?"

Earl swallowed, found his voice.

"This isn't about whites and Indians," he said.

"Then what is it about? Why're we standing here? Justice, shit! There ain't any. What do you think it's about, Walks Alone, since you know so much?"

Earl felt the old familiar withering under the force of Ted's fury, and for a moment his throat swelled and tightened, and a radical silence seized him and made him abject and ashamed. But he forced himself to meet Ted's eyes and saw in them, beneath the fury, despair. Sorrow. And he realized that Ted was right. Things were aligned against them. He'd known it in Greggy Longwell's office. Why was he denying it here? In a traditional culture this kind of thing wouldn't happen. Even if some rogue individual chose to hurt horses like this, he could not hide his actions or put himself at the end of a single response. Family and kinship and interlocking relationships would form varying pathways to action.

"All right," Earl said quietly to Ted. "Maybe it is the system. So let's change it, you know? Can we get that done before these animals starve to death?"

They stared at each other. Ted's face worked, and his hands turned to fists at his sides.

"I'm not your enemy," Earl said.

Ted's eyes widened. He hadn't known he was prepared to strike. Recognizing it, his face went slack. His fists slowly uncurled. He stared at Earl, breathing hard.

"A lot of things are trying to make me your enemy, you know?" Earl said. "But I'm just someone with a different opinion."

Ted's shoulders slumped. Earl was almost sorry for it. There was a greatness in Ted's anger and Earl regretted that he'd subdued it. He turned his eyes to the horses. He heard their ragged breathing, the dry phlegm inside their throats, and he wished that Ted would always keep his sense of injustice and that it would sustain and not destroy him. And perhaps because he hoped for this, he said to Willi,

"Did you mean it? You brought it up. Killing Magnus. Did you mean it?"

Abraham and Isaac

∿∿∿∿

WILLI WATCHED TED'S HAND reach up again and stroke Surety's mane. Bury itself in the dark hair. He watched the horse's ears move back and forth. Did he mean it? He thought of his father's face turning from the window when he'd come back from his grandmother's funeral. His father's voice speaking his name. And how he'd looked at his father across the room, thinking still of the sad little funeral and how he'd had to support Aunt Marti, who had been grim-lipped and white. Her nails had dug into his elbow. He could still feel their sharp pressure, could imagine the red, half-moon indentations in the skin.

"Willi, I need to ask you," his father said haltingly. "You went to see her, yes. And I assumed. But maybe not. Did she tell you?"

"Tell me what?"

Willi knew. But he did not feel forgiving. He wanted to force his father to say it.

"*Lebensborn*. Did she speak of it?"

"I've just come from her funeral. Is this . . .?"

But his father held up his hands. "Please. I've been waiting for two hours. It has taken all my courage to ask."

This shook Willi. That his father would speak of courage.

"Yes," he replied. "She did."

Something frozen in his father thawed. His breathing became visible. Willi realized his fear had been that Willi would not know. And he would have to tell him.

"She told you, then, that I was . . .?"

"She told me," Willi said. He was not used to his father stumbling over sentences. To have difficulty naming, giving voice.

His father nodded. Willi moved across the living room. They took up familiar spots, looking out the window. Only this time they were speaking. Or trying to. Each of them half-speaking, making a whole of it.

"One must go a long way to leave such a thing," his father said.

Willi remembered standing outside his grandmother's house in the darkness beneath the invisible stars. He spoke what he had thought then, though the words seemed strange, aloud.

"They sacrificed you, didn't they?"

A muffled sound came from within his father's chest. He cleared his throat.

"Yes," he said. "Yes. That's it."

He gazed upon the darkening city. "It is the other side of it all," he said. "An evil coin. Two sides, but the same false metal. Death and birth both made wrong. Death to those we chose as scapegoats and foreigners. And life to ourselves."

"But not life."

"Not life. Just more death. Pretending to be life."

The first lights in the city came on, out of their nowhereness. Willi and his father had always before watched the morning city, the lights blinking off in the sun. Willi wondered if the last one to turn off was the first to turn on. And if it was always the same one. Or if the smallest variations of shadow, of cloud, changed things, so that the pattern never repeated.

"I've tried to understand what they did," his father said. "My parents. I've tried to understand how they could. I look for models. I can't help it. Perhaps it's why I became a historian. The stories of history image each other like photographs and their negatives. But I have to go almost beyond history for a model for what they did."

He paused, gathering strength and thought, and Willi waited.

"I think of Abraham," his father said. "With Isaac bound before him. Abraham did not know his god was merciful. He thought his god was hard and unforgiving. Those who see Abraham as an example of faith forget the god he knew as he raised the knife. That god desired blood. People imagine only the god who stopped the knife. But Abraham raised the knife for a god greedy for the blood of his son. Think of it. His god was more than he knew. But he didn't know the more when he raised the knife."

Lights were popping on in the near and distant dimming now. They ran in parallel lines above the walking path along the Rhine and smeared their reflections in the river. They ran in other parallel lines outlining the streets. They lost their order in the distance, became a jumble, anything the eye wanted them to be.

"So much is never known," Willi's father said softly. "What did Sara say when Abraham came to her, full of wonder at what had been revealed to him? How far did he get in his story before Sara grabbed the child from him? The story we have exists because it is incomplete. It could not survive"—he paused, his voice became a thin, weak reed—"a real mother's words."

Willi's last resistance dropped away: to hear his father want his mother. To realize how much effort it still took him to resist her. Below them an S-bahn train, coming up from Frankfurt, rumbled along the Rhine, its windows flickering with interior lights. There were people on that train, looking out the windows, seeing the world like a movie, the castles along the Rhine like fairy tales, things imagined, unreal. Did those people look up and see this window, its light, the figures standing in it? A glimpse. Did they wonder why the figures stood so still?

Willi's father spoke again, things long on his mind. "Inspiration is as much deletion as it is revelation. Our knowledge of anything comes not in the fullness of the word but in its careful canceling. The words by which we know are defined by words unsaid. And those unsaid words might be the ruination of faith. The ruination of God Himself."

He paused and then said, *"Lebensborn."*

That single word. He breathed it out and let it stand and let it disappear and let the silence cover it. Then he went on. "Well of Life. Indeed. Isaac's story is never told. Only the story of the god. Or the demon. Isaac asked his father where the sacrifice would come from. Abraham answered that God would provide it. What did Isaac think of his father's faith when it dawned on him what that answer meant? We never hear. The story of God might not survive our hearing it.

"And then history shuffles the negatives, and the story reappears, reversed. My parents, and thousands like them, reenacted it—thousands of Isaacs just like me, sacrificed to a demon who knew no mercy. The angels of a different god had to appear to stop the knives. If you can call bombers angels. Swarms of them over our cities."

He reached out and placed his arm around Willi's shoulder. The gesture was awkward, stiff. They didn't move toward each other or away, the arm like a bridge between them. Not close, not even comfortable. But connected. The city below them was nothing but light, and their own faint reflection floating, imposed, above it.

"I've never been able to say these things," his father said. "How can Isaac not be ashamed? He's seen his life reduced to nothing but his death. The whole meaning of his life nothing but his death. Life, but not life. Every thought and dream he might have had swept away. Made meaningless. And then he is untied. What life is he to live now? How can he not be ashamed? How can he not be silent? The story we have never considers God's cruelty to the boy—to wait until Isaac has seen the knife raised. Where can Isaac go from there? Perhaps he chooses to forget. But when the story is its negative, and Isaac is sacrificed to a demon who intends no mercy . . ."

He stopped, unable to finish. Then he gathered his emotions and went on, his voice husky, "When you were very young, you gave me back the life my parents stole from me. I didn't think anything could do that. I didn't know such mercy was possible. Didn't know it could still come."

Willi's throat swelled up.

"But I didn't know what I was doing," he said. "I don't remember thinking. Don't remember . . ."

"It doesn't matter. Mercy is a mystery."

For a moment Willi couldn't see anything but a great, round blur of light.

"I only wish I'd told you these things long ago," his father said.

Willi blinked, lifted a hand to his eyes. The individual lights returned.

"Do you know what the Nazis called the Jews?" his father asked, his voice dryer now, as if he had to divert them both to something more abstract. "Do you know what name they forced every Jewish man and woman to take? Along with the yellow stars, the names? The men they called Israel, the women Sara. Israel is another name for Jacob, Isaac's son. They spoke of so many Israels, so many Saras, put on trains, taken to camps."

He let the image sink in.

"And then," he said, "they reversed the story. Perverted it and created it anew."

WILLI WATCHED TED'S HAND in Surety's mane, and he thought of all these things. He listened to the slide of cartilage and tendon as Orlando lifted a hoof, and he looked at Earl, who had asked him if he meant it, that they should kill Magnus, and he thought, *Here it is again. The same story. Sacrifice and gods. Or demons. But if this is the same story, who are we in it?*

Was the story so much a part of him that he carried it with him? It seemed he had chanced upon things here, stumbled up from that fire and followed Earl. Almost foolish. Almost bumbling. But what if all along he had pushed events before him? An envelope of influence he carried. It frightened him to think of it. Could it be? He couldn't make the thought diminish, couldn't make it dwindle and go.

He felt his grandmother close. Hovering. Waiting, like Earl and Carson and Ted, for his answer. Why had he spoken of killing Magnus Yarborough? Did he mean it? Or was it just a thing he'd said? Found it in his mind and spoken it?

No: He'd meant it. It was a real possibility. And if he'd been surprised to find it in his mind, he had spoken it deliberately.

"Yes," he said to Earl. "I did."

"You agree with Ted? You think we should actually do it?"

This was a different question—the difference between possibility and actuality, between choice and decision. A fifth person here awaited his answer—not just these friends of his, and not just his grandmother, but his father, too, somehow and somewhere— maybe only in Willi's mind, but still present, listening and waiting. *Cages are everywhere,* his grandmother would say. And his father would say, *Maybe. Or not. But even then you can make decisions. Cages do not determine what you do.*

He'd said it, Willi realized, to have the choice. To define, if that's what it was, the cage. To see its limits, its size and scope. And then to say, *I will not be my cage. My blood. My history. My story. I do not have to be these things. Do not have to be driven to the one thing, the only. There are reasons beyond the cage.*

"No," he said. "I do not think that we should do it."

Ted glared at him. "Why'd you say it, then?"

"So that we know," Willi said.

"Know what? What the hell's that mean?"

Willi shrugged. He couldn't explain. Even in his native language he couldn't explain. Even if they were going to do the same as they would have done if he hadn't spoken and hadn't considered the choice, still, it was different. Maybe someday he would tell his father. His father would understand. Willi felt his grandmother, like a dried-out wisp of thistle seed, leave his mind, leave the land here, the horses, the story they all lived, and slip away, unseen.

The Badlands

THEY WAITED FOR A NEW MOON. Carson drove to the church of abandoned cars and sat in his pickup behind it. The dark, humped shapes of the cars, like raised burrows of large animals, rose out of the ground all around him. Starlight glittered off bumpers and windshield wipers and windows, off the backs of mirrors, off hubcaps and grills—dozens of softly shining blurs scattered on the hillside. Carson's grandfather, even in the dark, could probably identify each car. He might have been the last person in Twisted Tree who could narrate the story of the county by naming the cars abandoned here. Carson wondered how long it would be before the land itself lost its stories, the names of places and families disappearing, until deserted buildings were scattered more widely than these vehicles but in similar disarray throughout the county. And how long after that before all the people who might recall those buildings and the people who lived in them were also gone—moved away or dead?

He couldn't afford to think the thought. He stepped out of the pickup, stood in the cold, his breath white, listening. A car with a bad muffler pulled off the highway and labored up the hill, then unsteady headlights splashed the grass near him and shut off entirely, and Ted's car rolled out of the dark like one of the abandoned hulks come to life. Carson walked toward it, opened the door before it had even stopped moving, and stepped into the back seat. Ted had already picked up Earl and Willi. "The fewer cars the better," Ted had said. "I'll drive."

"Smells like tacos," Carson said, settling into his seat beside Earl.

"Supper." Ted unwrapped another Taco John's burrito, crumpled the greasy paper, threw it on the floorboards at his feet, and pulled around the pale white rectangle of the church. He turned his face sideways to eat, peering out the windshield over the limp burrito in his hand. He waited until he was on the highway to turn on his headlights, and when he did, they immediately dimmed, then brightened again. The loose wire under the dash sizzled, and the faint smell of ozone mingled with the smell of taco sauce and fried hamburger.

"How many of those things are you eating?" Earl asked.

"Five."

"Five?"

"I'm hungry." Ted took another bite, looked at what remained, then stuffed it all in his mouth.

"I haven't had a drink since we took those horses to my place," he said, still chewing. "But now I'm addicted to burritos."

"You haven't had a single drink?"

"Not one. It just didn't seem right. Those horses and all. Didn't seem right."

They honored this with a moment of silence, thinking what they were gathered to do. Then Carson broke the serious mood. "You eat that many burritos, I hope we're out a this car before they take effect."

"Small price to pay for being alcohol-free."

"Small price for you, maybe."

They came to the Lostman's Lake turnoff and drove past the lake, gray in the moonless night, ice creeping out from its shores toward the center where, barely visible, a few waves moved in a patch of open water. The cold weather had come hard and unrelenting, and stock ponds were frozen over, the entire land, within the space of a few days, turned to a sheet of iron.

Ted's flickering headlights discovered the old section line road, untracked, two snowy trails leading away into the darkness, ragged grass growing between them. The car plowed forward.

"We're going to leave tracks," Earl noted.

"Supposed to snow," Carson replied. "Should cover 'em up."

They silently watched the road unspool in the wan light and the occasional bush march by, skeletons of snow and ice against the darkness, whitely reflecting the headlights, redly the taillights, and then fading into the distant dark behind them. The snow crunched, the car's suspension creaked, the muffler pounded. Once a bird of immense proportions loomed in the windshield, appearing first as a faint vapor in the sky growing quickly to a cloud and then, before Ted could stop or any of them could even clutch a door handle, becoming suddenly a bird with white undersides of wings flung hugely out of the light and into the brief darkness between hood and windshield, filling the glass, obscuring all vision with out flung feathers and great eyes peering in at them before swooping upward, soundless and gone, and the road still reeling out of its long distance.

"Holy shit!" Ted whispered. "What the hell was that?"

"Musta been 'n owl."

"Never seen an owl that big."

"Musta been a big owl."

They all felt they had traveled a long way into the darkness before Ted stopped and shut off the engine. For a few moments they sat, listening to the immense, sudden silence, the darkness so complete outside the windows it seemed to be pressing against them. Finally they opened their doors and stepped out, and as their eyes adjusted, they saw the Badlands wall, a blacker blackness than the night itself, looming in the near distance, thrusting out of the plains and going straight up, solid and impenetrable. They angled toward it, feeling their way toward the horses.

"Still think it's half crazy, takin 'em in there," Carson said.

"Maybe," Ted said. "But what else we got to do?"

"Than be crazy?"

"Yeah."

"Not much, I guess, way things're goin."

It had been Ted who'd insisted they take the horses into the Badlands—the concession he'd demanded if they wouldn't go after Magnus. Carson had argued against it. "Ain't no point," he'd said. "The more complicated we make this, the more chances we got a bein caught. We ain't tryin a hide it. Just want a make sure no one knows we're the ones did 't. You think the horses's goin a care?"

Ted had surprised him. "Yeah," he'd said.

Then, as the other three looked at him, he'd said more quietly, a little abashed to be speaking of such things, "They're spiritual beings. It makes a difference how we do it."

"That is right," Willi said immediately. "I with Ted agree."

"We ain't takin 'em to church."

"That ain't what I mean."

"Point is, the end result's the same either way."

"There's nothing good in any've this. It's just one, long, ugly road, enit? And we just can't seem to get off it. So the least we oughta do is walk it the right way."

Ted said this with a vehemence that silenced them. They felt beneath his words a grief that would not end, a fog of loss and bereavement so thick he didn't understand it and so wide he couldn't remember if he'd ever been out of it, and what he was speaking now was a single, clear idea that cut through some of it—did not disperse it, but showed a way, for a while, to move within it. All of them suddenly looked up and saw each other and felt inside themselves the same kind of grieving, the same fog of loss, and each knew, without knowing the sources, that the others felt it, too. It almost frightened them—that they were so close, that what they each held secret was so nearly known and yet not known. They all felt that they had plucked the others out of the night, held the others in their eyes, and that each of them was so held, visible and yet transparent, and the feeling hushed them, made them stare at each other with a strange and humble wonder.

"You're right, Ted," Earl said, his voice like a noise carried by the breeze out of his own fog.

"What we are doing," Willi said. "It should be hard, and it should be so that we almost cannot do it. So that whatever might stop us in the world, we have to give it every chance."

Carson, feeling it all, too, yet resisted a while longer, clinging to practicality, which for so long had been his reliable guide. "I just don' know," he said. "You might be makin this more 'n it is. I'm the one trained these animals, but I ain't seein any pilgrimage here. Just a thing's gotta be done."

"Just because you don't see a pilgrimage doesn't mean you're not on one, you know?"

"It is the Red Road. And the Black Road. Both of them. And Ted is saying how we walk is what makes the difference. Is what makes one from the other."

"Yeah. Maybe I'm sayin that."

"There were horses here way back, you know? My uncle says their spirits are still in the Badlands. I think these horses would want to go there. To be with their ancestors."

"*Mitakuye Oyasin*. It's how we gotta treat 'em, enit?"

"Mitak what?"

"All my relations," Willi answered. "It is a Lakota saying meaning we are all related. Everybody, every being, every thing."

"You learn that in Germany?"

"Many people know it there."

Carson shook his head. "I been livin here all my life, an I ain't never heard it. I don't know which one a us is weirder, Willi. But OK. We'll go."

GUIDED BY LANDMARKS they had memorized the first time they'd come, they found the horses in their lonely draw. The horses came out of the darkness and allowed themselves to be bridled, and Carson took a hatchet from a sheath at his belt and chopped through the ice and managed to find some water underneath. He led the horses to it and let them drink. They slurped noisily while he pulled fence staples and removed clips, and when the horses were satisfied and the wires loose, the seven of them set off, Willi and Earl holding the wires down while Ted and Carson led the horses over them, then replacing the staples at Earl's insistence.

True to the forecast it began snowing, the night so dark they were aware of the snow first by its touch on their faces, and only then did they look and see the flakes appearing briefly in the nearer dark before disappearing again into the white earth. The wind increased, pushing the snow along the ground. All over the land, hori-

zon to horizon, they heard snow moving, millions of flakes in a
massive hush and shuffle. They walked through it, guiding themselves by the wall of the Badlands looming nearer. They knew each
other as presences of darkness moving nearby, at the same pace, in
the same silence. They lost track of time, and none of them cared
to track it. They walked the abandoned section line road, and when
it ended, they went cross-country, taking down fences when they
had to and putting them back up. Whenever they stopped, the
horses lowered their heads and grazed and then, feeling the tug of
reins, lifted their heads again and plodded on.

"Why's he doing it?"

Ted's voice startled them all, coming disembodied and sudden
from the darkness. It even startled him, and he lowered it into the
register of wind and moving snow. "These animals. What's he got
against 'em?"

There were few boundaries on such a night. There was only passage, negotiated together, and Carson replied, "He saw what he
wanted a see. That's the nearest I can come to explainin it."

And he told them, briefly, with the snow descending all around
and pinging against their jackets, what had happened, knowing they
would hold it to themselves alone. He spoke of Rebecca, and of
Magnus's presence, and how he didn't know any longer whether
Rebecca had been driven toward him, Carson, and he toward her,
by that presence, or whether they had been impelled by their own
internal gravities. He didn't know, he said, how much two people
could be attracted to each other by forces outside themselves, and
he said he had to be careful not to blame Magnus for everything,
yet he had come to think that if Magnus hadn't insisted on seeing
what he wanted to see, Rebecca would not have seen it, though he
didn't know about himself. In any case, what Magnus saw happening hadn't, after all, happened, and a man who could see what
wasn't there and could refuse to hear what was, or to acknowledge
any need for reform in his own behavior or vision, was also a man
who could confuse happiness with the exercise of power and the al-
leviation of anger with revenge, and such a man might have no way
to stop himself when circumstances of revenge and the exercise of

power formed a vicious circle. For such a man could never see beyond that circle. And these horses had come within that circle and
gotten trapped in it. Therefore, Carson repeated, all he could do to
explain why the seven of them were walking in the snow and dark
this night was that Magnus saw what he wanted to see and had the
power to go on doing so, and so he could not see that these horses
were merely horses. He had turned them into something else, into
symbols that spoke the world as he believed it was. And that, it
seemed to Carson, was a dangerous thing—to turn the things of
the world and the beings that occupied it into statements to convince yourself and others of your own notions of the world. And
Carson said he was not even sure what he meant when he said all
this, that he was himself merely trying to grasp it, and he wasn't
sure he ever would.

He spoke all this slowly, and all the time they walked, and the
wall of the Badlands grew closer so that it now loomed above them,
a black background behind the descending snow.

"I can't seem to get away from the sonofabitch," Carson said.
"Anymore I don't sometimes know if I'm thinkin somethin because
it's me thinkin it, or if it's a thought comes out a him. The last thing
he did is he's buyin our ranch."

The storm increased, obscuring even the wall before them, and
they walked for a while invisible to each other, in a world of all
sound, where only feet and hooves striking the snow and lifting
from it again served as evidence for any kind of presence at all.

"He's buying your ranch?" Earl's voice came filtered through
the snowfall.

"Offering two and a half times what it's worth. Like somehow
the sonofabitch knows that ranch's all that matters to me. Same way
he knew these horses mattered to his wife. Hell, I don't know. Ain't
no way my parents can resist that kind of money, though."

But suddenly he was seized by a great doubt that coiled in his
stomach and uncoiled like a broken spring, and he stumbled under
its force and had to fight to regain his stride. What if resistance was
the very thing his parents needed—and he'd denied it to them? What
if they needed to see what forces were aligned against or with them?

What if his silence, which he'd thought protected them and prevented him from using them, merely left them ignorant, without the information they needed to do what they might otherwise do? What if Magnus was making all the rules and setting all the structures precisely because, as Rebecca had said, he was rich enough to hide himself? Because lying was easy for him? What if he, Carson, was merely being a fool, feeding Magnus's power by his silence? Letting him take over more and more land and influence by offering to others what he knew, and perhaps only he knew, were cheap dreams, a cascade of coins cast on the floor, rolling in unsteady circles. Kneel and pick them up. And stand to find your self gone: your land, your family, your past. And think yourself a winner.

For the first time in his life, Carson felt panic rising inside him. His heart wobbled like an unbalanced pulley. He'd let Magnus convince his parents they were winners. He'd forgotten what to keep his eyes on, and he'd fallen. Fallen bad. Maybe let his parents fall, though they would never know it. Let the land fall. His grandfather. All. And maybe he had done it out of love. Maybe out of care. But it didn't matter. Maybe they were short-term things, love and care, and people like Magnus depended on people like Carson and his parents not seeing that, depended on them thinking love and care mattered beyond death and change. But what if they didn't? What if only the land did? And Carson had let Magnus have it.

If it hadn't been for Orlando's reins in his hands, Carson would have fallen when he stumbled, but he clutched at the reins, and Orlando's neck, though weak, held him up. And the horse's warm breath against his neck dampened his panic. In any case, it was too late. His parents, as he'd known they would, had decided, and his father had already signed the first papers. There was nothing to be done. Nothing at the moment but to walk forward through the snow, on this mission that was unchanged and irrevocable. And maybe he was wrong about his fears. There were no clear lines to follow. No boundaries he could be absolutely sure of. He'd done what he'd done. He hadn't spoken of the cow, and if he'd been silent out of weakness or shame as well as out of honor, there was nothing to do but accept it. Go on. But without even knowing he was speaking

aloud, without even knowing he was continuing the conversation
he'd been having with the others, that it had mingled with the realization inside his mind, he spoke in a voice of wonder and loss.

"Everything I know's on that place. How can it all get turned
into money?"

They all sensed what he meant. Not just the survey, the plat, the
spaces marked by legal definitions and fences, but the snowy surface of things ironhard right now but moving always toward
changes: the prairie flowers that would rise small and shy in the
spring, the mallards and canvasbacks that would drop into the stock
ponds, the work that defined the way one moved in the world.

"About everything can get turned into money," Earl said.
"Maybe all you can do is try not to be miserable, you know?" The
snow decreased a little, and a few stars appeared, the high clouds
scudding downwind behind them as they marched forward, the wall
rising imperceptibly higher. Earl thought of the string of cars going
down to the liquor stores in Nebraska across the reservation border—a place of black magic where even misery was turned into
money and multiplied and then carried back up across the border
stronger than when it went down. Misery was an endless resource,
inexhaustible.

"My grandmother lived her whole life miserable, I think," Willi
said. "For her, being miserable was maybe the only way she knew
how to be happy."

"Sounds pathetic," Carson said.

""It's what happened to us," Ted said. "Losing land like you're
saying."

"Us who?"

"Indians."

"Yeah. I guess it did."

"Just goes on. Guns or money. However it works. No one much
cares what land means to the people who don't keep it."

"That makes me feel better."

"I'm just saying."

They walked in silence for an indefinite time. Then Earl's voice,
lilting, questioning, arose out of the night.

"There wasn't anything you could do, you know?" he said. "It's hard to fight a robber. Our grandfathers tried about everything, you know?"

For a moment Carson was flooded with emotion. What a strange, quiet guy Earl was. In one way his words meant that Carson's own ancestors were robbers of the land. Yet Earl intended comfort. And, oddly, Carson felt better. He wasn't sure Earl was right—that there was nothing he could have done—but the words nonetheless relieved him, in some nameless way forgave him.

THEY STRUGGLED UPWARD through narrow corridors of clay and sand, the dark escarpments of the Badlands rising above them, finding their way with no idea where they were going, only knowing they had to go and believing they would recognize their arrival. The walk had weakened the horses, and the climb slowed them. They plodded with their heads down, needing constant urging. With the passing of the storm, the stars shed enough light on the whitened ground so they could see obstacles and stones in their way. Ted walked ahead, guiding, and the others followed, each holding reins, leading the horses single file. They went inward and up, through narrow channels that sometimes dead-ended, forcing them to retreat and try another. They felt as if they were walking into the sky and would emerge in some skyland where nothing was familiar. They lost their sense of direction. Though the Great Bear wheeled above them around the pivot of the North Star, they did not bother to read that direction or to be guided by it. The land controlled where they could go, and they moved within its maze.

It might have been evening yet, or midnight, or early morning, and their memory of leaving Twisted Tree and arriving together where the horses were held seemed like a vision from another world, a faint and foregone era. And as they passed through the broken land, changing yet always the same, space, too, seemed to end, so that they felt they were moving without moving, heading toward a destination at which they'd already arrived. Somewhere within all this the voice of the Badlands began. It came so much out of the land and wind that when they realized they were hearing it, they did not know whether it had just started or whether it had been going on for a long time already. It was a low moan of many different pitches coming from all around them, emanating from the walls rising beside them, dropping out of the spaces between the stars. It rose and fell, increased and decreased without ever ending, a sound so constant and varied, so deep and thin, that it seemed an element they moved through, and they all grew calm, and they imagined at times that the earth produced the music and at other times that the music shaped the earth and carved the dark escarpments around them.

Even Willi, who had never heard the voice of the Badlands nor read about it, accepted the music as part of the place, but after a while he asked, "Where does it come from? This sound? How is it made?"

"It depends on who you ask," Earl said. The horses plodded onward, their hooves like soft drumbeats keeping some kind of rhythm. "Maybe it's an organ, you know? The wind coming through these canyons. Or maybe, like my uncle says, it's spirits singing. The wind is Tate, the breath of the Great Mystery. Maybe this is the music of Mystery. It sounds that way, you know?"

Willi thought about this, then said, "Maybe it is Inyan and Taku Skanskan singing together."

"Inyan an who?" Carson asked. They were all talking in voices of dream, and they all heard each other's voices as if coming from a dream or entering their own dreams, voices crossing the threshold of sleep.

"Inyan is rock," Earl explained. "The power of rock, you know? The stillness. You know how you can't believe sometimes how a rock can just be and be and be? Just stay that way? That is Inyan. And Taku Skanskan is the mystery that moves. You know?—moves the things that move. How sometimes you can't hardly believe clouds? Or migrating birds?"

They walked in silence.

"Yeah," Carson said, after a time that might have been a long time or might have been short, a time in which they might have moved far or not at all. "I know."

"And Willi is saying they get together sometimes. And sing," Ted said.

"And listen," Willi said "you cannot tell if the music is moving or is still."

And then, at some point, they were moving downward, bracing against the pull of gravity, loosened pebbles rolling ahead of them, the earth jarring against their spines and the narrow lanes of land widening, until they emerged from one of those lanes into a barren meadow set around with sky and with the broken peaks of the Badlands jutting into it. They each knew, without any of them speaking, that they had arrived, and they stopped and circled to face each other. Beasts and men huddled, breathing their white breathing into the circle they formed, until the circle they formed filled with white breath that rose upward out of it and was filled again.

"We come this far," Carson said. "You all sure?"

By their silence they spoke. But because they were human, tricked by Iktomi, inventor of language, and knew the word as the beginning and the end, the holy and the strange and the daily and the everlasting, Earl spoke for all their silences. "We can't let them go. They'd starve out here. And they wouldn't make it back. And if they did . . ."

Nevertheless they stood and waited. The voices of the spirits that inhabited this place, voices of air and earth, voices of all the numerous animals that had died in the long centuries here and whose bones rose up in the rain's erosion, the Wakinyan calling forth the Unktehi, the present calling forth the past, and all speaking—these voices filled the circular meadow, and Carson's and Earl's voices became part of the chorus. And then through it all came the howl of a coyote and then another, answering. The horses raised their heads momentarily and let them drop again.

"I'm wondering," Carson said, "what did the old-time Lakota do when they had a sick or dying animal? All my relations. What'd they do?"

Had this been a place or moment for surprise, they might have been surprised at the question, but they were not.

"I don't know," Earl said. "I've never heard."

"Me, either," Ted said. "You know, Willi? You read that some-where?"

Willi shook his head: a knowledge lost to all of them, having failed all means of transmission, at least to their small group.

"Listen to them coyotes," Ted said. "There used to be wolves all over out here. And grizzlies and mountain lions. The old-time people had a lot of help."

"Wolves," Carson said.

He thought of his grandfather again, sitting on that hillside lis-tening to the coyotes calling. And he remembered a picture his grandfather had shown him, of his own father, bearded, rifle in hand, outside a shed that had long since disappeared from the ranch, the corpses of twenty-five wolves hanging head down, nailed to the wall behind him. That old ancestor of his stared at the camera with a look of grim pride and accomplishment. Some of the wolves had their mouths open. Some had them shut.

Carson wondered how many other hundreds of such pictures there were that he'd never seen, and how many hundreds more such scenes that had never been photographed, in how many other such places now swallowed by time. The memory of that photograph filled him with sorrow. He thought of what Ted had said, and he thought that the way of life he now feared losing was itself built on something vanished and gone, and his family in its early ignorance and hope, its eyes cast only on the future, had been a cause of that earlier vanishing. So much gone, he thought. So much going. The wolves had been strangely white in the photograph, white against the dark shed, and his great-grandfather's face was dark under its hat, the rifle dark, only the pelts of the lifeless wolves shining in the sun, as if the last life within them resided yet in their fur and reluctantly left this world, clinging on, a thing of too much beauty, even after the heart had stopped and the feet no longer ran and the flesh had been nailed to the shed. And Carson himself now feeling like something vanished and gone, though his blood still ran in his veins and his feet walked the earth and his voice came out of him in the shape of words.

He felt the spirit of those vanished wolves gathered here, spirits ferocious and merciful and strangely moral, speaking that the starving and the weak shall be the first chosen. And that life shall stumble on.

Then Ted, speaking his words for him, said, "It was different back then. We're doing the work of wolves. They ain't here to do it. We got to do it for them."

FROM INSIDE HIS COAT Earl removed Norman's .38 pistol, not the same one he had pawned in his drinking days but one he had bought after he sobered up, "kinda to remind myself," he said, "that that's not something I want to get close to again." Earl had asked Norm if he could borrow it. Norm had waited to answer, then said, "Were you thinking you might tell me what you want to borrow it for?"

"I was thinking I might not have to, you know?"

Norm nodded meditatively. "That's a warrior's tool," he said. "Are you going to use it like a warrior?"

"I am."

"Be careful, nephew."

"I will be."

"I don't just mean the pistol. I mean being a warrior is a hard thing. It is. Guard your spirit well."

"I will try to, Uncle."

Now he removed the .38 from his coat, a gray, lumpish thing that during the long walk had knocked against his ribs like a cold, exterior heart. He held it in his hands, looked down at it. They all did.

"You know?" he said. "This scares me."

"It's not goin a be easy."

"I meant, for myself. What's this going to do to us?"

He looked up and met their eyes. A moment of realization and wonder. Quiet and cold and the moan of the land, and their eyes shining and bewildered.

"We'll be OK," Carson said. "It's the right thing to do."

"That is not enough," Willi said.

"Not?"

"Being right is not enough. Even if this is the best thing to do. Even if it is the only thing. We must not think we are pure. Maybe not even OK."

He looked up, at the peaks of the Badlands thrust into the sky all around them, and the bright, indifferent constellations, and then he looked down again at the attentive faces of the others.

"My grandfather did terrible things," he said. "He put people into trenches. He shot them. And the Nazis, they said they could do those things and keep their hearts pure. My father says they thought the Reich would be a perfect world. He says we cannot trust perfect worlds. Or a man who believes his heart is pure."

Willi's father had said these things during their long talk after the old woman's funeral. Willi had never spoken of his grandfather to anyone. He had never repeated anything his father had said, never taken it as his own. It all felt a little strange and frightening. The wind blew, the horses stamped, the earth revolved, the stars cast their vast quantities of light and energy into the void. In the silence Willi watched the others, half-afraid.

Then Ted winked at him, and Ted's sly grin appeared. "Original sin, enit?" he said.

"Original sin?"

"Hey, I'm the Pope's man. My parents made me take classes and go to church when they weren't too drunk to remember. I know all about original sin. The whole damn world's fallen. So even if we do the right thing here, it still might be a bad thing. And we're all guilty as hell for doing it."

"Yeah," Carson said. "And maybe we oughta be."

"You know what we have to do?" Earl said. "We have to burn sage."

HE HADN'T KNOWN UNTIL NOW why Norm had given him the Ziploc bag with dried sage in it.

"Take it along," Norm had said. "You might just need it."

Now Earl removed the bag from his coat pocket, opened it. The smell rose and spread to them, pungent and aromatic. At the bottom of the bag was a disposable cigarette lighter. Earl fumbled for it, brought it out, flicked it to test it. It sprang to life, a tiny flame, and they were all surprised to see each other's faces so near, composed of moving shadow. Then Earl lifted his thumb, and the moving shadows flowed back into the darkness they'd come from. They moved in a dreamlike fashion. Earl handed a few sprigs of sage to Ted, who held them toward him, and Earl lit the dried leaves with the lighter, all of them gathered near to form a windbreak around the flame. Finally the sage glowed and smoked, a powerful and sacred smoke that they all breathed in. None of them knew quite what they should do, whether there was or had ever been a proper ceremony for what they were about to do. Their movements were uncertain, and they looked to one another for guidance. Earl nodded to Ted, and Ted looked at Earl. Then he stepped forward into the small circle they all formed.

He waved the sage slowly. It made red streaks in the air, as if he were writing some indecipherable thing there, instantly gone. Its smoke mingled with their breath. Ted looked to the sky to locate himself, then held the sage to the west, then north, then east, then south, then down to the earth and straight up to the sky, and he passed the smoke over them all and spoke of how they did not wish to do what they were doing, and of their willingness nevertheless to do it. Then he ceased, unsure what else to do or say, and handed the sage to Earl.

Earl turned and passed its smoke over Surety. He walked entirely around the horse and asked for courage for it, and bid it goodbye, then returned and blessed its head again and gave the sage to Willi, who blessed Jesse in German and English and Lakota, and as he walked around the horse, he told it they could not know whether it assented to what would shortly happen, but he wanted it to know they had considered its assent, and that was the best that humans in their ignorance could do, because the gulf between their acts and their awareness was so wide, and yet they had to act, unlike the horse, which had only to live. He told the horse how fraught with peril were their actions and how little they could really know. Then he handed the sage to Carson, who looked at it in his hands, so unfamiliar, then looked at the others, who encouraged him with their eyes, until he turned to Orlando. Holding the sage in his right hand, he reached up and touched the horse on its long and narrow forehead with his left and reminded it of how wild it had been when they first met, how the world had looked like nothing but danger and threat then, but how it had learned to order and trust the world, and how he, Carson, had been honored to be its guide in that ordering. He removed his hand from the horse's skull and walked around it, imitating Earl and Willi, and as he walked, he told the horse that he had perhaps been wrong, after all, in teaching it to trust the world or to believe in the order Carson had taught it, for that order and trust had brought them here, and if the horse could have kept itself wild and suspicious and unwilling to do anything Carson had asked, perhaps things would have been different. But they weren't.

He returned to Orlando's head and returned the sage to Ted, who once again passed its smoke over them so that they all breathed it in, and then he extinguished it by pressing it into the earth.

"It's time," Carson said.

They all looked at Earl, who again reached into his coat where he had returned the pistol.

"We got to do this one at a time," Carson said. "In different places. Otherwise we got a panic. I'm willin to do it all, if you want."

"No," Earl said. "It's all of us."

"We'll take one," Carson said. "Someone's gotta stay with the other two here."

They looked at each other, unsure. "I will stay first," Willi said.

Carson handed him two sets of reins, took the other set in his hands, stepped away from the circle they all formed. The horse turned and followed, and Earl and Ted caught up, and they all walked forward into darkness.

The Work of Wolves

~~~~~

ONE BY ONE THE HORSES FELL in separate canyons, collapsing and losing shape and sinking into the ground until they looked as if they would go through the soil and disappear, kicking and twitching until the kicking and twitching stopped, and they lay immense and still.

Fire and Ice

∧∧∧∧∧

THEY DIDN'T SPEAK the whole long walk back. The mute way the horses had faced the pistol and the mute way they had fallen had infected the four of them, so that when they thought of speaking, the words rose like underwater things in their throats and sank back down to silence. Above them the Dog Star loped down its lanes of loneliness. They felt they would never leave what they'd just done. It would always be close. Always proximate. None of them knew a word in any language for what they were feeling: regret that is not regret, regret that points not to futility and uselessness but to necessity and so demarcates the stark but not barren outlines of the world. None of them had a word for this. They had to let their silence speak it. They walked side by side when they could, sometimes touching, letting the accidental drift and bump happen and maintaining the contact a fraction longer than mere accident would allow.

In the dark of early morning, they emerged into time again and stared at Ted's car parked where they had left it—a vague memory, almost familiar, from another life. They milled around it and did not enter it, until slowly the future returned to them, and they knew its urgency and remembered the coming light. Then they opened the doors and settled into their seats, and Ted started the engine and turned the car around and drove back the way they had come.

"We're just making new tracks," Earl said at one point.

No one answered him for a long time. The car ground onward. The lights of Twisted Tree appeared in the sky, a faint glowing, and high against them the red, blinking lights of Tower Hill, on and off and on.

"Maybe it will snow some more," Willi finally offered.

"Maybe."

But the thought of being found out no longer mattered to any of them. They couldn't bring its consequences into their imaginations. Their minds were consumed by the recent past and couldn't shape any detailed future.

"He wanted 'em gone," Ted said. "Why would he bother to report 'em?"

"Maybe he won't. But then why did he let them starve in the first place?"

Another long silence. The red lights rose over them, and Red Medicine Creek, off on their right, began to widen, and they were back in familiar territory—above them, the fence they had crossed so often when the horses were pastured by the artesian spring, and below them, the ice of Lostman's Lake spreading inward from the shore to the dark, lapping waves at its center. Ted drove out of the old road, and the swish of frozen grass bending under the car turned to the crunch of gravel under cold snow.

"Jesus," Carson said, "I'm tired."

Suddenly they were all exhausted. Drained. The words provoked weariness from their veins and bones, and they slumped against the doors and seats momentarily like drunks. They were halfway past the lake, the shoreline just a few yards from them, when Ted's burritos had the effect they had feared. His hands loose on the wheel, Ted leaned back in his seat, bracing his left leg against the floorboard, to lift his butt from the upholstery.

"This'll wake us up," he said.

And ripped an enormous fart.

As he did, his braced foot caught one of the burrito wrappers he'd thrown on the floor earlier and pushed it upward. At the same time the headlights dimmed, the wire under the dashboard sizzled, and then the headlights died entirely and the car erupted into flames. It all happened at once, the lights from outside the car suddenly sucked inside to become flame, and they could no longer see out at all. The flames rose up from under the dashboard, spreading from the pile of greasy wrappers as if they were gasoline. They

caught Ted's pants leg and the car's upholstery, so quickly the air itself seemed to have caught fire.

For a moment they were stunned. They sat in the burning vehicle
staring at what was happening, all four of them, and in that time the
fire leapt from the upholstery to the roof and ran backwards in a sizzling sheet. They ducked. Ted rammed the transmission into PARK,
and all four doors opened, and they tumbled onto the frozen gravel
headfirst, reaching out with their arms to break their falls, spreading
away from each other and from the burning car in four directions.

Earl, who was on Ted's side, lay for a moment in the snow. Then
he thought of the possibility of the gas tank catching fire. He
jumped up and heard flames outside the car and then Ted's voice,
shouting, but oddly calm and unconcerned.

"Shit! I'm on fire!"

Earl looked up, and the sight that met his eyes was so strange,
grotesque, and unexpected that at first he didn't comprehend it.
When Ted fell from the car, the snow had extinguished the fire on
his pants cuff, but his coat had ignited, and he was crawling around
on his hands and knees in a little circle, proclaiming loudly that he
was on fire—flames shooting out of his back and rising into the air
above him. His hands and knees were scurrying frantically, and
snow was flying from them, and the fire on his back was casting
shadows that doubled his limbs, so that he looked to Earl like a great
and grotesque and flaming spider spinning some notionless spider-
web in the snow.

Earl walked over, put his foot on the side of Ted's ribs, and
kicked him over.

He pushed so hard Ted lifted off the ground, his legs and arms
still flailing, and flipped onto his back. The fire sizzled in the snow.
Ted lay staring up at Earl, slowly waving his arms and legs as if they
were winding down, while the car blazed behind them, throwing
lurid, orange light.

Earl knelt next to Ted. "Are you all right?"

"I think so." Ted wiggled his back against the ground.

Earl held out his hand. Ted grasped it, and Earl pulled him to
his feet. The fire had burned the outer shell of Ted's coat but hadn't

burned completely through the insulation and inner membrane. The back of the coat was a charred hole, with blackened filler sticking out of it, but Ted was unharmed except for his long hair, which had curled from the heat, leaving the nape of his neck exposed.

Carson and Willi had come around the car. Carson slapped some of the char off Ted's coat. "Nice haircut," he said.

"Look at my car!"

They suddenly all recalled the car, which by now was a flaming wreck, fire bursting from all four doors, sheets of hot vapor lifting into the air.

"We must the doors shut!" Willi ran to the car, shielding his face with his hands, and kicked the driver's door shut, backed away for a moment, then did the same thing to the back door. Earl and Carson, seeing what he was doing, ran to the other side and did the same thing. Immediately the flames, deprived of oxygen, diminished, and within a few seconds the car darkened and filled with smoke, and the last orange light within it died.

"What do we do now?" Willi asked.

Though it was still dark, the eastern horizon was graying.

"Damn good question," Carson said.

Their predicament slowly became clear to them all. "Even Longwell might just figure out a connection between that"—Earl nodded at the car—"and those horses disappearing. If it comes to that."

"If the fire did not the engine reach," Willi suggested hopefully, "maybe we could drive it."

"Be a bit hot," Carson said.

"Sure is full a smoke, enit? If we opened and closed the doors, we could send messages. Sell it to the phone company, improve service on the rez."

"There you go."

"Or we got us a Port-a-Hell. We could sell tickets. All them born-agains? What'd they give to ride in that? Take it to Rapid City, Denver. Better 'n winning a bingo game."

"Has anyone noticed morning is coming?" Earl asked.

They all looked at the eastern sky.

"Truth is," Ted said, "that car ain't worth a thing. Maybe we should just make it disappear. Use some old-time Indian magic. What they used to do when they needed a vehicle to disappear."

"They did not have vehicles in the old-time days," Willi informed him.

"They didn't? Well, they used this on travois, then."

"What the hell you talkin about?" Carson asked.

Ted started to grin. His face was covered with streaks of soot, and he looked like a demented clown who'd had an accident with his makeup.

"Time for a magic act," he said. He pointed with his lips to the open water in the middle of the lake. "Courtesy the Army Corps of Engineers."

THEY GATHERED AT THE CAR'S REAR, with Ted in the open driver's door to steer. They feared that when he opened the door, the car might burst into flames again, but all that happened was that Ted disappeared for a moment in the cloud of smoke that rolled out. Then they all pushed. The car moved slowly at first, gaining momentum, then rolling down the slope of the shore as they stopped and watched it. They expected it to break through the ice and sink, but instead it rolled ponderously off the frozen gravel and with a squeak of springs and a sigh and crack of ice, squatted on the lake. They stared at it.

"What do we do now?"

"Hafta keep going," Ted said.

"Walk out there an push that sonofabitch? Are you nuts? If we're pushin when it sinks, we're gonna go with it. Unless you got some way we can walk on water."

"We'll push it until we don't think it's safe, enit? Then we'll start it and put it in gear and let it go the rest of the way on its own."

"Why not just do that right now?"

"Can't be sure it'll go straight. It's gotta go toward that open water. We get it going, and it turns and just drives around on the ice, we really got a mess."

"I can't swim. You know that?"

"Don't matter. You fall through that ice, the cold'll kill you even if you can swim."

"Well, hell, let's go then. I thought I had somethin to worry about."

They walked tentatively onto the ice, one at a time, and approached the car. The ice creaked but held, and they put their gloved hands to the trunk lid and began to push. The car moved slowly out toward the center of the lake.

They were about fifty yards from shore when the first crack came, loud as lightning splintering the sky. It started at their feet and boomed away, the lake suddenly and dangerously alive, the ice shuddering and vibrating in the soles of their boots. Sound and space were sucked into the splintering and then suddenly given back, and they jerked their hands off the car and stood completely still, letting the vehicle roll a few feet away from them.

"We're still here," Ted noted.

"And so's it."

The car crouched on the ice like an obstinate animal. Behind Tower Hill the sky was lightening, the clouds above the towers glowing faint orange.

"We gotta get that damn thing sunk before someone drives by on the highway."

"Go on back," Ted said. "I'll take care of it."

The open water was thirty yards away, lapping quietly at the ice, chuckling and subsiding. The cold smell of it came to them.

Ted started to shuffle toward the car. The others didn't move.

"Go back," he said.

"What if you fall through?"

"Then you probably ain't gonna be able to save me anyway."

"I wish we had a rope brought."

"We didn't expect to be drownin a car."

Ted shuffled forward, taking baby steps. His diminished hair blew about his ears, and the hole in his coat widened in the wind like a mouth opening, full of blackened teeth. The ice trembled. Underneath their feet the water was so near. A few inches. And then it went down. To a cold and rocky bottom, where trees stood upright yet, their naked branches lifting leafless to a sky that had been withdrawn from them. If the car would go through and open the ice to all of them, and if cold and weight would take them, they would drift down to hang like misshapen fruits in that forest of desert trees. Earl thought of how the spirits of that world, wandering between barkless trees and branches, might come upon them hanging head down. He thought of how silent it would all be, how silent the four of them and how silent the spirits contemplating this detritus from the upper world where they themselves had once moved and acted. It was the thought of that silence more than anything that made Earl shiver. How the spirits would look and pass on.

Ted reached the car and touched it and opened the door, and the ice held, though the creaking of the hinges seemed enough to shatter the world.

"Ted," Carson called. "Don't get in the thing. Start it standing."

Ted stared into the blackened interior of the car. They saw his head bend down to look, saw his burned and matted hair fall forward over his face. Then he stood erect and gazed at the open water. A breeze shivered over it, and it broke into a million points that then went still, and empty blackness settled there. Ted stood stock still, his back to them.

"Ted?" Earl called.

Ted turned slowly around, his face somber as stone. He didn't seem to see them, though he looked right at them. Earl, seeing his eyes as empty as the water's surface behind him, felt a jolt of fear. "Ted," he said again, more quietly.

Then Ted's teeth suddenly flashed white in his blackened face. "You're all supposed to be back on shore by now. You know what? I wouldn't get in this thing for a dozen burritos and a beer."

He reached inside the car and wrapped his arm around the steering column to find the ignition key. Gritty snow scampered along the ice and struck the car with a sound like sand.

Ted turned the key. The whole lake shook beneath the engine's rocking, and a second great splintering thundered through the ice, echoed off the hills surrounding the lake, rebounded and echoed again. They stood within the sound, paralyzed.

"Sometimes it don't start right away," Ted said.

"Christ!"

Ted turned the key again, and again the ice trembled as the starting motor rocked the vehicle. The lake felt like gelatin beneath their feet. Then the engine caught and smoothed and ran, and the ice stopped moving. Ted waited a moment to be sure the car would keep running, then pulled the gearshift lever down. The car lurched forward. He stayed with it for three steps, his hand inside the door, holding the steering wheel.

"Let the sonofabitch go," Carson yelled.

Ted looked back, grinning. Then he withdrew his arm and stood on the ice, hair ragged around his head, coat gaping as the car rolled forward, the door wide open. Finally Ted turned and shuffled away from it, spiderlike, his feet scurrying over the ice.

The car was only about ten yards away from him when the lake made a sound like a sigh.

The car was gone, nosing down without a splash, its taillights for just a moment pointing upward like red eyes as the water poured in the open door, and then the ice was barren except for snow upon it. And the four of them.

Ted looked back over his shoulder at where the car had been. Then he looked down to his feet. He lifted his face and stared at the other three, halfway between them and the open water. They stared back at him. Willi unconsciously lifted a hand toward him, as if to pull him in. For a moment more Ted stood, a statue carved and frozen. Then a grin spread on his face, and he turned into a crazy, sooty magician whose magic was a danger and who hadn't escaped unscathed but who nevertheless had triumphed. He waved his hand as if to erase the world, then walked grinning up to the others.

"Let's get off this ice," he said.

They gathered around him, wrapped him into their group, and all four turned toward shore.

"Like the old Lakota used to say, if your car burns up, drowning don't hurt it much," Ted said.

"I told you the old Lakota did not have cars," Willi informed him.

They grinned at each other.

"That right? Did you know that, Earl?"

"No. I never realized that."

"I knew it," Carson said.

"Well," Ted mused, "they're gonna say it when I'm an old Lakota."

They reached the shore, climbed the bank.

"Now we gotta get home without attractin attention," Carson said.

"We can go across country to my place," Earl said. "If we stay in the draws, we might be OK. Then I can take you all home."

"I hope my mother here is not up yet," Willi said.

"What are you goin to tell her if she is?"

"I do not know. What would happen if I told her the truth, do you think?"

No one could guess.

The Invisible Cop

∧∧∧∧∧

OUR DAYS LATER Earl was at his desk at school, trying to concentrate on the math problem scrawled across the board. He had seen the solution before Mr. Edwards finished writing the problem, but he was trying to pay attention anyway, to sink into the mundane step-by-step of the problem's working out. If he didn't, he kept seeing the horses falling under the thin gold ring of the new moon above the Badlands. He kept smelling the dust their bodies raised when they fell. When he'd gotten home after taking the others to their houses, he'd stepped into the shower, and dust had run off him like mud off a pickup. It had collected in the bottom of the shower, and he'd had to use the soles of his feet like squeegees to force it down the drain. He'd found blood on his clothes and had washed the garments in the shower, too, and seen the red streaks turn pink and drain away.

When he'd walked into school this Wednesday morning, the place seemed quieter—or more, it seemed that he carried a bubble of silence around him that caused people to stop talking when he neared and to glance at him and glance away. As he was hanging his coat in his locker, he felt a touch on his shoulder and turned around, expecting some prank, but instead it was Meredith Remembers Him, walking by, reaching out and touching him, letting her fingertips slide off his shoulder and across his shoulder blade, a line of touch he felt all morning, and looking back over her shoulder as she walked and saying, "Morning, Earl." And when he walked in the door of his first-hour math class, he felt that envelope of silence, momentary, fleeting, before the buzz in the room resumed. No one said anything to him as he took his seat, but he felt eyes on him. He wondered if there was something wrong with him. Were the dust and blood he still felt on his skin actually visible? Were people seeing something about him that he didn't see when he looked in the mirror?

He was trying to concentrate on the steps to the math problem when he felt another hand on his shoulder, immediately erasing the residue of Meredith's easy fingers. It was Tyler Ellison, whose favorite relief from boredom was pulling a hair out of his head and tickling Earl's ear with it, or poking Earl in the back with a ballpoint pen or writing on his neck. Tyler made no bones about disliking Indians. His grandfather had disliked them and so did his father, and Tyler was determined to maintain the family tradition. It troubled him immensely to be seated behind Earl in math class, and it troubled him even more that Earl surpassed him in the class by leaps and bounds, though Tyler had no qualms about peeking over Earl's shoulder during tests, and Earl had often felt Tyler's hot breath against his neck and heard his small, raspy breathing as he leaned forward, trying to see Earl's answers.

Feeling Tyler's hand now, Earl braced himself. He pretended to ignore the touch. But as usual Tyler wouldn't accept such displays of ignorance. He pressed harder, and Earl heard his own name whispered, faint as passing wings. "Hey. Walks Alone."

Earl still didn't turn around. He saw the students immediately surrounding him surreptitiously turn their heads and glance at him, but he pretended not to have heard Tyler whisper his name. Then the hand left his shoulder, and he thought that perhaps for once Tyler was going to give up.

Then he heard Tyler's whispered voice again, words fluttering by, moth wings at night, recognized only after they were gone. "Way to go, Walks Alone. You done all right."

AND SO THE KNOWN and the not-known got mixed up, until it seemed no one in Twisted Tree could tell the difference. Or those who could weren't speaking. Silence began to say more than words. Stories became random—bats at dusk, flickering, yet intent, impossible to follow. Goat Man was here. He was there. Mrs. Germain even reported seeing him in the Donaldson's Foods parking lot, a thin, moving shape under the blue, static lights, crouching for a moment behind the glowing wires of the carts in the cart corral.

When Greggy Longwell entered Jerry's Place, things were almost the same as they'd always been: the men at their dice cups casting for breakfast, the early-morning women lifting and setting down their heavy mugs stained with lipstick, people lifting their faces and greeting him as he walked to his favorite booth, and the men who occupied it with him as hearty or subdued in their "good mornings" as they always were. Except that Greggy noticed the conversation in his booth lost all speculation. No one seemed to have opinions any more. Conversation was all crop prices and weather. Greggy got tired of hearing about snow.

FOR SEVERAL MILES headlights had been in Earl's mirror. He'd taken Ted to talk to a man about a car for sale, but Ted and the owner couldn't reach an agreement, and Earl was taking Ted home. The headlights behind him maintained an even distance, just close enough to partially blind him whenever he glanced in the mirror. He was happy to get to the turnoff to the little-used gravel road that led to Ted's place. But the headlights followed him onto it. What were the chances? He was about a mile down the road, having just topped a rise and descended into a dip, when the headlights were joined by new lights, red and blue ones, stabbing out of his mirror and into his eyes. His heart leapt in his chest. He looked at his speedometer, found nothing to accuse him. He pulled to the side of the road.

"What the hell's this about?" Ted asked.

"I don't know."

"A cop stopping us on a gravel road? What'd you do?"

"Nothing. I don't know what's going on. I was being careful, you know?"

Ted opened the glove compartment. "You got your registration in here?"

"I don't know. Do I need that?"

"You ain't ever been stopped before?"

A car door slammed behind them.

"Here it is." Ted lifted the registration and proof of insurance out of the glove compartment. As he handed it to Earl, Greggy Longwell's face appeared, gazing through the side window.

"Longwell," Ted murmured. "What the hell? He can't stop us on the rez, can he?"

"He just did."

Earl was suddenly aware that they were at the bottom of the depression and that no one could see them from anywhere, unless someone just chanced to come down this forsaken road. Outside the window Greggy now stood upright, his hand on the holster of his gun, waiting. Earl rolled his window down.

"Evenin, gentlemen," Greggy said.

"Good evening."

Ted poked Earl on the shoulder, made a backward motion with his fingers to indicate Earl should show Greggy the vehicle registration. Earl handed it up, but Greggy didn't take it from him. He merely looked down at it, but kept his hand on the butt of his pistol. Earl let the registration rest on the window frame.

"Mr. Walks Alone and Mr. Kills Many," Greggy said. "Out for a drive."

Ted poked Earl again, and Earl held the documents up toward Greggy, but Greggy ignored them. Earl let them drop onto his lap. An ominous silence descended.

"We're on the rez," Ted said. "You can't stop us out here like this."

"Probably true," Greggy said.

"We want, we can just drive away."

"Probably true, too."

Earl thought, however, that would not be wise.

"The thing is," Greggy said. "I ain't even here."

Ted and Earl glanced at each other, then at the dark hill in front of them. Earl realized Greggy had shut off his rack and even his headlights. They were in deep darkness, with only the cone of Earl's headlights to give any vision, and the thin half-moon sliding across the sky.

"Like Goat Man," Greggy said pleasantly. "Ain't that how he is? He's there, and then by God he ain't? That's me right now. Wouldn't surprise me none if you two could see right through me. That's how much I ain't here."

"What do you want?" Ted said tonelessly.

"Just wanta talk. Want some good conversation."

"Right." Ted's belligerence surfaced. "You got lonely. Decided you needed to talk to a couple Indians."

"Something like."

Earl and Ted stared out the windshield.

"Thing is," Greggy continued, hooking one thumb in his belt, leaving the other hand on his holster, "no one else seems a wanta talk to me any more. I ain't just Goat Man. I'm the goddamn Maytag repairman. Lonely as hell. Goddamn shame, ain't it? Gotta stop a couple fine gentlemen like you out here in the middle a nowhere just to find someone who'll talk to me."

"Let's go, Earl."

"Bambi died."

"Bambi died?!" The unexpected news shocked Earl.

The sheriff's flat eyes gazed at him impassively. "Got hit. What you'd expect. Kid says he didn't turn one way or the other. Kept a straight line. Dog was gettin old."

This news was a final drop. Sorrow overflowed in Earl. The dog wasn't even his. But he felt that if he opened his mouth, sorrow would leak out of it like a milky, vaporous liquid. He knew for sure tears would come. He looked away from Greggy. It was just too much.

"I shoulda stopped that game, maybe," Greggy said. "Trouble is, wasn't my jurisdiction. What I think is, that dog just liked those lights. Musta filled the whole world for him. And he just finally forgot they weren't the whole world. What I think, anyway."

Earl looked back up at the sheriff, startled. Greggy met his eyes directly.

"Sometimes those lights can't be avoided, I guess," Earl said.

"Sometimes they can't."

Ted interrupted. "You telling me you followed us out here to tell us Bambi got hit?"

Greggy reached his left hand to Earl's outside mirror, twisted it so it stuck out away from the car, and looked into it. "Like I said, I ain't even here. See? Can't even see myself. Nothing but night in that mirror."

"If you got no reason for stopping us, I think we oughta be going."

"Didn't you usta have a car? That Citation with them bad headlights?"

Earl and Ted looked at each other.

"I was always waitin for them headlights to give out entire. Ticket you. What happened to that car? Why's Mr. Walks Alone chauffeurin you around?"

"A relative's got it. My cousin."

"Your cousin." Greggy pushed the mirror back in Earl's direction. "There. That about right?" It wasn't even close. The mirror shot out into space, catching a single star in its center. "Your cousin from around here?"

"New Mexico."

"New Mexico. You got a Navaho cousin, do you? And I'm guessin he's borrowin that car for a real long time."

"Something like that."

"It's good havin relatives, ain't it?"

Ted only nodded. For a while silence reigned. It was awfully dark. It was awfully quiet.

"You stopped us because you wanta know my family tree?"

"I'd be fascinated. But no, that ain't really it."

Greggy looked into the cast of Earl's headlights, the gravel road with its small pebbles throwing shadows ten yards long.

"No," he said. "I'm mainly just lonely. No one's talkin to me any more. 'Course I always got things to think about. Puzzles, you might say. Part a the job, puzzlin is. Most a the job, really. So even on nights when no one's speedin or crossin the center line, and everyone's headlights are workin fine, I'm not generally bored. Spend all my time puzzlin."

"That right?" Ted asked. "I always thought you were doing cross-stitch."

"I never cross-stitch in my car. But here's the thing about puzzlin. Usually I get all sortsa help. Most of it ain't worth a damn, but still. Anywhere I go, people're offerin me advice. Clues. Half my job is sortin it out. Most things, I got 'n *excess* of information. Too damn much. Confuses the issues. Makes it harder to figure out what happened."

"Fascinating," Ted said, truculently. Earl had withdrawn from the conversation. He watched the star in his mirror creep slowly off center as the earth turned.

"Oh, it is," Greggy said. "But there's a thing goin on right now that's more damn puzzlin than the puzzle itself. You two heard anything about them horses disappeared off Magnus Yarborough's place? Again?"

Earl had reached out with his fingertips to push the mirror and bring the star back into the center. He jerked his hand at Greggy's question, and stars streaked through the mirror as if all the heavens were falling.

"Ain't them things hard to adjust, though?" Greggy asked.

"No," Ted said, "we ain't heard about that."

Greggy whistled. "Now that's just what I'm sayin. You're as ignorant as everybody else in this county. Ignorance is rampant around here. Never seen it so profuse. How 'bout you, Mr. Walks Alone? You heard about them horses?"

Earl shook his head. "It's an ignorant county," he said.

"You got that mirror the way you want it now?"

Earl looked into it. It was pointing to some far point of the sky, full of stars. "Yeah," he said. "I think it's pretty good."

"Well, a proper adjusted rearview mirror is vital for safe drivin. What I was sayin, though. I ain't never since I been sheriff seen such a load a ignorance. Usually around here, somethin happens, the gossip's reportin it before the dispatcher is. And the case gets solved a hundred times before I solve 'r. But this horse thing—you'd think people been inoculated against knowing anything. Just like you two."

Greggy sucked his teeth, then whistled lowly again. In the far-off distance, so faint it seemed an echo to the whistle, changed and modulated by the land, a coyote's howl made its faint comment.

"Still," Greggy continued when Earl and Ted had nothing to say. "Like I said, sometimes the more people tell me, the more confusing things get. This much silence, it ain't as hard to read things, in some ways."

Earl suddenly realized what Greggy was saying. He felt such huge relief he couldn't prevent the beginnings of a smile tugging his lips upward. He looked up at the sheriff, who looked back.

"So what's your reading telling you?" Earl asked.

"Oh, hell, I'm still half-illiterate. About as illiterate as an invisible man can be. Take these tracks I found on this old road, for instance. Maybe a week-old set a tire tracks. But still a guy could prob'ly compare 'em to some real tires, if he could find the tires to compare 'em to. You might say truth is a *relative* thing in such a case, now."

Now it was Ted sitting silent and stupefied while Earl and the sheriff talked.

"I know what you mean," Earl said. "Very relative."

"I've even been doin some trespassing," Greggy said. "'Course I'd never admit that if I was actually here. Against the rules, you know. Trespassing is. Amazing the things you notice if you do, though. Trouble is, you can't ever make it official. Anyway, I'm beginning to think the guy first told me about them horses was tellin the truth. Shoulda listened to 'm. 'Course that guy'd be a suspect right now, if I knew who the hell he was any more. But an invisible man don't have much for memory. And his handwriting—shit! It's invisible, too. Don't hardly pay to take notes."

Earl remembered his name in big block letters pressed hard into the notepad on Greggy's desk. He thought that what Greggy had just said was as close to an apology as he was going to get. He decided it was close enough.

Greggy lifted his head. "Listen to that," he said.

Silence rang all around them.

"I don't hear nothing," Ted said.

"Me, neither. I don't hear nothin at all. Heard some yappin from Wagner Cecil a while back, an some growlin from Yarborough. But they sure as hell ain't louder 'n *that*." He jerked his head backwards at the vast, dark, quiet land, and the lights of the town below the hills shining silently into the night sky.

"Maybe Goat Man took those horses," Earl said.

"Now there," Greggy said. "You're the first person said somethin useful since I started puzzlin this whole thing over. I think you could be right. Could be like a few years ago in Harding County when them aliens was mutilatin cattle. I oughta go work on that theory. Don't bother to wave. I ain't even here."

He turned, walked back to his car, opened the door, called out, "Say hi to Carson Fielding for me, you happen a see him. *Gute Nacht.*"

His headlights filled Earl's car momentarily, then swung around, cutting a wide swath of brightness that faded in an arc across the prairie. Then Earl saw his red taillights in the interior mirror creep up the hill and disappear. He looked into the other mirror, at the stars framed there.

"What the hell was that all about?" Ted asked.

Earl thought there was a documentary to narrate somewhere in all this, but he couldn't think what it was. He felt the cold air pouring in the window and rolled it up. He looked at Ted. "What are you talking about?" he asked. "I didn't see anything. What'd I stop here for?"

He reached over, grinned, socked Ted on the arm, and started the car.

Another Fire

~~~~~~

NONE OF THEM KNEW WHY Carson wanted them to come to his place. He had called each of them, said he had some work that needed doing and could use some help. Ted hadn't yet found a car at a price he wanted to pay, so Earl picked up both him and Willi, and they drove out to Carson's ranch on a gray day, a few stray flakes of snow falling so slowly out of the sky they seemed suspended. Carson's place appeared deserted when they got there. Earl pulled up in front of the house, and they were about to get out when Carson came out of a small, ramshackle house they hadn't noticed when they first drove up. It was in plain sight, but their eyes had been fixed on the main house, and this other was so much smaller, perhaps half the size of the main one, with such a sagging roof line that it had the look of a natural thing and their vision had passed right over it. When Carson stepped out the door, though, the house leapt into their recognition—an old house, worn, small, poorly built.

They all got out and greeted each other. In their greetings they felt a common desire to avoid what they all remembered, to just be who they were at the moment, doing whatever it was they were being asked to do. Carson came to the point.

"I got some furniture needs movin," he said. "My parents 're gone, signin some papers. Thought I'd get this done while they're away."

He took them to a round tin shed, led them past an old Case tractor and some other machinery to the back of the shed, and pulled back a plastic tarp so thickly coated with dust it looked gray until he lifted it and the dust shook off and revealed the tarp's blue color. Underneath they saw furniture—end tables, stuffed chairs, beds and mattresses, lamps.

"This stuff needs a go back inta that old house," Carson said. "You willin a help?"

It took them two hours, back and forth from the shed to the old house, in the door, set something down, go back for more. Carson didn't care where they put things. "Anywhere," he told them. "Just so it's in."

When they were done, the space in the shed looked strangely barren—a big hole, surrounded by machinery staring like petrified bystanders having witnessed some remarkable vanishing. And in the old house there was a chaos of furniture, a bed in the kitchen, a table in a bedroom, chairs scattered without pattern or order, things tipped on their sides.

They looked at it. Carson offered them water, soda, a sandwich. They drank and ate. In the moving, Carson had been all business, saying little. They had all sensed some portent in what they were doing, but had stiff-armed the feeling with the work. Now Earl asked, "What's this all about?"

"It's my grandma's furniture," Carson said.

Earl waited, finally said, "That doesn't tell us a whole lot, you know?"

"Grampa moved it out to that Quonset when she died. I'm movin it back. They're sellin the place today. My parents are. Those papers they're signin? That's it. What I told you about that night. But I ain't lettin 'em have this house."

"Yarborough?"

Carson nodded.

"I guess I don't get it."

"That fire in your car?" Carson looked at Ted. "I been dreamin about it. Finally figured out why." He looked around the disarrayed room.

"Wasn't the work I needed so much," he said. "Just wanted the three a you here."

They were silent for a long time, Earl sitting at the old table across from Carson, Ted sitting in an overstuffed chair in the middle of the room, holding his half-eaten sandwich in one hand, Willi slouched in a ladder-back chair, his feet stretched before him, a can of pop dangling from his fingertips.

"Gonna make a hell of a fire, enit?" Ted asked quietly.

Wild, Freed

~~~~~

CARSON HAD THE FEELING it was all happening again: the knock on the door, the waiting, the sound of footsteps inside the house. Except that it was winter now, and except for memory. Winter and memory. It had been only a few months ago that he had stood like this, with no idea what lay before him. For a moment memory pretended to be the future instead of the past, and just before the door opened, the footsteps inside the house nearing, it seemed that within a couple of days he would see her opening the corral gate, stepping inside, wearing boots that had never been in a stirrup.

Then the door was opening, and Magnus Yarborough's eyes gazed at him through the storm door. He was reaching for the latch when he recognized who stood on the porch. His hand fell. Other than that, he didn't react. Carson might have been a salesman, neither welcome nor unwelcome until his wares and prices were known.

Then Magnus grunted. "Huh. You looking for work?"

Carson heard the derision—that he no longer had a ranch.

"Not hardly," he answered. "Won't be needin to work for a long time."

Give the man nothing. Pretend to be, like his father, glad for the money.

"You got some balls coming here, don't you?"

"I got somethin to tell you."

"So tell it."

"I ain't gonna talk through a door."

The wind drove snow from a drift in the yard, a white stream peeling off the top of the drift like ocean spray off a wave, clattering against the house.

Magnus's jaw hardened. He wanted to shut the door in Carson's face. But he also wanted to know what Carson had to tell him. Carson saw doubt in his eyes. Everything had become so complicated. Magnus couldn't be sure of anything Carson might or might not know—about Rebecca, the horses, the land. And he couldn't resist his need to know. His mouth moved as if he had tasted something sour. Then he stepped away from the door.

"It better be good," he said.

He didn't open the screen door for Carson. He just stepped into the dimmer light inside the house. Carson reached out, pressed the screen door latch. Magnus had left the foyer and was in the living room. Carson stood for a moment in a pool of blue, golden, and reddish light transformed by the stained glass panels above the door.

It was the first time he'd been inside the house. For a moment he gave in to thinking about Rebecca here—the routines she managed, the way her face would look sitting in a chair reading or wrapped in thought—and he realized he'd never seen her face in interior light. The only house they'd ever come close to entering had been Elmer Johannssen's, and that had ceased to be a house, had become something else.

Carson couldn't afford these thoughts. He closed his mind to them, walked to the living room.

"It's your visit," Magnus said.

He didn't sit down or offer Carson a chair. They stood: ungainly, stiff, wary.

"Ain't really a visit. I just got a thing to say."

"So say it."

"What you think happened didn't happen."

"I'm supposed to know what that means?"

"Between her an me. It didn't happen."

Magnus's head jutted forward almost imperceptibly. So suppressed was the movement that Carson wouldn't have noticed it at all except that a chance ray of light shifted from his forehead, brightening his coarse hair with the suddenness of a switch thrown.

"You come to me with that?" he asked. "And I'm supposed to believe you?"

"That don't matter to me."

Magnus's pupils dilated slightly. He hadn't expected that reply.

"I'm just tellin you," Carson said. "Whether you believe it, whether it makes a difference to you, that don't concern me."

"Why the hell should I believe it? Coming from you?"

Carson refused to respond to the belligerence. He wasn't here for that.

"I ain't offerin reasons," he said calmly. "Like I said, it don't matter to me if you believe it. I just want a say it. That's as far as I need a go with it."

"You know what that sounds like? Bullshit. You think coming over here and saying that will make things all right?"

Underneath Magnus's anger, Carson heard that he was hurt. He was trying to hide it, but he was hurt. Even if he'd played a role in hurting himself, still Carson wished it wasn't so. But that, too, was beyond Carson's purpose. He wasn't here to convince Magnus of his integrity or to excuse himself. He wasn't here to make either of them feel better.

"I ain't tryin a make things all right," he said. "I'm tellin you because I'm guessin she said the same thing."

He met Magnus's eyes, saw them shift—surprised again by Carson's answer and his refusal to get drawn into confrontation and its predictable paths. Magnus didn't like being surprised. He lifted his hands, placed them near his back pockets, elbows sticking out, shoulders and jaw leaning forward.

"What she said isn't your business," he said.

"It ain't. I'm just tellin you the truth because I think she mighta, too. Personally, I don't care if you believe me. I don't like you. I don't like the way you treated her. I don't like the way you treat animals. I don't know what goes on in your head. So it ain't like I need you to believe me so I can feel good about myself. I just come here to say it in case she said it, too. In case it matters to her. It don't to me. But it might to her."

If antagonism lay in the words, it lay in the words alone. The tone was factual, a mere report. If Magnus took offense at the report, it couldn't be helped.

And he did. He stiffened as Carson talked, a slow fossilization that locked his knees and spread upward through his body. With his elbows out and jaw jutting forward, he resembled the skeleton of an ancient bird trapped in mineral. But he also looked dangerous. He projected the sense that if he broke from that pose, it would be toward some explosive end.

"You come into my house and talk to me that way? Where the hell do you get off?"

Carson held up his hand—brief, conciliatory, but refusing to accept Magnus's challenge.

"I never wanted a come over here in the first place," he said. "Was you insisted. I'm just needin a finish it. Friend a mine claims that's important."

"Well, you've finished it."

"Just about. I'll go in a sec. I'm just sayin, she's your wife. Still. And she might still want a be your wife. That's a thing I don't know. What I'm tellin you's the truth. You don't believe it, that's fine with me. But it might matter to her. That's all."

"Are you trying to tell me all you did was teach her to ride?"

"I've already told what I've got to say. Anything else you wanta know is hers to tell. If she wants."

"What makes you think I want to hear anything from her?"

"What you want ain't nothin to me. I ain't concerned with you."

Magnus jerked his head, a movement so full of suppressed emotion that Carson had the impression Magnus had snapped bones in his neck controlling it, and he realized with a start that Magnus wanted his concern. Wanted Carson's attention. His notice. He didn't care if Carson hated him, as long as Carson noticed him. And all Carson had ever done was ignore him. With the horses, even with Rebecca, Magnus had been merely beside the point.

Carson stared at Magnus with a dumbstruck wonder. He remembered how Magnus, swollen with a rage he'd barely contained, had come down to where Carson was working the horses and tried to bully him the day after Carson had kicked Rebecca out of the corral. It dawned on Carson like something that had always been there but that he hadn't recognized, a thing taking shape out of the background before him, that Magnus had tried to bully him not because Carson had treated *Rebecca* like anyone else, but because he had treated Magnus Yarborough's *wife* like anyone else. Carson hadn't been enough concerned with Magnus.

They stared at each other across the space of the living room, Magnus trying to hide what his movement had revealed, Carson hiding the fact that he'd recognized it. In Carson, astonishment replaced realization: he had the oddest power over Magnus he could imagine—the power to ignore him. To find him beneath notice. Carson had come here to speak of Rebecca, and everything he'd said to keep the conversation on her, to avoid any confrontation with Magnus himself, had the opposite effect. It antagonized Magnus even more. Had everything—the fleeing cow, the horses, the purchase of the ranch—been a demand that Carson notice him? Was that possible?

But the thought was too pathetic to be borne. Carson had to get away from the man. He turned to go. But Magnus had one thing yet to keep him. In a voice tight with anger he said, "What'd you do with them?"

Carson knew what he meant, and he thought he could ignore this, too. Just keep going. He hadn't come to talk about the horses, either. He'd come to say the one thing, for Rebecca's sake, if she wanted it. He hoped with every cell of his body that she didn't want it. But he couldn't forget that moment of doubt when the sunlight off her mirror had stabbed his eyes, and the sound of her car door shutting had come across the field to him. He didn't know what she was doing, what deciding. He knew what he wanted, whether it was right to want it or not—but he wouldn't be part of preventing whatever she might decide. That's the only reason he'd come: to let her be. And to free both of them—to let Magnus have a choice, if that were possible, so that if Rebecca did refuse him, Magnus's influence would be over, the spell he cast—if he cast it—broken, and nothing Rebecca and Carson might do would then be his.

Still, Carson turned back to Magnus. He knew the man was trying to make him acknowledge his power. He wanted to force Carson to admit it. Carson turned back not to admit anything but because by speaking he could say less than silence would say.

"They're safe," he said.

With their relations, he thought.

"Safe, huh? I knew you were involved. That goddamn Longwell claims there's no evidence."

"Guess you oughta get him fired."

"Maybe."

Carson turned to go again, but Magnus said, "Safe like that cow, maybe."

Carson felt rage, and he turned back to face Magnus and in that instant knew that, in spite of Magnus's greater size, he could physically annihilate the man. Destroy him. Leave him a crumpled heap bloodying the cream-colored carpet of this living room. He saw fear leap like a flame into Magnus's eyes and knew that Magnus had just realized he was alone with Carson and not at all in control of what might happen, confronting a man boundless and unpredictable and with an energy greater than his. Magnus stepped back, away from what he saw, and stumbled, and almost fell. And all Carson had done was look at him.

But Carson reined his fury in.

"Truth is," he said, "we thought a killin you. It was an option. But we did another thing."

Magnus had just regained his balance. But at Carson's words he swayed, steadied, stared for a moment in disbelief. Then his face went slack, the flesh suddenly hanging from his cheekbones like soggy newspaper caught on a fence.

In ways he had never imagined, his manipulations had turned against him. What he thought he controlled had freed itself from him. Become wild. Going its own direction. Carson's words left no room for doubt or disbelief. Magnus's mouth opened and closed. He licked his lips.

But he pulled himself erect. Tightened his features, though he couldn't quite firm up his cheeks. He tried to take back the offensive.

"That's a direct threat," he said. "I could get you arrested for that."

"Who's listenin?"

"If anything happens to me."

Carson shook his head, dismissing it. "We decided it wasn't worth doin."

As if it were a minor thing. Beneath notice.

"We?"

Magnus, for the first time, picked up the implications of the word.

"There's a few of us got involved. One guy was a bit hard to convince. I think we talked him out of it. Least for now. Hard to say, though. He's out there."

Carson nodded vaguely, swung his head to indicate all of space.

Magnus had no words. He stared at a world he didn't know, with a random being in it whose attention he didn't want but whose attention he had gathered. It could be anybody—the next person he talked to, the next person he tried to look in the face.

Carson left him. He was in the foyer when Magnus tried to recover, to shout away what couldn't be known or faced.

"You've got nothing," he yelled. "You hear me? I'll even get her back."

Carson didn't know. It seemed doubtful. Rebecca wouldn't come back to this, would she? But now it was up to her. That's all he'd come here for—to make sure it could be up to her.

He reached for the door handle.

"I hate gutless people who won't even go after what they want," Magnus called.

"Yeah. Me, too."

Carson opened the door. His response had silenced Magnus momentarily as he tried to understand what Carson meant.

Then he called again. "You sonofabitch. You can't just walk out of here."

But Carson already had.

A Moment of What Remains

~~~~~

I N MAGNUS'S YARD Carson opened the door to his pickup, climbed behind the wheel, and suddenly lost the strength to turn the ignition key. He sat there with the sun pouring through the windshield out of the cold winter air, and he broke into a sweat that turned icy on his skin. He shivered. He was landless and womanless. All he had was money. He didn't know what he'd do with it. Didn't know what its point could be.

Some Set of Vectors

ARL'S GRANDMOTHER LIFTED the moccasins off her lap, held them up to the window light, out of the sphere of the incandescent bulb.

"There," she said. "Finished."

They were like no moccasins Earl had ever seen: red horses, blue water, green hills, and four human figures, young warriors, guarding them. Out of the straight, geometric lines of the beads, using only the variation of color, his grandmother had created a sense of movement and space and running things and wind. Yet nothing moved. All was still.

"They're beautiful," he said.

"They're yours."

He took them, as one should take a gift, with humility and thanks and without protest. He looked at the moccasins in his hand, and he wanted to ask her how she'd known, and what she'd known, and for how long. But then he didn't want to know. It was a mystery, best left so.

"They're not traditional," his grandmother said. "I kind of made up the pattern."

Earl nodded. The moccasins gleamed in the light. "Are you allowed to do that?" he asked.

"I think so," she said. "I never asked."

WILLI TOOK THE PHONE upstairs to his bedroom. He sat on the bed, began to punch in numbers, then looked up at the ceiling and stopped. But he saw only texture, only the ceiling spreading away from his eyes. He stared at it for several long moments, but his eyes didn't circle into the whorls up there, didn't start and stop and start. It was just a ceiling. Just texture and relief. He looked back down at the phone in his hand. Punched in the last two numbers.

In Koblenz his father heard the phone ring and took his gaze away from the city outside the window, walked to the phone and, without waiting for it to ring again, picked it up.

TED SAT HUDDLED IN A WINTER COAT under the largest cottonwood outside his trailer house. He had his arm over the neck of one of the greyhounds. He looked up at the secondhand car he'd just bought. The muffler wasn't great, but the lights worked. He'd bought a bag of burritos to celebrate. He wrapped his arm tighter around the greyhound's neck to bring the burrito in his hand to his mouth. The dog's head was right next to his. Ted bit the burrito in half. The dog whined.

"Want some?" Ted asked.

He held out the other half. The greyhound wolfed it down. Ted held his face against the dog's and felt the dog's jaws working, bone against bone. He shivered again. He thought how a few beers or some wine would warm him up. Longing and emptiness that nothing would fill gaped inside him. He remembered the ice on Lostman's Lake, that open water, and how the car had gone down so soundlessly. So easily. There had been that moment when he'd almost jumped inside. The car was moving and he was moving with it, running alongside, and it was just a quick little swing, a pull on the wheel, and he would have been within the ruined hulk, behind the windshield, watching the water near. And then a sudden falling.

Instead, here he was. Just here. Why? He didn't know why. Ted clenched his eyes closed. The darkness swam with blood. He clutched the dog. Held it to him. Clutched the dog so hard it whined.

AND EARL WALKED WITH HIS MOTHER across the frozen cemetery grass, past the prairie dog mounds that no one seemed able to rid the cemetery of. It was the first time he and his mother had ever visited the cemetery together. She had been surprised, saddened and pleased, when Earl had asked her to go with him. She had dressed for the occasion and had on dress shoes with slippery soles. She held his arm on the uneven ground.

He felt her grip tighten when she saw Norm standing in front of Cy's grave.

"Norman's here," she said.

"I know. I invited him."

"Earl."

"You said you should have him over for a meal."

"Yes. But—"

"But it just wouldn't have gotten done, you know?"

She'd stopped when she saw Norm. Now she started walking again. "You're right," she said. "It wouldn't have."

Then she said, "Earl. This kind of scares me."

"And him."

"You think?"

"I know."

Then with great dignity, Lorna let go Earl's arm and walked on her own to Norm and reached up. And at first he didn't know what she was doing and a look of great confusion came to his face. And then he saw and he opened his arms, and they fell into each other, and if it hadn't been for that, they both would have fallen. But their collapses canceled each other out somehow. That had to be it, some set of vectors, some equation that could be solved. But the truth was it looked to Earl like they were suspended, clear of the ground, floating.

Wind

~~~~~

IN THE KITCHEN OF THE NEW HOUSE, Marie Fielding stood alone, looking through the window at the empty space where the old house had stood, and she thought of her son watching it turn to flame. She thought of the heat against his face, his open eyes, and how within them there must have been the whole fire burning, compressed. Heat and light, he wouldn't have shut them. Would have watched. She knew that.

She and Charles had come back that day and found a pile of scorched rubble. Ash. Still-smoking timbers. Smoke curling up in various wisps before being swept away by wind. She'd been shocked. Charles had been shocked. It wasn't just the physical difference, the way the ranch place seemed almost unrecognizable without the old house there. It wasn't just the way that, without it, perspective seemed skewed, distorted, everything out of relationship. It was also that they felt the landscape of their lives had changed. As if things had shifted in their hearts and they couldn't quite recognize, suddenly, who they were. Couldn't quite navigate their own memories, couldn't quite steer a clear way through them, with that smoking absence before them, and the sky, the horizon, the snowy land visible where painted boards had been, sagging roof, silver wooden shingles. For a moment Marie had the disconcerting sense that she saw the outlines of the old house still standing, as if the smoke for a moment rose up and framed it, and it was there and not there both.

While she and Charles were staring at it, Carson drove up from the pasture where he'd carried hay to the cattle. He drove right up to where they were standing, opened the pickup door, stepped out.

Marie felt a small astonishment: He looked as he had always looked. He moved as if he'd just come from carrying hay to the cattle and would now go to another thing that needed doing.

"Carson!" she cried. "What happened? Are you all right?"

"I burned it," he said.

"You . . . ?" Her voice halted. "This wasn't an accident?"

"I just couldn't see lettin 'm have it. So I put the furniture back in and did it. There's room in the Quonset now."

There was no bitterness in his words. No blame. Marie understood this was no act of revenge, no childish calling for attention, no protest or message.

"You just burned 'er down," Charles said. He was staring at the ashes, anger in his voice. Disbelief and anger.

"Yeah," Carson said. "A bit a gasoline, and there it was."

"All their furniture, too?"

"It, too."

"Christ!" Charles looked at his feet, raised his hand to the top of his head, ran it down to his neck as if trying to press something out of his skin, or hold something in. "You just . . ."

He stopped, shook his head, his hand still on his neck.

"Just burned 'er down," he said, his anger suddenly and completely gone, only wonder left, some sadness. "Well, hell. I guess that's one way a doin it."

Marie couldn't speak. Charles and Carson agreed. But didn't understand each other. Did and didn't. Those years ago Charles had been going to take the house down, nail by nail, saving what could be saved, but he'd never got around to it. Now Carson had simply started a fire. The two of them finally agreed the old house had to go. Agreed it was best gone. But Marie understood, though vaguely and without words, that its going was Carson's way of keeping the past and Charles's way of leaving it. Charles's sudden anger had come from being forced to confront, without preparation, that leaving. Being forced to recognize what it meant. And he had turned his head to the ground and thought, and then accepted what had to be. He was a relatively rich man now. And he wasn't going to regret it, or what it meant. But Marie wondered if he should.

To divert her mind from thoughts that she couldn't, at the moment, get clear, Marie asked, "How did you get that furniture in there by yourself?"

"I didn't. Had some friends come out 'n help."

The way he said it, and the way he didn't name the friends, echoed in Marie's head. She'd heard some rumors about Magnus Yarborough mistreating horses and about how some local men had taken care of the problem. Vague things. Hard to know what stock to put in such stories. But Louise Rafferty, a friend of Marie's, had just a couple of days ago asked her, as if she should know, what had really happened. Marie had stared at her blankly.

"I have no idea," she said.

"Oh. I thought Carson—"

Then Louise had clammed up. "Nothing," she said. "I don't know what I was thinking."

That incident echoed now. "What friends?" Marie asked.

"Doesn't matter. Just friends."

She knew he wouldn't tell her. No sense pursuing it. If she had guesses, they would have to remain that way. Guesses and wonders—sometimes it seemed that was what her relationship with her son was. More wonder, perhaps, than guess. But both.

She stood alone in the kitchen now and stared at where the old house had stood, at the section of horizon it had hidden, this new, empty thing in her view, and she remembered it all and was able, she thought, to make sense of many things but not all of them. She remembered her way back to a time that seemed not that long ago but was. Or maybe wasn't that long ago. She felt she could no longer tell near from far.

Carson was five years old. He was with her outside, in a blowing wind, and she was trying to tie sapling oaks to steel posts to keep them from breaking. Carson wouldn't stay close. There were horses watching them, their faces sticking over the top rail of the corral. The corral was too far away, and she didn't want Carson going down there by himself. But he kept moving toward the horses. She would call him back, and he would stop and then take several more steps away, and she would finally have to leave the saplings and the posts and twine and go across the yard to retrieve him and bring him back. And the whole process would start over again.

Charles came out of the machine shed. He'd been working on the starting motor on the Case. He had the old motor out and was going into Twisted Tree for a new one. He came out of the Quonset and stood watching them. Now, standing in the kitchen, listening to the wind blowing outside—the way it picked the ashes up, how black they were at first, black air, and then they simply disappeared—Marie imagined what Charles had watched. She saw herself as he had seen her: her hands tying baler twine around the trees, which even as she tied them blew back and forth as if to flee her help, her hair whipping around her face, her calls to her meandering son—calls like the calls of small birds that Charles often told her of, flocks of them held stationary in the wind as they tried to fly against it, crying to each other until they suddenly all gave up and were swept away so swiftly in the direction they were trying not to go that they seemed, like that ash out there, to simply vanish. Every time Charles saw such a flock, he told of it. "They keep callin to each other," he would always say, every time. "Call until they're gone."

Carson drifted away again, down toward the horses, and Marie looked up from the tree she was tying, and the wind swept her hair into her eyes, and when she reached up to peel the hair away so that she might see her rebel son, the knot she was tying around the sapling unraveled, and the sapling bowed forty-five degrees to the ground, and the twine sailed away like the tail of a mythical animal. Marie let the tree bend. Let the twine sail. She gathered her hair in her hand and held it like a rope and called, "Carson. Come back now."

He turned and looked at her. Then turned back to the horses. And walked toward them.

And she knew, standing in the new house now, how her patience and calm and her call, and Carson's ignoring of them all, had ignited Charles's rage. She felt it whump inside her as he must have felt it: like a propane furnace flame. And she knew what he had thought, though he would not speak it, would not let her ears hear it: *The goddamn tree, the goddamn wind, the goddamn place, her goddamn hair, why in hell doesn't she wear a goddamn cap to hold it anyway in this goddamn wind? Everything flying away from her, everything her hands tried to do out here disturbed, deferred, diffracted. This goddamn country. And the kid, not even caring about any of it, not even noticing what his mother has to deal with, just interested in those goddamn horses.*

"Carson," Charles called, stepping toward the boy. "Obey your mother."

The boy turned and looked back. He faced directly into the wind and looked at his father. Had he been older, the gaze might have seemed disdainful, but he was too young for that. It was merely a gaze that took in all before him and judged in favor of the horses.

He turned back to them.

"You stop right there!" Charles yelled. He was suddenly moving so swiftly that to Marie watching he seemed to be reeling Carson backwards toward him. The horses in the corral flared in alarm. Still the boy kept walking. Charles called again, neared him, raised his hand.

Then Carson turned around again and looked up at his father standing above him. There was no fear in his face at all. There was nothing but curiosity. To see what new thing the world held.

Marie saw Charles's whole body go limp. His hand dropped out of the air, and he stumbled in stopping himself, and Marie knew that he recognized that he was pregnant with violence toward his son. But Charles would not let that violence be born.

He bowed his head, and she saw how he felt defeated. She saw how he didn't want her to see it. But she couldn't turn away her eyes. He couldn't look at her, though she wanted him to. She knew he was ashamed of his upraised hand, and more than that, ashamed of the wind he could not stop and how it bent the sapling she so wanted to grow nearly parallel to the ground, like she herself when she washed her hair in the kitchen sink of the old house. She knew how he stood behind her and watched her when she washed her hair, how he looked at her neck, the water making the tiniest piano music against the sink, and how he wanted to come to her and kiss her vertebrae and yet was so angry at himself that he couldn't afford to put a shower in the house that all he could do was set his coffee cup down on the counter and go outside to the work his father had long ago given him to do.

Marie held her hair in her fist, motionless, while the sapling's leaves beside her threw themselves straight out, whitely, before the wind, and made ragged, incessant noise. She stood motionless and gazed at her husband and couldn't believe the fullness of her love.

She'd watched him stride toward Carson. She hadn't called out to stop him. She'd felt no need. She'd seen him raise his hand. But even then she knew he would lower it slowly. Knew it when he didn't. Before he did.

Charles couldn't meet her eyes. She saw him look down at his hand. Saw his expression change—a look of disgust: that gnarled, knuckly thing he'd just tried to make an extension of her voice. She knew he thought his hand was ugly. He thought she thought so, too.

"Goddamn, Charles, no," she wanted to say. "You've got it all wrong."

But everything except for the wind seemed frozen. She couldn't make her voice work. And he wouldn't meet her eyes.

He looked down at his son.

"You got to listen to your mother," he said. "She's got reasons. You understand?"

The boy nodded: the steady eyes, the bald face, the serious expression.

"But you just gotta go to those horses, don't you?"

The solemn nod again.

"I'll take you, then."

Charles put his hand down to where Carson could reach it, and Carson put his hand up and into his father's, and they walked together across the gravel to the bowed heads of the horses, and Charles lifted Carson up so that the boy could touch those velvet noses.

Acknowledgments

‸‸‸‸‸

DOROTHY DEDMON, A STUDENT OF MINE, provided the initial inspiration for this story.

Black Hills State University supported me in numerous ways: with sabbatical leave time that allowed me to travel to Germany for research, with a monetary award from the Black Hills State University Foundation that helped pay for that travel, and with class-release time.

The South Dakota Arts Council provided me with a Project Grant that allowed me to take an entire summer off and to reduce my teaching load during one fall semester.

Along with being a source of constant support, Noah Lukeman, my agent, made a crucial comment concerning the fourth draft that forced me to resee much of the story. Kati Steele Hesford, my editor at Harcourt, read the novel the way it was supposed to be read. A conversation I had with her about an early draft allowed me to continue working at a time when the book seemed intractable. My copy editor, Lee Titus Elliott, clarified the book and allowed me to make final changes.

Gene and Marion BlueArm helped me understand why many Europeans, Germans especially, feel connected to the American West and the Lakota people specifically. Jens Doerner and Hilke Schubring, as well as Michael Schlottner, made me welcome in Germany and shared their lives and ideas with me. I have never known more generous and hospitable people.

Gitta Sereny's *The Healing Wound*, Richard Rhodes's *Masters of Death*, Stephan and Norbert Lebert's *My Father's Keeper*, Gerald

Posner's *Hitler's Children,* Peter Sichrovsky's *Born Guilty,* Dan Bar-On's *Legacy of Silence,* and Catrine Clay and Michael Leapman's *Master Race: The Lebensborn Experiment in Nazi Germany* were all instrumental in helping me understand either the *Lebensborn* program or the Nazi legacy and its lasting effects on society and individual families. James Walker's *Lakota Belief and Ritual* clarified Lakota ideas for me. These are only a few of the authors who have helped me shape this novel.

John Nelson, Al Masarik, Scott Simpson, David Cremean, and Bill Kamowski all read early drafts and provided both encouragement and insights that helped shape the novel's final form.

Jace DeCory and Ronnie Theisz gave me invaluable advice concerning Lakota ways, spirituality, ideas, and symbolism. They corrected my errors and misperceptions and gave me new ways to see the material.

Every time I write anything, Wendy Mendoza says one or two perfect things that reveal what I really could be doing instead of what I am. She did that again with this book.

No one has influenced the shape, texture, and meaning of the novel more than Vince King and Amy Fuqua. They read not one but several drafts. They have been involved almost from the beginning and believed in this book when there was little evidence it deserved that faith. If the novel has clarity, much of that clarity I owe to them.

My wife, Zindie, and my children sustain me.

Tom Herbeck and Stewart Bellman, to whom the book is dedicated, were close friends. Both died recently. They were sources of inspiration, wisdom, and ideas. They constantly challenged me to think and to see beyond my abilities. I owe them, and this novel owes them, in myriad ways, many so deep I cannot even recognize them myself.

Finally, a fourth-grade class in Mission, South Dakota, introduced me to Goat Man when I was conducting an Artist-in-the-Schools residency there several years ago. I will never forget the stories they told of Goat Man, and the picture of him one of them drew. Turning from the chalkboard, this young artist asked me, "You don't believe us, do you? You don't believe he's real." Perhaps this novel is my answer to that question.